Ian Skewis was born in Scotland in 1970.

He wrote articles for a local paper and had his first poems published at the age of 19. He trained at the Royal Conservatoire of Scotland and became an actor, appearing on film and television, and providing his voice for radio. He performed in numerous stage plays that toured internationally, including *Like Thunder*, which received a Fringe First Award in 2001.

He is the author of several short stories, including 'The Circular Memory', 'Leviathan', 'Borrowed Time' (finalist in The Temporal Logbook international competition) and 'Inkling', which was published in an anthology, *The Speculative Book*, in 2016.

He lives and works in Glasgow.

A Murder of Crows is his debut novel.

Praise for *A Murder of Crows*

'Ian Skewis deftly mixes gritty urban settings with sinister countryside in a multi-layered plot that keeps you guessing right up to the end. Strong characters and a finely crafted sense of unease lend this debut the star quality that will surely make it one of the standout thrillers of 2017.'

—Dr Brooke Magnanti (previously known as Belle de Jour), author of *The Turning Tide* and *Diary Of A London Call Girl*.

'*A Murder Of Crows* is a dark and disturbing excursion into the Scottish Highlands. Skewis skilfully creates an atmosphere of foreboding from the opening and doesn't let go until, breathless, you reach the last page.'

—Michael J Malone, author of *Blood Tears* and *A Suitable Lie*

A MURDER OF CROWS

A MURDER OF CROWS

IAN SKEWIS

To Ruairidh,

[signature]

Unbound

This edition first published in 2017

Unbound

6th Floor Mutual House, 70 Conduit Street, London W1S 2GF

www.unbound.com

ISBN (eBook): 978-1-911586-25-8

ISBN (Paperback): 978-1-911586-02-9

Design by Mecob

Cover image:

© Shutterstock.com / Oksana Mizina
© iStockphoto.com / Julie Macpherson

For Mum and Dad.

And in loving memory of a dog called Jill. X

Dear Reader,

The book you are holding came about in a rather different way to most others. It was funded directly by readers through a new website: Unbound.

Unbound is the creation of three writers. We started the company because we believed there had to be a better deal for both writers and readers. On the Unbound website, authors share the ideas for the books they want to write directly with readers. If enough of you support the book by pledging for it in advance, we produce a beautifully bound special subscribers' edition and distribute a regular edition and e-book wherever books are sold, in shops and online.

This new way of publishing is actually a very old idea (Samuel Johnson funded his dictionary this way). We're just using the internet to build each writer a network of patrons. Here, at the back of this book, you'll find the names of all the people who made it happen.

Publishing in this way means readers are no longer just passive consumers of the books they buy, and authors are free to write the books they really want. They get a much fairer return too – half the profits their books generate, rather than a tiny percentage of the cover price.

If you're not yet a subscriber, we hope that you'll want to join our publishing revolution and have your name listed in one of our books in the future. To get you started, here is a £5 discount on your first pledge. Just visit unbound.com, make your pledge and type JACKRUSSELL in the promo code box when you check out.

Thank you for your support,

Dan, Justin and John
Founders, Unbound

Super Patrons

Justin Ahmed
Camelia (Maddi) Alexa
Sandra Armor
Gabriele Bittner
Mark Campbell
Stuart Carter
Stephen Christopher
Roncavel Ciavaglia
Angus Wilby & Rob Collins
Ann Cowie
John Cowie
Charlene Cross
Anne Cunningham
Deirdre Davis
Nicola Dawson
Marc de Launay
Derek Devine
Stephen Driscoll
Jane Dunbar
Mary Dykes
Kirsty Edwards
Claudia Fonda-Bonardi
Martin Frame
Shirley Frame
Rosalba Franchi
Deborah Franco
Debra Fraser
Cathey & Hazel Gillies
Arthur Gough
Michael Grimshaw
Lisa M. Harney
Laura Hayes

Greg Herren
Sam Heughan
Edie, Jude, Acadia & Alora Holve
Nikki Jay
Angela Johnston
Leona Joiner
Dan Kieran
Alasdair Lay
Paul Le Poidevin
Keir Liddle
Brian Lunn
Kirsty Macara
Yvonne Maddox
Dr Brooke Magnanti
Graeme Malcolm
David McColl
Nikk McCurdy
Tracey McMillan
Kay McNee
Susan McVey
Daniel Meikle
Lindsay Mitchell
Gillian Mitchell
John Mitchinson
Greg Moore
Katrina Morrison
Christine Mugnier
Chris Nicholson
Sara Park
Eve Bethan Park
Justin Pollard
Greg Powrie
Marc Rees
Claire Reynolds
Phyllis Richardson
Jack Riddell

Barbara Robotti
David Seath
Claire Semple
Sandra Silvester
June Skewis
Ian Skewis Snr
Lisa Skorupa
Keith Sleight
Babs Steele
Thompson Sunerton
Georgina Taylor
Ruth Taylor
Emma Thomson
Janie Thomson
Anne-Marie Timoney
Sarah Ritchie, Craig & Paul Tomlinson
Christine Wanamaker
Mary Wells
Karim Rhemani White
Esther Williams
Erik Zoha

With grateful thanks to Mark Campbell and Stephen Driscoll

Prologue

September 1st

Nothing ever ends, not really. Everything is a prelude, a prologue, to something else…

    These words break the surface. I'm not sure why. I'm in pain, a hell of a lot of pain – so maybe it's a way of distracting myself from it. I'm aware of what's going on around me, but I see it only in brief flashes: I'm lost in the woods, searching for my girlfriend. There's a thunderstorm overhead. And I can't find her.

    I have no idea how it got to this stage. It has simply become fact. Nothing more, nothing less. It's being presented to me like a consolation prize: let's see what you could have won. And I can see her. Frightened. Panicked. Caroline, my lover, running through the trees, trying to escape from the storm that rages all around us. I remember the moment it happened. When she let go of my hand. I lost her then. I was going to be a dad. I want to scream but no sound comes out.

    And there is blood.

    I can see it. Spreading through my clothes, dripping onto the bracken. I can feel the agony of my injury searing through me. It's so intense that my legs are threatening to give way. Then I fall to the ground, amongst the leaves and the ferns, panting like a frightened little animal. Except the initial fear is gone. Now I'm being drowned by the weight of a feeling I can't yet describe. Sadness perhaps; disappointment maybe.

    All my senses tell me that this is it. I'm finished. And that's when those words bubbled up from the depths.

    I can't recall who said them or why. Either way it doesn't matter now, for it provides scant comfort as I lie here. This story is ending. I'm fucked. And I'm very bitter about it. I loved Caroline. Where's the justice or sense in all this?

And I remember now. It was my mum who said those words. Funny how we all go back to our mothers in the end.

Just make sure this isn't the end, will you? Give my life some meaning. And make my story a good one. A prologue for better things to come.

Part One

Chapter One

It began as a black dot.

DCI Jack Russell could just about see it through the windscreen as he manoeuvred along the winding country lanes of Hobbs Brae – the small village on the west coast of Scotland that had been his home for more than 20 years. He was feeling tense. Perhaps it was the heat. The air hadn't cleared despite the storm of two nights ago. He could feel his palms sticking like glue to the steering wheel. The sweat trickled down his ample back, gathering amongst the mound of flesh at the base, which mushroomed out rather more than he would have liked. *I need to go on a diet*, he thought, and had a quick look at himself in the mirror, catching sight of the shadows under his eyes, but focusing instead on his irises, which were large and brown. He imagined they gave him an almost Mediterranean look. *Still got it though*, he dreamed. He sighed restlessly and lazily concluded the black dot was nothing more than a squashed fly on the glass.

He glanced into the mirror again to have a quick look at his son, Jamie, who was in the back seat behind him, texting.

'You getting that hair cut anytime soon?'

Jamie never replied, and Jack started humming tunelessly to himself before seeking company from the mild-mannered but insistent tones of Radio Four. *It's a curious trait of teenagers, that they can be sitting only inches away and still make you feel utterly alone*, he thought.

He caught sight of the black dot again. It wasn't a bug because it had moved its position and now seemed larger. It was something in the sky. He peered ahead, shifting in his seat. At over six feet tall and with the build of a rugby player, albeit one past his sell-by date, Jack had never felt comfortable in the police car, and the leather upholstery was making him sweat all the more. The object grew in size, winging its way towards him at an alarming rate. *It's only a bird*, he concluded, and was relieved, though he felt a little foolish. Suddenly the huge crow swooped down and dive-bombed his car, its great black wing flicking across the windscreen with a *thwack*, causing him to swerve and narrowly miss a ditch. 'What the fuck,' he shouted as he ground to an abrupt halt.

He wiped the sweat from his hands and muttered, more from habit than anything else, 'Sorry.' His wife didn't like him swearing in front of the kid, even though he knew from experience that his son had learned a few choice swear words himself. A teenager, to the hilt. Jack was about to turn round to see if he was all right but decided against it. He didn't need to. He could feel Jamie staring at him accusingly with his mother's eyes. Therein lay the other reason he chose not to turn round. The estrangement from both wife and son hurt like hell. He stayed still for a few moments, thinking about bad omens and impending doom – it seemed as if the crow had been flung at him from afar by the hand of God.

Feeling his son's eyes boring into his back, Jack pulled himself together and attempted to start the engine up again. It complained loudly, refusing to budge. The last thing he wanted was to be stuck in the middle of nowhere – but at last it staggered into life. With his composure regained, he was soon back on the road. It was only some time later that he realised the radio signal had disappeared. He fiddled with the knobs but nothing came, only a distant static and the hiss of white noise. Finally he switched it off, and as he drove towards his destination he began to settle into his usual mode of forecasting bad things for himself. For a long time he had been haunted by the idea that he'd been cursed with some kind of second sight, but as the years went on he perceived that with so many doubts and fears fluctuating inside his psyche, it would only be a matter of time before at least some of them came true – a law of averages. Even when good things happened to him he'd immediately expect the worst.

'What's wrong?' Rachel had asked him. 'Aren't you happy? You got promoted.'

'I know that,' he began lamely. 'It's just, well, it seems too good to be true, you know?'

'No. I don't,' she said tersely, and he watched his wife stomp off into the kitchen.

He couldn't help it. How could he tell her that, yes, he was very happy to be promoted, but that he still had the nagging worry that any minute now a pile of horseshit might fall on his head.

'Stop worrying,' said Jamie, as if reading his thoughts.

Jack smiled at him in the mirror, startled at first by Jamie's perceptiveness. 'How did you know I was worried?'

'You had that look again.'

Jack's smile became fixed, rueful. He was almost but not quite glad when he saw his partner waiting for him at the red telephone box. He pulled over.

'Jesus, Jack, you look as if you've seen a ghost,' DC Clements said, with an expression of barely concealed glee.

'Shaken but not stirred, Colin,' replied Jack. 'Get in.'

Jack watched with some amusement as Colin awkwardly got into the passenger seat, his red face reddening further with the effort. Pulling the seat belt over his pot belly, he turned and gave a very insincere smile, his broad-rimmed spectacles hiding his true intent. *Here it comes*, thought Jack, and braced himself as he put the car into first gear.

'So. Your final case,' announced Colin. 'What are you going to do with yourself when you retire?'

'Exactly the same thing I told you yesterday, and the day before,' replied Jack evenly.

'Now don't be like that, Jack. I'm sure you've got loads to look forward to.'

Jack gave another in his long catalogue of smiles, a patient one this time, and focused on the road ahead, glad he didn't have to look at Colin. Every comment the detective constable uttered seemed like a thinly veiled attack. They had known each other for so long, they understood each other's weaknesses intimately. Jack's weakness was that he had no idea what to look forward to when he retired. And Colin knew it. Their partnership felt like his marriage. Made in hell.

'Now, I've done some work on this Mispers case as you

requested, but I'm not entirely convinced we should take it seriously yet.'

Jack drew a sharp breath. He hated the way Colin abbreviated everything. 'The *missing persons* case is up and running regardless of what you or I think about it. Someone has reported it and so we must investigate.'

'That's my Jack, always being official.'

'Professional, Colin. I'm professional.' *And I know you meant officious, you little prick*, he seethed.

Their journey settled into silence. As far as Jack was concerned, they had very little in common and any attempt at small talk had all but expired. Jack preferred it this way. It gave him time to think, though he was aware that his thoughts were often the result of an unsettled mind. Today he felt particularly unsettled. Despite the fact that the leaves were turning brown, the remnant summer heat was stifling and he was more tense than before. He wished Colin wasn't there beside him. His close proximity made him feel suffocated.

'I need to pee,' announced Colin eventually.

'What? You've only been in the car for ten minutes.'

Colin tightened his mouth in an effort not to look displeased.

Jack, sensing his embarrassment, continued with his mild protest. 'There isn't a public toilet for miles out here, Colin,' he said with a smirk.

'Stop the car, will you?'

'Sure, Colin. Will here do?' replied Jack, his voice as sincere as he could allow.

'Aye. This'll do.'

Jack watched as Colin's little legs hurried him over to the best place he could find – some bramble bushes. As he stood by the roadside, Jack realised there was a distinct possibility of Colin being seen, but right now he didn't care – the opportunity to see the little bastard lose his dignity was too good to pass up. He heard Colin cry with relief as his piss hit the tarmac. Jack turned away discreetly. A Mini Cooper passed by, an elderly couple hunched in the front seats, their faces agog and aghast. All Colin could muster was an unapologetic shit-eating grin. As the car disappeared around the bend, Jack watched in embarrassed silence as Colin shook himself off, popped his manhood back into his trousers, zipped up and sauntered back to the car – not caring a jot.

'There. That was most refreshing,' he announced as he got back inside.

Jack became aware of something moving and looked up to see two figures coming towards him from around the bend – the elderly couple from the Mini Cooper. What Jack assumed to be the male of the species chapped its knuckles hard against the passenger side window. Clements slowly wound it down and Jack observed the man's wind-blown, papery skin, rosy at the cheeks, making him appear somewhat androgynous. His wife simply scowled, manfully holding a large Tupperware box that was presumably filled with food. Whatever it was, it was brown and looked like shit.

'It is against the law to urinate in public places,' the man said with a slightly contorted nasal whine, his thin lips stretched into a triumphant smile.

'I am the Law,' Colin replied, in a deep authoritarian voice. 'Detective Constable Colin Clements.' With a quiet, restrained tenor, and to get right up their hunched little backs, he added, 'And I can do what the fuck I like.'

Jack cringed and gave them a pained smile, then drove off. He smarted when he caught sight of the smug look on Colin's face, obviously happy that he was leaving the couple agog and aghast for the second time that morning. Jack frowned in disapproval when his son yelped with delight and appreciatively kicked the back seat. Jack felt his support of Colin's behaviour was not only misplaced but a sure sign of betrayal.

They arrived at Hobbs Brae Police Station and got out of the car.

'Wait here,' whispered Jack to his son, but he was oblivious, texting endlessly.

At the top of the stairs, Colin tried to get in through the door first but Jack beat him to it.

'Jack be nimble, Jack be quick,' Colin quipped, and with an overtly dramatic flourish, opened the door a little wider for him. Jack looked down at the detective for a brief moment, enjoying the fact that he towered over him. Colin was only five feet four. *A few years ago he wouldn't even have been eligible for my job*, Jack thought. *If only I could turn back time.* He knew Colin could barely conceal his longing for Jack to disappear. Every exchange he had with the man felt like a hand on his shoulder pushing him back out the door. He watched as the DC marched his squat little frame down the corridor. *I wish I could work alone, just once*, pined Jack, and headed to his office.

As he sat behind his desk, his paperwork neatly stacked on either side of him, Jack mused on his pending retirement. *Your final case*, he heard Colin say gleefully again. *I'm sure you've got loads to look forward to.* But it didn't feel like that. He sighed heavily and considered calling his wife. *What would I say?* he wondered, then noticed that time was moving on as he wasted it deliberating. He pulled himself together and recalled his conversation with the Chief Superintendent of the Police Constabulary.

'A young couple have gone missing.'

'I see,' said Jack patiently, glancing at the Chief's numerous trophies in the glass cabinet, framing him in polished silver, an imposing sight.

The Chief cleared his throat, absentmindedly thumbing through some files on his desk. 'Alistair Smith and Caroline Baker. They were last seen on the night of September the first at a petrol station just outside this village.'

'Who reported it?'

'Helen Patterson. She looks after Alistair's mother.'

'What about the girl's parents?'

'Her family have been informed. Should be a nice, easy case for you to conclude your career with.'

I don't need a nice, easy case, sir, Jack wanted to say, but thought better of it.

Maybe that was Jack's problem. Even now he felt swamped by his own ambition. He wanted to end his career on a high, not with some nondescript case that any old policeman could solve. It was patronising and it made him feel worthless. The entire conversation felt as if he was being handed his coat.

'To be unappreciated in one's own lifetime,' said Jamie airily as Jack got back into the car. Jack turned and looked at him, surprised at his ability to seemingly read his thoughts.

'Where did you learn that kind of talk?'

'Can't remember,' replied Jamie distantly, already texting someone, his face flushing red; a lie, obviously.

'Do you mean I don't appreciate you?'

Jamie glanced at him contemptuously.

'That's your mother talking,' Jack concluded, his chin raised defiantly against the outside world and the private domain of his own doubt as he drove off into the autumn sun.

Chapter Two

Alice Smith woke with a start. She sat up from her day bed and sipped from a glass of water that had turned warm in the heat. She breathed deeply and tried not to mull over the disturbing dream she'd just had.

Helen, her carer, appeared in the doorway. 'Are you okay?' she asked.

Alice hated the patronising way Helen always cocked her head to one side when she enquired after her well-being. 'I'm fine,' she snapped, getting up and putting on her cardigan.

'You were talking in your sleep,' commented Helen.

Alice noted her tight little smile that seemed far removed from genuine concern. 'Did I say anything interesting, dear?' she replied sharply.

'I wasn't listening, actually,' she heard Helen say impatiently.

Alice gazed back at her steadily. 'Isn't it time for you to go now?' she suggested.

Helen made a point of looking at her watch. 'Oh, yes it is.'

'See you tomorrow,' purred Alice with a smile of pleasure. *And good riddance*, she thought.

'Yes, see you tomorrow,' replied Helen, running her fingers through her long, dark hair as she left. 'Don't forget to take your pills now.'

Alice glared as Helen waddled out of the room. 'Fat cow manages to make everything sound like a competition,' she muttered, and sat back down on the edge of the bed. She couldn't shake off the cloud that hung over her – a remnant from her dream, whose subject she couldn't remember, but it made her feel on edge nevertheless. She was in no mood to dwell on it and made her way through the house and outside onto the front doorstep. The early evening air was warm.

Must have been a beautiful afternoon, she thought. She resented the fact that she had missed the sunset again.

Her memory had been failing her for a while. Simple things like the date and time, and rather more embarrassing things like her own name and the birthdays of family members. She kept this fact hidden, for she didn't want to worry anyone, least of all her son. *An early onset of dementia*, she had been told by her doctor. She had been forced into taking early retirement from her teaching job. Her memory loss was a frequent visitor, a decidedly unwanted guest that kept gate-crashing her mind at the worst possible moments. Helen was brought in to help. Alice hated her. Initially, she had seemed an easy target; overweight, quiet, almost mousy. The opposite of Alice.

'I've no idea why you're here,' was Alice's opening shot. And she spent the rest of that afternoon berating her helper, who she observed went about her duties with tight-lipped toleration. Alice was surprised to find that at the end of the day, Helen had found her voice.

'I'm here to protect you,' she explained, in a tremulous tone, but with a hardened stare. 'To help clothe and feed you when your memory really starts to fail. To wipe your arse if need be. And if you want to bark at me all day, then fire away. I can take it. Plenty of years' experience under my belt for that.' And with this as her parting shot, she left.

Alice was furious. 'How dare she speak to me like that in my own home,' she shouted, but no one was there to listen. As the night went on she recalled all the things the doctor had told her to expect and she felt the fear creeping in on a series of *what ifs.* By the next morning she couldn't wait for Helen to come and rescue her from her own fragile state of mind.

'I know I can be a grumpy old so and so,' she explained, 'but it's because I'm frightened. Sometimes I don't know where I am. Or who I am.' She wept at the admission and was grateful that Helen sat with her for the rest of the day. 'I owe you so much,' she said.

Helen smiled kindly and replied, 'I can be a grumpy old so and so too, you know.'

They both laughed.

But she didn't feel like laughing now. Something was wrong. It wasn't that her memory was failing or that she could not recall the contents of her dream. It was that the dream had left her feeling disturbed. Unsettled. She was vulnerable once more and she wished that Helen was still around.

Then the dream came back to her. *Something to do with my son.* She concentrated, pictured him: his green eyes; the scar on his forehead. She was upset without quite knowing why, agitated because she couldn't summon up anything that would make sense of it all. *Did something bad happen to him in the dream?*

She gave up trying to think about it and smiled fondly as she saw him turn and look at her, his eyes narrowing shrewdly as he decided on his next act of mischief. Twelve years old. She recalled the day he left home, a young man with his whole life ahead of him. She had watched tearfully from the top of the hill as his form receded into the distance, until he became nothing more than a dot, then disappeared.

Alice sighed, the encroaching night zephyr ruffling her thinning, white hair. She hadn't heard from her son in a long time now. She couldn't recall how long, but figured it must have been several months now, maybe even a year. She remembered he was seeing a girl, though. *Carol? Caroline?* She couldn't be sure. Alice recalled that she had never met her, never been introduced. But her mind kept going back to that dream, and the feeling of utter dread. She wanted to call him. But what would she say? *I think something terrible is going to happen.* Her mother had been a strong believer in premonitions and such like, but Alice was made of sterner stuff. Becoming a teacher meant that any influence her mother had once exerted was totally eclipsed. Alice had no time for such nonsense. She sipped at her glass again and grimaced at the warmth of the stale water. *Perhaps it's just this heat,* she thought, and wandered off to get some fresh lemonade from the kitchen.

Chapter Three

September 3rd

Colin was growing impatient. He viewed with furrowed brow the mountain of reports he had to get through, which frustrated him because he was no office junkie. The stifling heat and the lack of space only served to make him claustrophobic. He squirmed in his seat, noting all the details of each person he had interviewed, hating every minute of it. For, despite his short, fat appearance, Colin regarded himself as a man of action.

'Tell Campbell and Driscoll I need to see them both now. The usual place.' He slammed the phone down and aggressively scratched his scalp.

A short while later he was in the pub, the Crow's Beak. 'I'm sweating like a rapist,' he complained, and wiped his brow.

'I've got to separate the cranks from the genuine callers,' Campbell stated despairingly.

Colin raised an eyebrow. 'Oh, poor you,' he said contemptuously. 'It's your job. Deal with it.'

'But there's shitloads – sorry, hundreds of them.'

'No more than usual,' replied Driscoll pointedly.

Colin gazed at Campbell, the younger of the two officers who were part of his team, and noted his constant attempt to look serious by frowning and self-consciously stroking his embryonic beard. A failed attempt to be in two camps at the same time – the police officer and the artful West End bohemian. He was standing at the bar, unconsciously mimicking Colin's pose and eyeing up just about every female within a 20-foot radius. The DC observed him with a wry smile, and saw that Driscoll, an older officer with a sly look and dyed-black greasy hair swept behind his ears, had opted for sitting on a stool opposite. *Anything to be different*, thought Colin.

'What about you, sir?' Driscoll asked.

'Aye. I've got to take statements,' said Colin. 'In other words, I'm doing Jack's dirty work.'

'And I bet that eats you up like a cancer,' said Driscoll through a grin.

Colin gazed at him steadily for a moment. He scratched his head and pondered on how to respond. Then he lowered his voice. 'Aye, it does. And you know the only cure for it?'

'What?' Driscoll asked, leaning in to him, with Campbell following suit.

'High doses of fucking alcohol!' he shouted, and they laughed loudly.

'But seriously, I'm being forced to tail this investigation when I should be in charge of it. Jack should have retired by now. I'm fed up being his underdog.'

Driscoll smiled thoughtfully and said, 'He's good stock, though, don't you think? Never put a foot out of place in all these years.'

Colin snorted. 'Since when did you start admiring Jack Russell? He's a do-gooder with a whiter than white track record and a degree in self-fucking-importance!'

His colleagues gave a hoot as he slammed his beer onto the bar for effect, the froth spilling across the tarnished surface.

'But you have to admit he's very well respected,' Driscoll said.

Colin stopped him with a stare. He could tell when an ambitious officer was trying to marginalise him and he smiled at Driscoll's subsequent look of discomfort, for they both knew what was coming. 'And you like whiter than white role models, do you? Think you might be in a position to get my job when all this is through? Move up the ranks two places at a time, maybe?'

It was Driscoll's turn to snort. 'Don't be daft,' he said, laughing nervously.

'Don't forget I know you, Driscoll. I know all your dirty wee secrets. So don't get too upwardly mobile just yet. I'll tell you when there's a gap for you to fill. But right now, I'm thinking of number one.'

'Don't hold back, Colin,' Driscoll said sullenly.

'I fucking won't,' he answered, turning to the bar and calling to anyone who was listening, 'Same again.' He turned back to face his small entourage, who were both looking for the door.

'I need to get back…' began Driscoll.

'That bastard's always got the upper hand,' grumbled Colin.

'Who, Jack?' Campbell asked innocently.

Colin looked at him, trying to figure out if the officer was quite the full shilling. 'You're right,' he concluded to Driscoll. 'You need to get back to work.' Then he looked markedly at Campbell. 'Both of you.'

'Understood,' said Campbell, and he left, following in Driscoll's wake. Colin remained at the bar, alone. He wondered at the investigation that was now unfolding: *Alistair Smith and Caroline Baker. Local kids. Both on a trip from Glasgow and went missing on their way to Hobbs Brae.*

'Hobbs what?' the Glasgow office had asked.

'Brae,' replied Colin, almost shouting down the phone. 'Hobbs Brae.'

'Weird name for a village,' came the reply.

'Aye. That's what everyone says, but are we going to discuss the finer points of the origins of village nomenclatures or get on with the case in hand? We need CCTV footage of the missing couple on their journey from Glasgow to here. Might give us a clue as to their whereabouts.'

Colin smiled to himself. *I'm not the type to use big words but that was impressive.* 'Nomenclature,' he repeated, then realised that he had sunk one too many pints. 'I'm away for a piss,' he said to no one in particular, saluting unsteadily with his empty glass. Afterwards, he hit the fresh air outside and whispered, 'Fuck. I need to sober up.'

Returning to his office brought all the bitterness of his situation back to him. He couldn't stand the way the Chief placed Jack Russell on a pedestal, revering him like some kind of latter-day saint – *holier than thou.* It was as if Jack had somehow managed to hypnotise all who gazed on him. As a result, Colin's ego was put in an impossible position. He was jaded, jealous. He hated Jack more than words could say. He couldn't help himself. Jack was taller and better-looking than he was. Jack was more successful. Jack was jammy. He could not wait to see the back of Jack. As he endured sifting through the files, trying to sober up quickly with a bottle of water and mug of black coffee, he jotted down reams of notes with his own special kind of shorthand – a habitual use of abbreviations that had got him through his endurance test as quickly as possible. Only he could read them and so it served as a nice *fuck you* to Jack. DCI Russell had a lot to answer for. The longer his investigations dragged on, the more paperwork Colin had to do.

There wasn't enough room in his office for the hate he felt, so he got up and stormed out, marching quickly down the corridors despite his short legs, narrowly avoiding bumping into the officers and secretaries with their starched collars and their sensible shoes, their bundles of papers and their files, their ringing phones and their constant chatter, and finally into the one place where he could find sanctum:

The mortuary.

He pushed open the heavy double doors and walked inside, past the empty stretchers with their rubber lining and the gleaming surgical equipment, and found himself a corner to retreat to. He sat down heavily with a sigh and the padded chair let out a mutual sigh of air. He took off his glasses and rubbed his tired eyes. He pictured Jack lying dead on one of the stretchers. *If only*, he thought.

Colin knew full well that his hatred of Jack was bordering on the pathological and that Jack was somehow always destined to be 10 steps ahead of him. He needed some way of undermining the DCI. He reminded himself how ridiculous it was and that this was to be Jack's last case anyway, but he wanted to get back at him for all those years of being in his shadow. He wanted to see that long and distinguished career ending in disgrace. He would steal Jack's glory at the very last hurdle if necessary. *It shouldn't be too difficult*, he thought. *After all, I've worked under the bastard for long enough. I know all about him. One thing in particular. But how? The application must be perfectly timed.* He sat there for a while and fidgeted. Then he made his decision.

It would be risky, he concluded. *But it would be worth it, if only to see the sanctimonious smile wiped off Jack's face.*

Feeling somewhat refreshed, Colin marched back out of the mortuary with a benign smile concealing his malignant ideas, leaving the doors swinging shut behind him and disappearing amongst the bustling corridors of Hobbs Brae's finest.

Chapter Four

August 30th

Something the boy said… what was it he said?

Alice could not remember. Yet she recalled everything else about that day: the blazing sunshine; the scent of rosemary in her garden; the way the field of rapeseed undulated in the breeze around the scare-crow in the centre. But she could not for the life of her remember what the little boy had said. She could picture his face, wide-eyed and stark, but it was the distinct tone of his voice, awed and hushed, that haunted her, for he had been frightened, so petrified he could barely speak.

There had been nothing to explain his plight. It was just another day. Another long, hot summer in the village of Hobbs Brae, and she had been in the field – the one that stood below her house, the one that no longer got used so it was overgrown, unkempt, like her garden. She looked around at the abandoned shrubs and the untended bushes – a horticulturist's nightmare. Her ruined, abstract flowerbeds and the confusion of dense weeds were an echo of her mind's state, which sometimes made her feel that it was best not to tend to it anymore, for it was like looking into a mirror. Yet she viewed her garden as a medicine of sorts; it helped her to remember. In every nook, in every corner, there were memories – mostly happy, sometimes sad, and in today's case just plain odd.

What did he say?

Alice could see the boy's face; already a little weather-beaten perhaps, but still soft, smooth. A child's face. Yet his stare seemed indicative of a knowledge way beyond his years. *Had he seen something?* She closed her eyes, tried to picture his lips moving, speaking – but she still could not remember his words.

She blinked her eyes open again and realised with a start that she was in the bathroom. *How did I get here?* she wondered. Alice clutched protectively at the pearls around her neck and felt her heart thudding under her cardigan. Her breathing was laboured. *I must have come up the stairs*, she thought to herself, *but why? There's a downstairs bathroom.* Perplexed, she tried to focus by training her eyes on the mirror in front of her. The face that looked back seemed old before its time; a face that had suffered, and yet somehow retained a flush of colour in the cheeks, a youthful tightness around the eyes, and a naïvety in the gaze. The lost look that she now beheld made her stomach lurch at the thought that she had just suffered another fugue. As always, this would be followed by the fear of the knowledge that her memory had been hijacked yet again. And then the depression would set in. And then poor Helen would receive the brunt of her subsequent anger and frustration.

Her dream about Alistair had long since disappeared into the deep, uncharted ravines of her mind. But she could picture him back then, on that hot summer's day in the field, shoulders back and looking much like his father – a thought that brought her considerable pain. Since her husband had left she had been on her own, making do, *and succeeding nicely, thank you very much* – an independent woman – but her blackouts were becoming more frequent and the reflection that looked back at her from the mirror was an increasingly vulnerable one. The light seemed to pass so quickly into dark and back again. It was difficult to tell one day from the other. Every now and then Alice had a moment of clarity and she remembered things, like the way her husband used to nod his head slightly when he talked, or the sound of the doorbell before it broke – or an ominous message from a little boy. That single note of disquiet resonated inside her.

What. Did. The. Boy. Say?

She tapped her fingers impatiently against the edge of the sink. *Why is it so important for me to recall such a minor detail?* Alice was exasperated with herself because she already knew the answer to that one. She needed to be able to remember because she had a private point to make: *If I can recollect this one tiny component then it's a sure sign that my mind is still strong, in good working order.* She closed her eyes tightly, trying to think back, trying to picture his lips opening and closing, the words coming out. Still nothing. The soundtrack to her recollection was muted, so all she could summon up was a tone that implied fear, as if the boy was party to something that she was not even remotely aware of, something that she had ignored for all these long years, but which had now resurfaced for a reason, though for what reason, she did not know. It was a puzzle that refused to piece itself together, rendered inoperable by a distinct lack of mental prowess on her part.

It made her angry, frustrated, and she was about to slam her fist against the sink when she found that she had a trowel in her hand. She stared at it, as if it had suddenly materialised. Blinking furiously, she heard the sound of seagulls crying in the distance, felt the wind billow around her slight frame, teasing at the corners of her faded white dress.

She was outside.

Her heart thudded, faster now, and she looked around, confused, searching for something tangible, something to cling on to. She ran her fingers through her flaying, wispy white mane in an effort to try and control something, anything, and instead her fingers settled on the small, soft flecks of soil in her hairline. Then she heard something behind her and spun round, the trowel raised as a makeshift weapon. *Nothing there. Just the floorboards creaking again.*

The floorboards?

With a startled cry it dawned on her that she was indoors again.

'Helen?' she cried out, and was alarmed at the way her voice sounded strangled with fear. She edged out onto the landing and stared long and hard for the slightest movement. But there was nothing. Numbly, she returned to the bathroom, dropped the trowel into the sink and gripped the edges for support as she tried to summon her memory back. 'Think,' she said out loud. 'Try to remember.' *What was I doing?* She licked her dry lips and gathered herself, dredging up the evidence: *I was in the garden. Then I came up here. Then I went into the garden again. Now I'm in the bathroom. Again.*

She laughed a little at the ridiculousness of it all and was more than a little relieved that at least she could recall the day's events, even if she couldn't actually string them together. Then she caught sight of something on the floor – and her eyes followed a trail out onto the landing. She moved automatically, as if her eyes alone were steering her towards an unknown destination. By the time she was downstairs, the trail was more obvious, in large dark spatters and smudges across the varnished floorboards. She stepped outside. The light had changed. *Almost sunset*, she thought. *Where did the rest of the day go? Where is Helen?* The trail of dirt led to the flower garden. There was a basket sitting on its side on the broken paving stones.

And a large mound of freshly dug earth.

She frantically scanned the garden for evidence, desperately trying to piece the visual clues together.

Was I in the garden digging? Have I just buried something?

Fearfully, she looked around. The wind moaned through the treetops. She felt a chill up her spine as she recalled the boy's timid face, his dark brown eyes seeing something that she could not even begin to fathom. She realised now that they were the same, for she too was in the grip of fear. In constant dread of losing her memory and by default her entire mind. Her hold on reality was slipping as fast as the sun was now sinking below the horizon, the lengthening shadows encroaching like predatory fingers around her frightened, widowed heart.

Suddenly she remembered: sunshine; rosemary; the field of rapeseed – and the scarecrow at the centre of it all. It came to her in a flash, took her breath away. *It was the very same day we built the scarecrow. How could I have forgotten?* She gasped. *Those words. He said them. It happened here on this very spot.* She could see it now as clearly as if it was yesterday. She had just returned from the field. The sun was setting then as it was now and Alice had taken his hand, but he wrenched it free with such ferocity that she had turned to him and was about to ask what was wrong, when she saw that he looked terrified.

She wondered, aghast, why she hadn't remembered it before; that frozen look on his little face and those words that haunted her even now. Those three seemingly insignificant words. And the way he'd said them.

'Something is coming...'

Chapter Five

It was a perfect day.

The sun was shining warm and bright, and Caroline was in the passenger seat of a rented Ford Fiesta, being driven by her boyfriend, Alistair. They were heading along the A82, bypassing Dumbarton, and out into the country. She noted that Alistair was unusually talkative, jumping from one subject to another in quick succession. Caroline wasn't really listening. She smiled and nodded at what she perceived were the right moments, but she was feeling light-headed and couldn't concentrate. Just then, a wave of nausea seemed to come out of nowhere.

'Let's stop at that service station,' she said quickly.

'Hungry?' he asked as he pulled into the car park.

'A wee bit,' she lied.

Returning from the toilet, where she managed to suppress the urge to throw up, she sat down in front of him. The smell of greasy food and coffee began to make her stomach churn again.

'Could we sit at the window?' she asked innocently.

'Sure,' said Alistair with a smile.

She was relieved that he agreed so readily, for she had deliberately chosen the table nearest the door, and the fresh air that wafted in with every customer was a welcome respite. Caroline committed only to small talk, furtive glances and tentative laughter, as if she was on her first date, not her umpteenth. She was waiting to choose her moment, as she had something important to tell him. After only picking at her food, she went to the bathroom to prepare her speech, and noticed that her long blonde hair looked lank, in need of a wash. She fished out a hair band from her handbag and tied it back. Her face was hot and flushed. She placed her hands under the cold water tap and patted her cheeks with her damp palms. When she came back out she took a deep breath, feeling ready to tell Alistair her news – but he was nowhere to be seen. She glanced up and down the café and saw him waiting outside. She sighed, disappointed that he hadn't stayed put; now the moment was ruined, for she had wanted to be sitting facing him when she conveyed her story. She suggested they go for a walk somewhere.

'Where to?' asked Alistair.

'Loch Lomond's not far from here,' she said, thinking there were plenty of secluded areas on the surrounding shores. Just the place for an important conversation.

'Loch Lomond it is then,' he said with a trusting smile.

They walked along the pebbled banks. Caroline thrust her hands deep inside her coat pockets and playfully nudged Alistair with her shoulder. She knew how well he understood the manoeuvre and she smiled as he dutifully placed an arm around her. The sun was beginning to set, casting their long shadows in front of them like ghosts of the future, stories yet to be told. She felt ready to tell hers and took a deep breath, bracing herself, and turned to him.

She saw a brief flicker of a question on his face as he stared at her. She stared back at him, her eyes following the scar on his pale forehead that emerged from under his dark hairline and ended where his eyebrows met in the middle. It surprised her that she had never noticed until now that one of his pupils was a slightly darker shade of green than the other. Somewhere in the distance she could hear ringing.

'Is that an alarm going off?' she asked. Then she blacked out.

She came to inside the car and found that she was in the back seat with Alistair, who was holding her hands and looking intently at her. Caroline struggled to sit up and she smiled sleepily when he helped her, his arms around her waist. She tried to form words but none came.

'You fainted,' he explained, and she saw him searching her face for a response. 'You okay?' he asked.

His voice seemed to become clearer. The veil lifted and Caroline looked around, trying to remember where she was, what she had been doing.

'You scared the shit out of me,' he said. 'I was thinking all sorts of stuff.'

Caroline forced herself to smile. 'I'm fine,' she replied weakly, and then she said without thinking, 'I'm pregnant.'

She waited nervously for a reaction. Alistair threw her a wary glance and she looked back at him, attempting a smile, but it felt clumsy, lopsided. Alistair suddenly smirked mischievously and said, 'C'mere you,' and drew her closer. She hugged him tight and kissed him, long and deep. 'Alistair,' she said softly, and took his hand and gently placed it on her belly. His eyes were wide, like a little boy's. He remained there, staring down at her midriff. She could see the telltale tremble of his top lip.

'I can hardly believe it,' he said in a hushed voice.

Caroline smiled broadly. She felt safer now that Alistair had accepted with enthusiasm that he was going to be a dad. She was amused but also touched by how gently he escorted her to the front seat. Then, as they pulled out and were back on the road, she saw that mischievous grin again.

'I'm taking you to Hobbs Brae to see my mum,' he said softly, with a sly narrowing of the eyes. 'Don't worry, she's expecting us.'

'I wondered why you were so intent on me packing my bags,' replied Caroline. 'You kept saying it was a surprise. I just assumed we were going away for a romantic weekend. We're going to your mum's? Seriously?'

Alistair began fumbling for words and Caroline understood how disappointed she must have sounded. She didn't want to appear ungrateful, so she rescued the situation and interrupted with, 'So why all the secrecy if we're just going to your mum's?'

Alistair cleared his throat and said mysteriously, 'Because there's more to it than that.'

Then it suddenly occurred to her.

'You knew I was pregnant already, didn't you?'

She watched, amazed, as he grinned and casually reached out to stroke her hair, his other hand on the wheel.

'I suspected as much, but I couldn't be sure. I was waiting for you to tell me.'

Caroline said nervously, 'Your mother's going to die when she hears about this. And keep both hands on the wheel, you.'

She frowned with annoyance as Alistair laughed, making a show of obeying her instructions, and said, 'Don't be daft. She'll be thrilled. She's a grandmother now.'

'And you're a dad,' Caroline replied, and she couldn't help but smile with delight. Then she noticed a flash of doubt flit across his face. 'What?'

'I was thinking about your mum.'

Caroline gave him a measured stare. 'The last thing I want to talk about today of all days is my bloody mother.'

'She's not going to like it.'

'She's going to have to lump it,' Caroline replied, with a bravery that she didn't really feel. She saw Alistair exhale heavily and roll his eyes, then reach out once more and squeeze her hand.

'Happy?' he asked with mock innocence.

'I'd be happier if you kept both hands on that bloody wheel,' she replied, then caught that roguish look in his eyes again. 'Delirious,' she said eventually, with a smile, then thought back to how dizzy she had been earlier and laughed at her own words.

Chapter Six

August 31st

Jerome was in his favourite armchair, staring soulfully at the fire as it crackled and danced before him. Puffing on a joint, he sighed loudly, trying to relax. Bessie, his border collie, was lying curled up at his feet. Now and then he caught her glancing at him, every regard implying a readiness for obedience, but tonight he thought her gaze was different, troubled. *She can pick up on my mood no matter how much I try to hide it*, he observed, and patted her head to put her at ease. Bessie wagged her tail a little and settled down.

He resumed watching the flames and trying to unwind, but the pain in his back was making him restless. He glanced at his walking stick, which leaned against his chair. *As constant a companion as my dog*, he brooded. *The cannabis has never been enough to ease this perpetual pain. God only knows how I've managed to pull through. Fifty-four years old. My wife long gone. And there's no one left to help me. There's my son, of course, but he's never shown any enthusiasm, so I'm forced to do all the work by myself. But I can't run the farm efficiently anymore, not with my back, and I'm struggling to make ends meet. It's affecting my health. I blame my son entirely for it.*

He shifted uncomfortably in his seat. *Scott was wrapped in cotton wool from the outset*, he pondered bitterly, replaying an age-old argument in his head.

'I'm not having any son of mine being brought up to expect an easy life. I never had one so why should he?' Jerome had said this with rather more vehemence than he had intended, and as soon as he saw the look on Elspeth's face he instantly regretted it. His late wife had stared at him long and hard, her right eyebrow hoisting itself upwards as if pulled by an invisible thread – always a sign that a torrent of retribution was on the way.

'You never had an easy life? And what about me? Do you think I have it easy? No, I don't. But do I ever complain? Do I make your life a misery because of it? Of course I don't. I just get on with it. I get up well before you every morning. I cook your breakfast. I milk the cows and collect the eggs. I clear out the barn. I send Scott to school. You do remember that he's still at school, don't you?'

Jerome shifted uneasily from one foot to the other. 'Of course I do, but I don't think that means we should be—'

'I'm not making his life easy,' she continued over him. 'I'm treating him as he should be treated – he's still a child. And given that the farm is doing well under my supervision – we've got plenty of food and money to spare, almost entirely thanks to me, then I get a say in how things are run here and that includes my son – and I say he can have a day off every now and then. God knows one of us should.'

'He has every day off,' Jerome grumbled, but Elspeth shot him a look and he slinked off outside. He'd been scolded enough for the time being.

As he sat in front of the hearth, absentmindedly stroking Bessie's ears, he felt a pang of regret, for he knew that Elspeth had been quite right in her assertions; the farm was in better hands when she was in life. He smiled fondly at the memory of her formidable skill in dealing with the daily stresses of running the business – rising before dawn and getting on with it, all without complaint; balancing the accounts and completing the necessary correspondence late at night. Elspeth Jennings had been a one-woman powerhouse. She had more than earned her stripes.

Unlike our son, thought Jerome, and he felt his blood pressure rise as he pictured Scott sullenly doing nothing. *I tried to warn her but she never listened.* He took another impatient draw from his spliff as he recalled how Elspeth did everything for their only child.

'That boy's turning lazy. He's a daydreamer.'

'Nothing wrong with dreaming,' replied Elspeth sharply. 'That's how all successful people begin.' Jerome felt slighted once more as she affectionately ruffled Scott's hair and they both looked at him with that same dull-eyed defiance.

Jerome regretted that he hadn't put his foot down and showed the pair of them who was in charge. He was painfully aware of just how much he was paying the consequences for his own lack of assertiveness. Elspeth had ruled the roost and Jerome watched disapprovingly as his son became more and more indolent.

'We're blessed to have a boy like him,' Elspeth had said defensively.

'Oh, he's blessed all right. Blessed with the knack of disappearing whenever a job needs doing.' Jerome walked out in disgust and stared long and hard into the woods. *And no amount of shouting his name seems to bring him from out of the undergrowth*, he concluded.

As he sat in his chair, his physical discomfort manifested itself in his thoughts. *There's something else. It's not that Scott doesn't touch the breakfasts I cook for him anymore – that's not what bothers me. Nor is it that his disobedience seems much more blatant, again that's not what bothers me.*

What bothers me is the silence.

Scott has always been on the quiet side. That's not a surprise. We've spent our entire lives isolated on our small farm on the edge of Hobbs Brae with only our livestock for company. Our nearest neighbour, Alice, is over a mile away. Elspeth spoke to her on occasion but neither myself nor my son ever made the effort. In fact, Scott and I rarely speak to anyone. I used to think that was the explanation, that perhaps the silence was simply a trait that Scott had learned – a case of like father, like son. Or perhaps it was because Scott had no brothers or sisters to talk to. These explanations would have been so wonderfully normal and therefore easier to deal with, but none of them seemed to fit. Since approaching adolescence, Scott's wall of silence has become insurmountable. I used to think he was simply at that awkward age when kids' hormones go haywire, but as time has gone on and Scott has reached his nineteenth year, I can no longer find excuses for his conduct.

I worry that it's increasingly unlikely that Scott will want to take over the farm when I grow too old and infirm to work on it myself – and that day is approaching much faster than I anticipated. Scott's growth into maturity has resulted in a struggle of wills between us, putting the family business in jeopardy.

Jerome shook his head and made a concerted effort to try and stop thinking about it, fearing that the cannabis was making him paranoid. He flicked the remainder of the spliff into the fire. He sat further back in his chair. Soon, he felt becalmed and his mind began to wander, making its way down to the cemetery, where Elspeth's grave lay in the shadows of the old abbey. In his relaxed state he could smell the fresh breeze from the North Atlantic that wafted in through the ruins. He smiled at the amusing sight of Bessie darting in and out of the tombstones and sniffing at the decaying bouquets of flowers. He could see everything as clear as day, could feel the sun on his weather-beaten face. All at once Jerome was euphoric.

'Plenty of old bones for you here, girl,' he shouted happily to Bessie, then felt guilty for speaking out of turn, amongst the dead, and in the presence of the one person who had made his life bearable. Jerome composed himself and sat down, resting his head on her gravestone.

'I don't know what to do about our son, Elspeth. Ever since you left I've tried so hard to be a good father to him and in return I would have expected some loyalty, a vested interest in our livelihood, but there's been nothing.'

He looked around helplessly. The wind whistled through the gaps in the ruins where the stained glass windows once stood, and he could only imagine what her response would be.

Jerome wasn't sure how much time had passed when he came out of his chair-bound reverie, but he could feel his mood begin to bruise once more, the old anxiety arriving like the spectre at the feast. He watched Bessie rest her chin on her front paws and give out a loud sigh. He could see that she was getting old and it saddened him because it was beginning to feel like the end of an era. He wondered if his life's work would be forgotten. *I don't know what the future holds. When Scott is asleep upstairs I quietly despair. I still can't find a motive for his behaviour. I'm no good at this. I can't keep second guessing anymore.*

He winced as the pain in his spine began to recur. He tried to turn his attention to something else and dreamed of a period when he was more able-bodied. *I was too busy to worry about anything back then. All I did was work. Now I have to rest all the time and all I do is worry.* He thought about the bare facts of his predicament: he and his son were as strangers and they had barely spoken in months. Something was wrong with Scott and it infuriated Jerome that he could not figure out what. He couldn't rid himself of the idea that his son was planning something. There was no proof, nothing tangible. It was just a feeling he had. Yet the clues were there in his actions: the long absences, the uneaten breakfasts – and the wilful destruction of the snares.

Jerome had been trying to catch a fox that had been attacking the hen coop. Feeling positive, he had hobbled quickly through the grass with Bessie trotting alongside him. His hopes were dashed, however, when he found that his snares had been deliberately destroyed. Each and every one. Jerome was furious and stomped back to the house to confront Scott, for he knew that his insolent son was responsible. But then something happened that changed everything. When he flung open his son's bedroom door, he saw the fox lying there in a cardboard box, being looked after like some sort of pet. Jerome's face flushed with shame when he saw that one of its hind legs was bandaged. Scott glared at him with such hatred that Jerome lost his words and hobbled silently back down the stairs, all the while blaming Elspeth for his predicament. *Wrapped in cotton wool*, he reminded himself. Either way, the message was clear: his son resented him and would do anything to spite him.

Not bad for someone who doesn't talk, Jerome mused, attempting to see at least some humour in the situation, *but what did I do wrong?*

The question was loaded with implications he dared not think about. Instead, he turned his attention to the sky. It seemed to be ablaze. It reminded him that tomorrow was the beginning of the field-burning season. Every September he would set fire to one of his crops in order to germinate new growth for the following spring. He tried to imagine Scott helping him, but found he could not conjure up such an unlikely work of fiction. He smiled ruefully at this and watched as the bloodstained clouds threaded their way across the horizon.

Red sky at night, shepherd's delight…

Elspeth had rhymed off that old proverb on many occasions. *So tomorrow will be a nice, dry day*, he thought. *Ideal for burning the field.* But as night fell, and the first chill of autumn approached, his fears

Chapter Seven

September 1st

I'm going to be a dad!

As he waited to buy some coffee to keep them going on their long journey, Alistair couldn't help but feel excited. The queue seemed to be taking ages and he kept glancing nervously at Caroline sitting at a table, texting on her phone. He was fuelled with the irresistible urge to abandon the coffee and go straight back to her, sit with her – guard her.

But from what?

He watched as she sat there, innocently messaging her friends. From his vantage point she did not look any different from any other person in the café. Her downturned face partially hidden by her hair, concealing her beautiful regard, and making her seem almost anonymous, almost but not quite ordinary. He glanced across the room. People were sitting at their tables chatting or texting, drinking coffee, eating. Just a typical afternoon. And yet every fibre of his being told him that today was anything but, for his heart was filled with pride because he was going to be a daddy. And there in the middle of the room was the whole reason, his touchstone. Only he knew how truly special she was. It was a delicious secret between them that was hidden in the humdrum of café life. The course of his life had now changed forever. And it was all because of her. He peeked over his shoulder at his girlfriend yet again as the line in front moved like a viscous river; he longed to be beside her, protecting his own. Yes, he was most definitely a father now. Who would have thought?

He had come a long way in the past year or so. Ever since that first day he had been drawn inexorably off course, away from the lanes and alleys where crime was a currency, and onto the busy pavements where the good people walked, the ones who paid their taxes and obeyed the rules. It was as if he had been summoned from darkness into light.

Alistair wondered at how things had turned out. That first sight of Caroline walking quickly across George Square: the books clutched to her breast; the long winter coat; the calf-length boots; the long blonde hair that flowed behind her pale face; the troubled brow and the shadows under her startling blue eyes, giving her the demeanour of someone on an important mission, sleepless and secretive, mysterious, perhaps vulnerable – and distinctly out of his league. Unapproachable. And now she was sitting only a few tables away, carrying his child. Whatever had happened between these two states blew his mind.

He remembered how cold and sunny it had been that day. He had lost her in the glare and was forced to wait impatiently at the traffic lights, shielding his eyes with the back of his hand, peering anxiously through the moving buses and cars, trying to find her again. Then she reappeared, further away, walking quickly through a flock of pigeons that rose up uniformly into the air, making way for her. His heart thumped as he saw his chances receding with her slender form. And he just stood there, unsure what to do next, held fast by inhibition, so that by the time he had weighed one option against the other, by the time he had plucked up some courage, the traffic lights had changed again.

And again.

And again.

And though he kept returning to the same spot at the same time, it was now several days too late and she had long since disappeared; forever, it seemed. He was furious with himself. He'd blown it. But in time he got used to the fact and kidded himself that maybe she wasn't so special after all. It was the hard-hearted rationale of someone who had made up their mind that they would never have that chance again.

Then, quite unexpectedly, their lanes crossed.

He was entering a newsagent for some cigarettes when a purse dropped right at his feet. He instinctively bent down to snaffle it but when he stood up she was there.

'Thank you,' she said, taking the purse from him, and he just looked at her, dumbstruck. She smiled politely and left. And that was that. He bought his cigarettes on autopilot and went outside, cursing himself.

And there she was, waiting for him.

She smiled again and he nervously smiled back. With a sudden surge of confidence that came from nowhere, he adjusted his baseball cap and started to walk towards her when the look in her eyes stopped him. Her gaze was fixed on something behind him. He was about to turn round to see what it was, when a tall, handsome man with a deep suntan and a whiter-than-white smile marched quickly past him, said, 'Sorry I'm late,' and kissed her on the cheek. Alistair's stomach sank as they both disappeared around the corner, hand in hand. He could see those damned traffic lights again, could see his chance receding fast into the distance. But in an instant he was being propelled into forward momentum, and before he knew it, he was following them as they walked down the street, observing how the couple were matched in terms of height and wearing mutually expensive clothes.

West-Enders, he thought.

And he was right. They went into a restaurant on Byres Road called the Glasgow Grand, and he waited outside, nervously fixing his baseball cap and trying not to feel like some kind of mad, jealous stalker. Of course, he was fluorescent green with envy but he didn't want to lose her a second time, such was the strength of his feeling.

There's always a chance, he told himself. *She can either say yes or she can tell me to fuck off. At least I've tried.*

Emboldened, he turned to look through the restaurant window, when he saw the boyfriend coming towards him and he darted back out of sight. He heard him call in a posh, private-school accent, 'See you tonight – and I promise I won't be late again.' Alistair watched with a predator's eyes as the boyfriend hurried out with an air of unbridled confidence and swaggered down the street, disappearing around the corner. Alistair deftly caught the restaurant door just as it was swinging shut. The moment seemed providential.

Why not? he thought, and ventured inside. The Grand was warm and filled with the aroma of coffee and the industrious chat of people who, judging by the sharp suits and Prada bags on display, all had top-tier jobs. He furtively scanned the room for any sign of her, but all he could spy were customers sipping their sparkling mineral waters and nibbling on their salads. Two attractive young waitresses were bustling up and down with bread baskets and fine wine. He couldn't see her. *Maybe she's in the toilet*, he reasoned. *I could always wait* – and he wondered if he had enough money for a cup of tea. He was about to finger for some loose change in his jeans when he caught sight of her, but she was dressed differently. Then he realised.

'She works here,' he blurted, then self-consciously placed a hand over his mouth. He watched in awe as she manoeuvred gracefully through the tables and chairs, her hair tied back and an apron around her petite waist. He thought to raise his hand to catch her attention, but he felt inhibited, and could only watch helplessly as she sashayed through the door and disappeared into the kitchen.

'Next please!' someone shouted, and Alistair looked up to see he was now at the front of the queue and a member of staff was waiting impatiently on him.

'A latté and a cup of tea,' he said, and turned to see Caroline watching him from her table. He gave her a nod and she gave him a little wave back. Moments later he was seated in front of her, wishing he had bought something cold to alleviate the stifling heat.

'What's happening?' he asked distractedly, referring to her phone.

'Nothing much,' she said, stifling a yawn and putting the phone back in her bag. He watched as she leaned forward and cupped the latté in her hands. 'I think I felt him kick,' she said quietly, and gave him an impish smile.

'Don't be daft. You're only a few weeks gone. You can't feel it that early. Can you?'

He waited keenly as Caroline looked from side to side conspiratorially, as if about to tell him a secret. 'No, of course not,' she laughed, her blue eyes bright and watery. Then she fished out her mobile again and went straight back to texting. Alistair watched as her fingers flicked rapidly across the phone, the very same phone she had used to tell her posh boyfriend that she wouldn't be seeing him anymore and that she was with someone else. Alistair relived the moment when Caroline had told him about it, the thrill that went through his heart when he learned that her fancy man was history.

His thoughts drifted back to the restaurant and how he had waited for her to come back out of the kitchen. When she reappeared he bit the bullet and introduced himself, reminding her that he was the one who had picked up her purse. He was relieved when she remembered instantly.

'Alistair,' she repeated, as if it sounded foreign on her tongue. 'That's a nice name. Simple.'

He frowned, unsure what she meant.

'I mean uncomplicated,' she said, smiling, but her azure eyes drifted downwards, and Alistair quickly surmised that something was troubling her.

He became aware that he was being watched. Customers were giving him the once over because of the way he was dressed.

'You might have to remove your baseball cap,' Caroline whispered.

Alistair took it off and ran a hand across his cropped hair in order to conceal his scar. Then, in a moment of annoyance at being singled out, he said loudly, 'Actually, this is Glasgow. They don't really bother about that kind of thing, even in the West End.' He took pleasure in seeing the startled look on Caroline's face and briefly wondered if he had taken his defiance a little too far, but now he couldn't stop himself. 'It's all right everyone, I'm not a drug dealer,' he announced, mimicking the serious and self-important tone of a BBC news correspondent. He heard someone tut, but by and large they all went back to their business.

'See?' he said, arms folded in mock defence but smiling broadly.

'You'll get me fired,' whispered Caroline through a nervous giggle. 'I'll get you some tea, then you'll need to go.' And she gestured for him to sit down. After he'd finished he was about to pay when she said that it was free of charge.

'Thanks,' he said, secretly relieved that he could keep whatever minimal loose change he might have for another day. Then he added, 'I'd like to see you again.'

He tried not to appear too nervous as she paused before looking up from the till. He witnessed that same troubled look again. She seemed to be trying to read him. 'Well, you know where I work now, so I suppose I can't stop you,' she said, and gave him a wary smile.

In other words, yes, Alistair thought, and it was his turn to feel unbridled confidence when he walked out of the restaurant.

After another cup of tea at the Grand, Alistair decided his face didn't fit and suggested they meet at Kelvingrove Park instead. They sat on a bench looking at the Stewart Memorial Fountain, with its gilded cherubs defending a circular moat of water supplied from Loch Katrine, the Neo-Gothic tower of Glasgow University rearing up behind it in the distance. Caroline talked about her job. She hated it.

'No, really I do,' she said earnestly. 'It's just not very... me.' And she self-consciously stroked her hair.

Alistair was bemused at how she could be down to earth one minute and full of airs and graces the next. He could see why she had chosen Matthew, the guy with the Colgate smile. They had a lot in common, right down to the private-school accent. *But what the hell does she see in me?* he wondered.

'So what do you want to do with your life?' he asked.

Caroline shrugged. 'I don't know. I just want a better one.' She stared right back at him, as if still trying to read him.

Alistair avoided her gaze and wanted to ask, *Am I on parole or something?* He could tell that she was not yet convinced about his motives. She was very guarded and seemed to be weighing up the odds, deciding who was the better man – him or Matthew. The possibility that she might even contemplate sticking with that posh twat was too much for him to bear. He speculated that she might be cooling off on him already and was about to confront her on the issue when she moved a little closer to him.

'It's my fucking family's fault,' she said tersely.

Alistair inwardly sighed with relief. *I'm still in the game*, he thought, but felt himself seizing up at the prospect that Caroline was about to go off on yet another tirade about her mother. *Here we go again.* Bracing himself, he sat through her entire monologue, pretending to listen, as she described in great detail how her mother had kept her ambitions in check by constantly interfering and bringing her down. She loathed her brother, too.

'He's a moody little mummy's boy,' she grumbled. 'If he had his way he would have me killed for dishonour.' And her father was something of a nonentity, too, it seemed. Alistair stared into the middle distance, waiting patiently for her diatribe to conclude.

'I keep feeling that I've got to please them. Is it the same for you?'

'It's the same for all of us,' Alistair lied.

'I don't think they see me as someone to be reckoned with, you know? Nothing I ever do is good enough for them. I feel like a performing seal sometimes.'

Caroline paused for reflection and Alistair cast a sidewards glance at her. She touched her ear lobe, and said quietly, 'I just want to make something of myself, you know? In order to do that I need to focus and work as hard as possible. But I want to do it for myself, not for them. And I want no distractions. I can't afford to be veered off the straight and narrow.'

Alistair sat silent, unsure what to say. Something brushed up against his leg, and he turned to see Caroline smiling slyly. 'Well, I don't mind the occasional distraction,' she said softly. Her lips were brushing against his and they kissed, in full view of everyone in the park. *I guess this means we're serious now*, he thought as he concentrated on not getting a hard on.

But it was something of a mystery to Alistair at first. Why would someone like Caroline opt out of a relationship with a well-bred restaurant owner and opt in for a pale-skinned wee man who had left his middle-class roots behind and settled for surviving in one of the poorest parts of Glasgow with no job and hardly any money?

Am I just a bit of rough to her?

A few more park meetings later she answered his question. 'You make me smile,' she said, without prompting. 'You're genuine. You don't have to speak fancy or anything. You're just... you.' She shrugged and laughed helplessly.

'I've got working-class charm,' he said, putting on a grin and puffing up his chest and arms in a parody of pride, whilst trying to subdue the doubts and fears he carried about his newly declared status.

Her resulting laugh empowered him. He had something that Matthew didn't – he wasn't sure what it was but Caroline seemed to like it. Spurred on by her belief in him, he spent the next few days searching laboriously for a job – any job – but to no avail, so he did what he always did – and picked someone's pocket. There wasn't much cash in the purse but there was enough to fund his planned night out. He harked back to the moment he had found Caroline's purse and he felt his face redden with shame at the thought that he had almost stolen from her, too. He marvelled at how things had turned out.

Two months passed and they had become inseparable. As a direct result of her existence in his life, Alistair felt his self-confidence blossom. He no longer looked in the mirror and saw a friendless 21-year-old staring back at him, the scar making him look much harder than he actually was. His expectations were raised and so was his view of the world around him.

Several months later, the all-too-brief Glasgow summer was coming to an end. The light was already so cold and clinical it cast a scientific glare on the buildings, making them seem hyper-real, their angles rendered stark and clear-cut. The glass fronts of the metropolis towered into the blue, rising towards the broken rays of the sun and mirroring wedges of dazzling light across the city, whilst freezing fog transformed the distant office blocks into monolithic ghosts. As Alistair walked amongst the throng and towards the iconic Victorian bridge of Central Station, he noted the looks of derision and fear. It was a curious dilemma that he had tolerated for most of his young adult life – that perfect strangers should give way to him – as one does a leper – because his matching blue tracksuit and trainers and the scar above his brow gave him the look of the lowest common denominator. But he was used to people's narrow assumptions by now. Their prejudice would have been justified once upon a time – but not anymore: he was a sales rep for a sports shop; his tracksuit was his uniform. He was earning a wage and paying his tax. He had passed his driving test, first time. He was just like them now. One of the good people.

Reminding himself of this fact gave him an increased vigour as he strode under the bridge with its neon shopfronts and rank smell of stale chip fat. Now that they were an item, there was no need for secrets and doubts, no need to deflect any more questions. She knew about his missing father. She knew about the fight Alistair had with a policeman that resulted in him requiring 14 stitches across his forehead. She knew about his old friends who were petty criminals. There was nothing she didn't know about him. Caroline had encouraged Alistair to open up and let her further into his private world. Now he felt unburdened, liberated from a self-imposed prison. He smiled dopily as he came to the startling conclusion that Caroline had done the impossible. She had actually made him happy.

And then, only hours ago in the car, the announcement that she was pregnant. It was the absolute confirmation of his hopes and dreams. The highest of peaks, surmounted, vaulted over in one giant step.

They were back on the road once again, the windows rolled down to let some much needed air in.

'I've got a new job, in a book shop,' she said. 'I've left my parents' plans for me on the back burner.'

'Good for you,' he replied, admiring her new-found confidence.

'I'm twenty. I can do what I like now,' she said evenly. 'I start as soon as we come back from your mum's.'

'Great,' he said, suddenly sounding less enthusiastic than he intended.

'You okay?' He felt her looking at him now, frowning with concern.

Alistair sighed. 'A wee bit tired, that's all.'

'Do you want to stop off at a hotel or something?'

He felt her hand on his knee and glanced at her. 'Nah. I'll be fine,' he replied, smiling faintly. 'Glasgow to Hobbs Brae is an easy ride.' A moment passed and he felt her hand lift away, an indication that she was not entirely convinced with his explanation. He decided to tell her something that had been on his mind of late.

'I've got a surprise for you,' he began. 'A special surprise.' He cast a quick look at her and caught the beginnings of a smile on her lips as she tried to keep her eyes on the road ahead. He tapped his fingers playfully on the steering wheel and waited for the suspense to become unbearable.

'Okay,' she relented, 'what is this special surprise?'

'It's a secret,' he said, and burst out laughing. A split second later he felt a stinging sensation on his thigh from the slap that she gave him. He looked at her questioningly and saw her mocking smile.

'So intriguing. And keep your eyes on the road, lover.'

He gave an obedient nod of the head and stated, 'Everything is a prelude, a prologue, to something else.' He smiled cryptically.

'That's deep, for you.'

'Not me,' he replied. 'My mum.'

'Thought it was too good to be true,' she quipped.

'Besides, I'm not deep.'

'What are you then?'

'I'm deeply shallow.'

Caroline's resulting laughter was disarming. It pealed loud and clear like a bell, temporarily taking his mind off what had been nagging at him. A car had been tailing them for some time now. A Porsche. He thought he recognised the registration plate, but he didn't want to jump to any conclusions just yet.

He felt Caroline looking at him concernedly again. 'Another coffee?' he quickly suggested.

'You know me so well,' he heard her reply warmly.

They arrived at another service station. Alistair allowed Caroline to walk ahead of him, then opened the door of the café for her.

'How gentlemanly,' she commented, and adopted a simpering pose.

'After you,' he said, not really paying heed, for he was too busy looking around to see if there was anything suspicious. He was relieved to find that the car had vanished.

'You must have been desperate for a break,' she remarked once they'd sat down, 'given how quickly you turned off that road. I nearly got whiplash.'

'Sorry,' he said, and changed the subject by making an observation that she was drinking camomile tea.

'Coffee's not so good when you're pregnant,' she said, looking down at her cup. 'I read that somewhere.' A pause, then he heard her say quietly, 'Of course, neither's whiplash.'

Alistair exhaled. It was obvious she knew that something was wrong and she wasn't going to give up until he told her. 'Maybe I'm just a wee bit more tired than I thought,' he said, hoping that would be the end of it.

Caroline stared at her cup a little longer, then said, 'You don't wear your cap anymore.'

'Guess I don't need it anymore,' he said flatly.

She stared at him. 'Are you sure you're okay?'

He nodded.

'Are you worried about me meeting your mum?'

Alistair thought, *Give it a rest, why don't you?*

'Yeah, that's it,' he lied.

'Don't be. She can't be any worse than mine,' Caroline began, and Alistair braced himself for another onslaught of mummy issues. Pretending to listen, he self-consciously touched his forehead as he thought about how sullen he must have sounded. True, he hadn't visited his mother in a long time, but right now what worried him the most was Caroline's ex-boyfriend. *Why would he follow us?* he wondered. *Jealousy? Obsession? Something else I don't know about?*

He sensed Caroline had stopped her diatribe and he felt the urge to fill the silence with something, anything, that would maintain some semblance of normality whilst his mind raced with the possibilities.

'How you feeling? Tired?' he asked, trying to sound upbeat. No response. Thinking that she had caught him out for not listening and was in a mood, he was about to apologise when he saw that she had fallen asleep.

Alistair sat there for a moment and watched as she slept. He smiled to himself. Here he was once more, amazed to be sitting opposite the mother of his child, her eyes closed to the world, her trust in him implicit. He loved her. It had become the defining fact of his life. He loved everything about her: the shape of her posture in the bed-clothes; the casual grace of her walk. Sometimes he could taste her, could detect the memory of her scent, even though she wasn't there. It disturbed him the way he felt. Caroline's absence could be every bit as overpowering as her presence. She left a huge fingerprint in his small world.

Which made the continued presence of Matthew all the more difficult to accept. It was his car that had been following them, he felt sure of it. Alistair suspected he was being paranoid, but he knew that her ex was never quite out of the picture, and the sight of the Porsche all but confirmed it. He had learned that they still remained good friends, even saw her in Matthew's flashy vehicle once in Glas-gow, and this after they had supposedly split up. He wondered why she hadn't told him but at the same time he understood; she didn't want to make him jealous. *But what if she's still seeing him, in that way? And what if the child isn't mine at all? Does she have any more secrets, or surprises in the waiting?* He shook his head a little and dispelled once more the ghost of his insecurities, reminding himself that he'd given Matthew the slip. Just then Caroline jolted awake. Alistair didn't dare to ask what or who she had been dreaming about.

Back in the car, his spirits lifted. He passed a sign for Loch Ness and distracted himself by talking about the mythical monster and what if it was really true. Before long he decided to cut out such crap and stop at another service station. They went for a meal and more tea. Trying not to notice the suffocating heat, he turned the conver-sation to his mother and he wondered how she was. He was looking forward to seeing her expression of surprise and delight when he told her that she was going to be a grandmother.

'Can I borrow your phone?' he asked.

Caroline looked blank.

'I'm not getting a signal,' he explained.

'Sure,' she said, after a pause, and passed it to him.

'I need to call my mum to let her know what time to expect us.'

'Of course. I think it's really good that you're staying in touch with her now. I know it's not easy. Mine is a… well, you know what I think about her.'

He nodded, not really listening because there was a strange tone at the other end. He waited.

'That's odd,' he said finally. 'Phone's dead.'

Caroline's eyes widened. 'Is she not in?'

'No, it's not that. It's like it's been cut off or something.'

'Power cut maybe? I did hear someone say there's a storm coming.'

'Guess so.' He brooded for a moment, then hung up and passed the phone back to Caroline.

'I'm sure everything's okay,' she said, and touched his knee again. 'So, what is this special surprise you've got me?'

'I'm taking you to see my mum, remember?' He kicked himself at how sarcastic he sounded.

'I know that, silly,' she said, laughing. 'I mean the other surprise.'

He managed a smirk. 'Just you wait and see.'

'Okay, man of mystery,' she replied, and they left the station café.

Alistair rubbed his tired eyes. A four-hour journey and we've done nothing but stop at service stations, he thought. But he was finding it difficult to concentrate. He could feel a headache coming on.

'There's no air out here,' complained Caroline, looking up at the sky, which had begun to cloud over.

Something about her tone made him turn to face her. He saw that she had that troubled look again.

She touched his arm and said, 'There's something you should know. Me and Matthew are still friends, but that's all we are. And I know today has been something of a shock to you, what with me being pregnant and all, but I love you.' She looked at him with an expression of hope.

He looked into her eyes and thought to tell her about the car he had seen following them. But he knew there wasn't much point. He had lost him, if it was him at all. 'You look pale,' he said, changing the subject. 'You okay?'

'Don't worry about me,' she replied. 'I'm not going to faint again if that's what you think.'

And they both laughed.

A short while later they were nearing the outskirts of Hobbs Brae. The wind was buffeting around them, whistling through the trees that towered on either side of the motorway. Nearly there, thought Alistair with relief.

Then Matthew's car reappeared.

Alistair felt his stomach lurch. Where the hell did he come from? He thought back to his first sighting of Matthew outside the newsagent's. He had recognised him then. It took a moment at first, but he recalled that Matthew had worked for his father a long time ago. Odd that their paths would cross again in Glasgow all these years later.

He stared intently at the Porsche that tailed in the background as the rain began to pelt against the windscreen.

'Are you okay?' Caroline asked, sensing his mood.

'I think you were right about that storm,' he said, and drove off into the encroaching darkness.

Chapter Eight

August 31st

Scott had been woken up at dawn, as usual, by the sun sliding in through his bedroom window – and the smell of burning pig.

He got out of bed and stretched. Heaving a sigh, he stood for a moment, gazing out at the fields and hedgerows, his palms resting on the bare windowsill, which already felt warm from the sun's rays. He savoured the sensation of sleepiness and the inhibition of standing naked at the window. Seconds later the truth of his existence weighed heavily on him.

'I've removed the curtains so that you won't be late for your work in future,' his father had said. Scott was 11 years old at the time.

His bedroom was positioned on the side of the farmhouse that caught the morning's light. As Scott grew up, it dawned on him that this was no accident. It also became clear that the bacon his father prepared for breakfast each day was nothing more than a bribe – another method of enticing him downstairs and getting him ready for the day's work. And then there was the hen coop that had been strategically placed below his window with the cockerel perched inside, ready to wake him up just in case.

'See how thoughtful I am, boy?' Jerome had said with a smirk when Scott had once dared to confront him about it.

Over the years Scott obeyed the rules that his father had laid down, but in time he began to quietly rebel. He made a point of getting up well before the cockerel each day. He took to making his own breakfast. He set to work before his father was up and about. And he always made sure he finished his work exactly 10 minutes after his father had finished his. Scott was successfully beginning to prove a point – that he was his own man now.

For, despite his 19 years, he was well able to work independently on the farm. The proof of his efforts was evident in his broad shoulders and in his complexion, which was tanned from toiling outside and in all climates. At the end of each working day he would sit and eat the dinner his father prepared, a necessary compromise, because he had been working so hard that his fingers were becoming calloused and he was barely able to lift his knife and fork, let alone prepare an evening meal. It was also down to a habit forged by Elspeth, who had cooked all their meals when she was in life, and who made them sit at the table as a family – regardless of how they felt about each other. There existed between Scott and his father a respect for her memory that was embodied in the silence that stood firm against every corner, every wall.

But between father and son lay a grudge that began when Elspeth died. Scott was just seven years old and her death left a huge gap in the family tree. With no brothers or sisters to fall back on, her responsibilities were passed directly to him. Under her tutelage he had learned the basic tasks of how to feed the pigs and collect the hens' eggs, but he couldn't do her paperwork or any of the other tasks of farm life. That required skill that could only be attained with years of training. Despite his father's best efforts to teach him, Scott was simply too young to understand.

Jerome was blind to this and lacked his late wife's patience. Scott would often get a beating from him because he could not learn quickly enough.

'You'll thank me for it, boy, one day,' he had once said afterwards, still breathing heavily with the exertion of delivering his punishment.

Scott missed his mother.

He knew only too well that his father regarded him as a total disappointment, but in turn Scott regarded him in much the same way. He was no longer his dad – he was a dictator who seemed to grow more oppressive by the day.

'You good-for-nothing layabout! What do you think you're playing at? You left the barn doors open – the cows are all over the place!'

'That wasn't me, it was you,' Scott replied timidly, shrinking back from the stench of whisky on his father's breath.

Jerome took a step forward, and was now inches away from his son's face. 'Don't you answer me back, boy,' he warned, glowering at him.

'It's not my fault,' Scott countered, his voice and knees quivering. 'It's yours. You got drunk and left the doors open, again.'

A split second and everything went black.

When he came to, his face hurt and he could taste blood in his mouth. After that Scott withdrew more and more from his father's aggressive behaviour, while his confidence died a slow and painful death.

The years dragged by and the drinking and the violence escalated. Soon after Scott's 18th birthday his father was once more spoiling for a fight.

'You think I don't know what you've been doing, boy? You think you can flout my authority by wandering off whenever you feel like it?'

'I didn't wander off,' Scott explained quietly, his legs threatening to buckle under him.

'Don't answer me back!' Jerome screamed, and he raised his fist.

Scott braced himself for the onslaught. But the blow never came. It took Scott a second to realise that he was holding his father by the wrist. A reflex action had kicked in from somewhere and he watched, a little amazed at his own sudden prowess, as Jerome tried to break free. Scott caught his other wrist and held him fast, and their eyes became locked in a mutual struggle of wills. But Scott began to push his weight forward until the balance of power finally shifted and his father lost his footing. The dictator was overthrown and fell backward into the mud.

He was howling in pain. At first Scott thought he was *crying wolf* but then he realised the disagreeable noise was genuine. He tried to lift him up but the rise in pitch and volume informed him that the pain was only being made worse, so he called for an ambulance. His father was taken to hospital. He did not go with him.

Instead, he stayed and looked after the farm and came to terms with the fact that his father was no longer his keeper. He could stand up to him now and this gave him confidence. He decided there and then that things would change. With his father gone, for the time being he could enjoy his freedom. Though he wished him no real harm, Scott couldn't help but pray that he would not return for some considerable time.

He was back the following morning.

However, his father was somewhat sheepish. He was hobbling about on a walking stick and he didn't say much.

Then the following day: 'You think you've got the better of me, boy?'

Scott looked at him blankly. 'Sorry, what?'

'You heard. Your time will come, boy. Make no mistake about that.'

Scott retained a dignified silence even though he felt like punching his lights out. They both knew it was the last attempt by an ageing bully to get the upper hand. But Jerome's threats were no longer effective. Scott was running the show now.

By the time Jerome was fully recovered, some three months later, the old accusations were in full flow. Even though he no longer needed it, the walking stick never left his side. Scott feared that the verbal abuse would degenerate into violence once more and that he was going to have to defend himself all over again. However, it soon became apparent that the stick was simply an excuse for his father to leave all the heavy work to him. Scott obliged, as he always had done – but only because he chose to. He was bigger and stronger than his father now and there were no consequences to fear anymore.

But there was little satisfaction in any of this and he began to wonder what life was like beyond the confines of the family business and his father's rule of thumb. He hated himself for it, but his father still held a psychological control over him. Above all, he feared that in some small way Jerome was right about him. Scott had lost interest in the farm and as a result he no longer did much work. Now he seemed destined to become the person his father had always said he was – a layabout. He needed to escape. *But where would I go?* he wondered.

Scott remembered the fox that he had rescued from one of his father's snares, and he imagined she was still out there somewhere. He knew how important it was to protect the hen coop from predators, but he had felt a compulsion to destroy not only that trap, but all of the traps that his father had laid. It seemed right somehow. A symbolic fantasy – breaking free of the constraints that his father had so tightly bound around him.

But I'll never escape, he thought bleakly.

It was with that same bleak outlook that he welcomed the sun as it cast its warmth on his bare chest. Scott wondered what the day held for him. September was almost here again and autumn was coming. It was evident in the trees that were already beginning to change colour. But there was no dawn chorus – the birds were curiously silent today. He thought about his own silence. As dignified as it appeared, he knew that it was a warning that his father had won the long battle of wills between them. For all his desires had long since been beaten out of him and he was already exhausted by it all.

Chapter Nine

August 31st

Alice Smith was in the living room, reading her book, when she was startled by a loud thump from the hallway.

'Good god, what was that?' she exclaimed, throwing her volume on the sofa and stomping into the lobby to see what had happened. She looked around and saw nothing out of the ordinary. She opened the front door and stepped outside – nothing there either. It was warm and sunny but airless. And there was something else, something not quite right. She hummed nervously to herself as she padded around the exterior of the house, via the back garden and round to the front again. By the time she got to the garden gate she concluded that it would remain a mystery. Then she realised what was wrong.

It was as quiet as death.

She looked back at the house and her garden again, at the treetops and the bushes. No sign of life anywhere, save a few bees flitting in and out of her wilting carnations. She sighed, thinking that she should really get the place in order, use a watering can at least, if only she could find it. Mildly irritated, Alice turned her attention to the abandoned field below and the scarecrow that stood tilted at its centre. She decided to venture out a little further and opened the creaking gate. A short walk and she was near the edge of the steep hill, surrounded by yellow scented broom and looking out to the village and the sea beyond, which was calm, as blue as the sky above. Something caught her eye – a brief flash of light in the distance.

Someone opening a window and catching the sun, she thought.

She removed her cardigan, for the heat was prickly, uncomfortable. Eventually, she decided to go back indoors. She had just closed the gate, and was halfway up the garden path, when she saw something shaped like a paper fan lying on top of the flowerbeds, just in the shadow of the steps of the front door. She approached cautiously.

It was a dead seagull, its wings outstretched as if in parody of its own flight.

Alice groaned pityingly, and moved it with her slippered foot. She looked up to see blood and feathers smeared against the glass window above her front door. She thought back to the times when it had happened before. Living so high up and near the sea, it had become commonplace. She thought to bury it and turned to look for a good place to do so. It was then she noticed a mound of earth had already been dug out. There was something familiar about this, and the basket that lay beside it.

Another blackout, she thought, blinking confusedly, and went back indoors, wondering what she had done with that trowel.

Chapter Ten

September 1st

Red sky in the morning, shepherd's warning...

Jerome could see the signs in the atmosphere. It was one of his late wife's pet phrases, and one that reflected his foul mood, so it seemed particularly apt. His son was nowhere to be seen. *Today of all days*, he thought, his hands bunching into fists.

'You throw me a gauntlet and you've got a fight on your hands, boy,' he shouted.

Jerome felt sure it was no coincidence that the increase in hostilities happened to manifest itself on the first day of a new season, which they both knew meant more work. Exhaling heavily, he fished out a small bottle of whisky from his trouser pocket and gulped almost half of it down in one go. Coughing and hacking, he threw Scott's uneaten breakfast into the bin, snatched his walking stick and hobbled out the back door, Bessie at his heel. It was already a close morning and this only accelerated his temper.

He looked around for any sign of his errant son. He bellowed his name and was answered with nothing but silence.

'No change there then,' he muttered, and spat on the ground before launching into his work: opening the barn to let the cows into the field, sweeping the floor and chopping firewood. He shepherded the sheep into their pen and pictured the look of defiance that was the cause of so much of his grief. Scott's taciturnity seemed every bit as impenetrable as the reason behind it. Jerome sweated and toiled as the hours slowly passed and the sun reached its zenith. At the end of another laborious day he herded the cows back into the barn with his walking stick, Bessie doing her canine best to assist by circling round them and, with her master's permission, barking out the occasional order of her own. He smiled sadly, wishing that he could inhabit her dog's life for just a few moments – unclouded by grievance and ill temperament.

If only he could have been more like his late wife. Whenever he visualised their marriage it was almost always when they were having a heated debate about something – usually their son.

'*Moley*? What kind of a name is that? Call him by his proper name for god's sake,' Jerome had snapped.

Elspeth looked up from her accounting, her buxom figure squeezed between the table and chair, watching him, reading glasses perched halfway down her nose.

'Don't you sit there and judge me,' he warned.

'He likes being called that,' replied Elspeth calmly, and went back to her bookkeeping.

'Well I don't.'

'It's only a nickname. Hardly any worse than yours, *Jerry*.'

'You know I won't tolerate being called that,' he barked, pointing his finger at her. 'My proper name is Jerome. That's French, after my father.'

'He likes his nickname, Jerome. He invented it,' she replied, eyes still fixed on her paperwork.

'That's what bothers me.'

'It's harmless. He likes digging for things. Like a wee mole, he is.'

Jerome snorted.

Elspeth stopped her work and removed her glasses. 'Do you remember when he came back with a fossil?'

'That was no fossil.'

'I know. But that's not the point.'

Jerome raised his eyebrows expectantly.

'Do you recall that he returned home all excited because he thought he'd found a rock with fossilised raindrops? Do you remember how excited he was?'

'I do. Except it wasn't fossilised bloody raindrops – it was a piece of concrete with holes in it.'

'I know that,' she said patiently, 'but my point is that he was so enthusiastic about it. It was so sweet to see him like that, so happy.'

Jerome frowned in disapproval. 'I feel you're leading up to something here.'

Elspeth looked right at him and said, 'He's still a child, Jerome. Our child. Don't work him so hard all the time. Give him some room to breathe.'

Jerome shook his head sadly. 'That boy is in a world of his own. He doesn't mix at school. Never seems interested in girls. Instead, he sits in the trees and watches birds. And he hides his thoughts with the expertise of a poker player.'

'He gets that from us, Jerome. I mean, look at us. We live in the middle of nowhere. We're all he's got as role models.'

Maybe I've been too hard on him, Jerome thought as he shut the barn doors behind him and headed back home with Bessie. *When Elspeth died I got it into my head that I needed to be twice the father. Maybe that's the problem. I've pushed him too far, alienated him with my strict ways. Tact and diplomacy aren't exactly my strong points and perhaps my temper has got the better of us both.* He stopped and turned, gazing steadily into the forest. He knew Scott would be in there, idling his time away, while Jerome suffered.

The field isn't going to be burned today, he thought bitterly, and took a long swig of whisky.

Bessie started barking so furiously that Jerome fought hard to control her. He noticed that she was sniffing the air and Jerome thought he detected a strange smell, like something metallic. He calmed her and looked around. He had the odd notion that he was being watched, as if the natural world around him had become preternatural somehow. There was total silence. It was then he realised that his cockerel hadn't crowed. Alarmed, he hobbled quickly to the hen coop and found that his pride and joy was dead. He kneeled down to take a closer look. It had been partially devoured. He knew immediately from the bite marks what animal had done it – a fox.

Jerome was livid. Shaking with fury, he threw down his walking stick, went over to the wood pile and pulled the axe from the tree trunk. Ordering Bessie to stay where she was, he stumbled into the woods in search of his son.

'Scott!' he shouted, his bloodshot eyes wide with hate. 'Daddy's coming!'

Chapter Eleven

September 1st

Alice suddenly woke up from her afternoon nap.

Something's wrong, she thought, and looked about her. It was silent except for the ticking of the grandfather clock in the hall. The air was still and hot. She got up from her armchair and went into the kitchen to pour herself a glass of water and drank it down in one go. The atmosphere in the house was oppressive, as if about to ignite, and the clock seemed to be counting down to something explosive.

'Oh, stop it,' she whispered and clucked her tongue at her over-wrought imagination. *Hard to believe I used to be a teacher*, she thought scornfully, and put the kettle on. Feeling hot and suffocated, she decided to go outside for some fresh air.

It was even worse outdoors. The air felt thick and heavy. The sun was hidden behind a haze of heat and the blue sky looked dirty, tinged with a strange colour, almost green, like verdigris. She breathed deeply and wondered, *What's that smell?*

She looked at the seagull beside the front steps. It hadn't been dead long enough to give off an odour, despite the heat, she concluded. This was something else, something coppery. It permeated the air around her.

Better get rid of it soon, though, or it'll attract flies, she told herself, and glanced at her watch, which read 3.05pm. Alice wore it all the time now to try to keep track of things in case she suffered another fugue. She checked the watch against her grandfather clock and realised that it should have chimed by now, but its pendulums had mysteriously stopped. She picked up the phone and was about to dial the speaking clock when she heard an odd tone – the line was dead.

The kettle started screaming.

When she came back out with her cup of Darjeeling, she stood at the front steps and left the door open. It struck her that the air smelled almost exactly like the inside of her kettle. She heard seagulls screech-ing overhead, looked up at the now darkening sky, and watched as they flew away from a bank of brooding cloud that had materialised in the distance. There was a flash of light – she knew this was no win-dow being opened.

'Looks like I won't need to find that watering can after all,' she said to herself with a smile.

Chapter Twelve

September 1st

Scott had been spending his time in the woods, pottering about, happy with his freedom from all that the blunt instrument that was his father had held dear and which he despised. He was alone with his favourite tree – a 700-year-old oak. Thanks to his mother, and the natural history books that she had provided him with, he knew its real name:

Quercus robur.

And he knew the name of the bird that had built a nest there – the Eurasian jay:

Garrulus glandarius.

And the rodent that lived inside it – the red squirrel:

Sciurus vulgaris.

And that of the plants that grew below it – liverwort:

Conocephalum conicum.

And reindeer moss:

Cladonia rangiferina.

Under this tree he had grown from a precocious little boy to an inscrutable young man. He had played and daydreamed and slept under its protective branches. He had cried under its canopy of leaves when his mother had passed away. Scott knew the contours of its surface and its blemishes as intimately as a lover. He climbed its reassuringly thick arms and when he got to the top he could see for miles around: his father toiling on the farm, looking so small and distant, like an ant that he could crush between forefinger and thumb, his beloved Bessie investigating every interesting smell in the vicinity, and the fields beyond that swept to the horizon where a premature twilight seemed to be descending.

That's when he noticed it. Everything was still and hushed as if in anticipation. The birds had been strangely silent all day and their silence now seemed to intensify. The air was stifling. Something down below caught his eye – his father coming towards him, but at such surprising speed that it took him a moment to realise that his walking stick was gone and in its place there was something sharp and shiny, which he was swinging back and forth in his hand.

Then he saw what it was.

As if in league with his thoughts, the birds sounded the alarm. To the untrained ear this would have been but a random chorus of chirping and chattering, but Scott knew better. He had observed their behaviour and listened to their songs for years. They were warning of something approaching.

But it wasn't his father, or some other predator.

From high in his treetop he looked to the sky. And he saw the birds flying back to the safety of their nests because something was coming from the west. A strange mountain was forming on the horizon.

'Cumulonimbus,' he whispered to himself. 'Storm clouds…'

As Jerome made his way through the dense undergrowth, his blood was racing from the whisky and all the indignities he'd suffered at the hands of his own son. The snares tripped. The work never done. And that insolent silence.

'You fucking little bastard!' he screamed, with a face the colour of beetroot juice, his voice almost hoarse with the effort. 'You broke my back, you evil little cunt. I'm going to get you. I'm going to cut you in half!'

He advanced through the trees, swiping branches out of his face, his heart thumping hard with the bitter memories of all those years he had spent harbouring doubts about his own conduct.

'All that time I wasted, worrying that I hadn't done enough for you, making excuses for you, when all the time you've been laughing behind my back whilst I sweat blood every fucking day to keep you in the manner to which you're accustomed. You ungrateful little brat!'

There in the dark he could see Scott perched up high in his favourite tree, illuminated by the curved arc of the moon above. He thought his son looked right at him for a moment, but then seemed to turn away, as if disinterested – his head, quite literally, in the clouds. Jerome snarled and advanced towards his quarry, tightening his grip on the axe that was swinging to and fro in his hand.

He arrived at the base of the tree. 'You think you're untouchable up there, do you?' he yelled. Then he smiled broadly, maniacally, and said matter-of-factly, 'Well, Daddy's here. And he's going to cut you down to size…'

Alistair was driving through a tunnel of dark, towering trees, when suddenly an explosion jolted across the roof. Caroline screamed and Alistair put his foot hard onto the brakes, skidding the car to an abrupt halt. For a few seconds they both sat there looking at each other.

'What the hell was that?' Caroline said breathlessly.

Alistair didn't reply. Instead he waited and listened. There was nothing, except for the rain being blown against the windscreen. He looked in the mirror to see if there was any sign of Matthew's car. Nothing there. He made a move, ignoring Caroline's protest, and signalled for her to remain where she was.

Warily, he slid out of the car to investigate, craning his neck to see what had happened. He saw something resembling a hardback book lying on the roof, black and shiny, thrown with such force that it had created a dent in the metal.

Before he could even begin to comprehend what it was or how he was going to explain the car's damage to the hire company, another one flew out of the darkness. Alistair jumped back to avoid it, slipping and falling on the wet grass as the object shattered the front windscreen.

Caroline gave another terrified yell, and he quickly picked himself up. He was about to run round to get her, but she had already climbed out of the car. He took her hand in his and considered what they needed to do next. They were exposed and being buffeted by the elements, but the car was no longer the safest place to be. His first thought was to take shelter amongst the trees, but another piece sailed past, narrowly missing his head, and landed with a whump in the grass verge. He ventured towards the thing and tentatively picked it up, turning it over in his hand.

It was a slate from someone's roof.

He peered into the darkness to see where it had come from. As if in answer there came a deep, threatening growl of thunder, followed seconds later by a blue-white flare that lit up the trees ahead.

Caroline squeezed his hand. 'Let's get out of here,' she said.

But Alistair wasn't listening. He was speculating on what had caused the flare – he knew it wasn't lightning…

From his vantage point Scott watched as the storm approached steadily – vast strata of clouds towering on the horizon, mushrooming into the shape of a blackened anvil. The outer layers of the cloud bank spread across the night sky, snuffing out the stars like celestial candles, one by one, creeping rapidly, like some gigantic and unstoppable organism, until it swallowed the moon.

The silence became electric.

Scott could detect the warm metal smell of ozone surging up from the earth, could feel the hairs on the back of his neck stand up as the humid, charged air billowed around him. A deep, ominous rumble sounded in the distance, followed by a flash of lightning that briefly lit up the skyline, startling him. He watched, hypnotised, as nature's drama unfolded. Plump, warm drops of rain smacked heavily through the trees.

Scott snapped out of his reverie when he saw that his father had arrived at the foot of the oak, and was screaming something incomprehensible. A moment later and the axe was embedded with a sickening thud into the trunk. Scott looked on dumbfounded as his father wreaked havoc, chopping furiously. With each slice it dawned on him that it wasn't so much an attack on the tree itself, but rather an assault on all that he cherished. Each blow was a blow to his heart. He turned away, unable to watch any more. The wind began to howl and the rain grew torrential and the thuds continued; again and again and again, until they finally staggered to a stop.

Scott looked down to see his exhausted father looking up at him in the rain. Their eyes met in a silent confirmation that Scott had won – king of a very peculiar castle. But as a victory it was meaningless. Scott watched with regret as Jerome hobbled away, the axe held limply in his hand. He felt pity for him. His father seemed so small, so utterly alone. And Scott, ever the optimist, climbed down the tree and called out to him.

'Dad?'

Jerome stopped and turned round. Scott saw there was a strange expression on his face, one he'd never seen before – a look of crazed hatred.

'I'm not your dad, any more than you're my son,' he growled – and he raised the axe once more…

Alistair and Caroline watched numbly as another blue-white flash lit up the road ahead. The wind grew stronger, embarking on a dismal chorus, moaning and whistling through the tired limbs of the surrounding trees – as if the dark heart of the natural world were awakening from some ancient slumber and threatening to exact some awful revenge on mankind. In the midst of this orchestra of hell, there was a single note, barely perceptible, but steadily increasing, like the murmur of a swarm of strange electronic bees.

Caroline saw Alistair was deliberating whether to go back to the car, but it was fast disappearing in a flurry of wet leaves and broken branches. So she tightened her grip on his hand and led him off the road and into the relative safety of the woods. The droning was much louder now and seemed to be coming from above. Another bluish flash lit up the trees, accompanied by a spurt of sparks.

'I was right,' exclaimed Alistair, and Caroline wondered what he meant. She followed his gaze and looked up to see an electricity pylon standing in the dark right above them, emitting an angry buzz as the wind tore at its cables.

She felt Alistair tugging on her hand and turned to see him shouting something to her – but his words were lost in the wind. There was a sudden din of grinding metal from overhead and something scraped across the treetops, ripping branches off as it went, the debris falling around them. They both ran for cover. Caroline tripped, and with her arms in front of her face to break her fall, she landed awkwardly amongst some bushes, her fingers catching on the thorns. She realised she had lost her grip on Alistair.

And when she looked back, he was gone…

Scott ran as fast as he could, away from the madman with his brandished axe and his bloodshot eyes, away from the murderous screaming of his name. Through trees and branches he stumbled, slipping on wet leaves underfoot, but moving apace and never looking back. He came to a river and saw a little humpback bridge, and he crouched underneath, panting like a frightened animal. He knew his father wouldn't be too far behind – he was more able-bodied than he made himself out to be – and so Scott held his breath and waited.

And then he waited some more.

He could hear nothing except the storm.

Perhaps he's given up, he thought hopefully.

He was about to come out from his hiding place when he heard *Daddy* stomping across the bridge, the sharp end of his axe striking and dragging the flagstones directly above Scott's head…

Alistair was desperately trying to find Caroline. He cried out her name again and again, but there was no sign of her. His stomach lurched at the thought that she might be lying injured somewhere. He ran through the rain-soaked forest in search of her, and even when he realised he was lost, he kept going, up an incline, still shouting for her, until he came to a clearing. A farmhouse and a barnyard stood barely visible in the violence of the storm.

He wondered if perhaps she might have taken shelter there. As soon as he was out of the woods and into the open air, the full force of the storm hit him hard. He was almost lifted off his feet, but he fought on, battered by the ferocious wind and the pounding sleet. He was assailed by a bewildering array of broken branches and snapped twigs and conifer needles, which flew towards him on their deadly trajectories. Nature had gone berserk, but heroically he stumbled on amidst the shrapnel, almost losing his balance in the wind and the slippery hailstones littering the ground. He could see the trees moving from side to side and their shadows dancing furiously on the roof of the barn. The wind was howling through the eaves and the cattle inside were braying and bellowing. Suddenly the barn doors were flung wide open and the panicked cows bolted; he had no option but to bolt with them. He was trapped between their heavy flanks as they stampeded into the forest, taking him with them.

Alistair stumbled, and watched in abstract as the world seemed to turn on its axis. He was falling, tumbling breathlessly through the air, catching glimpses of treetops and dark clouds, and hearing the intimate muffled, crumpled sounds of his own body crashing through thickets, before landing with a thump on his back.

For a moment he just lay there at the bottom of the incline, dreamily looking up to see how far he'd fallen. He began laughing uncontrollably when he saw the cows dispersing in an orderly fashion to take shelter in the trees, as if nothing was out of place.

Above all this, in the night sky, he could make out the last remaining stars, like eyes that were now closing in shame at what was happening to the mortal world below. All the forces of nature seemed to conspire, creating a singular tempest, which was rising to a crescendo all around him.

A sudden and overwhelming sensation of anguish brought Alistair to his senses. He could hear water. There was a river nearby. He picked himself up, gripped as he was with the urgency of getting back up the slope to finish searching the farmhouse.

Something was coming for him, from out of the shadows. He tried to escape, but it held him fast. A searing pain jolted into his side that made him cry out one last time for Caroline.

And the storm raged. And the lights went out across Hobbs Brae.

Alistair's pain quickly subsided and he was overcome by seemingly insignificant thoughts: it was payback time; this was his punishment for not looking after his mum when his dad left; for his past life as a petty criminal. And the bitter irony that this is what he'd got for trying to stick to the straight and narrow, for he'd ended up off the beaten track again.

As the ground rushed up to meet him, he was struck by the unfairness of it all – he didn't stand a chance. He lay there on broken bracken and saw the debris of the gale flying over him, and he imagined Caroline's beautiful face, and the unreal way her long, blonde hair seemed to writhe in the wind.

Lost her again, he thought sadly. *My story is ending.*

And then he saw her guide his hand to her belly and he was overwhelmed with desolation.

I'll never see my own child.

As his synapses closed down and the river disappeared into darkness, he was inundated by once-forgotten memories: his father closing the garden gate behind him; his mother staring wistfully at the sea. And then one final, fleeting recollection of Caroline walking quickly away across George Square, and the sorrow he felt because he never did get to tell her about his special surprise…

The storm soon faded away. The water dripped from the trees.

And then silence, like a breath held.

The stars twinkled, and dappled shadows lay flat, like flock wallpaper, on the barnyard roof. The cows began herding themselves back into the barn. Only the brief shriek of a fox in the distance delivered a moment's relief from an evening that was now suddenly and inexplicably humdrum.

But from under the bridge, in the night, in the dark – *Moley* saw something that breathed rapidly, heavily…

A monster that leered over its kill.

It cackled to itself – a pure sound – like water being decanted into crystal. He watched in horror as a trail of red snaked from Alistair's dead body into the icy river, turning its flow pale pink in the near monochromatic light. In dread and shaking, *Moley* averted his eyes and saw, high above, a distant satellite that moved differently from the others. But he could not avert his eyes for long, could not resist the awful truth that a man had just been murdered in cold blood, on this, the first night of September.

Chapter Thirteen

September 1st

In a hotel situated less than a mile away, a doorbell rang, and the land-lady, Margaret Crawford, sat bolt upright in her bed, her shock of grey hair a tangled mess.

'Who on earth is that at this ungodly hour?' she muttered.

Sighing loudly, she reached over to switch the bedside lamp on, but it wouldn't work.

Bloody storm, she thought, and turned to look at her husband, who she could see was oblivious to what was going on, half-hidden under the bedclothes, snoring. The bell rang again.

'Wake up, you!' she shouted, trying to nudge him awake.

Another chime came from the front door.

'For god's sake, it's the middle of the bloody night,' she moaned, clambering out of bed and putting on her dressing gown. She turned to her husband again. 'Thanks for nothing,' she snapped, and tramped downstairs in her slippers.

'Who is it?' she called when she arrived in the hallway, trying to sound more confident than she actually felt, for there was a sinister silhouette on the other side of the glass-fronted door. Margaret was answered with a distant rumble of thunder, and she bit her lip, wondering what to do next.

Suddenly the hall lights came on and she yelled with fright.

Pulling herself together, she picked up an umbrella from the nearby stand, pursed her lips and marched sternly to the door. When she yanked it open she was surprised to see a handsome young man standing there. He was suntanned and well dressed, but soaking wet – and had a killer smile.

'Hello,' he said brightly. 'My name is Jason Black and I'm looking for a place to stay…'

Part Two

Chapter Fourteen

September 2nd

Alice rose early and switched on the kettle. She felt tired, restless. The storm had kept her up all night, but she had enjoyed watching it from her conservatory. She had lived in Hobbs Brae for almost 50 years and had never experienced such a display of fireworks as the storm of September the first.

The kettle began to whistle urgently and she took it off the hob. As she poured her morning tea, she began to feel settled. The act of carrying out a mundane chore had instilled in her a feeling of normality. Everything seemed right again.

Then a thud came from upstairs.

Another bird flying into the window, she concluded, and ventured up to investigate. Just as she was halfway there, the phone rang. She sighed impatiently and came back downstairs. It was Helen.

'I'm sorry about yesterday,' she began. 'I tried to call to remind you that your son was due to pay you a visit?'

'Oh,' Alice replied blankly.

'Yes. I remember you told me that your son was going to be coming to stay and how excited you were about it. I figured you would want some quality time with him as we discussed. So how is he?'

'He's fine,' Alice lied, wondering what on earth she was talking about.

'Good. I'm glad. Like I said, I did try to call you but the lines were down. Probably the storm.'

'It's all right,' replied Alice, trying to sound perfectly normal, but unable to stop herself from adjusting and readjusting the pearls around her neck.

'Same time later today, then?' Helen asked.

'Yes, fine,' replied Alice. She was about to replace the receiver when Helen said, 'I'm so looking forward to meeting him.'

'Me too,' Alice said, and realising how odd that must have sounded, she hastily put the phone down again. *Me too*, she brooded. Then she remembered the noise from upstairs.

'Alistair?' she shouted hopefully.

There was no reply.

'Alistair?'

Lost in thought, she went back to the kitchen and picked up her cup of Darjeeling. She looked around and listened to the silence.

And she wondered. *Why didn't he come home?*

Chapter Fifteen

September 2nd

Matthew White stared into the mirror and saw reflected back at him the face of someone who felt distinctly out of their depth. *What the hell am I doing here?* he wondered.

He checked his watch. 7am. *Too early for the landlady to prepare my breakfast*, he thought disdainfully, so he went for a walk and surveyed his surroundings. Nothing much had changed since he'd left Hobbs Brae as an ambitious teenager, heading for the bright lights of the city.

The Crow's Beak was still there, a pub that he had rarely ever set foot in. He preferred to drink in proper wine bars. *That's city life for you*, he thought. *It gives you airs and graces.*

He strolled past the rows of houses and hotels and inspected each and every one, noting the neat flowerbeds and the baskets that seemed to hang above every doorway. Beyond them there was nothing but trees. It was sunny, but the cold air, and the fact that there wasn't a living soul in sight, gave Matthew the impression that he'd arrived in a village that was in a state of torpor, waiting to be revived from its long, deep sleep.

His thoughts were distracted by a gentle clacking sound. At first he had the romantic notion that it might be deer rutting in the distance, their antlers locked in battle, but he looked up to see the bare branches of a dead tree coupling in the wind, clasping and unclasping, like a pair of gnarled hands in anxious and repetitive prayer.

As he continued on his way, he noticed that the houses were largely bungalows with names like the Glen Coe or the Lothian. His adopted Glaswegian sensibilities sneered at the suburban pretension of it all. The hotels had equally false-sounding names like the Rest And Be Thankful or the Queen's View, and most had vacancies, given that the summer season was coming to an end. Nevertheless, he noted that the Scottish Tourist Board was very much alive and well as he passed a quaint little craft shop, a small newsagent's and an even smaller post office, which were all well stocked with tartans and butter tablet, postcards and pottery. He walked past another hotel – Arthur's Lodge.

Arthur's arse more like, he thought, and he harked back to the copse of conifers that almost completely obscured the view of the hotel that he had chosen to stay in – a modest little two-up two-down called the Warm and Friendly. It had sounded more like a pub than a standard bed and breakfast, but it also sounded more honest than its counterparts. He liked the fact that it appeared low key, discreet. It suited his purposes nicely.

Getting his belongings from the car to the front door had proved to be more difficult than expected, with the high winds and the rain lashing down upon him, and by the time the landlady had finally arrived he was soaked through. He realised the lateness of the hour when he saw that she was in her nightgown and he gave her what he thought was a charming and mildly apologetic smile. She didn't seem too pleased to see him, and wordlessly let him in. Once inside, he found that she had an umbrella in her hand.

If that's for me then it's way too late, he brooded, and watched as she went through to a back room. He took a look around. The hallway was gloomy and silent, and there was a stale smell of mildew in the air. It caught in his chest and he gently coughed. He could make out a vase of wilted yellow chrysanthemums on the reception desk, which was defined by two rhombuses of light that flashed through the discoloured net curtains every time the storm's electrical bolts cracked across the night sky. The flowers – apparently there to cheer up the place – only served to make it appear funereal.

'This is about as cheery as the Bates Motel,' he muttered.

He had decided to leave when he heard her come back out of the room, shuffling slowly, huffing and puffing, with a scowl on her ancient face. She stopped behind the desk and looked at him steadily.

'I don't do breakfast before nine,' she stated baldly. 'I don't do lunch. And I don't do dinner.'

'That'll be why it's so busy here, then,' he replied, with an impudent smile.

'What?' she asked, her hooded eyes narrowing suspiciously.

'Nothing.'

'Sign here.'

Matthew filled in his personal details on the form and signed the guest book – *Jason Black*. His keys were slammed on the desk.

'Can I have a room with a double bed, please?'

The landlady just looked at him.

'I can't sleep in a single bed. Not at my age.'

She sighed loudly and found another set of keys and slammed them on the desk as well.

'Room seven. Upstairs. I'll get Hugh to take your stuff.'

'I can manage, thanks.'

But she had already turned and was shuffling back out to find *Hugh*.

After his decidedly cold reception, Matthew hesitated for a moment, unsure whether to just cut his losses and go. But given that he was desperate for a bath and a bed, he decided that he would stay for one night. *I can always find another place tomorrow*, he reasoned. So he left his belongings at the desk with *Hugh*.

Whoever he is. Her hen-pecked husband probably, he surmised, and went upstairs and found his room.

On opening the door, the first thing that struck him was the smell – that same damp odour he had breathed in downstairs was now much stronger. The entire room stank of mould. The walls were covered in faded, floral-patterned paper, pink in colour and peeling at the edges. There was a double bed with an old yellow candlewick bedspread and a table beside it, upon which stood a lamp fringed with small tassels. Opposite the bed was a battered old wardrobe. Under the window, with its faded pink curtains, was a dressing table with a mirror, and a stool in front of it. Adorning this apparition of female decadence were ornaments on lace doilies, which were as curled as Matthew's lip at the sight of it all. He frowned at the small chair that had been sent to the corner of the room, presumably for being so *bloody tasteless*.

In despair, Matthew turned to the en suite bathroom and walked straight into an explosion of avocado – the bath, the sink and the walls were covered in the same dull green colour. The shelves were littered with numerous products from Crabtree & Evelyn. Floral-patterned towels hung from a rail and he spied one of those Spanish señoritas hiding toilet rolls up her flamenco skirt. *It doesn't take Columbo to figure out that Hugh doesn't wear the trousers in this house*, he thought darkly.

He stripped off his wet clothes and stared at his pristine reflection in the mirror, obsessively checking the even tan, the white teeth and the blonde highlights of his neat, side-parted hair. Satisfied that all was well on the surface, he fell back onto the bed and submerged into a dreamy, fitful sleep.

Matthew's tour of Hobbs Brae ended when he found himself at the foot of a hill. He looked up and saw the house of Alice Smith, silhouetted against a pink sky, as the sun began to rise. He shivered in the chill and his mind carried him back to another time, when he was young and valiantly trying to forge a decent living, before it was all so ruthlessly taken away from him.

Chapter Sixteen

September 2nd

'I have a confession to make,' said Alice, falteringly.

She paused, unsure how to break her news. 'I don't remember Alistair telling me he was going to visit.' She shrugged.

She was relieved when Helen gave her a compassionate smile. 'You told me that he was due to arrive yesterday.'

'I forgot,' said Alice, blinking furiously, holding back the tears. 'I tried to phone him just now but there was no answer.'

She watched as Helen thought for a moment, her fingers toying with her hair, an act which Alice found irritating. *For god's sake don't just stand there. Do something!* she wanted to scream.

'Where does he work?' Helen asked finally.

'In Glasgow,' replied Alice.

'Yes, but where?'

Alice exhaled loudly. 'Well, I don't know where exactly. A sports shop.'

'That could be anywhere.'

I don't like your tone, Alice thought.

'And he didn't phone to tell you he was going to be late?'

'No. But the lines were down, though mine seems okay now.' Alice fumbled at her necklace, trying to delay the obvious. 'What should I do?'

'Does anybody else have his number?'

'I don't know,' replied Alice, feeling defeated.

'We'd better phone the police.'

Alice's heart thudded hard, and she tried not to appear alarmed.

'It's only a precaution. I'm sure he's all right,' reassured Helen. 'But better safe than…' She bit her lip and smiled apologetically.

Alice contemplated the unspoken word and its implication. Then she shook her head and said quietly, 'I can't. Could you do it?'

She watched as Helen seemed to grow taller before her and marched efficiently to the phone in the hall, trying to suppress a smile as she did so. *You're actually enjoying this*, Alice observed. *Making yourself useful for once. Busybody.* She watched as Helen spoke on the phone, her tone light and girly, almost excitable. Alice clucked her tongue. *I just can't help myself*, she thought. *The slightest stress and I take it out on her. I don't know why she puts up with me*, Alice contemplated. *The pay, I suppose.*

A short while later, they were sitting in the living room, a cup of tea in their hands, waiting.

'You're doing the right thing,' said Helen, touching her shoulder.

Alice flinched. 'I'd totally forgotten he was coming. I haven't even made his bed.'

'I wouldn't worry about that just now,' replied Helen briskly. 'We just need to make sure he's okay, which I'm sure he will be.'

'There was a noise upstairs,' Alice said ominously.

'Well, I'm sure that was just your gardener,' explained Helen.

'My gardener?' Alice repeated.

'Yes, you said you were going to hire someone to tend to your garden?' Helen smiled patiently and tilted her head to one side.

She always looks at me as if I'm an object of curiosity, thought Alice. But she knew her intolerance of Helen was merely an attempt to hide her revulsion at the thought that she had no idea what was going on anymore.

There came a knock at the front door. Helen made a show of pretending to try and heave her bulk out of the chair, but Alice ignored her play-acting and answered the door herself. Two men stood there, dressed formally in suits. She didn't like the look of either of them.

'Hello, Mrs Smith. My name is Detective Chief Inspector Colin Clements.'

She heard his associate suppress a snigger. 'And this,' he said disparagingly, 'is Constable Driscoll. We are here because you reported a Mispers?'

'Mispers?' Alice repeated, blankly.

'Missing persons,' he replied, with a slight lack of patience.

Alice saw Driscoll smile a little patronisingly. She looked from one to the other as if they were a pair of delinquent schoolboys and said, 'You must first understand that up until now I have had no contact with the police and as such I have no concept of their use of abbreviations.' She then smiled sweetly at them both and continued, 'Do come in.'

'I think you've met your match,' she heard Driscoll mutter to the detective.

'Shut up,' came the terse reply as she led them into the living room, where she noted that Helen had finally managed to hoist herself out of the chair and was standing, waiting.

Clements strode into the room with Driscoll as if he was some kind of dignitary. He puffed up his chest and said pleasantly, 'Now then. Let's start at the beginning, shall we?'

Chapter Seventeen

September 3rd

DCI Jack Russell was sat in his office, surrounded by the statements that had been collated from everyone who knew Alistair and Caroline. But it amounted to nothing. As a last resort, he impatiently flicked through Colin's statement from the boy's mother. However, he couldn't help but sneer at it, for he knew how the DC liked to write his reports in shorthand. He wondered why certain details were omitted from his paperwork and yet still found their way to the Chief. Jack wondered if he was being deliberately marginalised. He noted that Colin always pleaded ignorance, citing an error on his part. But it had happened once too often and Jack began to question if there was a motive behind it. Colin was certainly ambitious, competitive even. Jack no longer trusted him, but he couldn't figure out why, couldn't quite understand what was going on in his partner's mind. It bothered him to such an extent that he was desperate for an excuse to get out of the office and away from his own dark suspicions. His excuse came almost immediately when the phone rang. It was Campbell. He sounded excited. Said he had found something. Would Jack take a look at some CCTV footage?

'Sure,' replied Jack. 'Be there in five.' He switched on his sceptical persona and made his way to the main office.

'So, anything interesting?'

'Yes, sir. We found this,' replied Campbell eagerly, and he played the footage.

Jack scrutinised it. There, in ghostly colour, was a car pulling up and a young couple getting out. 'So this tape shows Alistair and Caroline's last known movements at the service station,' confirmed Jack. 'Any witnesses?'

'A few have come forward, sir, but nothing suspicious has been reported. However, we then found this.'

Jack watched as Campbell fast-forwarded the tape. The young officer then sat back, and with a little flourish, paused it. Jack leaned over his shoulder for a better look. There on the screen was a grainy close-up of a number plate.

Jack peered at it. 'That's the registration of the vehicle that Alistair hired?'

'No, and that's what's so interesting about it,' replied Campbell, a little too fervently for Jack's liking. 'It's from a car that appeared to be tailing his. We've traced its journey back to Glasgow. It followed them all the way.'

'And do we know who it belongs to?'

'We've traced the registration plate back to a guy called Matthew White. He resides in Glasgow and owns a restaurant there.'

'Name of the restaurant?'

'The Glasgow Grand, I believe it's called, sir.'

'Well, that is interesting,' replied Jack, smiling.

'We've looked into further details regarding Matthew White, sir, and it seems that he was born in Hobbs Brae and went to the same school as Alistair Smith.'

Jack thought for a moment. 'Is it possible they were travelling together?'

'Unsure. After all, they were in separate cars. And Matthew's car seems to disappear off the radar once he leaves the petrol station. We're looking into other footage since there are at least two other routes he might have taken.'

'Good work, Campbell,' said Jack. 'Keep searching.' He left the officer beaming with pride, like a puppy performing his first trick and receiving a biscuit as a reward. He then spoke to the Chief Superintendent.

'We've tried repeatedly to contact Alistair Smith directly on his phone, but there's been no response.'

'And what about his family and friends?'

'They too have stated that they tried but with no success. His mother has been harping on about there being a ringing tone when she phones him, but we know from experience that this is just a basic recording by the carrier and not the actual phone itself. It may well have been destroyed for all we know at this stage.'

'Well,' began the Chief. 'How about something to distract you?'

Jack sat up politely and clasped his fingers over his ample belly. 'Yes, sir?'

'I spied the press snooping about.'

'Ah,' said Jack, deflated.

'Yes, I think they've got tired of reporting the storm damage. They're looking for something juicier. Give them something, anything. But not this.'

'Sure,' replied Jack. 'I'd like permission to search the woods near the service station where the missing couple were last seen.'

'Any particular reason?' asked the Chief.

'I just want to be thorough,' replied Jack.

He waited patiently whilst the Chief eyeballed him, and was quietly relieved when he was eventually given the nod. On his way out, Jack realised that he was now the puppy being given the biscuit.

Later that night, Jack was in his office at home, assembling his report. Jamie came wandering in.

Jack looked up. 'Don't you ever knock?'

'The Glasgow Grand – that's the same restaurant that Caroline worked in, isn't it?' asked Jamie.

'That's right,' affirmed Jack, stopping his work and smiling patiently.

'The same restaurant that Matthew owns?'

Jack nodded.

'So I reckon they were an item.'

'And?'

'He was jealous of Alistair.'

'And?'

'He made them disappear.'

Jack sat back in his chair and regarded his son for a moment. 'You have the makings of a very good detective,' he replied, with a cunning smile.

Chapter Eighteen

September 2nd

Matthew was trying to eat his breakfast but without success because the landlady was all over him like a rash. As soon as he had come back from his walk it was *Jason* this and *Jason* that. The alias he had chosen was fast becoming tiresome, overused by a mad old woman who now treated him like some kind of celebrity. *I can't get rid of her*, he thought. *It's as if she's had some kind of overnight surgery on the brain – last night misanthropic and morose, today sociable and sprightly.*

'My name is Margaret Crawford,' she announced, her face stretching into a somewhat unnatural smile, 'but you can call me *Maggie*.'

It wasn't exactly the name he had in mind for her as she went on to speak at length about her ingrown toenail, before moving on to the equally dull subject of her next door neighbour's badly tended garden. Matthew strained his tea – as he strained his smile – and wondered if perhaps her medication was kicking in. He made a mental note that he hadn't properly unpacked his belongings yet. He thought back to the previous evening and the sight of an old man – Maggie's better half presumably – labouring upstairs with those self-same belongings. So when Maggie started on about her supposed *poor excuse for a husband*, the accusation struck him as unfair, and he made his excuses and left. She followed him out the front door, and was still yapping away as he walked quickly down the garden path. He left her beating the hall rug against the doorpost, her hunched form disappearing in a cloud of dust – quite apt, given that this was exactly what he had wished for.

Once well away from the hotel, he slowed his pace down and stopped at the bottom of the street. He surveyed the litter-free kerbs and perfectly aligned flowerbeds – a picture of quiet suburban normality. And yet the silence seemed furtive, conspiratorial, as if something sinister was being deliberately hidden behind the twitching curtains. Hobbs Brae increasingly seemed like the estranged Scottish sister of Stepford.

As he continued on his way, he dwelt on his separation from Caroline. *I was too passive*, he thought angrily. *I should have put a stop to it sooner.* By *it* he meant Alistair. He recalled his journey from Glasgow in his Porsche, deliberately disappearing from time to time by taking alternative routes so that it would seem he was not following them both. He stopped and looked around. *I'd rather stick needles in my eyes than see this place again.*

He recalled the house on the hill and that's when it all came back to him. The memories. The water.

And the blood.

Chapter Nineteen

September 3rd

Colin had been summoned to Jack's office, but once there he was forced to sit impatiently for a full five minutes with barely a hint of acknowledgement from his superior. He watched with contempt as Jack pored over his notes and finally looked up to give him a somewhat predatory smile.

'So, what have you discovered so far?'

Colin held his gaze, thinking, *Didn't you just read my notes?* 'Well, as you know we interviewed Alistair's mother and her... carer. Caroline's family have been interviewed, too. The local press have taken a keen interest...'

He was stopped by Jack raising his palm, a self-important gesture that annoyed him, the hand held a little higher than necessary, as if he was passing a benediction to the masses. 'The local press have taken a keen interest in Caroline because she's pretty,' he stated. 'They're not so keen on Alistair, presumably because he is not so pretty. Keep them in line, will you?'

'Right,' said Colin, perturbed.

'Good,' replied Jack. 'So, any further with the statements?'

'My statement is right in front of you,' Colin replied coolly.

'Yes, but I want to hear you tell me in your own words, if that's not too much trouble.'

Colin sighed loudly. 'We took a statement from Alice Smith and her carer. Some fat bird called Helen Patterson.'

He watched with a wry smile as Jack bristled.

'And?'

'Nothing conclusive,' began Colin, then he leaned forward and said secretively, 'Between you and me, Alice is a wee bit *Gone with the Wind.* Lights are on but no one's home. She's got premature white hair. Very prickly person. Bit of a battleaxe to be honest.'

'I know Alice well. She's no battleaxe.'

I know you do, thought Colin, taking delight in his boss's displeasure. 'Well, she got very defensive when I questioned her today.'

'Yes, she phoned to complain about your interview skills, or lack of them.'

'Cow,' muttered Colin.

'What did you say?' demanded Jack.

'Sorry,' whispered Colin with an exaggerated tone, then he gave a defiant sniff. 'What did she say about me?'

He watched as Jack seemed to gather himself. *He's enjoying this*, Colin surmised.

'She said you intimated that her illness was, and I quote, *bound to have an effect on her ability to recall the facts.* Do you remember saying that?'

I remember every bit of it, you self-righteous prick, he thought.

'No. I don't recall saying that.'

He watched with narrowed eyes as Jack began to use the big boy voice. *Predictable as ever*, he judged.

'May I remind you that Alice is not a suspect. She reported her son as missing and that is why you were there to speak to her. Not subject her to an inquisition. You do realise that I have to follow it up. Nothing personal, of course.'

'Of course,' replied Colin. Moments later, he walked out of the office with a crimson face and a huge chip on his shoulder. *I'm going to destroy you, Jack*, he promised himself as he marched out of the station.

Chapter Twenty

Jerome was staring emptily into space. Sitting on the edge of his bed, shoulders stooped, his posture deflated, haunted by the previous night's events.

He had slept in for the first time in years. He was hungover, more so than usual, but even if his head felt like it would explode, it had never stopped him from getting out of bed before. It was already midday and he could barely move a muscle. But the longer he remained there, inactive, the more his brain went on overdrive, collating everything that had happened. Finally, in the late afternoon, he forced himself up and found his walking stick lying on the ground where he had discarded it. He picked it up and toured the farm, accompanied by Bessie, who padded alongside him as he looked for signs of damage from the freak storm.

Now that he was actively engaged in his work again, he could feel his old self returning, his head beginning to clear. He approached the hen coop and felt a wave of nausea when he saw that the corrugated metal roof was missing. He took a closer look and heaved a sigh of relief when he found that the hens were still inside, their eggs incubating and intact. He wiped his brow and wondered if he was sweating out his hangover or whether it was just the incessant heat. *Both*, he presumed. Then Jerome remembered that the cockerel was gone. He pictured the bird strutting proudly about the perimeter, guarding his brood – only to be ripped apart by a fox. Jerome felt once more the resentment swelling inside him.

He closed his eyes tight and tried to regain control. A moment later he continued with his inspection, noting that the barn doors were wide open. The lock was broken and he feared the worst – but his cows were all present and correct. Jerome congratulated himself with a quick swig of whisky. As he made his way along the wooden fence, he drew comfort from the fact that there was comparatively little damage done to the farm despite the ferocity of the wind. He stepped back to take a look at the roof of the farmhouse. Remarkably, there were only a few slates missing, and so his spirits lifted. He watched as his sheep made their way across the field, browsing on the grass as they went, but he grew increasingly aware that the black sheep of the family was missing.

'*I'm not your dad...*'

He leaned against the shed, his reddened eyes welling with tears. Angrily, he thumped his fist against the wall and shambled off into the undergrowth until he arrived at the scene of the crime. His anger soon turned to guilt when he looked up at the old oak tree, and his fingers traced the deep, horizontal cuts in the bark. He thought about those harsh and completely false words and he wondered if he would ever see his son again.

His back was aching and he took a long sup of whisky, feeling the hatred rising in his gorge again. Soon, the old accusatory thoughts were in full flow, his sore head pounding to the beat of his heavy heart, maddening him. As the sun set and the shadows lengthened he downed more and more alcohol, and came to the conclusion that Scott was up to his old tricks again. Jerome went deeper into the woods, angrily slashing at the undergrowth with his walking stick and shouting for his son until he was hoarse – but to no avail.

That night, driven wild with whisky, he stumbled inside Scott's room. It was a disorganised mess: an unmade single bed under the bare window; the battered old shelf unit opposite, filled with books about dinosaurs and natural history, and littered with pebbles and sea shells. Amongst the clutter, he spied a dog-eared copy of *Gray's Anatomy*. Beside it, an outdoor survival guide and the piece of concrete pitted on its surface with *fossilised raindrops*. And proudly displayed on the top shelf was a sheep's skull, complete with lichen-encrusted horns. The floor was littered with dirty clothes and sketchbooks that could no longer be squeezed under the bed. Drawings of the surrounding countryside plastered the walls. A desk and chair stood beside the bed with a computer positioned in the centre. Attached to the top right-hand corner of the screen was a faded colour photograph of Elspeth, her small brown eyes almost disappearing as she smiled back at him from another, happier time.

'You always bring me roses, never sunflowers,' she had said.

'That's because they're common,' Jerome replied petulantly. 'There's plenty of them growing in the fields. They're just weeds as far as I'm concerned.'

'Well, I like them,' said Elspeth, placing the roses in a vase and casting a glance at him. 'Sunflowers are my favourite.'

'Can't do anything right,' Jerome grumbled. Then he felt her hand on his shoulder.

'Thank you anyway,' she said softly. 'It was a lovely thought.' And she kissed him.

His heart sank at the memory of her. 'If only you knew what you gave birth to,' he said quietly.

He went over to the wardrobe that stood beside the desk, opened it, and took out Scott's wallet from the top shelf. He fished out his son's bank card and put it for safe-keeping inside his pocket, then carefully placed the wallet back on the shelf.

'I reckon Scott will need his money sooner or later, Elspeth, and when he returns, I'll be waiting for him.'

Chapter Twenty-One

September 3rd

Jack was sitting behind his desk, preparing for his investigation in the forest. Jamie sat restlessly in the corner, sullenly watching him.

'I see you,' said Jack, without looking up.

'What are you doing?' asked Jamie, through a yawn.

'Pulling some stray threads together.'

'What does that mean?'

'It means there's more to this than meets the eye.' He looked at Jamie and winked.

His son got up and perched himself on the edge of the desk. 'So, tell me.'

Jack sat back and locked his fingers together. 'Alice Smith.'

'My old schoolteacher. What about her?'

'Well, I've just read Colin's statement from her and it appears that she said to him that she has never had any dealings with the police before. But in actual fact she has.'

He smiled when Jamie leaned forward, his interest now well and truly aroused. 'You mean that she is somehow responsible for her son's disappearance?'

'God no,' laughed Jack. 'She's just a bit forgetful these days, that's all. No, it's just that once upon a time she reported her husband as missing.'

'How did you find that out?'

Jack paused for a split second and said, 'Local knowledge gained a long time ago.'

'So you think there might be a connection between her son and her missing husband?'

'It's certainly worth looking into,' replied Jack, standing up and playfully ruffling his son's hair. 'Time to go,' he added, putting his jacket on.

'Are we going into the woods?' asked Jamie excitedly.

'Yes,' Jack answered, 'into the woods.'

'I need to pee first,' said Jamie.

'The toilet is first on the left,' replied Jack, and he watched, bemused, as his once estranged boy exited the office. *Things are looking up*, he thought.

Once Jack was on the road, however, he decided to make a detour and visit Alice.

'I need to apologise to her,' he explained to his son, who was once more sitting in the back seat, texting.

'Whatever,' came the reply.

Jack rolled his eyes and parked his car at the foot of the hill. Jamie looked up. 'We've got to walk all the way up there?'

'No, only me. It's best you stay here.'

Jamie shrugged and smiled as if this was the best news ever, then went straight back to texting.

A seagull screeched overhead as Jack emerged from his car and he watched as it flew over the gentle golden swell of the Jennings's fields and the jagged forest beyond. By the time he got to the top of the hill, he was out of breath and decided to stand and look at the view in order to compose himself. He could make out the shops and houses in the middle distance, and if he narrowed his eyes he could just about see the Warm and Friendly. And, yonder, there were some hazy, heather-covered hills, and beyond that a dramatic aspect of the sea stretching into the distant horizon, interrupted only by the ruins of the old abbey – all this crowned with a sky so impossibly blue it seemed to have been imported from the Mediterranean.

Not bad for September, thought Jack. He wiped the beads of sweat from his top lip and breathed deeply what there was of the air, for it felt close, too close.

He opened the gate, which creaked ominously, and was met with the somewhat foreboding view of Alice Smith's house. It looked like the kind of dwelling a child would draw: two windows above and one below, with a path winding its way to the front door. It was very quiet, but Jack kind of liked it. He pictured living there, far from the madding crowd and in perfect isolation. He strolled leisurely up the trail and through the garden, which had been left to grow in wild abandon. A chaos of dead weeds draped the cracked paving stones like ancient, dusty cobwebs. Growing on either side were clusters of rosemary, thyme and other fragrant herbs, which had grown into disarray, festooned with brambles and rambling roses. He saw a monkey puzzle tree standing to the right of the house, towering up into the blue and looking like it had been transported there from some Jurassic age. He observed a seagull in the distance glide behind the upturned green branches, and imagined it reappearing on the other side as a pterosaur, lazily flapping its wings towards the cliffs. To the left of the house stood a clump of conifers and several silver birches. Amongst these there were some rhododendrons and broom.

Now that he was at the front door, he realised that the house was in a state of abandon too. The once white paint was cracked and peeling, and the windows on either side were filthy – so much so, they almost looked like they'd been deliberately tinted to block out the sun. He knocked on the door. It opened immediately.

Alice stood there; elegant and thin, not quite frail, though her white hair tied loosely back, the tarnished dress and the cardigan that hung on her slight shoulders gave her an untidy appearance, not unlike her garden. He waited for some sign of recognition, but none came.

'Detective Chief Inspector Jack Russell,' he said eventually.

Her eyes brightened and she smiled graciously, opening the door wider.

'Thank you,' he said, and stepped inside.

It was like a sauna.

She shut the door and walked straight past him, singing 'This way' as if to a child.

He smiled witheringly and followed her through the hallway and into the dining room, then through to the large Victorian kitchen, with its antique hob and blue and white display plates. Jack had difficulty keeping up with Alice, who was moving at such a pace that she momentarily disappeared from view. He was about to beg her to slow down – when he suddenly found himself walking straight into a jungle.

Alice was already seated on some white wicker furniture as if she'd been there all the time. She was pulling a loose thread from her cardigan when she seemed to hear him approach. She looked up and gave him a cheerful smile.

The conservatory was large and white and cluttered with plants of all shapes and sizes, some in huge, cracked glaze vases on the uneven paving stone floor, others in terracotta pots that crammed the window sills; several were sitting on piles of old newspapers, ready to be re-potted. He suspected they had been sitting there for some considerable time, judging by the amount of dust on them. The whiteness of the place gave the illusion that the conservatory was well ventilated and cool, but all the windows were closed and the humidity was almost unbearable. As he sat down, he could hear the tiny snap, crackle and pop of moisture burrowing into the soil of each pot, could see the condensation dripping from the plants hanging from the rafters and landing in irregular-shaped spots on the floor.

He was sweating profusely and about to suggest she keep a few windows open in her house, when she reached for a glass jug of lemonade that sat partially hidden by the overgrown spider plant on the table.

'Homemade,' she said with pride.

He smiled with relief as she poured him some and handed him his glass, the ice clinking satisfactorily. He drank deeply and felt a little sheepish as he realised he had downed it all in one go. She smiled kindly and pushed the entire jug towards him. As he poured himself some more she seemed to read his thoughts and said, 'I never open the windows because my plants don't seem to like it.' Then she added, 'You can take your jacket off.' Her tone made him feel somewhat admonished, but he was more than happy to comply and he hung it on the back of his chair. After that there was an uneasy silence.

'I just wanted to apologise for how you were spoken to by my associate. We always endeavour to try and maintain good practice when speaking to members of the public, Alice, but unfortunately that was not the case this time. Please accept my sincerest apology.'

Alice had sat bolt upright in her chair during his speech and by the time he had concluded, he could see that something was troubling her.

'You mean there was another police officer here?' she asked cautiously.

Jack frowned a little with concern. 'Yes, there was. But you won't be seeing him again, I promise you. Which is why I'm here.' He flashed her a reassuring smile and she seemed to relax a little. 'I just want to say that we're doing everything we can to find your son but I need to ask you a few—'

'Okay, fire away,' she replied, with sudden impatience.

'When did you last hear from him?'

'Last Christmas. He phoned to say he couldn't make it.'

Jack sat back a little, perplexed. 'Sorry, but wasn't it more recent than that? I mean, Helen, your carer, said you had told her that he was coming to visit you.'

'Well, if Helen says so, then she must be right,' replied Alice, with an unexpected coldness.

Jack cleared his throat and allowed the uncomfortable moment to pass. 'And when did you last actually see him?'

'Two years ago.' She smiled bitterly. 'Out of sight, out of mind.'

'As I'm sure you're aware, a car that he had hired was discovered abandoned not too far from here. You had no idea that he was on his way to see you?'

He watched keenly as Alice sipped her lemonade. 'I didn't, but then Helen reminded me.'

'And Helen cares for you on a daily basis?'

Alice nodded.

'Did he tell you what the purpose of his visit was?'

'He's my son, he doesn't need a purpose to visit me,' she replied defensively.

'Of course,' replied Jack softly. 'But if there was anything specific it might give us a clue as to his whereabouts.'

'Helen told me that he had said something about a *special surprise*.' She shrugged, and as she placed her glass back on the table Jack noticed her wedding ring. He braced himself before asking his next question.

'And your husband, William?'

'Who?' she asked. 'Oh. Gone, a long time ago.'

Jack avoided her gaze. 'What do you think happened to him?'

'He died, Mr Russell.'

Jack heard that same impatient tone again and it struck him that this version of Alice was markedly different to the one he had once known. He recalled an occasion when his son had come home from school, saying that *Mrs Smith* had taught him all about the migrants of the First World War. Jack looked sadly at her, for it was plain to see that she could barely recall her own recent movements, let alone that of another generation.

'He was a fisherman,' she explained, 'so I was used to him being away for long periods of time, but then one day he didn't come back. My son believes that he just walked out on us. He's probably right.'

'So you think he might be alive?'

'He might well be. But he's dead to me.'

Jack glanced at the ring she still wore on her finger. He took a breath.

'Do you remember calling the police all those years ago to report his disappearance?'

'Yes.' She glared at him, then sipped some more of her lemonade.

'Do you think there might be a connection between the disappearance of your husband and now your son?'

'Yes.'

'You think someone is responsible?'

'Without a doubt. And I know who.'

Jack leaned closer. 'Who do you think is responsible, Alice?'

'The police, of course – they've done sod all about any of this.'

Jack sat back, disappointed.

Alice exhaled loudly, 'First my husband, now my son. Suppose it'll be me next.' Then she broke into a smile. 'The bane of my life,' she exclaimed, as if it was something wonderful. 'All dead ends and undergarments now.'

Jack was puzzled at her turn of phrase and he took a quick gulp from his glass. It caught the sun and cast a halo of light above Alice's head – somehow it made her martyrdom seem complete.

'Did you know Alistair had a girlfriend?'

'I can't remember,' she said, blinking furiously.

Jack began to wonder if maybe he had caught Alice in a rare moment of clarity because now she appeared to be degenerating before his eyes. He decided to get to the point before she turned into the hopeless case that Clements had so dismissively described.

'Do you think that maybe someone was after him, I mean, did he have enemies?'

'He hasn't spoken… to me… in…'

Alice slumped in her chair and Jack managed to catch her glass just before it fell from her hand. He watched, disturbed, as she seemed to fall into a state of paralysis, staring into space, and he wondered if he should call for an ambulance. A nervous flicker of the fingers in her left hand suggested she was beginning to come back to life. A few moments passed, then she came to and looked at him blankly.

'I've forgotten… What was I trying to say?'

'It's all right,' said Jack. 'Let's get you out into the fresh air.'

He helped her out of her chair and through the house. By the time they had reached the front door she was sufficiently recovered to manage by herself, but all the while Jack was thinking how sorry he felt for Alice. *To lose her husband is bad enough*, he surmised, *but to lose her only child as well, and to never know what really became of them, is a terrible burden to bear. She can't even grieve for them.* He wanted to tell her that everything would be all right, that he would find her son and her husband, but he knew he couldn't, at least not yet.

She seemed to fully revive and looked at him. 'Sorry,' she said, embarrassed. 'There's not much air.'

Jack noticed it too. There was a humidity in the atmosphere, a closeness that was almost claustrophobic.

'That storm isn't finished yet,' Alice said, staring vacantly into the distance.

Jack looked at her questioningly.

As if reading his mind again, she turned and smiled. 'Oh, there's nothing mysterious about it, Mr Russell. It's because we live in a valley. The weather remains *in stasis* here. If it rains then it rains for days, likewise if it's sunny, we get a long spell of it. The weather gets stuck in Hobbs Brae, like it's on a record.' She gave a self-satisfied sigh, getting her old teaching habits back.

A stuck record. Jack knew the feeling. He couldn't wait for the case to be closed so he could go home and sort his life out. *Who would have thought?*

'I'm sorry about what happened in there,' said Alice. 'I have dementia. If you find my son, please don't tell him.'

'Of course,' replied Jack. 'Is Helen taking good care of you?' He suddenly felt like he was intruding. He had hoped that Alice would have remembered him by now, but there was not the slightest hint of recollection.

'We have our moments,' she replied, 'but Helen's a good egg. She looks after me most days. I'm at my worst in the late afternoon, when the sun is setting. I don't know why. She calls it *sundowning*. Apparently it's not uncommon with people in my condition, but I know very little about it. I know very little about anything these days.'

Jack watched as her eyes seemed to glaze over.

'*Alfred*,' she said quietly.

'Who?'

'*Alfred*,' she repeated, a little louder.

'Who's *Alfred*?'

Alice came out of her reverie and said fondly, 'We built him a long time ago.'

Jack gave a careful smile as he saw her laugh warmly at his confusion. 'This way,' she said, in that patronising tone again, which proved she was back to her old self, and she led him out into the wild wilderness that was her garden. Everything was bathed in a honeycomb glow as the sun reached its zenith. He followed Alice down the path and into the abundant undergrowth. Midges danced in lazy circles. High above, a lone ice-cream cloud slowly melted in the sky.

He observed with curiosity as Alice stopped suddenly and pointed, smiling broadly. Something about this pose made her look like a little girl. Perhaps it was the way her long, flowing dress reminded him of an old-fashioned smock, the kind that female Victorian artists would once have worn. He followed the line of her arm to her finger, which was pointing towards one of the abandoned fields. In the middle stood a wooden cross.

'A scarecrow,' he said flatly.

'*Alfred*,' she replied brightly. 'We built him in remembrance of things lost.' She suddenly looked rueful. 'There he stands and watches the sea in case my husband should ever return.'

Jack looked at her and said what had been on his mind for some time now.

'You do know it's unlikely that your husband will return.'

'I know,' she replied, and laughed as if he'd said something funny, yet he saw her brush a tear from her face. A breeze picked up and the leaves of the nearby bushes gaily showed their silvery undersides. Jack was reminded how peaceful it was. He didn't want to leave, but time was marching on and he knew that he must go soon.

'Why did you call him *Alfred*?'

Alice laughed again and clapped her hands together. 'Because he was so useless at scaring the crows. They just use him as something to perch on. So we called him *Alfred*, as in Hitchcock, the film director.'

'Ah.' He smiled. '*Alfred*.'

'What was your name again?'

'Jack,' he said amiably. 'Jack Russell.'

She smiled faintly and took a step closer, scrutinising him. 'The *dogged detective*,' she said with a smirk and Jack laughed. Then she added, 'You have kind eyes.'

He watched sadly as Alice appeared to become distracted and resumed staring out to sea. She suddenly seemed so lost, so utterly alone. Jack knew he had to go, but it felt like an act of cruelty to leave her.

'We'll do everything we can, I promise,' he said, backing off.

'Can you feel that?' she asked, without taking her eyes off the ocean.

Jack shook his head. Then Alice turned and looked right at him.

'Something is coming.'

Her delivery of this mysterious statement confounded Jack, but he didn't have the time to consider what she had meant by it. *Perhaps she is just* Gone with the Wind *after all*, he mused. *And yet…*

He reached the gate and she called out to him, 'Drive carefully.' He nodded and smiled pityingly at her. He closed the latch and walked quickly down the hill, still haunted by her parting words and the fact that, despite him having lived in Hobbs Brae for more than two decades, she no longer remembered him.

Who do you think is responsible, Alice? he heard himself say. Jack was saddened that she could not recall that he had been in charge of her husband's case at the time. A masochistic part of him wanted her to remember, wanted her to blame him. It was the only case he had never managed to solve. And the guilt haunted him even now. But there was more to it than that. Jack believed that if she had pointed the finger at him, recognised him for what he was, then it would have meant that there was still hope for her and her memory. But he walked away feeling despondent.

He arrived back at the car and nodded to Jamie, who looked up dead-eyed with concentration from his mobile, then went back to texting. Jack saw Colin's car pull up in the distance and his mood brightened. *This is going to be fun,* he thought, and he enjoyed the sight of the DC impatiently patrolling the outskirts of the woods, awaiting further instructions. *I could watch this all day*, Jack thought smugly.

Completely unaware that he too was being watched.

Chapter Twenty-Two

September 3rd

Scott jolted awake from a nightmare. He shuddered, remembering that it had taken place somewhere dark and that something had been with him. He tried not to listen to its phlegmy, rattling breath against his ear. He shut his eyes tight and drew his arms and legs into a foetal position in order to protect himself. He felt safe at last. But then it giggled, so close that it seemed to come from within. And the rest he couldn't recall, for that's when he woke up.

Groggily, he felt the memory of it recede with the encroaching daylight that filtered through the trees as the sun began to rise. He emerged cautiously from his hiding place and folded his arms across his chest to try and keep warm. He had been sleeping rough under a piece of corrugated iron that he'd found in the treetops. It was large and flat and folded in half, and when he had pushed it with his foot it had fallen to the ground with a crash, landing in the shape of a huge open book. On climbing back down he saw that there were some feathers clinging to its underside and he recognised the roof from his father's hen coop. *I can't escape him*, he mused.

Scott had pined for independence for so long, but he had never envisaged it would manifest itself in such a negative way. He had no food and no money. He ate apples foraged from a tree that had taken root at a dumping ground near the edge of the forest, and he drank from a nearby waterfall. He was effectively homeless and knew he couldn't exist for much longer. His only viable solution was to return to the farm, but he feared what might be waiting for him there.

'Scott!'

His heart leapt. It was his father's voice. Instinctively, he crouched down in the undergrowth.

'Scott!'

He heard Jerome shouting his name repeatedly until his voice tired out. Once he was sure that he was gone, Scott ventured out from his den and breathed a sigh of relief. Yet, as time passed by he found that he could not relax, could not venture too far from his hiding place, lest his father be somewhere in the vicinity still, waiting, perhaps, to trap him. Hours passed and he finally convinced himself to make a move, because now the onset of hunger was irrepressible, so when he felt certain that his father would be out working in the fields, he took his chance and crept towards the farmhouse.

Entering via the back door, he bounded quickly and quietly upstairs to his bedroom, grabbed his jacket and his wallet, then ran back down – straight into Jerome.

For a moment Scott saw his father look blank, dumbfounded to see his own son standing there. Then a look of shame flickered across his face. 'So you're back,' he said.

'I came to collect my things,' said Scott, chin held high, trying to sound braver than he actually felt.

'You were supposed to help me.'

Scott was horrified. It was as if nothing had happened between them. He stepped back from him a little. He felt his legs shaking so he widened his stance. 'Then you came at me with an axe,' he replied, surprising himself with his assertiveness.

A moment passed between them. Jerome looked almost impressed, then he cast his gaze downwards for a second. He seemed about to confess, but when he looked him in the eye again his face hardened a little.

'We need to burn the field, remember?'

'I don't need to do anything for you anymore,' replied Scott, and he turned to leave.

'I think you'll find you won't get very far without this,' he heard his father say, and Scott turned back round. There, held aloft in his father's cruel hand, was Scott's bank card.

Scott stared at him, and in that moment there was a silent agreement between them to put aside their differences and get back on to the task in hand. 'When do we start?' he asked, reluctantly.

'No time like the present,' Jerome replied. Scott watched enviously as his father, who now literally held the ace card, hobbled busily around the farm, emerging moments later from the shed with a can of liquid fuel. 'We'll work in parallel. You on one side of the field, and me on the other. Remember to light the fire downwind. I don't want the whole farm going up in flames.'

Scott gave him an ironic smile.

'Any problems, contact me on this.' Jerome threw him a two-way radio.

'I do have a problem,' said Scott.

'If you're referring to your bank card, boy, you'll get it back when I'm satisfied that you've done the job, and done it well.'

Scott shrugged and set to work, only too happy to be building a wall of flames between them – another symbol of his bone of contention. He knew he could never be satisfied with such an outcome, could never shake off the feeling that despite the few acres that stood between them, it still felt like they were a million miles from one another.

Chapter Twenty-Three

September 3rd

Jack was marching briskly down a dirt track towards the forest, with Colin trying to keep up with him. He was amused by his sidekick's laboured breathing and constant complaining. As they made their way towards the place where he suspected Alistair and Caroline had hidden from the storm, he suppressed a laugh when he heard Colin slip in the mud and curse loudly. It was moments like this that made his job worthwhile.

'Breathe in that fresh air,' he cried.

'Smells like shit to me,' grumbled Colin.

'Manure,' Jack corrected. 'It's good for you,' he added, with an unusual spring in his step.

'What do you expect to find here?'

'Well, that's the question, isn't it?'

'Wait a minute, will you? You're going too fast.'

Jack stopped and turned to face him. 'There are two people missing. We are in a race against time, so I suggest you get some more exercise unless you want me to report that you're no longer fit for the job?'

Colin scowled at him, but Jack didn't care. They both knew that he was right.

'This is just a wild goose chase,' Colin griped. 'Why are you even here? You're supposed to be overseeing this investigation and instead you're going on a hunting expedition in a bloody forest.'

Jack stared at him. 'Are you finished?'

Colin sniffed.

'First of all, *Clements*, I don't need to be told how to do my job. I am overseeing this investigation and I have a very, very good reason for being here. We've found, or rather Constable Campbell has found, an abandoned vehicle matching the one that Alistair was driving on the night he and his girlfriend went missing. Secondly, there is a likelihood that they took shelter from the storm in this forest, so there may well be clues.'

'But why are you here? You're not going in there are you?'

'No, Detective Constable Clements. You are.'

Just then, several police cars pulled up and a team of officers with tracker dogs arrived on the scene. Jack watched as Driscoll sauntered up to Clements and gave a small, helpless shrug.

'I want you men to assist Clements here,' said Jack loudly. 'We need to scour the entire forest if necessary. The forensics team will work alongside you.'

Colin marched up to him and said quietly, 'And so what are you going to do then? Swan off and push some pens across your desktop?'

Jack smiled patiently. 'No. I'm going to speak to some of the locals. In fact, I've just come from Alice Smith's house. We discussed the derogatory way that you addressed her concerns about her missing son and I'm pleased to be able to inform you that she accepted my apology on your behalf. So don't sweat it. But be careful how you speak to me, Clements – you are next in line for my job and right now I have serious doubts about your future. Your friend and subordinate Constable Campbell seems to know what he's doing. Look to him as an example.'

Jack watched triumphantly as Colin spat with contempt on the grass, then turned and went to join his colleagues. Jack made his way back up the dirt track, and wondered about Colin. He had known the DC for years and he acknowledged that theirs had never been an easy alliance, but he had never seen him so bitter, so resentful, before. It worried him that he couldn't figure out what was really going on behind those spectacles of his.

Once he reached his car, he saw Jamie sitting in the back seat, waiting. Theirs was an alliance that seemed to be growing stronger and it touched him that his son now wanted to spend so much time with him.

Before getting back into his vehicle, he found that he had a good vantage point and he looked around. He could see his officers making their way into the woods. Then he saw something else.

There was smoke billowing out from behind the trees. A fire had been started.

Chapter Twenty-Four

September 3rd

Something had caught Matthew's eye. He could see a huge plume of smoke spiralling into the air. The field in the distance was in flames.

He had been trying to trace Caroline's whereabouts. He looked around for any signs of the car that Alistair had been driving. He went to the Crow's Beak and ordered some lunch and discreetly dropped Caroline's name – but there was nothing.

Then he saw the morning paper. Alistair and Caroline had gone missing. He wondered what to do next. Then he spied the police.

I'll tail their investigation, he decided. He watched as a burly detective went to Alice Smith's house. And he watched as the same detective went to the forest some distance away.

Then he saw the smoke.

There was something else that at first he could not easily fathom. In the field where the fire was burning, there was a ghostly figure at the centre. It seemed to be gliding. He couldn't be sure, but something about the languid way it moved gave him the impression that it was a woman. He peered into the distance, trying to decipher more, but she seemed to disappear, quite literally, in a puff of smoke.

Chapter Twenty-Five

September 3rd

Jack drove the car up to the farm. Telling his son to stay where he was, he marched past the house and made his way towards the location of the smoke. He noticed that the windows of an old lean-to shed were covered with tin foil. Ignoring it for the time being, he reached the site of the fire. There, in front of him, were huge flames, the length and breadth of the field, rearing and snaking upwards like a many-headed hydra, the clouds of smoke floating and gliding outwards, casting shadows across the trees.

He saw someone – a teenager – hurrying away from the scene. On seeing the detective, the boy suddenly changed course, disappearing into the undergrowth. Jack's suspicions were aroused and he went after him. The boy kept glancing over his shoulder at Jack, who was careful to keep his distance. Then the boy broke into a run. Jack had no option but to increase his pace too, otherwise he would lose him amidst the trees. As he followed him deeper into the forest it became increasingly difficult to make his way through the thickening bracken. Then the boy suddenly stopped dead in his tracks. Jack did the same and watched as the boy began to back off from something or someone that remained unseen. The boy abruptly turned and fled deeper into the woods, bounding through the greenery with surprising speed, leaving Jack alone to face whatever or whoever had frightened him off. His adrenalin surged and he felt his muscles tense, ready to defend himself. He peered into the darkness that filled the narrow gaps between the tree trunks, but he couldn't see anything.

An old man with a walking stick suddenly emerged from the shadows. Jack stood scrutinising him and the man stared right back, his mouth twisted into a sneer. Jack took a step towards him.

'Detective Chief Inspector Jack Russell,' he said by way of introduction. 'Why did that boy run away from you?'

'Only thing he runs away from is work.'

'Didn't look that way to me.'

'Looks can be deceiving.'

'Now isn't that the truth,' Jack quipped, and took another step closer, noticing that the man instinctively tightened his grip on the walking stick.

'Are you his grandfather?'

The man shook his head, smiling smugly, and for a moment Jack felt uncomfortable.

'Father, then?'

Silence. Jack looked him up and down. Then he twigged. The farmer's reputation preceded him. He seemed too old to be the boy's father.

'You working on the field today?'

'I am.'

'Seen anything suspicious?'

'Only you.'

Jack smiled at the retort. 'Know why I'm here?'

'To find them missing kids,' the old man spat contemptuously. 'We had another of your type here yesterday – DCI Clements.'

Jack snorted, 'He's not a DCI.'

'Said he was.'

'That doesn't entirely surprise me.'

'You won't find them,' said the old man.

'What makes you so sure?'

'Because you've just let that kid slip through your fingers,' he replied, and turned to go.

'Hang on mister,' Jack called after him. 'You're not out of the woods yet.'

'I've got work to do,' he called back. 'A field doesn't burn itself.'

'You didn't happen to see those kids, did you?' shouted Jack, but it fell on deaf ears and he noted that the old man moved very quickly for one so apparently disabled. 'Jerome – you do realise that I could make life very difficult for you if I chose to. After all, I'm aware that you have a history of illegal activity on these premises.'

Jerome stopped and turned. 'You and I on first name terms now? That's cosy,' he said.

Jack sauntered up to him. 'It's like this, Jerome. There's now a lot of publicity surrounding this case and it's up to me to find out what happened that night, and I will, because I'm a tenacious bastard. And no one is going to put any obstacles in my way. You can forget about burning any more of those fields of yours. We don't want any evidence going up in flames now, do we?'

Jack smirked at Jerome's fuming silence.

'I'll want to have a word with your son, too,' he added.

'You leave my son out of this.'

'I'll leave him – and you – out of this when I uncover exactly what happened here. In the meantime, destroy the cannabis plants you've got tucked away in your shed. See you both, very soon.'

Jack strolled off, satisfied that he had put the unpleasant farmer in his place. But as he made his way back out of the forest, something kept bringing his attention back to the walking stick. He'd noticed how Jerome had held onto it very tightly, yet he seemed relatively able-bodied. He couldn't think why this bothered him so.

His phone rang. It was Colin.

Moments later, Jack was driving as fast as he could back to the dirt track.

'Show me,' he ordered.

Colin nodded obediently and led him into the woods. They approached a river and he found that the area had been cordoned off with police tape. The forensics team were waiting nearby.

'It's right here,' said Driscoll, and pointed to a plot on the ground which had been marked out with numbered plastic stands and covered with a clear tarpaulin.

Jack was given some paper shoes, and once fitted, he took a closer look. There, on the ground, was a large dark stain, a yardstick lying beside it for scale.

'Blood,' confirmed Colin. 'Copious amounts of it.'

'Has a sample been taken?'

'Already done, sir,' said Driscoll.

Jack noted that he hadn't been called *sir* for some time by his inferior, who usually took a leaf out of Colin's book and avoided giving him his place whenever he could. It was obvious that the discovery had knocked the insubordinate tendencies out of everyone. Even Colin looked suitably solemn.

Jack was aware that they were all waiting on his instructions. He couldn't help but enjoy the thrill of their anticipation. *Guess this isn't going to be the nice, easy case the Chief thought it would be*, he mused happily. He took a deep breath and said to everyone, 'You've all seen the evidence. As of now this is no longer a missing persons case. It's a murder enquiry.'

Chapter Twenty-Six

September 4th

Scott was thinking hard about what to do next. He had committed to helping his father burn the field and, as he had anticipated, Jerome ensured he did countless more tasks, so that by the end of the working day Scott was too exhausted to even think about leaving. Instead, he stayed one more night in the forest and tried not to think about his father's final act of cruelty. Once Jerome was satisfied that he had wrought every last drop of labour from him, he then casually threw his son's bank card into the dying flames of the field. Scott ran into the embers, frantic, scrabbling for his card. He managed to rescue it just in the nick of time. As he scanned it for any signs of damage, he found that it had been blackened, but it was only superficial and the soot was easily wiped off. Immediately afterwards he ran from the place where his father had held such a historical grudge against him. The only solace he took was that he was free from the old bastard at last.

Scott could hear several voices shouting in the woods. They seemed to be calling for someone. He cocked his head to one side and listened, but they were too far away for him to hear distinctly. Somewhere a dog was barking and he could hear a helicopter in the distance. Moving further into the woods, he was stopped by the feeling that he was being watched.

He turned and was alarmed to see a man standing there, staring threateningly at him. He was short, fat and bespectacled, wearing a suit, and flanked by two other men wearing similar attire and with the same look on their faces. Scott fearfully surveyed his chances of escape as the three men seemed to size him up and then advanced towards him.

'DCI Clements,' Colin stated, wiping beads of sweat from his hairline, which was the colour of Irn-Bru. He seemed out of breath and was somewhat red in the face. 'Now I've got some questions for you and you are going to answer them.'

Scott nodded obediently. Widening his stance slightly, he prepared to make a run for it if he had to, for he could sense aggression in the tone of voice.

'Who are you?' asked Colin.

'Scott,' he replied quietly.

'What?'

He cleared his throat. 'Scott Jennings.'

'And what are you doing here?' Colin enquired with mock politeness.

Scott mentally scanned through a back catalogue of violence and repression and found that he was in a quandary. *Where do I begin?* he wondered.

'Well?'

'I'm camping,' he answered. *Well, it's sort of true*, he thought to himself.

Colin irritably wiped the condensation from his glasses. The air was growing humid. 'I find that hard to believe,' he replied.

'I've got no reason to lie,' said Scott, his heart thumping hard.

'Really?' said the detective, replacing his glasses and exchanging a doubtful look with his officers.

Scott felt his patience begin to run out. 'Why am I being questioned?'

'I'll be conducting this interview,' Colin said, his voice hardening, and his claret face seeming to inflate. 'Where were you on the night of September the first?'

'I was at home,' replied Scott, staring him straight in the eye.

'At home? With your father, in the farmhouse?'

'Yes.'

He saw the detective smile disbelievingly. 'So, if you live nearby, why are you out here, *camping*?'

'We don't get on,' said Scott uneasily.

'Continue,' replied Clements.

Scott looked at him warily, then said, 'I don't know what else to say.'

The detective regarded him for a moment, then replied, 'It's like this, Scott. Two people have gone missing in these woods. Alistair Smith and Caroline Baker. You didn't happen to see them by any chance?'

'No,' replied Scott flatly.

'That's odd, Scott, because your father said you were here on the night they both disappeared.'

Scott's stomach lurched and he felt his face flush. Then came the anger. *You bastard*, he thought, *I cover your back, despite everything you've done to me. And you throw me to the dogs.* 'I was in the forest but I never saw anything,' he lied. Just then Scott had a flashback to something that he couldn't easily form into words.

'What are you hiding?' asked Colin, through a pleasant smile.

Scott shook his head. 'Nothing. I never saw anything.'

The detective constable stared at him for what seemed the longest time – then he suddenly lost interest.

'Okay. You can go,' he announced.

Scott blinked. 'I can go?'

'Of course you can. There's nothing stopping you, is there?'

Scott waited a moment, unsure, then cautiously edged past.

'Is your father a violent man?' Colin asked suddenly, stopping Scott in his tracks.

'When he's got a drink,' said Scott carefully.

'I can't abide violence myself. I was never very hands on, you see.' He nodded to Driscoll, who sidled up to Scott. 'Of course, I can't speak for both of us.' And with that as his exit line, Colin left with Campbell, leaving Driscoll with Scott.

Scott glared at him and was ready to defend himself if necessary. But Driscoll simply looked him up and down, the expression on his face implying that he thought Scott was no match for him. He gave him a wink and sauntered off with a smirk.

Scott was furious. He was sick of being threatened. He was also very hungry, having not eaten properly in days. He marched out of the woods and went into a nearby café and ordered a hot meal. He wolfed it down, all the while wondering why his father had tried to frame him. Was the old bastard so twisted that he would do anything to get at him? It certainly seemed so. *What have I ever done to him to cause such hatred?*

Scott's optimism and hopes for reconciliation were all but extinguished, and he decided there and then that it was time to leave for good. He finished his meal and got up to pay.

His card was declined.

Scott phoned his bank.

'I'm sorry, Mr Smith, but someone has reported that they found your card lying in a street so we had to take a course of action in order to prevent it from being used without your authorisation.'

'But it's my card. It was never lost in the first place,' argued Scott, heatedly.

'I'm sorry, sir – we can send you a new one within twenty-four hours – but you won't be able to use the old one.'

After much arguing, Scott reluctantly agreed, and after supplying his details, he hung up.

Dad must have kept a record of my bank details, he thought darkly. *Why won't he leave me alone?*

He stared long and hard into the woods. Something seemed to cackle quietly in the shadows. *A bird perhaps,* he reassured himself. But it was cold comfort at best. *I'm trapped here. Game, set and match to dad.*

Chapter Twenty-Seven

September 4th

Alice Smith was doing her housework, flicking the dust off the great-grandfather clock in the hall with a small feather brush, when she noticed that her telephone had been moved. She always left it at what she felt was a *jaunty* angle, but now it was sitting a little too near the edge of the table. When she approached, Alice found that the receiver was no longer on its cradle. It looked like it had been deliberately taken off the hook.

I must have moved it when I was dusting, she thought, unconvinced, as she continued with her chores, her mind wandering furtively through all the distinctly creepy possibilities. Then she stopped.

Something upstairs. She listened, staring at the ceiling. It came again. The sound of creaking floorboards.

I've heard this before. Probably just the house cooling off. But Alice wasn't particularly good at reassuring herself. Her mind would not let her rest. She just had to go up and see.

On arriving at the landing, there seemed to be nothing there. She sighed impatiently at her own paranoia and went back down the stairs.

The very next moment she was humming a tune to herself as she sprinkled water on the herbaceous border of her garden. Alice knew something had happened, but she did not know what. It just felt wrong somehow. She looked at her watch, but the time meant nothing to her anymore.

Another fugue? she wondered vaguely, and Alice suddenly felt lost, for her life was becoming a secret that she was no longer part of.

She went back indoors and struggled for a full 20 minutes to comprehend the fact that the clock in the hall had stopped working when the storm had struck. When she finally understood this, she fell exhausted on the front doorstep and cried.

Just then she discovered that the dead seagull was gone.

The revelation jolted Alice back to her senses and she pulled herself together. Steadfastly trying not to think about her disturbing lapses of memory, she got up and continued watering the soil, which was bone dry from the heat that still permeated Hobbs Brae, despite the recent thunder. She breathed in what air there was and wrinkled her nose when she smelled something acrid, like smoke. She looked down at her dress and was shocked to see that it was covered in strands of straw. Alice was struck with a hazy memory of something that made no sense; she could see a blue cardigan and she remembered flames, but nothing more.

Something caught her eye and she stood stock still, watching the upstairs bedroom window closely. The curtain flicked back suddenly and she gasped, dropping the metal can onto the paving stones with a clatter, the water pouring out until it sputtered to a stop. Alice clutched at her pearls and backed off, shocked that her suspicions were true.

Someone is in my house.

It explained everything that had happened: the floorboards upstairs and the dead seagull disappearing; then the phone. *And now this.*

Alice felt her feet sinking into something soft and found that she had retreated into the soil. The basket was still lying there on its side and she wondered what was buried nearby under the telltale mound of earth. With a sudden act of boldness, she marched round to the back garden and pulled out a spade from the shed and marched round to the front again. Digging furiously, she discovered a pile of terracotta pots under the soil. Alice realised with an involuntary laugh what she had done. She had buried them there because she thought they would somehow grow. 'Not one of my better days,' she remarked. Alice was so disgusted with herself that she left the pots scattered in the soil with the spade sticking crookedly out of the ground.

She looked up at the window again. *And I thought I was going mad. I've been blaming myself for all these strange little things that have been happening. When all along someone has been here with me the whole time.* For a moment, Alice felt confident, for the evidence behind her bedroom window told her that she had more nous than she gave herself credit for.

To think I thought it might be the ghost of my husband.

Alice almost laughed at the idea, her no-nonsense teacher's sensibilities kicking in again.

This would be the last place he would return to, she thought cynically, and stared up at the window once again, silently challenging her trespasser to appear before her. When nothing came, she pressed her lips together determinedly, and went straight back inside.

'Who's there?' she shouted, and waited for a response. None came. She stood for a moment and wondered what to do next. 'I'm calling the police,' she yelled.

But, by the time the sun began to rise again, Alice had already spent the entire night in her garden, shivering in the cold, and exiled from her own home.

For just as she was about to pick up the receiver, someone had run heavily across the hall upstairs.

Chapter Twenty-Eight

September 4th

Despite the sunshine, Scott had retreated once more to his green dominion. It was the only place where he felt reasonably safe. In the relative gloom of the trees, he could move around unseen, and the masses of moss, which were reassuringly soft and springy underfoot, served to muffle his movements. He found a glade of ferns and hid amongst their fronds, lying back on the forest floor and staring up through the leafy canopies at the sky. Two vast clouds were slowly coming together like two huge armies joining forces – a massive, silent drama of reconciliation taking place in the air above. And here on *terra firma* he wished that he and his father could do the same. It pained him deeply to think that they had always been on opposing sides. Unlike the clouds above, it seemed they would not be reconciled until one or the other was defeated. There was no going back now.

He was getting used to his life as an outcast. It didn't seem that different to how his father made him feel at the best of times. He had no money and no home, and he was now playing a distinctly uncomfortable waiting game for his bank card to arrive. Uncomfortable, because he would have to try and intercept the postman before it was delivered into Jerome's callous hands.

Yet he had discovered a crude sense of independence and his confidence was growing as a result. In some ways he had his father to thank for this, given how he had pushed him out into the real world. He just wished that it hadn't been done so maliciously. In any case, he knew that he would soon have no choice but to leave because his dominion was shrinking. The forest had too many visitors and he could hear one of them approaching now. He sat up quickly, alarmed by the heavy, laboured footsteps coming towards him through the trees. A figure appeared. As it approached Scott was relieved to find that it wasn't Jerome.

'DCI Jack Russell,' the detective said gruffly, looking down at Scott and cloaking him in his shadow. Scott looked up, observing that the investigator had a stern expression, but his eyes betrayed an empathy with the world. Scott thought there was something clumsy about him. He seemed to be putting on a stance, his chest puffed out deliberately and his voice forcibly deeper than it ought to be.

'And you are Scott Jennings,' Jack added, intending, it seemed, to intimidate him. Scott smiled patiently and waited. Clements had been playing *bad cop* and he suspected this one would soon tire of being a bully and would revert to being the kind soul that was so evident in his eyes. He wondered what was lacking in the officer's life that he felt the need to play-act. Scott's patience was wearing thin. If it wasn't his father threatening him with an axe, it was some nosey detective with an axe to grind. He never seemed to get a moment's peace. Once more he was being driven from his bolthole. He felt endangered, close to extinction – a future fossil.

Scott watched carefully as Jack sat down heavily beside him and wiped his brow. He could see that the man was exhausted. His shoulders were slumped, as if a lead weight rested on them. There were shadows under his eyes, and he had a haunted expression, as if trying to conceal some private malady. *Doubt perhaps*, thought Scott.

'Still on the run from your dad?' Jack quipped.

Scott flinched slightly. 'I'm not running away from anybody.'

'You ran away from me. And it did appear that you had been running away from him too, no?'

There was an awkward silence, then Scott stammered, 'I thought you were that other detective – Clements.'

'Yes, we often get mistaken for one another,' said Jack good-humouredly. 'We're practically twins.'

Scott noticed the detective suddenly scowl.

'So let me get this straight. DC Clements has already questioned you?'

Scott looked at him cautiously. 'Yes.'

'I see. And how did that go?'

Scott fidgeted uncomfortably. 'I was scared,' he said finally.

This seemed to strike a chord with Jack. 'Nothing wrong with being scared.' Then he leaned closer and whispered, 'And between you and me, I don't like Clements either.'

Scott giggled involuntarily and twigged how childish he must have sounded. His face flushed with embarrassment.

'I'm worried about you,' said Jack. 'This isn't a good place to be right now. Two people went missing here. You do know that, don't you?'

Scott shrugged. He felt Jack nudge him.

'Do you remember the storm a few days ago?'

Scott replied, 'The storm isn't gone. It'll be back.'

He saw Jack look at him questioningly. 'Someone else said that.'

Scott felt a charge of excitement. Somebody was on the same wavelength as him. 'They did? Who?'

'It doesn't matter,' replied Jack. 'What makes you think the storm is coming back?'

'Can't you feel it?'

He looked right back at the detective, who seemed to be observing him closely, as if trying to figure him out.

'Where were you, Scott, on that night?'

'I was here.'

'Did you see anyone?'

Scott shook his head.

'If you saw someone, then you must tell me. You'll be protected.'

'I only saw my dad.'

'Why were you running from him yesterday?'

Scott didn't respond.

'Did you have a fight?'

'We're always fighting.'

He watched with a degree of quiet cynicism as Jack attempted an amiable smile.

'I had a little chat with him. He likes a drink, doesn't he?'

Scott remained guarded.

'I could smell it,' explained Jack.

'Whisky,' said Scott simply.

'I guess he's got quite a temper on him when the whisky kicks in. Am I right?' An attempt at a laugh.

Scott gave Jack a wary look, then nodded.

'Does he frighten you?'

'No,' answered Scott quickly.

'And yet you hide out here alone, on cold nights, with people going missing all around you. Bit dangerous, is it not?'

'That's why I did it,' claimed Scott with a winning smile, but he could tell that the officer wasn't convinced. He self-consciously plucked the leaves from some plants, waiting for the next question.

'Your dad doesn't really need his walking stick, does he?'

This unexpectedly touched a nerve and Scott blinked away an oncoming tear. He was startled when the detective seized him by the shoulders and put his face close to his.

'Did you see anything suspicious that night – the slightest thing – anything at all?'

Scott felt under pressure to give him some kind of answer, but he didn't know what to say. He frowned and pursed his lips, trying to think fast.

'Did you see anyone else in the forest on the night of September the first, other than your father?'

Scott saw himself in the woods. He could remember the rain soaking through his clothes and the wind howling through the arch of the bridge. A glimpse of water. And blood. He recalled averting his eyes to the cosmos above. 'I saw a strange star in the sky,' he blurted.

'A *star*?' Jack repeated impatiently.

Scott hung his head. 'It moved differently from all the others,' he added quietly.

Jack let go of his shoulders and Scott could feel the air of regret between them. They sat together in silence for a while, then they both heard footsteps. Jack got up, absentmindedly ruffling the boy's hair. Then he shouted, 'Come out of your hiding place.'

Scott was preparing to make a run for it, lest it was his father. But instead, DC Clements came out of the shadows. Scott watched as Jack marched towards him and then there were raised voices. It appeared that Clements was getting a bollocking. Scott was relieved not to be on the receiving end of someone's bile for once. He moved a little closer so that he could hear them more clearly.

'What the hell are you playing at?' demanded Jack.

'I don't know what you mean, *sir*,' Scott heard Colin reply, with a look of defiance.

'That boy has just told me that you have already questioned him. So why did you not take him to the office for a formal written statement?'

Scott didn't like being referred to as a *boy*, nor did he like the look of contempt that DC Clements gave him at that moment. He worried that he had inadvertently got the detective into some kind of trouble with his superior. He observed him move closer to Jack and tell him something, but he couldn't make out what it was.

Scott moved a little closer too, his eyes cast downwards as if disinterested. He cocked his head to one side in order to eavesdrop.

'... and what about the blood?' he heard Jack say.

'Nothing yet, sir.'

Scott saw Jack heave an impatient sigh. 'What do you mean, nothing yet?'

Colin appeared to bristle. 'Well, as you know, it can take weeks to find the DNA in such a sample.'

'Yes, I do know that, but there is nothing stopping you from finding out the blood type and matching it with his medical records. They are easy enough to find, are they not?'

'Well, aye, but we need a warrant first and if it's a common blood type it hardly gets us much closer to a match.'

'But it does narrow it down, so get it done.'

The DC glared at his superior for a moment, then shrugged and stomped off.

Jack watched him go, and turned his attention to Scott. He walked up to him and smiled apologetically. 'I'm sorry, Scott. But I need you to come back to the station with me in order to make a statement. Once done, we can then take you out of our enquiries.'

Scott felt his stomach sink. *Out of the frying pan and into the fire*, he thought, as he reluctantly followed Jack back to his car.

Chapter Twenty-Nine

September 4th

Matthew White was watching and waiting, collating every scrap of information he could get. He observed that the local press were reporting on the case, but only seemed interested in Caroline. He didn't mind too much. *She's worth ten of Alistair*, he thought.

He pondered on whether or not to contact his own family, to let them know that he was back home in Hobbs Brae, but he felt it would only muddy his business. And what a covert business it had turned out to be. He'd become quite the detective these days, snooping about and following his respective leads. How could he tell them that he had come here for the sole purpose of stalking an ex-girlfriend? *How creepy would that sound?* he wondered.

Despite his concerns, he couldn't help but be a tiny bit pleased that Alistair had stumbled. The fact that Caroline had gone missing was proof, if ever proof was needed, that Alistair was simply not good enough for her, and that it would take a man, a real man, to come charging in on his white horse and rescue her from whatever or who-ever she needed rescuing from. As far as Matthew was concerned, he was the one to do it, for he had always been convinced that Caroline needed rescuing from Alistair.

It had struck Matthew as odd that his replacement had been a boy with the complexion of cement and an ugly scar on his face. Now, because Alistair had let Caroline slip through his fingers, Matthew felt forced to return home – the last place on earth he ever wanted to be.

'Too many bad memories,' he once said to Caroline, and he had left it at that.

Yet Matthew was well aware that he too had allowed Caroline to slip through his fingers. With his good looks and well-spoken charm, he had once thought of himself as something of a catch, but he soon discovered that Caroline wouldn't tolerate his misdemeanours and so she had moved on. Matthew had pretended to himself that he wasn't bothered, but as time ticked by he understood what he'd lost, and he could no longer cope with the idea of someone else taking his place. His jealousy took him by surprise and when he discovered that Caroline had gone missing, he surprised himself again with the lengths he would go to in order to find her – such as checking into a hotel under the guise of an alias. *Jason Black.* The alias ensured that no one knew Matthew had returned.

Being recognised was the one thing that had troubled him most on his journey home, but he quickly realised that he had undergone a huge transformation since his childhood in Hobbs Brae. Once a pale, skinny teenager, he had remade himself when arriving in Glasgow, and had bulked up in the gym, whitened his teeth and now had a permanent tan. He was barely recognisable anymore. He wondered if all this cloak and dagger was worth it, but he couldn't help himself because there was always the prospect that Caroline might appreciate his efforts and give him a second chance.

Something distracted Matthew from his thoughts – a shadow emerging from the trees. A large, suited man had come out with a teenager and was walking at pace away from the forest. Matthew watched, fascinated, as they both got into a car nearby, where another suited man was waiting at the wheel. He had seen the bigger of the two men before and knew he was in charge of the investigation. His fascination soon turned to alarm when he saw them heading towards the centre of Hobbs Brae. From his vantage point high on the hill, he watched as the smaller detective entered the Warm and Friendly.

'Why would he go there?' he whispered. *Have I been found out?*

Meanwhile, the officer in charge drove away from the hotel and off towards the police station, taking the lad with him. *Time to face the music*, Matthew thought, and he drew a breath and headed quietly back to the Warm and Friendly. On arriving, he stood outside the door and listened. There was nothing. Cautiously, he stepped into the gloomy hallway, his heart thudding with dread.

Margaret was standing there and staring at him.

His heart skipped a beat at what she was about to say.

Suddenly, she broke into a smile and said, 'Lovely to see you again, Mr Black, but you just missed a visitor. Said he was a police officer and that he wanted to talk to you. I didn't like the look of him and told him you were no longer staying here.'

Their eyes met and he thought he saw her blush.

Without waiting on a response, she then said, 'Would you like a cup of tea?'

You've just saved my bacon, he thought, and smiled broadly, switching on his charm. 'Maggie, I'd love a cup of tea.'

As he sat there at the table, waiting, he recalled an oar slicing through the waters of a loch.

'Whatever's wrong?' Margaret asked, startling him, a tea tray in her hands. 'You look a little crestfallen, dear.'

'Bad memories,' he said, almost to himself.

Margaret sighed and sat a plate of biscuits on the table in front of him. 'We've all got plenty of those,' she said. 'But let's not dwell on them. A nice cup of tea will solve everything.'

'Yes, a nice cup of tea,' he replied, and he watched vacantly as she poured the brew, his mind elsewhere, for all he could see in that moment was the oar striking the water – and the blood beneath the waves.

Chapter Thirty

September 4th

DC Clements was in the mortuary again, thinking long and hard about the humiliation he had suffered at the hands of Jack, *and right in front of that weirdo kid, too*, banging his knuckles against the metal surfaces as he moodily skulked about.

Driscoll came in, slyly looking behind him to ensure that no one had seen him enter. 'You rang, m'lord?' he joked.

Colin gave him a brooding stare and the smile fell from Driscoll's face.

'Campbell's becoming a liability,' he stated.

Driscoll stammered, trying to catch up. 'Well, he's eager to please, ambitious…'

'He's an arse-licker. He simpers after anybody who's in charge and pines after them like a wee puppy. I'm done with him. It's just you and me now.'

He observed Driscoll gain a few inches in stature and a smile of delight spread across his feline face. He almost heard him purr with pleasure.

'I had my arse booted today, yet again,' Colin growled.

'What happened?' asked Driscoll, stepping closer.

Colin paused for a moment and then said, 'I tried to explain to him that I didn't bring that kid in for questioning because I was tailing him.'

'Makes sense,' agreed Driscoll.

'Well, I thought so. I wanted to see what he would get up to, see if he did anything suspicious. I mean, how many nineteen-year-olds decide to stay in a forest, for fuck's sake? The kid blames his dad, but Jerome seemed all right to me. In fact, I quite liked him – a no-nonsense type of guy.'

'Just like yourself,' said Driscoll, smiling still.

'Don't push it,' Colin snapped irritably, trying not to scratch at his blotchy face, which he could feel was getting hotter and redder by the minute.

'Sorry, boss,' replied Driscoll.

'All his lordship is worried about is the fact that I didn't mention it in my report. Because I didn't mention it, he thinks I'm trying to withhold something from him. Paranoid prat.'

Driscoll suppressed a laugh.

'And now Jack wants the blood sample expedited.'

'Shouldn't be too difficult.'

'Naw. It isn't. I just wish he would stop micromanaging everything I do. I would, of course, have had that done, but Jack always has to get in there first. He loves the sound of his own voice, that one.'

'I tend to try to avoid him as much as possible to be honest, sir,' replied Driscoll.

Colin regarded him for a moment, wondering if Driscoll was as honest and transparent as he made himself out to be. 'I visited the Warm and Friendly today,' he said, letting his words hang in the air.

Driscoll's ears pricked up. 'Oh?'

It was Colin's turn to switch on the sly demeanour. 'Yes. I've been searching every nook and cranny for any signs of, well, anything that might help us tie up the loose ends. You see, there are four missing people here and they're all connected.'

'Four, sir?' enquired Driscoll, moving closer.

'Well, there's Alistair Smith and Caroline Baker. And then there's Matthew White.'

'Well, yes, but is he actually missing?'

'Well, Campbell has come in handy for something. The CCTV footage showed that Matthew was following the missing couple. He may well have been the last person to have seen them.'

'This isn't really anything new though, sir, if you don't mind me saying so.'

'I'm getting there, Driscoll. Allow me my moment of glory.'

He let Driscoll chuckle, then moved on. 'We contacted Matt's restaurant. Spoke to a supervisor who manages the place in his absence. It turns out that the supervisor was told that Matt would be away for a few days, but they were not told *where* he would be. However, we know he came here.'

'So?' asked Driscoll impatiently.

'So he's still here.'

He watched Driscoll's eyes narrow. 'I did a bit of snooping about. No one recognises Matthew White from the photo I got from one of his chums at the restaurant. He's a good-looking bastard as well, and in this hellhole of a place he should stick out like a sore thumb.'

'So…'

'He's incognito. I checked the recent signatures in the guestbook at the hotel. Know what I found?' He teased Driscoll with a pause. 'One signature. Dated September the first. Jason Black.'

'Jason Black, sir?'

Colin was enjoying this. Driscoll was now the mouse and he was the cat. 'Jason *Black*. Matthew *White*. A wee bit of a coincidence, methinks. But there's more to it than that.'

Driscoll licked his lips and moved closer still.

'I checked out that name, *Jason Black*. He lived here in this village at the same time as Matthew White and Alistair Smith. He died in an *accident*.'

Driscoll's eyebrows raised. 'You mean this is the fourth missing person?'

'No, he's not missing,' said Colin with a sigh. 'But Alistair's father is.'

Driscoll smiled. 'I see,' he said. 'Good work, boss.'

Colin smiled supremely. 'I found out that Jack had pursued that case years ago, but it was never concluded. William Smith has never been found. And Matthew White has been in the vicinity every time someone in Hobbs Brae goes missing.'

'But William Smith, Alistair's father?' Driscoll interjected.

'Matthew worked for him.'

'Bloody hell,' said Driscoll. 'So let's get him.'

'We need to catch him first. So keep an eye on that hotel. Margaret Crawford is the landlady. She's as mad as a box of frogs, but still a game old bird and might be hiding him for some reason. Watch her closely.'

'Absolutely, sir,' replied Driscoll, beaming with pleasure.

Colin allowed himself a rare little laugh. 'Do not, and I repeat, do not breathe a word of this to Jack. Knowing him, he's already ten steps ahead of us anyway and has something up his sleeve, but just in case, keep it to yourself.'

'Yes, sir,' replied Driscoll, preparing to leave.

'And remember this. If I crack this case ahead of Jack, there will be a reward in it for you, especially now that Campbell's out of the game.'

Driscoll nodded obediently and left.

Colin stayed for a while longer. He winced a little. There was a dull pain in his groin. He breathed deeply until it subsided. Then, feeling recovered, he made to leave. He was almost out of the door when he stopped dead in his tracks. *I wonder why Jack never cracked that case. Did he fuck up in some way?* He imagined saying this to Driscoll. It would be an easy thing to do. Just say the words and let the drama unfold. A self-satisfied smile appeared on his face. 'Well, I think I've earned myself a wee pint or two at the Crow's Beak.' And he left, the rubber-lined doors swinging shut behind him.

Chapter Thirty-One

He must think I'm stupid, thought Jack. He was sitting behind his desk, collating all the information he had received and noting one glaring hole in the paperwork. 'Clements,' he hissed.

Despite being reprimanded for it countless times before, he observed that Colin's notes on the case were written almost entirely in shorthand. Jack heaved a sigh and glanced over the pages of hieroglyphs and non-stop abbreviations.

'It takes reading between the lines to whole new levels,' he had complained to his wife once, only once, because from the look on Rachel's face he could tell instantly that she couldn't be less interested.

A snake slithering up the ladder, that's Colin, he thought. *Hard to believe that he actually started life intending to be a doctor, but changed his mind and became a policeman. So he gave up his Hippocratic Oath and became a hypocritical oaf instead.* He suppressed a laugh. *Jamie would have liked that*, he thought. *Shame he's not here just now.* He stared out of the window for a moment. The sun was still shining outside and his office felt humid, despite the open window and the fan revolving in the corner. *Would the air never clear in this place?* he pondered.

Once more, he thought to call his wife, but what would he say? They never spoke anymore. He had to read between her lines too, listen to what she didn't say. It was an intangible code that implied rather than stated what she was thinking. The clues were in the pauses, the hyphens and the dot, dot, dots.

No clues in the dot, dot, dots here, thought Jack, for Colin's notes were every bit as bad. *Why is he so lemon about everything?* he wondered. He thought back to their argument in the woods.

'We've been working partners for years now. I know we've never really seen eye to eye, but surely we can do better than this?'

Colin just sniffed, avoiding his gaze.

Jack felt his hackles rise and made a concerted effort to sound calm and reasonable. 'We have solved countless cases together but I don't understand what's eating you lately. Is it something personal?'

'Aye,' said Colin, and he turned to go.

'I haven't dismissed you yet,' Jack barked, and he immediately regretted his tone of voice, because he knew that Colin would not back down. As he predicted, the argument escalated and he watched helplessly as Colin stomped off. *I can't piece the clues together on this one*, he thought. It was an ongoing dilemma for Jack that his relationships with other people were 10 times more difficult to solve than the cases he had to contend with.

Which brought him back to Rachel.

The sound of the front door slamming shut still echoed in his mind. He could hear her footsteps outside, rapidly receding. 'It's not my fault!' he shouted, and smashed the mirror in front of him with his fist, instantly lamenting it, wondering if the next seven years could be any worse than what he'd already gone through. Then he saw that he was bleeding.

Jack frowned with displeasure at the star-shaped scar that still shone white across his knuckles. The telltale signs of old arguments that never quite go away.

Maybe that was it in a nutshell. He knew how much Colin loathed him for what he had said to the Chief.

'I don't think DC Clements is a worthy successor,' Jack had said, sitting in the plush office of his boss.

'And why is that?' replied the Chief, fingers interlocked defensively in front of him.

'I feel as if I'm walking on eggshells around him. He always seems to have an agenda going on, usually to my detriment.' He bit his lip. *Never begin a sentence with 'I feel'*, he reminded himself.

The Chief Superintendent smiled patiently and replied, 'Well, these are hardly solid accusations, Jack. I mean, where's the proof?'

'I don't think he likes me,' Jack said, and almost kicked himself. He knew how feebly he was coming across.

'Not much I can do unless you give me something of substance.

I mean, has he done anything to halt the progress of your case? Any proof of insubordination?'

'Nothing I can't handle,' replied Jack, a little petulantly.

'Well then,' said the Chief, and went back to his paperwork. 'You can go now.'

'Right,' said Jack, unsatisfied, and he walked out of the office and decided there and then never to mention it again. *He'll trip himself up in full view of the Chief eventually*, he thought, trying to find some cold comfort.

He cast his mind back to the broken mirror. He recalled taking it down just before Rachel returned. Their eyes met and she saw the pale shadow on the wall where the mirror had once hung, but he noted that she never mentioned it, nor did she say anything about his bandaged hand. They lived in a house where words were suppressed and this bad habit infected the discussion he had with his boss. He regretted not being more explicit when trying to advise the Chief not to promote Colin. He knew how trite his objection had seemed. On the other hand, the mere fact that he had visited his superior in order to talk about Clements would no doubt have sown a seed of doubt in the Chief's head. *Perhaps that would be enough*, thought Jack. And maybe that was what had got to Colin. *Did he find out about our conversation? Is that why he's been giving me daggers lately?* he wondered.

Someone knocked on his door.

'Come in.'

Campbell entered breathlessly. 'Sir, there's loads of journalists outside. They know it's a murder case now.'

'Fuck,' mouthed Jack. He drummed his fingers impatiently for a moment. 'Hold them off for the time being. No statement until I give the go ahead, okay?'

'Sure, boss,' replied Campbell eagerly. He was about to leave when Jack decided to ask the 20-million-dollar question, knowing full well the response he would get.

'Don't suppose you happen to know who blabbed?'

Campbell blushed and said, 'Sorry, I don't.'

Jack gave him a put upon kind of smile and Campbell quickly closed the door behind him. Jack got up and opened it again, feeling claustrophobic. He paced about irritably, mulling over everything he had seen and heard. Finally, he arranged a meeting with the murder inquiry team. He took a deep breath and prepared himself, for he had an agenda of his own this time. *I'm going to remind a certain someone who's in charge of this case*, he told himself, and he marched down the corridor and strode into the room.

The entire team were huddled together in the cramped office, men and women, sleeves rolled up, ties undone, some with a mug of coffee in their hands, all looking in serious need of a good night's sleep. His spirits lifted when he saw that Campbell was there amongst them and seemed as bright as a button. He even wore a smile. Colin was apart from the rest, with Driscoll beside him, both lurking in the corner, watching and waiting. Jack gave Clements a curt nod of acknowledgement and began.

'So Alistair Smith and Caroline Baker both go missing on the night of September the first during a thunderstorm. Their last known movements are caught on CCTV at a service station three miles outside of Hobbs Brae. They are followed by Matthew White, an ex of Caroline's. However, as we all know, what started as a missing persons case has now become a murder inquiry. We found blood.'

Jack paused, making sure he had everyone's attention before he dropped his bombshell.

'And it has been matched to Alistair Smith's.'

He looked around as the room became heated with conjecture, and noted with satisfaction the look of surprise on Colin's face.

Driscoll piped up. 'How can we be sure, sir?'

'Alistair had got himself into trouble with the law a long time ago. His blood was already on our records. You will note from the photo of him on the wall that he has a scar on his forehead. This was as a result of an altercation he had with a police officer. We now believe that, given the quantity of blood found, Alistair Smith is almost certainly dead.'

Jack gave his audience a moment for the information to sink in, then he continued. 'His body has not yet been found, however, despite tracker dogs, helicopters and countless officers combing the surrounding areas. His mother is yet to be informed. Campbell, will you undertake this?'

The young officer blushed and looked around him as if to say, *Why me?* But he was evidently pleased to be singled out for such an important task. Jack pressed on with his speech. 'We also need to assemble a team to take DNA samples from Alistair's room. By this, I mean his old bedroom here in Hobbs Brae and at his address in Glasgow. That way we can compare and get a probable ID. Alistair's mother reported him as missing, but her testimony is somewhat unreliable because she is suffering from dementia. This does not mean that we should treat her statements with anything less than our usual scrutiny. She is the boy's mother and there may well be something to be gleaned from her statements.' He looked pointedly at Colin, who stared right back at him with a firm smile. 'As for Caroline Baker, I believe she could be in grave danger.'

'That's assuming she didn't bump him off.' Colin had predictably decided to stir things up.

'Or she got Matthew White to do it,' said another officer, and within seconds the entire room was awash with gossip. Jack watched Colin maintain a steady smile, happy, it seemed, to be causing a drama.

'Yes, all right, all right,' shouted Jack, 'we've all read the article in the local paper, but right now it's irrelevant. This is about to go national.'

'Oh, and I bet you're loving that,' announced Colin.

A silence of anticipation settled against the walls. Jack felt all eyes on him. His audience were waiting for a response.

Jack took a moment. 'No. I am not *loving it*. And yes, it's true. It takes a certain degree of ambition to get where I am today. A few murder cases that become public property can have the effect of giving a detective a certain credence within the force, but at the end of the day a man has been murdered. Here, in our own village. I don't see anything to love about that, do you?'

Colin was about to say something in turn, but Jack was in no mood to stop. 'I have served my time in this building. And that's why

I'm running this operation. You'd do well to remember that.' *In other words, shut the hell up,* thought Jack angrily.

A few murmurs came from the team, who were enjoying the show and waiting eagerly for Colin to retort.

'I think you need a rest, sir.'

'I think you're enjoying this a little too much,' said Jack, growing red in the face.

'Oh, I'm *loving* it,' purred Colin. The room went into a roar of laughter and applause.

Jack eyeballed him and Colin stared right back. Jack gathered himself and said, 'I repeat, a man has been murdered. What is there to love? Unless, of course, you did it?'

A few gasps in the room. Jack felt uncomfortable, knowing that he had gone too far, but it was worth it to see the smile fall from Colin's face.

'I repeat, I think you need a rest, sir,' he replied, but without much conviction.

Jack felt guilty, but comforted himself with the knowledge that he had been backed into a corner and had no option but to fight it. He just wished he had done so with less emotion and more professionalism. He worried that the Chief would come to hear about it.

'Cork it, Clements,' he said, and looked around the room. 'Everyone settle down, please,' he shouted. 'Cabaret is over.' He waited until the room was silent again. 'Current suspects are Jerome Jennings and his son, both of whom were in the vicinity at the time of death. But there is no known motive. As you are aware, ninety per cent of all murder cases are committed by someone who knows the victim, therefore Matthew White is currently our prime suspect.'

He looked again at Colin, checking to see if he was now prepared to toe the line. He was relieved that his partner kept a tight-lipped smile. *Good,* thought Jack. *Time to go in for the kill.*

'I know that Matthew has been staying in the Warm and Friendly hotel not far from here under the alias of Jason Black.' He paused, observing with some satisfaction the consternation in the room. He especially liked the look on Colin's face, as if a scorpion had been planted on his lap. *You didn't think I knew that, did you?* he thought smugly. 'Now, Jason Black is the name of a child who died in a domestic accident many years ago. There was nothing suspicious about it. Though why this particular alias has been chosen remains to be seen. I also believe that William Smith, who was Alistair's father, may be connected in some way to this case. He, too, went missing some fourteen years ago, supposedly last seen in the area of Loch Ness. There is evidently a strong connection between these cases and we urgently need to find out what.'

'So where do we go from here, sir?' asked one of the officers.

'We must find Matthew White. Simple as that.'

'Is he no longer at the hotel?' asked another officer.

'If he is, the landlady is doing her best to hide him. And so far, succeeding,' replied Jack. 'Anything more on the abandoned car?'

'Nothing as yet, sir,' replied Campbell. 'Broken windscreen. Dent on the roof, caused by a slate from the farm. Judging by the angle of impact, it seems likely it was thrown there by the storm. A nearby pylon was damaged, too, which may be why they went into the woods – to take shelter there. Probably the safest place under the circumstances. Phone lines were temporarily down, too. Nothing suspicious found.'

'Except the footprints, of course,' Jack reminded.

Campbell smiled, as if expecting the question. 'There are two sets, sir. Presumably Alistair and Caroline's…'

'And we found a third set,' interjected Colin loudly. 'It might be the killer's.'

Jack watched with interest as both Clements and Driscoll smiled complacently at Campbell, who was clearly annoyed at being upstaged. Jack noted the shift in politics that he had just witnessed and, smiling politely, deliberately sidelined Colin with, 'Thank you, Campbell.' He was relieved to have someone who was so evidently on his side. Satisfied that the meeting was coming to a natural end, and eager to leave the boxing arena that the office had become, he cleared his throat and prepared to summarise. Then an all-too-familiar voice said loud as a church bell, 'You didn't manage to find William Smith then, sir?'

Jack regarded Clements for a moment and felt hurt. *Is this what it's come to?* he wanted to say, but he could find no comeback, no words. And in that moment he saw his son standing there, at the back of the room, staring at him with a mixture of accusation and sorrow. It was unsettling how much like Rachel his son seemed at times – the boy who gazed with his mother's eyes. He blinked the image away, swallowed hard and said, 'Get to work everyone.' He left the room, slamming the door behind him and leaned against it, feeling bruised.

Later that day, he was back in his office, mulling over the case. He received information from staff at a bookshop in Glasgow, stating that Caroline had been due to start work there. Her parents were making a noise about the time it was taking to find her. He considered Caroline, with her long, blonde hair and her startling blue eyes – a photogenic visage that occupied the front pages of the papers. He thought about Alistair Smith and his scarred face that made the press less than reticent to suggest he was more likely to be the perpetrator of a crime than the victim of one. It was curious the way the missing boyfriend had been marginalised by the media, as if his life weren't as important as the girl's. Now he was most likely dead, it seemed doubly unfair.

Then there was Scott Jennings. The boy seemed agreeable enough – he even kind of liked him – but he was a bit of a nonentity. He could see why Jerome had seemed so discontented with him. On the other hand, he wondered if perhaps the farmer had some kind of psychological control over his son. Scott was almost certainly hiding something and yet he was wilful enough to leave home. None of it made sense. Perhaps he was a silent witness, too frightened to open up about it. Or maybe he really didn't know anything at all.

And then there was Jerome. He could picture him, standing there with his bloodshot eyes that seemed to calculate every move well in advance. That barrel chest and the large, calloused hands. He sighed with impatience. The pressure was on to find the killer. *It's either Matthew or Jerome*, he reckoned. *It was most likely Matthew. The exboyfriend. The only one with the slightest motive.* But for some reason he kept coming back to Jerome. *What is it about that walking stick?* he wondered. *Why is it bothering me so?*

Chapter Thirty-Two

September 5th

Alice came to, standing in the hall with the front door wide open, the cold night air wrapped around her. Shivering, and annoyed that yet another fugue had robbed her of precious time, she slammed the door shut. She went into the living room and began preparing the fire, ripping up some newspaper and placing some kindling in the centre with logs at angles over each other, before striking a match. The flames sprung up quickly and within minutes she was warming her hands in front of the flickering light. Alice dwelled on how many hours she must have been out for the count, and tried not to think about the strange things that had been happening in her home of late.

Yet she couldn't help but replay it in her mind. Alice's excuse to herself was that, in her current state, remembering anything, good or bad, was better than nothing at all. She recalled digging in the garden with a spade. Then there was the seagull.

And her son.

There was no shock at being told that he was most likely dead, because somehow she already knew. It was nothing tangible. Just a feeling.

'Oh my god, Alice. I'm so sorry,' Helen had said, in a somewhat dramatic outpouring of emotion that Alice did not feel was in keeping with the circumstances. It wasn't until afterwards that she realised it was her own reaction that was wrong.

The police officer and Helen went to the next room to have a private discussion, but Alice could hear them talking about her.

'She's probably just in shock, Officer Campbell,' Helen gushed breathlessly.

'Yes, I'm sure that's it,' the policeman replied.

Alice snorted. *They're talking about me as if I'm a child*, she thought.

Helen said, 'Yes, I'll make sure she is well looked after,' and that was enough for Alice. She stomped off to her conservatory for some peace and quiet, hiding amongst the flowers and the foliage. *What am I supposed to say?* she wondered. *And why am I not upset?*

Helen called out her name, but she remained stock still and waited.

'I need to go now, Alice. I'll see you tomorrow,' Helen shouted as she left.

Bugger off and don't come back, thought Alice, as she came out of her hiding place. Later she went to the study and picked up a framed photo of her son. She stared at it long and hard, but no feelings of sorrow, or anything else for that matter, emerged. She wondered if perhaps Helen was right, after all. *Maybe I am in shock.*

As night fell, she became haunted by fears that seemed new and yet somehow familiar. She heard the floorboards creak above her and looked up at the ceiling, fingering the pearls around her neck. *Hasn't this happened before?* she brooded.

Meanwhile, the moon had climbed high in the sky, casting an ethereal light on her isolated house on the hill.

In her upstairs bedroom window a figure stood, gazing out at the stars – a young woman with long, blonde hair.

And piercing blue eyes…

Part Three

Chapter Thirty-Three

September 6th

Jack was covered in shit.

As he stood in the shower washing it all off, he reflected on the events of the past 24 hours. How it had started so promisingly and how had it ended with him being covered in crap?

He had been walking in the direction of the Jennings's farm when his phone rang. It was Driscoll. He waited a few seconds before he answered it. *So Clements is too coy to speak to me now*, he suspected.

'We've found some hair attached to the branch of a tree. Might be Caroline's. Might be a sheep's fleece.'

'Okay. Get it to forensics. Let me know as soon as possible, please.'

'Will do.'

Jack smiled wryly. *Unusual for Driscoll to phone. And was that an ounce of respect I heard in his voice? Colin must be feeling apologetic right enough.*

He breathed in the fresh air and sighed with exasperation. *Just as another clue turns up, the mystery of what's going on with Colin deepens.*

Jack worried about the people who had vanished in Hobbs Brae. Alistair; his father; his girlfriend – and now Matthew White. There was a common thread binding them all together, but the motive remained tantalisingly out of sight. Then there were the suspects: Jerome Jennings and, again, Matthew White. One possible witness so far, the detective concluded, was Scott. However, if he was a witness, then he was also a suspect, too.

His phone rang and he fished it out of his jacket pocket. Campbell told him that Margaret Crawford had tried to wake up her husband, Hugh – only to find that he had died in his sleep. *For such a small, remote place, Hobbs Brae has a lot going on*, he thought, aghast.

'Have you called her in for questioning?'

'Yes, I did try, but she is a bit upset about her husband,' explained Campbell sheepishly.

'I'm not interested in how upset she is. She's been harbouring a potential criminal in her hotel and she lied to the police. Haul her in.' Jack hung up. He was aware of how hard he had become, especially since his confrontation with Colin, but he required results. He replayed the events of the murder inquiry meeting. He had wanted to punch Colin's lights out. The DC had deliberately avoided him since then, it seemed. *Probably for the best*, thought Jack. He scratched his head. The midges were out in force today. The stifling heat was like a breeding ground.

Yet again he contemplated phoning his wife, but just then he became aware of something on the periphery of his vision. He remained calm and continued walking, relegating it to his own paranoid imagination. Suddenly he stopped in his tracks because he was certain something had come up behind him, treading heavily through the grass. Jack quickly turned round.

Nothing but cows.

The majority of the herd were behind the fence, but two of the posts had been pushed over and several of the cows had squeezed through the resulting gap and were now lumbering towards him, their grass-laden stomachs wobbling from side to side. At the centre of the group was a dominant female bellowing loudly, more like a bull than a cow. She pushed herself to the front of the group and trotted with surprising grace. Without quite knowing why, Jack's adrenalin began rushing. He laughed disbelievingly.

This can't be happening, he thought.

The sudden advancement of the matriarch, whose name must surely be *Legion*, had set in motion a single purpose within the entire satanic herd. It began to gather pace until Jack had no option but to turn and flee as the bovines thundered after him. He couldn't contemplate the ridiculousness of the situation because all his faculties were being used to avoid the danger of being trampled by their heavy hooves. He slipped and landed with a grunt on his side, tumbling over the grass and landing in the mud at the foot of the hill. He could hear nothing but a high-pitched ringing in his ears, then he gradually came to his senses. He slowly sat up and heard a sucking sound as his face and right hand came unstuck from the sticky wet gloop. Then he noticed the smell…

Jack had fallen head first into a mound of cowpats.

He sat there numbly for a moment. Then he pulled his other hand free, his fingers having gone straight through the dry, hard crust and into the glistening olive-green goo beneath. Through the halo of flies that darted around his head, he could see the cows ambling away as if nothing had happened.

He glared murderously at the matriarch, who regarded him vacantly as her jaws went round and round, chewing slowly on the grass that hung limply from her mouth. Jack picked himself up and looked around for the nearest object – a stone. He hurled it at her. It missed and struck the hide of one of her other partners in crime, who reacted by turning round to see where the supposed itch had come from, and with a brief flick of the tail, sauntered away. This mildest of commotions had aroused the interest of the others, who were now all watching him with that same level gaze, and he decided it was best not to tempt fate – they could just as easily chase him back up the hill.

Besides, he thought vindictively, *you'll all be going to the slaughter-house soon enough.*

He turned to go and was startled to see Jerome, leaning on his walking stick and smiling malevolently.

'How long have you been standing there?' Jack demanded.

'Long enough to watch you lose your dignity,' was the laconic reply.

'I think your cows need a good anti-psychotic.'

'This is their territory, Mr Russell. And you're trespassing.'

'I'm a cop. I can go anywhere I like.'

'Antagonising my animals, Mr Russell, is a criminal offence. Now you don't want me to be reporting this to your superiors now, do you?'

He had a point. But Jack wasn't going to be beaten by a lowlife like him.

'I'll be coming back to speak to you, Mr Jennings. Don't go any-where, will you?'

'Yes, you go and have a good clean-up, Mr Russell, and mind you give your nails a scrub – that stuff can smell for days.'

Jack let him have the last word for now and made his way back to the station, pretending not to be bothered by the copious amounts of shit that he was covered in, which had begun to dry to a thin scab. Nor bothered about the fact that everyone who saw him in the street gave him a wide berth. And certainly not bothered that he'd been humiliated by a *smart arse farmer and his herd of mad fucking cows*. In fact, he was so *not bothered* that by the time he arrived back at the station he found he was on the verge of bursting into tears. However, Jack manfully pulled himself together, opened the door and walked into the reception area, bumping straight into Campbell. And Margaret Crawford, who screamed at the sight of him – an apparition made of dung.

'Jack fell down and broke his crown,' he said, with deadpan delivery, and he was about to march off when he was stopped in his tracks by a cleaning lady, armed with a mop and bucket. She glanced at his shit covered shoes, then at her nice, clean floor – and then she gave him a warning look. Jack stared unflinchingly at her – and started undressing. He observed with detached interest her face growing red with embarrassment. She drew her mop closer, almost hiding behind it, as Jack then ceremoniously began to peel off his trousers. He out-stared them all, daring them to say anything, and gave the landlady a sarcastic smile. Her look of tear-stained accusation was one that he wasn't prepared to tolerate. He strode past them in his underwear, carrying his dirty clothes and his shoes. Padding down the corridor, head held high, he turned into the locker rooms.

Once in the shower he fumed about how he was going to get back at Jerome. He needed something that would wipe the troublesome smile from the farmer's face. He decided that he would take a leaf out of Colin's book. *With this being my final case, I really have nothing to lose, so why not break a few rules for once?* He supposed he could get at Jerome by bringing his son in for questioning again. He recalled something that the farmer had said. *You leave my son out of this.* Was this genuine concern for the lad or was he worried that Scott might tell all? Now was the time to find out. Jack felt he had been too soft on them both. The gloves were coming off. No holds barred. *I need to know what Scott saw that night. I'm sure he saw something. I'll break him in two if I have to.* And yet the tough guy act made him feel uncomfortable. *I feel less than human today*, he brooded guiltily.

He thought how dumbstruck Margaret had been and concluded that she was embarrassed at the sight of his near-naked body. Then he recalled that her husband had only passed away several hours earlier and he hadn't offered any condolences. Disgusted with himself, and the brown water that swirled at his feet, he stepped out of the shower.

It crossed his mind again to call his wife, but he couldn't bring himself to do it. He recalled the photo of her on his desk at home: her short, black hair, plump face; her determined look behind the smile. But it wasn't the photo of Rachel that was important – it was the person who had taken it, a person who wasn't there anymore.

Jack realised with a start that perhaps in some strange way he too had gone missing. He was no longer the man his wife had married, that was for sure. A stranger had taken his place. Absent Without Leave, that was Jack.

He finished dressing and left the locker room, intending on going back to his office to lick his wounds, when suddenly he remembered something. He phoned the forensics department.

'Given the amount of blood that was found on the forest floor and the distribution of splash particles, I would say that the puncture was caused by a particularly sharp object at least six inches long.' The forensic scientist spoke quickly and methodically, much to Jack's pleasure, for he was in no mood for hanging around.

'A knife?' he suggested.

'Almost certainly,' came the reply, 'but we can't be sure yet.'

'The kind you might find hidden in the handle of a walking stick?'

A pause. Jack began impatiently drumming his fingers.

'Well, I'd have to see it first, I suppose, but yes, it is possible.'

'Okay, thank you,' replied Jack, and he hung up. *Jerome seems quite able-bodied*, he mused, *so why does he always have it on his person? Can't just be for the sheep.*

'I'm on to you,' he said with a grim smile.

Chapter Thirty-Four

September 6th

Alice Smith was trying to remember something.

She was standing on the garden path, and had been for some considerable time. *Something strange happened here, on this very spot*, but Alice couldn't remember what the strange thing was, or even when it occurred. Increasingly frustrated, she scanned the scenery, searching for clues. In her mind's eye, the village below was smaller than it was now and the forest was bigger. The fields were no longer abandoned and overgrown. They were shorn and neat. So was her garden. It was hot and sunny and the air was filled with dandelion seeds. A small lizard darted across the paving stones. And there was a boy. Two boys. And she remembered.

It was the last day of summer and Alistair was about to start secondary school. His ascent into adulthood had taken Alice by surprise and it pained her to hear little Alistair's voice beginning to break. Already he seemed more grown up than any of the other kids at his school. Of course, he had to be, given that his father wasn't there anymore.

Alice felt a bitterness well up inside her as she cast her mind back to those sunny days that were clouded with sadness. William went missing towards the beginning of Alistair's final term at primary school. He was often gone for weeks at a time, she recalled, trawling for cod off the coast in all weathers, so she was used to him being away. Yet on this occasion his return was overdue and so Alice, thinking that there had been an accident out at sea, had phoned the coast guard.

'I can assure you, Mrs Smith, that if William had met with some mishap you would be the first to know,' came the authoritative voice at the other end. He went on to explain that William had finished his shift and, on arriving safely back in the harbour, he had clocked out as usual. Nothing out of the ordinary. Just another day. But that was the last anyone had seen of him. A fact that had haunted Alice ever since.

His disappearance, suspicious as it was, became doubly so when the police looked into his employment records and discovered there was a further anomaly. There was nearly always a two-day hiatus between him clocking out and returning home. This was a startling and somewhat embarrassing revelation to Alice. No one knew, or appeared to know, where he disappeared to on these little detours. There was a rumour he had been sighted fishing in Loch Ness, but it was never truly substantiated. Alice had her suspicions, and the gossip in town showed that the neighbourhood had similar ones. Inevitably, the rumours became rife. She thought back to how it had got to such a point that even one of the police officers had the audacity to suggest, ever so succinctly, that her husband might be having an affair. Naturally, she denied it, because it would be bad enough if he'd left her for someone else, but how could he leave their only child? Alistair was just 12 years old.

Alice could not explain to her boy where his father had gone, let alone why, and it caused her all the more pain to see him suffer as a result. She summoned up the difficult memory of how he had started missing classes, putting her into an awkward situation because she was a teacher at the same school. This was further exacerbated by the feeling that she was being quietly judged by her colleagues. It was evident in the way they all looked at her and what they insinuated in their conversation. They all offered their respective shoulders to cry on, but she had alienated them because she did not feel the need to weep about her husband. In fact, she had remained very stoic about it. His sudden and inexplicable disappearance had left her feeling numb, because she was still expecting him to walk in through the back door at any time, taking his boots off before he entered, as was customary. Besides, as far as Alice was concerned, it was a family matter and that meant it was private. But as time went on and her hope dwindled, she couldn't help but wonder why anyone would want to waste their energy grieving for someone who probably wasn't dead in the first place, and who had probably betrayed not only her but her son, too.

It all came to a head when the local minister approached her and suggested she might want to erect a headstone in remembrance of him.

She looked at the minister, and then said, 'Don't be ridiculous. Why on earth would I want to remember him when he forgot all about us?' Thus alienating him, too.

The truth of the matter was that Alice was done trying to figure out what had happened to her husband and why. She was exhausted by it, and there was no longer any time to consider the past. Her main concern was looking after her son, who was very much in the present.

She carried on regardless through the rest of term and could not wait for the summer holidays; anything to get away from the prejudice of others. Her intention was to go abroad somewhere, taking Alistair with her. But when the holidays finally came, Alice was struck with lethargy not of her own making. She had regarded herself as a very motivated person. Even when she had time off, Alice had taken pride in keeping herself busy – pruning the garden, shopping for groceries and generally keeping her house in order. Now she was spending her days lying in bed and her meticulously organised life soon fell into disarray. The dishes piled up, the fridge gradually emptied and the garden fell to wrack and ruin. She supposed it was belated grief of a kind.

By the time she pulled herself together, the summer holidays were coming to an end. Alice felt guilty because she knew she had neglected her son and reneged on her promise of some time away, so when she arrived downstairs and couldn't find him anywhere, she panicked, thinking that he had abandoned her too.

It was one of her school pupils who came to the rescue. A seven-year-old boy called Scott – a precocious kid who she didn't particularly like. One day in class, he asked her to call him *Moley* because his mother called him that. Alice's response was to give him a punishment exercise, ordering that he write his full and proper name 100 times. The exercise was never completed, though, because Scott's mother complained very loudly to the headmaster about it. As a result, Alice's own conduct was brought into disrepute, and so she took great pleasure in undermining Scott whenever she could. But when, after frantically searching the entire house and garden, she saw him that day

walking up the hill with Alistair – and he announced innocently that
they were going to build a scarecrow together – she could have kissed
him.

Alice could see them now, the two boys toiling in the waning
sun of the holidays. She recalled how eager she was to become
involved, given that she had been somewhat dormant of late.
Inevitably, the schoolteacher in her took over and she found herself
supervising the proceedings. They collected some wood and straw
from Scott's father's farm and they built the scarecrow in the garden.
First, Alistair began hammering two wooden planks together. This
would be the scaffold that the mannequin would be attached to. Scott
complained loudly that he wanted to hammer some of the nails in too.

Alistair turned to him and said, 'This is a man's job.'

'Never mind,' Alice interjected diplomatically. 'You'll get to
build the scarecrow's body – that's the best bit.'

Scott grinned eagerly and she took him by the hand. They went
upstairs to hunt for some old clothes, and found a jumper and a pair of
long johns that had belonged to William. She held them in her hands
for a moment, for it felt as if she was teetering on a precipice, as if
the very thought of utilising her husband's old clothes was somehow
an act of violation against some long-held belief. But once they were
out in the garden again, and she was showing Scott how to stuff straw
into the jumper, she realised that there was something quite cathartic about it. By the time Alistair had finished assembling the scaffold,
the feeling of guilt was forgotten and she began to discuss what they
should do about the scarecrow's head.

'A pumpkin?' suggested Alistair.

'This isn't the season,' replied Scott knowledgeably, to which
Alistair winked at his mother as if to say, *Kids, eh?*

But Alice was deep in thought. She went back into the kitchen
and came out again with some old sackcloth. 'We'll use this,' she said.

They got to work on stuffing the sackcloth and, once done, Alice
retreated to the peace and quiet of the new conservatory, which she
and William had only purchased the previous year. She stitched the
body parts together, whilst the two boys stayed outside and played. A

couple of hours passed, then the boys came to see her. She detected their impatience and said, 'Not long now,' in a sing-song voice.

Scott looked at the buttons she had stitched onto the head and remarked accusingly, 'You've given him blue eyes.'

'Yes?'

'He should have red ones. They're much scarier.'

'And he shouldn't be smiling, either,' added Alistair, sneering at the black wool mouth his mother had stitched onto the face.

'And we don't like the duffel coat, do we?' said Scott, turning to Alistair, who shook his head in agreement. Alice was a little put out by her son's disloyalty and her gaze fell on his favourite blue cardigan that he was wearing. She was about to suggest they use that instead, but she thought better of it. There was an uncomfortable silence during which she pursed her lips and raised her eyebrows expectantly – her displeased teacher's face – then the two boys turned and walked back out. Alice stuck out her tongue and resumed making her masterpiece.

An hour or so later, she was finishing off the last of the stitching when Scott entered, looking subdued. Alice put her handiwork to one side and went over to him. Scott had a permanent tan from being outdoors so much, but he was pale even by his own standards. She felt his brow. It was hot and damp.

'You've been out in that sun for too long,' she said. Just then Scott vomited and swallowed it back down again – an act which disgusted Alice.

He saw the look on her face and said, 'Don't worry. I'm just chewing the cud.'

'Chewing the…?'

'Cud. Dad's cows do it all the time. They eat the grass and then it's brought back up into their mouths to be chewed a second time and then they swallow it again. They've got two stomachs, you see.'

'Scott Jennings, shut up and sit down,' ordered Alice, in the voice she reserved for her most disobedient pupils. It had the desired effect. She observed him closely whilst Scott shifted uneasily in the chair and waited for further instructions. Then a thought suddenly occurred to her.

'Where's Alistair? I thought he was supposed to be looking after you?'

Scott smiled wanly. 'He's outside.'

'Where outside?'

'I don't know.'

'Wait here.' As she hastened out of the conservatory, Alice tried to ignore the feeling of panic in the pit of her stomach. But she couldn't help herself, and increased her pace as she went through the house, until she was running out the front door and down the garden path. Her worst fears were confirmed when she saw that the gate had been left open. She stumbled down the hill and into the valley below, the wind lifting her dress up in front of her face, momentarily blinding her. Then she stopped suddenly because she could see him, or rather his blue cardigan, making its way through the field of yellow rapeseed. Her relief was quickly replaced by anger because he had gone there without telling her and he'd left Scott on his own. She was about to call his name when she realised that he was bent double and carrying the full weight of the wooden scaffold on his back. The sight of him struggling, and yet determined to go on, evoked a tenderness in her. Alice's fears seemed unfounded, because for the first time her son was like an adult, straining under the will of the world and the burden of responsibilities yet to come. Nevertheless, the fear quickly resurfaced, for in her mind's eye she could see the weight of his father's abandonment bearing down on those all too young shoulders. She couldn't help but worry how it might affect him – and it seemed he was carrying his own crucifix.

As Alice made her way into the pasture, she saw him fall, disappearing amongst the reeds of rape. She shouted his name, and when he did not reply, Alice ran over to where she had last seen him and was relieved to find that he was all right. In fact, he was lying on his back and laughing. It was infectious, and she couldn't help but join in, and suddenly their endeavours that day seemed ridiculous. Eventually, they made their way to the centre of the field to finish what they'd started. Alice remembered that she'd left Scott alone in the house, and hurriedly made her way home as Alistair dug out a hole using a trowel from her garden that he'd put in his back pocket.

Chapter Thirty-Four

'Bring the tattie-bogle!' he shouted after her.

'Yes, Master Smith,' she muttered sarcastically, but nevertheless admired his new-found gift for good word usage, a gift she had given him.

When she arrived back at the house, Alice found Scott asleep on the living-room sofa. She touched his forehead again. His temperature felt normal. Satisfied, she fetched some old rope from the shed and hoisted the tattie-bogle over her shoulder. She carried it all the way down to the meadow, sweating in the setting sun. Together, they erected the scaffold. They hoisted the scarecrow up and tied it there with the rope. Afterwards, they stood back to admire their handiwork in the now slanting shadows.

'He's the wrong way round,' Alice concluded.

'Is he?' commented Alistair, sceptically.

'Yes. I want him facing the sea.'

Alistair looked at her for a moment. Something about his gaze made her feel naked before him, because she could clearly see that he understood her own silent purpose. So they got to work turning the mannequin round. When they'd finished, Alice picked a posy of flowers to put into the top right breast pocket.

The name of those flowers escaped her, but she remembered clearly the scarecrow standing there: a lone sentinel watching, waiting, with its creepy disposition and lopsided smile; its duffel coat billowing in the breeze, a tease of straw hair sticking out of its sackcloth head, its shadow lengthening, stretching across the field, which was now burned orange in the dying embers of the day. Alice looked at her son – and smiled.

'Have you had a good holiday?' she asked him.

'The best,' he replied. 'I don't want it to end.'

'Nothing ever ends, not really,' she explained. 'Everything is a prelude, a prologue, to something else.'

They headed back up the hill. Alice felt a pang of worry because Scott's mother would be wondering where her son had gone. When they got to the top of the brae, Scott was standing there, waiting. He looked troubled, as if unnerved by something.

'What is it?' asked Alice, concernedly. 'Are you still unwell?'

Scott didn't respond, and she looked to Alistair, but he just shrugged his shoulders and went back indoors. Alice saw that the colour had returned to Scott's face, but he seemed very distant. Finally, he snapped out of it, and turned to her and smiled. She could never get used to Scott's strange little traits, but she liked him more now than she had at the start of the day. However, she knew it was high time he went back to his mother.

The scarecrow had stood there for many years. A testament to time; the head and shoulders barely discernible amongst the weeds, and the duffel coat faded to beige, rendering it almost indistinguishable from the surrounding grassland. Once upon a time, Jerome Jennings would carefully drive his tractor round their ramshackle mannequin, which became affectionately known as *Alfred*. And Alice laughed out loud because she suddenly remembered the name of the flowers that she had put in *Alfred's* pocket.

Forget-me-nots.

She smiled at the irony because they were growing everywhere. Her sadly neglected garden and the overgrown fields below were full of them – a constant reminder of her missing husband. As she stood there on the path, she seemed to wake up to something new.

There was a man here, she thought suddenly. *A large man with kind eyes. That's right*, she recalled, *a detective. And he was looking for Alistair. He's missing now, too.*

She looked out across the fields once more and noted that the scarecrow had become a monument to her son as well as her husband. But the scarecrow was gone now. And so was the field. Burned away to a big black nothing only a few days ago. The pain of this conclusion seemed to wrench her heart from her breast. She caught her breath, for she could see Scott wrenching his hand free of hers when she had tried to take him home.

'Are you feeling sick again?' she asked, but Alice knew full well that this wasn't the case. It occurred to her that perhaps there was something wrong at home. She had heard that his father was very strict with him, but Alice knew she had to tread carefully and not jump to any conclusions, particularly when the boy's mother had all too clearly demonstrated her zeal for complaint. Alice bent down, and, gently holding his shoulders, looked right into his eyes and enquired, 'Why don't you want to go home?'

He didn't reply.

'It's all right, Scott,' she said, and attempted to take his hand, but he pulled free of her with such unexpected strength that it took her by surprise. Even more surprising had been the tone of his voice when he had said that *something was coming*. It was delivered in a serious and solemn manner that alarmed her to such an extent that she forgot her misgivings about the boy's mother and called Elspeth Jennings to come to her house immediately. When Elspeth's large frame waddled up to the front door, Alice found that she could not bring herself to ask the question that was eating at her. Instead, she lamely explained that Scott had taken *a funny turn* and that perhaps it was best to get him to bed.

Elspeth gave her a reproachful look, and Alice grudgingly apologised and left it at that, watching with grave concern as the boy reluctantly left with his mother to go back home to whatever horrors were awaiting him. Alice never slept that night. She couldn't bear the thought that something terrible was happening in the household that was but a mile distant.

It was the very next morning, when she went out into the garden and saw the smoke rising from the farm, that she found the courage she had been unable to muster the previous day. She ran down the hill and made her way to the Jennings's farmhouse when she stopped suddenly in her tracks. Elspeth was outside, seated on her doorstep and bawling her eyes out, a sound that cracked the air. Alice watched, horrified, but she felt like an intruder. Although she was desperate to find out what had happened, and if Scott was safe, her cowardice regained its hold on her, like an old habit, and she shamefully walked all the way back home. The following day she heard about the dreadful thing that had occurred: the Jennings's barn had burned down and all the cows inside had perished in the blaze.

Perhaps she was reading too much into it, but it did seem to her that Scott had suffered some kind of horrible premonition. Rumour had it that his father had deliberately destroyed his own property for an insurance claim. Yet there was something not quite right about that because of what Scott had said. Something was coming.

But what? What was coming…?

YES! I would like to subscribe to Cycling Weekly

Complete this coupon and send to: FREEPOST TI Media Limited (No further address needed. No stamp required – for UK only)

YES! I would like to subscribe to Cycling Weekly
Please tick your preferred payment method

☐ UK Direct Debit, get 6 issues for £6, followed on by £58.49 every 6 months, SAVING YOU 30% (full price £84.12)

☐ 1 year Cheque/Credit or Debit Card (51 issues), pay only £125.99, saving 25% (full price £168.23)

☐ 2 year Cheque/Credit or Debit Card (102 issues), pay only £235.49, saving 30% (full price £336.46)

YOUR DETAILS

Mr/Mrs/Miss/Ms: _____ Forename: _____

Surname: _____

Email: _____

Address: _____

_____ Postcode: _____

Home Tel. No: (inc area code) _____

Mobile: _____

Date of Birth: ☐☐ ☐☐ ☐☐☐☐

SEND A GIFT TO

Mr/Mrs/Miss/Ms: _____ Forename: _____

Surname: _____

Address: _____

_____ Postcode: _____

Please also fill out 'Your Details' above. To give more than one subscription, please supply address details on a separate sheet.

3 EASY WAYS TO PAY

1. CHEQUE I enclose a cheque/postal order made payable to TI Media Limited for: £ _____

2. CREDIT/DEBIT CARD

Please debit £ _____ from my:

☐ Visa ☐ Visa Debit ☐ Mastercard ☐ Amex
(I am over 18)

Card No. ☐☐☐☐ ☐☐☐☐ ☐☐☐☐ ☐☐☐☐

Expiry Date ☐☐/☐☐/☐☐
(I am over 18)

Signature: _____

Date: _____

By submitting your information, you agree to our Privacy Policy available at www.ti-media.com/privacy/. Please keep me up to date with special offers and news from Cycling Weekly and other brands within the TI Media Limited Group by ☐ email, ☐ post, ☐ telephone and/or ☐ SMS. You can unsubscribe at any time.

☐ Please keep me up to date with special offers and news just by email from carefully selected companies. Your personal details will not be shared with those companies - we send the information to them on your behalf, and you can unsubscribe at any time. Offer closes 4 February 2019. Offer open to new subscribers only. Direct Debit offer is available to UK subscribers only. *6 issues for £6 followed by £58.49 payable by 6 monthly Direct Debit. This price is guaranteed for the first 12 months and we will notify you in advance of any price changes. Please allow up to six weeks for delivery of your first subscription issue (up to eight weeks overseas). The full subscription rate is for 12 months (51 issues) and includes postage and packaging. If the magazine ordered changes frequency per annum, we will honour the number of issues paid for, not the term of the subscription. For full terms and conditions, visit www.magazinesdirect.com/terms. For enquiries please call: +44 (0) 330 333 1113. Lines are open Monday-Saturday 8am-6pm UK Time or e-mail: help@magazinesdirect.com. Calls to 0330 numbers will be charged at no more than a national landline call, and may be included in your phone provider's call bundle.

3. Pay only get 6 issues for £6, followed on by £58.49 every 6 months (UK only)

Instruction to your bank or building society to pay by Direct Debit. Name and full postal address of your bank or building society. For office use only.
Originator's reference - 764 221

Name of Bank: _____

Address of Bank: _____

_____ Postcode: _____

Name of Account Holder: _____

Account No: ☐☐☐☐☐☐☐☐

Sort code: ☐☐ — ☐☐ — ☐☐

Signature: _____ Date: _____
(I am over 18)

Instruction to your Bank or Building Society. Please pay Magazines Direct Debits from the account detailed on this Instruction subject to the safeguards assured by the Direct Debit Guarantee. I understand that this instruction may remain with Magazines Direct and if so, details will be passed electronically to my Bank or Building Society.

QYC CODE: NYP8

Chapter Thirty-Five

September 7th

'You didn't do anything bad, did you?'

The question had hit Matthew with the force of a sucker punch.

From his vantage point high on the hill, he could see several police cars gliding through the streets, their blue lights flashing. He could hear the sirens wailing, the distance reducing the sound to a tinny cry. He glanced to the east and observed a crowd of ants outside the police station. With a near aerial view he saw how the entire village seemed suddenly and inexplicably to be in the grip of a vast net, as if it were being trawled from end to end.

'What's going on?' he asked himself, and felt the urge to run all the way down the hill, for he was missing out on the action. But Matthew knew he couldn't, because of what Margaret had said.

'That man came back,' she began.

Matthew looked up from his newspaper, surprised by her tone. She sounded fearful. He saw her hands were shaking. 'What man?' he asked.

'The detective,' she whispered. 'He knows that you've been staying here.'

'How did they find out?' he demanded, with such vehemence that he realised that the old landlady was a little frightened of him. 'Sorry,' he said, and gave her a half-hearted smile. 'I just need to know.'

'They know because you didn't check out. But I thought you were a detective. Isn't that what you said?'

Matthew felt his face redden with shame. He didn't answer.

'That man, he frightened me. He said I was hiding a potential criminal. But you're not a criminal, are you?'

Matthew's stomach plunged and he watched pitifully as Margaret seemed to shrink away from him. 'I'm sorry,' he said helplessly.

She replied, wringing her hands with anxiety, 'It might have been my fault.' Hesitantly, she continued, 'I wasn't thinking straight, what with my husband and all.' She left it at that, afraid to say any more.

Matthew regarded her for a moment and heaved a sigh. Then he ran upstairs and packed his bag. When he went outside he found that his car was gone.

'The police took it away. I couldn't stop them,' Margaret explained, then burst into tears.

'You didn't do anything bad, Jason, did you?' she asked, approaching closer. 'You seem such a nice young man. Please tell me you didn't do anything bad.' She looked up at him with tear-stained eyes, her small frame trembling. Matthew felt a bitterness at the back of his throat and wordlessly left the hotel and Margaret behind.

And high on the hill he watched the drama unfold. Something else caught his eye. A police car had detached itself from the others. He watched with alarm as it headed further west and moved along the winding road towards Loch Ness.

Chapter Thirty-Six

Jack got out of his car, smiling and waving at the press like a Hollywood actor on the red carpet. He was enjoying himself. He had been preparing for this moment for the past 24 hours. He gestured for them to quieten down and Jack imparted his story. There followed a very brief stunned silence. Then, suddenly, a plethora of eager questions.

'Sorry, folks, I am too busy to tell you anything more right now,' he shouted brightly, and with a broad smile, went back to work.

Moments later, he was marching down the corridors of the police station, only vaguely aware that Campbell was trying to keep up with him because he was too busy replaying how he'd felt the previous day – anxious and pissed off, his fingernails stinking of cow shit. He'd been on a mission, for something had been bothering him, something that didn't quite fit. Once he had cleaned himself up he went to see Alice again. He felt sure there was something still to be gleaned from her, a clue, anything. He had unfinished business, and that business was William Smith. He knew there was a connection; he just didn't know what it was yet.

'It's not been this busy in a very long time,' said Campbell, interrupting breathlessly with a reference to the press call.

'You mean in the three years you've been here,' replied Jack, with a smirk. He was in good form today. He finally had the bit between his teeth. *I am a tenacious bastard*, he confirmed to himself. 'What's the latest?' he asked.

'Jerome Jennings has been brought in for questioning as you required.'

Jack stopped suddenly. 'Did you get his walking stick?'

Campbell looked blank. 'Sorry, I don't know for sure, but I can find out.'

Jack continued his stride. 'What else?'

'Margaret Crawford, the landlady at—'

'Yes, yes, I know who she is.'

'She's filed a complaint.'

Jack stopped abruptly once more and turned to face him. 'Why?'

'I have to confess it was because of DC Clements.'

'Explain,' replied Jack with a measured stare.

'Well, as you know she was upset when I tried to question her at the hotel and so DC Clements volunteered to help out as it were…'

'In other words you let him muscle in on the job because you weren't capable of doing it yourself.'

Campbell looked at his shoes. 'Sorry, sir,' he said quietly.

Jack set off again.

'Okay. And?'

'And the clump of hair that was found. It's human hair. But it will take weeks to find out if it's Caroline's, sir.'

Jack arrived at his office, leaned against the door and gave an airy sigh. 'Well, at least it ain't sheep's wool.'

'The press are still wanting more information from you,' added Campbell.

Jack placed his hand on his subordinate's shoulder. 'Then find something to keep them entertained, will you?'

Campbell's face went bright red with anxiety. 'How do I do that, sir?'

Jack thought back to the previous day again. 'Give them a striptease. They love that,' replied Jack over his shoulder as he went into his office, and without looking back, slammed the door shut behind him. Smiling broadly, he relived the moment when the Chief had read out to him the headline, 'Copper Caught With Pants Down'. The newspaper had been thrown at him along with a torrent of abuse, before the Chief told him in no uncertain terms to leave his office. *Bastard hacks must have been hiding in the bushes*, Jack surmised.

He had driven up to Alice's house, parking his car at the base of the hill and preparing himself for the tedious walk up to her front door. He was relieved to be out in the open air again, but there was a humidity that felt like being wrapped in a warm blanket. The midges were incessantly biting, and he spent much of his walk sweating and flicking them away until he reached her garden gate. He hurried up to the front door, eager to escape from the heat and the flies. He saw that Alice was outside hoeing the soil, pleasantly surprised to see her finally attempting to rectify the shambles that was her flowerbed.

'Alice,' he called. 'I'm sorry to come here unannounced but I need to have a chat, if that's okay.'

Alice didn't respond. She continued with her work, a broad-brimmed summer hat hiding her face, and making her deaf to the world, it seemed.

Suddenly, Jack felt as if he was suffocating. His heart was thudding rapidly under his damp shirt and he tried to get his breath back. 'If you don't mind… I need to…' he began, but his vision blurred and he had no option but to stagger in through the partially open front door. On arriving unsteadily in the hall, he sat at the bottom of the stairs, head between his legs, trying to recover. After a few moments, he raised his head and noticed a jug of Alice's homemade lemonade sitting on the hall table.

'Thank fuck,' he whispered, and was about to reach for some when he noticed there were two glasses.

'Helen?' he shouted upstairs.

There was no reply, so he quietly ascended to the landing. He looked around, searching each room quickly and methodically – but found nothing. He immediately felt silly and more than a little desperate, but he was so struck by the sensation that something wasn't adding up. He stood there, tapping the banister with his fingers, wondering what to do next. Jack didn't want to be accused of trespassing, and was halfway down the stairs when Alice came in and stifled a scream.

'Finished your hoeing?' he asked, as if nothing was out of the ordinary.

'What are you doing here?!' she exclaimed.

Jack smiled apologetically. He was about to explain himself when he realised something, stomped heavily down the remainder of the stairs, and, ignoring Alice, went straight out of the front door into the garden. He grabbed the other woman by the shoulder. She shrieked.

Alice, who had followed him, barked, 'What do you think you're doing?!'

But Jack was confounded by what he saw.

She was wearing Alice's clothes, but he noted that they were a little too small for her. He took a step closer and she backed off, removing the headphones from her ears.

He reassured her. 'It's all right.'

'It most certainly is not,' launched Alice. Jack raised his hand to try and silence her, but was taken aback when she slapped it out of her way. He turned angrily, and through gritted teeth, said, 'Back off,' to which Alice replied, 'Well, really.' Jack turned his attention to the girl again. Her face was unmistakable, her eyes as blue as he'd seen in the photos.

'Caroline Baker?' he asked, though it was not so much a question as a projection of slight disbelief.

Alice looked confused. 'She's my gardener.'

'Are you okay?' he asked.

'Yes...' began Alice.

'Not you – her,' he shouted.

'Well, of course she is!' retorted Alice.

Jack ignored her. He was too busy making his own mind up. He stared intently at Caroline, looking her up and down. Other than a slightly distant look in her eyes, she seemed all right. He turned to Alice. 'Where did you find her?'

'She found me. She was looking for a place to stay. I told her not to go to Margaret's horrible hotel. So she stayed here.'

'Did she tell you anything?'

'She's hardly said a word since she got here.'

He turned back to Caroline. 'Where is Alistair Smith?' he demanded.

'She won't talk,' Alice asserted. 'Why are you asking her that?'

Jack regarded Alice for a moment. He was about to question why she hadn't told him that her son's girlfriend had been staying with her all this time, but it was obvious that Alice didn't know who the girl was. Alice looked expectantly at Jack and he wondered if it would ever dawn on her. He saw her turn to look at Caroline. Something shifted in her eyes and she reached out and touched the young woman's face, then she turned away with a look of sadness, perhaps at the fact that her son was somehow so near and yet so far. Jack took out his phone and ordered that an unmarked vehicle be brought up.

When the car arrived a while later, Caroline was taken to Inverness Hospital to be checked and put under observation.

Jack then phoned Colin.

'DCI Russell,' drawled Clements on the other end of the line. 'You're carving out quite a wee niche for yourself. Terrorising little old ladies and flashing yourself in public. I wonder what you do for an encore.'

'This is what I do for an encore,' snapped Jack. 'Get in touch with Caroline Baker's family. Tell them I've found their daughter and that she's alive. She's being taken to Inverness Hospital.'

There was silence – the seething kind, fuelled with envy. Jack waited a few moments until his patience ran out. He was about to reprimand him when Colin replied quietly, 'Well done,' and hung up.

Jack suddenly felt utterly alone. *Any other officer would be congratulating me, but not you. A grudging 'well done' is all I get. What is wrong with the man?* he wondered.

Returning to the station, he marched off to inform the Chief and make amends.

'Well, I suppose this is marginally better than exposing yourself in front of all and sundry,' remarked the Chief without so much as a hint of irony. Jack smiled, knowing he was off the hook, and was then dismissed.

Back in the present, he pictured how Colin must have looked when the Chief had told him the news. He chuckled a little, relishing the childish image in his mind of a piggy little Clements squealing with rage and running off to his wife, tail between his short, fat legs.

Chapter Thirty-Seven

September 7th

'Jack has found Caroline Baker.'

The Chief Superintendent made the announcement quietly in his large, air-conditioned office.

'I know,' snapped Colin, immediately regretting it. He glanced at the Chief apologetically, but saw that he had a bemused expression on his face. He noted that, even when seated, the Chief was a tall, imposing figure, all the more so because of his numerous medals and awards on proud display in the polished mahogany wall unit behind him. Colin observed that the Chief was getting more and more over-weight from too many lunch meetings and charity balls. And, though bemused, his gaze was like steel.

'You look like you need a drink,' he said, and went to his over-sized cabinet and poured the DC a whisky.

'Ta,' said Colin gruffly.

There followed a long silence, during which Colin tried not to fidget. 'So, does this change anything?' he asked finally.

The Chief turned, planted two glasses firmly on the desk. Eventually, he sat back down and looked thoughtfully into his drink. 'That all depends on you, Colin.'

The DC looked at him expectantly.

'Jack has struck gold,' said the Chief.

'The little shit got lucky,' replied Colin, to which his boss raised an eyebrow. 'Sorry,' he then muttered, nervously scratching his nose.

'Luck doesn't come into it – at least not where Jack's concerned. Now, I'm none too happy about the press catching him with his pants down. But it's not too serious and either way it means we continue as planned. With the media interest now at fever pitch we can't afford not to. The discovery of Caroline will give them something to chew on. Might even reignite their interest in Alistair's whereabouts. You will speak to them in due course. And I'm sorry, Colin, but you're staying put.'

The detective was about to protest.

'It's only until the case is closed which, given how quickly he's come up with results, shouldn't be long. But I need to know, Colin – what's going on between you two?'

Colin was flummoxed and bought some time by taking a draw from his glass. 'Nothing's going on,' he lied.

The Chief's eyebrows knitted together. 'None of your cock and bull stories now. Is something troubling you?'

'Why? What have you heard?' Colin demanded, unable to keep the accusation from his tone.

'It doesn't take long for word to spread in this place, Colin. And the word is that you and Jack have fallen out.'

'We were never bosom buddies, anyway,' Colin replied, curling his lip.

'But it was never as bad as this. Why aren't you the one going out and knocking on the doors? You should be out there getting your hands dirty and instead Jack's doing it all. That's your job.'

'I did. I went to the hotel to speak to Margaret.'

The Chief's expression darkened. 'And she lodged a complaint about you. That's two this week. Are you going to try for a hat trick?'

Colin looked away, disgustedly.

'On second thoughts maybe it's best you don't chap on anybody's doors for the time being. Maybe it's best for everyone if you take some time off.'

'I'm fine,' replied Colin. 'It won't happen again.'

'Damn right it won't,' replied the Chief.

'He just wants all the glory, all the credit. Looks like he's going to get it, too,' Colin replied sullenly.

'Is it because you're not playing ball?'

Colin sniffed, took another swig from his glass.

'Answer the fucking question, Colin,' commanded the Chief, his voice hard as nails.

Colin regarded him with surprise. In all the years he had known him, the Chief had never once sworn at him.

'I'm having some problems, yes,' Colin said quietly. 'Nothing I can't handle.'

The Chief sat back a little. 'Fine. We all have our crosses to bear and you don't have to tell me if you don't want to. What I do want is your total and absolute support on this. Jack Russell has had an exceptional career and his loyalty goes without question – and I know we both want to make sure his final days in the force are unblemished, don't we?'

Colin scowled.

'Maybe he's had some luck, I concede that, but he goes out of this with his reputation intact. Understood?'

Colin gave a curt nod.

'Since Jack seems determined to hog the limelight, I want you to take care of operations here. And I know this might be asking too much but given his inexperience can we make sure Campbell uses some tact and diplomacy when dealing with Caroline's family? I want to avoid a hat trick at all costs.'

'Oh, of course.'

'Let me make myself clear,' said the Chief sharply. 'You will do this or you can kiss your promotion goodbye. Is that understood?'

'He got lucky,' Colin retorted.

'So what!' shouted the Chief, slamming his fist down on the desk.

Chastened, Colin eyed him sheepishly.

The Chief glared at him and then leaned forward. 'Jack is retiring after this is over, so just sit tight. Put up and shut up. You'll have his job soon enough.'

Colin tried not to smile, and instead finished his whisky, for it was the answer he had been waiting for.

'Good,' said the Chief pleasantly, sitting back and picking up his glass. 'Now that's settled, how is your wife?'

Chapter Thirty-Eight

September 7th

Jack was pacing up and down in the small interview room of the police station like a caged tiger. He was all too aware of the effect this was having on Scott Jennings and his twitchy, inexperienced solicitor. The pair of them were sat at the table like convicts waiting on their last meal.

'Scott Jennings, you previously gave us a statement on the fourth of September declaring that you never saw or heard anything suspicious on the night of September the first. You have been brought here because since you made that statement there's been a development. Alistair Smith's blood has been found in the forest. The very same forest that you've taken up residence in for the past few days. Therefore, I need to ask you again: did you see or hear anything suspicious?'

Jack watched closely as Scott looked to his solicitor, who nodded. 'No. I didn't see anything,' he said quietly.

'For the benefit of the tape can you explain to me what you were doing in the middle of a forest during a violent thunderstorm?'

He observed Scott shift nervously in his chair and try to make eye contact with Campbell, who was standing beside the door. Campbell stifled a somewhat dramatic yawn. There were no windows and the room smelled stale.

'Would you like me to repeat the question?' asked Jack impatiently.

'I was hiding,' said Scott reluctantly.

'Hiding from what?'

'My father, I told you already.'

'Yes, you did tell us. But what I don't understand is why you would go to such lengths to avoid him.' Jack forced a laugh. 'I know he's a bad-tempered old so and so when he's had a drink in him, but you could easily have defended yourself – I mean, he's got a walking stick for god's sake.'

'He came at me with an axe!' Scott pleaded.

Jack watched with keen interest as the solicitor placed her hand on Scott's, a sympathetic act that Jack felt was a little too personal. He suppressed a smirk as she gently shook her head at her client, her perfect curtain of black, bobbed hair swaying comically from side to side above her shoulder pads.

Jack sighed and glanced wearily at Campbell, who shook his head with a smile of disbelief. *You're taking to this well*, Jack thought, impressed by his colleague's acting abilities, but he needed to get to the root of his doubts about Scott, so he returned to his line of questioning. 'My colleague spoke to your father earlier today, Scott,' said Jack quietly, 'and though he might be a lot of things, I don't think an axe-wielding maniac is one of them.'

'You don't know what he's like,' muttered Scott, his deep-set eyes lowered in thought.

'I have a very good idea what he's like, Scott. And I don't think you're taking this seriously enough.'

'I am,' he insisted.

'Alistair is still missing,' growled Jack, 'his mother is worried sick and I think you know what happened.'

'I don't.'

'Yes, you do!' barked Jack so loudly that his voice reverberated off the walls.

'You don't need to answer that,' the solicitor said with a tremulous voice.

He spied Scott looking once more to Campbell for support, but Jack intercepted. 'And there's no point in eyeballing him because he's not going to help you.'

Jack prowled round him, deliberately disappearing from Scott's point of view. He stood behind him and marvelled at how someone with such a broad back could be so afraid of an old cripple and cave in so easily under pressure. It didn't seem truthful somehow. He suspected that Scott was made of sterner stuff than he portrayed. *Another actor, just like his father*, he surmised.

He watched Scott carefully gripping either side of the chair, as if preparing to make a move. He gave a warning glance to Campbell, who nodded. Leaning over Scott's shoulder, but keeping a short distance between them, Jack spoke softly but loud enough for the tape to pick up his voice. Sounding eminently reasonable, he said, 'Do you want to know what I think, Scott? I think you know what happened to Alistair. And I think you're frightened. But you don't want to get on the wrong side of the law now, do you?'

Scott shook his head. He began to cry. The woman leaned forward and whispered, 'Are you all right?' but he ignored her.

Jack smiled a little triumphantly and patted Scott's shoulder, then walked past him and stood on the opposite side of the room, beside his officer. 'So, in your own words, what happened to Alistair Smith on the night of September the first?'

'My client won't be answering that question,' replied the solicitor, who flicked her hair back defiantly with a snap of her neck. It bounced back and a few strands went into the corner of her mouth.

Jack suppressed a smile. 'Fine,' he said, 'but I'll be asking plenty of questions and if Scott doesn't give me a satisfactory response then this will count as evidence against him in front of a jury.'

He looked pointedly at Scott, who said nothing.

Jack suddenly felt irritated. 'Come on. You must know something. You've been staying there for days. You mean to tell me that in all that time you've not seen or heard anything?' He noted that the farmer's son flinched, but still remained stoic. Scott's eyes were wide, looking around him, as if in search of a suitable response. His gaze rested once more on Campbell, hoping for a lifeline. Jack frowned; his colleague had begun to look a little concerned. He deliberately stood between them, blocking their view.

'Know this in advance, son,' he said, imitating Jerome and bearing down on him, 'you gave me no choice.' Jack signalled with a jerk of his head for Campbell to join him. However, he did not move. Jack wondered what was going on until he saw the look on the officer's face. A split second later he heard a strange trickling sound. He abruptly turned back round to face Scott, who was sitting there whimpering, head bowed in shame as his jeans were rapidly darkening from the crotch.

The solicitor screamed, 'Right, that's it!'

Jack admired her outrage. *At last,* he thought, *her feathers ruffled.*

She tried to take Scott's hand but he refused to budge, perhaps in embarrassment. The stain spread down his inside leg, and the piss was pattering across his trainers and out onto the floor. Just then Campbell's phone rang and he sharply fished it out of his breast pocket.

'What the…?' said Jack, glaring at him as he hurriedly left the room.

'This interview is now being terminated,' said Jack reluctantly into the tape recorder. 'The time is 6.23pm.'

A moment passed during which he scrutinised Scott, observing how he had tried to cover his humiliation by folding his arms over his knees. Campbell crept back in and avoided his eyes. Jack ignored him and leaned forward so that he was almost nose to nose with Scott. 'This is your last chance to talk. Because if we find out that you've been withholding vital evidence your feet won't touch the ground. I'll be back shortly.'

'I think that's quite enough for now,' said the solicitor angrily.

Scott remained silent but began shaking uncontrollably. Jack paid no heed to the look of accusation from the solicitor and signalled for Campbell to open the door and call for medical help. Another officer sped into the room whilst Jack and his sidekick exited.

Slamming the door shut behind him, Jack snapped, 'Well, you fucked that up, didn't you?'

'I didn't know he was going to wet himself, did I?'

'Yes, I could see how mesmerised you were by his performance. But I'm referring to your bloody phone. You interrupted the proceedings. Do not bring that into the room again.'

'Well, we never got a confession anyway,' the officer retorted.

Just then Jack's phone rang. Campbell sniggered. The DCI stared at him measuredly and reluctantly answered the call. He listened for a minute, then hung up.

Campbell asked, 'So who was that?'

Jack looked right through him.

'I don't think we're approaching this the right way, sir, if you don't mind my saying so.'

'Really?' commented Jack with mock interest.

'Well, it just seems a little bit desperate. A wee bit out of character – for you, I mean.'

Jack watched him closely. The officer clammed up. 'Don't be afraid to say.'

'It's more the kind of thing that DC Clements would do,' added Campbell cautiously. He gave Jack a nervous smile.

The DCI looked at him steadily. 'I'll deal with you later,' he replied.

As the disgruntled officer marched off down the corridor, Jack leaned against the wall and deliberated on what to do next. He looked in through the small window in the door and saw Scott having his pulse checked. The solicitor caught his eye and glared at him. Jack pretended not to notice. Then came a look of reproach from the medic officer, and Jack felt a pang of guilt at what he'd put Scott through.

He's right, of course. I am turning into Clements, he thought. Jack recalled Colin's words to him on the phone. Terrorising anyone, let alone little old ladies, was something that Jack had never dreamed he would be accused of. And it galled him that someone like Clements had the nerve to bring it up, especially since the DC had received complaints from both Alice and Margaret for his own misconduct. But the sight of his near-naked body in the police station faded into obscurity when it transpired that Margaret Crawford was more upset about the fact that Campbell had allowed a bully to interrogate her. And this on the day of her husband's death. Given that he was in charge of the case, Jack was also implicated and his reputation was now running parallel to Colin's. A home truth that disturbed him.

But desperate times required desperate measures, he reassured himself. He was particularly desperate to find out whether Scott was somehow involved in Alistair's disappearance or whether he was simply a witness to it. There was no evidence either way. His intention had been to intimidate him, to soften him up. Neither he nor his colleague had bargained on Scott falling apart quite so easily. It disturbed him that Scott appeared so vulnerable and he pondered whether he should allow a proper doctor to see him in order to assess his mental state. Whichever way he looked at it, his entire operation seemed increasingly pointless as there was still no trace of Alistair's body. The case now hung on Caroline's recollection of events. He had arrived at the hospital bright and early, confident that he would come away with something to pin on Scott.

There had been a major setback.

Although it was only 24 hours ago, it now seemed an age since he had found her. Since then, Campbell had informed him how elated her family had been at the news that their daughter had been located. Jack, too, had been on cloud nine and seemingly in total control of events. His discovery of Caroline had implied that the case was about to be closed. Not so.

'I don't know what happened to Alistair,' she said apologetically, in her hospital bed.

Jack stared at her, his mouth slack, trying not to show disappointment. 'So... when did you last see him?'

'On the night of the storm.'

Jack felt irritated again. 'What happened?'

'We tried to take cover, but then we got separated. I looked everywhere. But I was frightened and I was soaking wet. I'm pregnant. I wanted to protect my baby – his baby – so I went to find somewhere safe.'

'And this is how you came to be at Alice's place?'

'Yes. I don't know how I got there. I was lost. I came out of the woods and there was her house, up on the hill. I went there to get shelter, hoping that he would have done the same, but when I got there I fainted, I think. Alice looked after me. So I stayed there.'

Jack watched as her blue pupils drifted like twin satellites descending into the Southern Hemisphere of her eyes. He remained there for a moment, tilted his head slightly, then said, 'You stayed there? That doesn't make sense. Didn't you think that your family would be worried about you?'

'Not my family,' she said with a sigh.

'Well, let me tell you that they were worried sick.'

The twin satellites reappeared, holding his gaze in their steady axis. 'I'm sorry,' she wailed suddenly, and hid her face in her hands.

Jack quickly fumbled for a box of tissues on the bedside table and placed them on the sheets in front of her. He watched as she blew her nose loudly, the noise grating on him. Deep down, he wanted to slap her face for putting everyone, including himself, through hell.

'And what about Alistair? Did you go back to find him?'

'Of course I did. I tried to phone him again and again. But there was nothing.'

'Okay, I get that, but did you actually go back to look for him?'

She remained tight-lipped.

'You were the last person to see him alive so you'd better answer me or so help me god.'

'Alive?' she repeated. 'What do you mean?'

Jack felt his face flush and he quickly changed tact. 'Look, Caroline, you've been staying here for several days now. Why didn't you tell anyone? Why didn't you return home?'

Caroline fingered the bed sheets nervously. 'I don't get on with my family,' she said simply.

Jack waited.

She tried to stare him out, but Jack was in no mood, and finally Caroline shrugged and relented. 'I knew the press were out there. I read about it in the papers. I saw them from the top of the hill when I was in the garden. I didn't want to see anyone. I was upset. I just needed some peace and quiet.'

'Somewhere to hide?'

She nodded.

'Why?'

'My parents don't hold me in high esteem. Nothing I ever do is good enough for them.'

'But they were at their wits' end,' Jack insisted. 'Your face has been plastered all over the papers, and on television – and I know for a fact that much of this was due to your parents' concern over your well-being.'

Caroline smiled cynically. 'They only care about how this will affect their social standing.'

Jack raised his eyebrows. She reminded him of his son: defiant and untrusting of the elders in her life. 'So you were hiding here to punish them?'

She thought for a second or two. 'I knew they wouldn't approve of Alistair. And they certainly won't be happy about my pregnancy, so yes, I hid from them. But that's not the reason I stayed here.' She glanced up at him, her lower lip trembling.

Jack forced a helpful smile. 'Take your time,' he said, though he didn't mean it.

'The day after the storm, it felt like I had been given a chance. It was like a new beginning for me. I did go back to the woods, but I stopped short of actually going in there because I got scared. I don't know why. It seems so silly now. But that's when it all changed for me. When I got back to the house, Alice's house, her carer, Helen, was there at the gate. I told her what had happened and she said I could maybe take care of the garden for a few days. It would take my mind off things. I said we'd better ask Alice first. Helen said not to worry about that. And she was right. When I met Alice again she didn't remember me from the previous evening.'

Jack sat back a little. 'So you mean to say that both you and Helen concocted a lie between you? You took advantage of Alice's illness?'

'No,' Caroline replied quickly. 'I mean, it was true that Alice needed help with the garden. And she did know who I was on some occasions. She knew I was Alistair's girlfriend, most of the time. It depended on how her memory was from day to day. I guess I arrived at just the right moment.' She smiled hopefully.

Jack regarded her critically, as Caroline then bit her lip, realising how lame she must have sounded.

'So, Helen knew about your circumstances?'

Caroline nodded.

'Let me be absolutely clear on this. You're saying that Helen knew that you were officially missing and she withheld that evidence?'

Caroline blushed. 'Please don't get her into trouble. It was my fault really. She saw the state I was in and took pity on me. Just as Alice had done the night before.'

Jack watched as she lowered her sights again. He could tell from the way she kept her face covered that she was preparing to offer another revelation. Finally, she said, 'Between you and me, Helen is a bit simple.'

'She's a trained nurse,' replied Jack disbelievingly.

Caroline looked up and smiled. 'I know. But she's lonely.'

Jack folded his arms impatiently. 'So are lots of people. It doesn't make them *simple*.'

'She confided to me once about it. She just wanted to take care of me, the way she does with Alice. It's all she has in life, really. Please don't blame her.'

Jack let out a long, slow sigh.

'I did help in the garden. You saw me,' she said eagerly, like a child.

'But you must have considered that everyone would be looking for you,' remarked Jack incredulously.

'Yes. But there's something about living up there on that hill,' she began, her gaze drifting dreamily up to the right. 'It's like nowhere else. You're divorced from everything. Real life is down there somewhere, in the village. On the brae it's so peaceful. There's no press, no gossip. Nothing can hurt me up there.'

Jack watched, a little crestfallen, as she started sobbing again. He gave her a moment to recover. As he sat there, he reminded himself that she seemed to be telling the truth, if the direction of her visual recall was anything to go by. *Up and to the right means a true visual memory. Up and to the left means an imagined one.* He observed her closely and wondered. 'Caroline. What do you think has happened to Alistair?'

Jack waited as she slowly lifted her head and peeled away the blonde hair that was clinging to her face. Her eyes met his. They were wide with fear, her pupils shrinking.

'I don't want to say.'

'You must,' replied Jack, quietly but firmly.

'He's the father of my child.'

'Yes, I know that.'

'I don't want him to leave me,' she said simply.

Jack bit his lip thoughtfully, wondering if that was a euphemism.

'There was another reason for wanting to stay there,' she added, shifting slightly in her bed.

'Yes?'

'I knew Alice was his mother. And it felt good to be with her. I could pretend that nothing was wrong and that he had managed to introduce me to her after all. He wasn't there, of course, but I could pretend.'

Jack looked at her long and hard, finding her story difficult to believe. Yet her tale seemed so banal in places that a part of him wondered if it was true. *If she is lying then it's a pretty feeble one*, he deduced. Jack reminded himself that she had displayed no tells, no signs of deceit. When it came to the feeling of tranquillity at the top of the brae, and the resulting desire to escape, he saw Rachel and he understood exactly what she meant.

'Your reasons for remaining in hiding are not going to hold up well in a court of law,' he explained quietly. 'By making this decision to remain hidden in plain sight, as it were, you may also have implicated both Alice and Helen.'

'Sometimes Alice forgets I'm there. I catch her looking upstairs, as if she's trying to remember who else is staying with her. I don't mean to scare her but it's good that she forgets.'

Jack clenched his jaw angrily. *She's not even listening to me now*, he realised. *Perhaps she received a blow to the head or something. She certainly seems traumatised.* 'What do you mean it's good when she forgets?'

'I'm not troubled by consequences when I'm up there. I'm a liberated woman.' She stared unflinchingly at him.

'Liberated,' he repeated, smiling at her naïvety. *You'll be feeling quite the opposite if the prosecution have their way*, he thought. As far as Jack was concerned, she wasn't a woman yet. *Old enough to give birth*, he decided, *but her emotional age is stifled by words and phrases that she carefully selects in order to make herself sound more of a force to be reckoned with than she actually is.* Her actions were passive aggressive too, he felt. He was certain that she was, to an extent, using the episode to punish her parents. But something about her story didn't quite ring true. Something between the lines. *What is she not telling me?*

'And what about Alistair?' he asked. 'You do realise that you must have vital information that could have helped us in our search days ago?'

'I don't think I do, to be honest. I'm as in the dark about this as anyone else.' Then she added, 'I'm a coward. I'm too scared to deal with whatever the outcome might be. You said I was the last person to see him alive. What did you mean by that?'

Jack remained silent, wondering why she hadn't seen the news in the papers. *Maybe she's being deliberately obtuse, blocking out the inevitable*, he thought. *It would explain her actions – her strange choice to remain hidden. Some people go mad not knowing if a loved one is alive or dead. Maybe she's dealing with it as best she can in her vulnerable pregnant state.* He reasoned that maybe she was more mature than he had previously thought and that in doubting her he had shown up his own quiet prejudice for what it was. Jack believed that he never gave women enough credit for anything. *My wife would certainly testify to that*, he thought with a knowing smile.

He leaned closer to Caroline and said softly, 'You are aware that there's a distinct possibility that Alistair is—'

Her raised forefinger prevented him from saying the obvious.

Caroline then rubbed her finger cautiously across her lower lip and said, 'I don't want to have this baby if he's gone for good.'

Her euphemism is a thinly veiled one this time, he thought. And he began to consider what his next move would be when she said quietly, 'Would you tell them that I'm pregnant?'

Jack looked at her, confused. 'Tell who?'

'My family. I don't have the heart to do it.'

'I don't think I should,' replied Jack. 'It's better if it comes from you.'

She touched his arm and looked right at him with her blue eyes wide and imploring. 'Please.'

Just then, an entourage arrived: a tall, red-headed, well-dressed woman in high heels that clacked loudly across the floor; a short, squat but sharp-suited man with receding dyed-black hair, who had difficulty keeping up with her; behind them a good-looking, dark-haired young man, who scowled at everything in sight.

Caroline swallowed and attempted a smile. 'Who needs enemies when you have families?' she quipped, and sat up properly in her bed as they approached. Jack gave her a complicit smile and intercepted, standing between Caroline and her unwelcome relatives. Introducing himself and launching straight into his well-used phrase of '*we're doing everything we can*', Jack gently ushered the brood into another room, whilst Caroline got some extended reprieve.

They were a funny lot, Jack thought afterwards. He noted that the parents were very polite and said all the right things, but, as is often the case, their eyes betrayed them.

'I just want her home,' the mother said anxiously.

'Yes, she's needed at home,' added the father, as if Caroline was late for the all-important task of darning his socks or something.

The brother remained silent, but it was plain to see from his folded arms and intolerant frown that he had already cast judgement on his sister and it wasn't a favourable one. Every glance between each member of the family seemed loaded with doubt and condemnation. As Jack continued with his explanation of Caroline's wellbeing, he noted the looks between them escalated and were now being exchanged faster than a game of catch.

Jack concluded that Caroline was right after all, for it was painfully clear that they were far less concerned with their daughter's welfare and rather more concerned with the damage her relationship with someone such as Alistair would do to their reputation, so much so that Jack decided to curtail his speech and get right to the meat. There was a part of him that actually relished the idea, and he was surprised at how quickly his mind had changed, that he now found himself fighting Caroline's corner and wanting to defend her. He, too, felt like punishing them.

'I also have permission from your daughter to inform you that she is pregnant.'

Cue a mutual gasp from the parents and a look from the brother that could melt steel. It was obvious that they did not approve of either Caroline or her boyfriend. Nevertheless, after a startled pause, the mother conveyed her gratitude to Jack, who then informed her that Caroline was in very good hands and that the doctors would do everything they could to get her back to normal. 'We will, of course, return her clothes to her after the forensics team has finished with them.' This wrinkled the mother's nose slightly, as if the reference to her daughter's garments being inspected by a bunch of strangers implied something distasteful, an invasion of privacy perhaps. A curious thing happened next.

The mother touched Jack's arm and said hesitantly, 'Thank you.' Her eyes were wide and filled with tears. Her lower lip trembled.

Jack didn't believe her. It was a performance that had no doubt worked many times for her in the past, whenever she wanted to get her own way. She did seem to rule the roost, if the relative silence of her male counterparts was anything to go by. Her approach smacked of melodrama and seemed insincere. Suddenly, the entire episode was about her. As she reached into her handbag and pinched out a handkerchief, her two subordinates flanked her defensively. Jack lost his patience at such shallow demonstration and, as much to end the sorry episode as anything else, fell back into his official authoritarian voice and closed the exchange with, 'It is also my duty to ensure that this and all other aspects of her physical and mental state are kept away from the prying eyes of the press.' They all looked at him, as if offended, for it was clear that Jack was giving them orders. He then smiled reassuringly, equally as insincere as the mother's performance.

The family exchanged looks once more, and the mother gave Jack a bitter citrus smile – not too happy that Jack was having the last word. She flounced past him, and Jack sighed inwardly; his instructions were as much to save his own reputation as Caroline's privacy. He needed a reliable witness and these were in very short supply. He watched the family leave, remembering the cow that had all but pushed him into the crap, and how much he disliked matriarchs.

Still leaning against the police station corridor wall and feeling quite literally up against it, Jack's doubts increased tenfold and he wondered how this mystery would resolve itself. His investigation had shifted back into an interminable cycle, going round and round, waiting to reboot and upload with vital new information. Never before had he felt so impotent.

'We will need you to make an official statement when you get better,' said Jack to Caroline. She looked at him oddly, almost haughtily, as if to say she was in no fit state. *Shades of her mother*, he thought. Disappointed that he now had nothing to pin on Scott, he reluctantly made his way back to the police station to question him.

Leaving the drama of the interview room behind him, he exited the station and went to his car, where his son was waiting for him. Jack drove off. He had no idea where he was going. He just knew he needed to get away for a bit. He was almost outside Hobbs Brae when his vehicle broke down and he was forced to call the rescue service.

He waited for a while, but time seemed to drag by and he thought to return the phone call he'd taken in the station. It had been from Rachel. Her message had sounded urgent – something about Clements's wife. Jack hadn't really been listening and he had cut his wife off mid-sentence. He knew he would get an earful from her for that, so he decided against phoning her back. He wasn't in the mood for yet more drama.

Instead, he turned and said to his son, 'Well, what next?'

Jamie just stared back at him, unmoved by his father's plight. Jack gave a little shrug, more in defence than anything else, for he knew how his offspring blamed him for everything, and maybe he was right to. Jack had too many things on his mind and didn't have the inclination for an argument. The minutes dragged by and he could feel his mood darkening. As a distraction, he looked outside and saw the clouds massing above him. He smiled ruefully.

For the sky was darkening too.

Chapter Thirty-Nine

September 7th

Matthew was returning to the scene of the crime.

As he walked along the dirt track, his footsteps faltering, uncertain, he wondered how everything had got into such a mess. He recalled the landlady's frightened face and how guilty he had felt. *What am I playing at? What did I think I could achieve?* It all seemed so stupid now, all his jealousy and subterfuge. But he had set the wheels in motion and now there was no going back.

I did it all for Caroline, he concluded, as if that somehow made his criminal behaviour acceptable. He shamefully recalled the details. Following his ex in the car that night and checking into the hotel under an alias. Lying to the landlady, who so obviously had some sort of horrendous crush on him. Spying on the police as they carried out their investigation.

And in the back of his mind there was the blood. Always the blood.

He had figured the police might find his car sooner or later. He had parked it a short distance away from the Warm and Friendly so that passers-by might assume it belonged to someone further down the road, but a neighbour complained that it was blocking their driveway and the police intervened. He guessed that he had got off lightly up until then. The landlady was easily coerced and his alias had worked for a time. He kept a low profile, only venturing outside when he figured that most people would be at work and the streets were quiet. No one who lived there would recognise the scrawny kid with the nervous disposition from all those years ago – a fact that gave him some comfort.

He recalled Caroline's last words. It felt like he had been stung and the venom was now coursing through his veins. But there was no time to make amends now. He had to leave. *But where would I go?* he wondered desperately.

His heart sank in realisation, plummeting down into the depths and anchoring itself to something terrible. There was only ever one choice. He smiled bleakly, knowing he was always destined to go back there. To the place he never wanted to see again. Hobbs Brae had been but a stepping stone into a dark, haunted past, it seemed.

He came to the end of the dirt track. And there it was. Down below. Where it all began. The scene of the crime. The place where blood was etched into his youth.

The murky waters of Loch Ness.

Chapter Forty

September 7th

Scott was in the forest, sitting beside his corrugated iron lean to, with Bessie dozing next to him, her chin resting on his thigh. He stroked her head, deliberately stopping every now and then to see her gently nuzzle his hand so he would continue petting her – one of her most endearing quirks. He wanted to remember Bessie this way.

Scott knew it would be the last time he would ever see her.

As far as he was concerned, there was nothing to keep him in Hobbs Brae anymore. He had been assaulted by his father so many times that he was at breaking point, and after his interrogation by the police he was feeling doubly bruised.

DCI Jack Russell has turned into a monster bad enough to rival my dad, he thought, trying to hold back the tears, lest Bessie sense his mood.

Scott felt he had no option but to leave his old life behind. The prospect filled him with dread because, despite everything, he still loved his father, even if the reciprocation of that love was as cold and remote as the light from the furthest star. He did not want to go, but it seemed he no longer had a choice. He looked down once more at Bessie, who was still napping, unaware of the momentous changes that were taking place in her young master. She was old now – in dog years far older than Jerome. It seemed an act of betrayal to leave her in the hands of an alcoholic who could barely look after himself. Scott couldn't help but wonder what might happen to her once he was gone.

Would my dad take his temper out on her? Hurt her?

Scott winced as he imagined terrible things happening to Bessie. Then he saw the blood as it ran into the river on the night of the storm. He shut his eyes tight, trying to block the anxiety he felt surge through him like a freight train.

Moley, not once has your father ever harmed our dog, so there is no reason to think that it will happen now, the soothing voice of his mother said.

Scott opened his eyes. He knew himself well enough to understand that he had a predilection for seeing the downside to everything. With the arrival of adulthood, he now had the added burden of conscience and the weight of responsibility that went with it. For the first time in his young life, he was about to pursue a desire that would affect those he cared about most. His leaving would cause pain, but he would suffer indefinite pain himself if he did not leave.

He knew just how much his father needed him. With the advent of autumn, it was a particularly busy time on the farming calendar, but Scott's life was beginning to revolve around an altogether different clock. His recent spurt of self-determination and the fact that he had already learned a trade had given him some confidence. He was acutely aware that he owed this trait to his father. Jerome had taught him in no uncertain terms how to work, and by being so tyrannical he had inadvertently pushed his son into the arena of the independent.

If it hadn't been for him, I would not be where I am now, preparing for a new chapter in my life.

This acknowledgement of his father's part in his own development made his decision to leave all the more difficult.

'If my mother was still alive, I reckon it would be easier because she would take care of things after I was gone. It was what she did best.'

Bessie's ears pricked up and Scott realised he had said this out loud. He smiled. As usual, thoughts about his mother always led him out of the dark tunnel of despair that he often found himself in. Elspeth Jennings – with her rosy cheeks and her good-humoured smile, her buxom figure and her fondness for cream teas – had taken care of the family business ever since the barn had burned down.

Scott remembered it well, but he had never heard her side of the story before, not until she told him one night, when Jerome was in a drunken stupor upstairs.

'It had been your father's turn to check up on the animals. He locked the barn door as usual and went to bed. Later that night both he and I were woken up by the smell of smoke and, there it was, the most horrific sight – the barn had turned into an inferno. I called the fire brigade. But it was too late. The barn and everything inside were destroyed.'

Scott recalled her shoulders shaking at the memory of it, her voice tremulous. 'But it got worse, so much worse. The firemen explained to me that the cause of the devastation was an oil burner. Jerome had used these to illuminate the inside of the barn because there were no windows or electricity. Well, the oil burner had been left inside still lit and had toppled over onto the hay. The flames spread so rapidly that the entire barn was ablaze in a matter of minutes.'

Scott recalled gently taking his mother's hand. She squeezed his palm tightly as she exorcised the ghosts from her past. 'The following morning, the smoke could be seen for miles around. And the smell of burned hide was carried by the wind into the village.' Elspeth wept after that and went outside to calm herself down. Scott sat there, mulling over everything that she had said.

Even now, Scott could clearly recall the remnants of the building still smouldering, the embers winking from deep within the ruins, and the near comical image of their new puppy, only recently named *Bessie*, walking stiffly on her little legs across the debris, like a wind-up toy gone astray, her tail sticking up like a small antenna.

'Jerome was stunned by the damage,' said Elspeth when she came back inside. 'He was usually so careful and he could hardly believe his own clumsiness.' She leaned in towards Scott and added quietly, 'But I knew. I could still smell it on his breath from the night before. He was drunk when he checked the barn.'

Scott watched sadly as his mother sat there, forlorn. Her arms were crossed limply over her knees, her pining gaze, distant, at the memory of it all. 'I never said anything, never blamed him. I pre-tended not to know. He later commented on how calmly I had taken it.' She sat up straight again, recomposed herself, and, brushing some-thing invisible from her lap, said, 'After that, things were never quite the same between us.' Abruptly, she got up and left the room to con-tinue with her chores.

Scott had wondered what she'd meant, but only now did he

understand; his father's drinking drove a wedge between them. *If only my mother knew how much worse it was now with her gone*, he brooded.

Over the months following his mother's death, it became clear to Scott that it had had a profound effect on them both. He understood that Jerome became harder on him because he needed him to fill Elspeth's shoes, but his teaching methods were infused with impatience. Scott was still only a child – he couldn't learn things quickly enough, so Jerome's impatience turned to anger. This, in turn, grew into violence. At night, however, Scott would often hear the painful sound of his father grieving in the privacy of his bedroom.

Scott was grieving, too. He yearned for his mother terribly. He missed the sound of her voice; her pet phrases such as, *'the way to a man's heart is through his stomach'*. He missed the smell of her perfume. And he missed being called *Moley*. He discovered that all these things could be summed up in one single fact – what he longed for most of all was his childhood. His father had needed a grown-up to help him run the farm, not a little boy, and Scott had resented him for that. His dreams had been all too quickly replaced by the harsh reality of working life, and the ever-present threat of violence that seemed to stem from every adult male who touched upon his existence. Now it had come to this.

Scott was standing on a tree-lined road, his haversack on his back, a new bank card and PIN number in his wallet, faced with an agonising decision. The road forked into two paths. One led back to the farm, the other led down to the open sea. Scott took a deep breath. He thought of how he had served his time alone in the forest, and what at first had seemed a kind of banishment he now saw as a rite of passage, for he had entered the woods as a boy and come out a man. In that moment he made his decision because he knew there was no need to delay any longer. There was nothing left to fear.

He looked at Bessie. She gazed back up at him and panted, gently wagging her tail with an air of expectancy. 'I'm sorry,' was all he could say, and Bessie cocked her head to one side in puzzlement as Scott turned and left. Some way further down the road, he heard her let out a little whine, but he kept walking until he knew he was about to disappear from view, trying not to hear her cries. He turned one last time to look at her and she was still there, waiting for him – a sight that broke his heart.

Once round the corner, he forced himself to keep moving, past the towering trees and the thick hedgerows, which gradually gave way to the freedom of the pastures and the sky above. In the distance, he could see the blackened field where the scarecrow had once stood, the one that he had helped to build at a time when life seemed less cruel.

He thought back to a few days ago, when he had noticed something black, like a shadow, hovering above the lone figure. It appeared to be changing shape, disintegrating and reforming. He guessed it was just a flock of carrion crows (*Corvus corone*) and he smiled at his own ability to still remember their Latin name. Yet as he made his way down to the beach, something bothered him.

Soon he was distracted by the sight of the sunlight dancing on the water, casting luminescent ripples across the ruins of the abbey, which stood like a huge set of broken, jagged teeth by the shore. He remained there for a time, watching the garlands of seaweed undulating in the salt water like clear soup, the tide inexorably dragging the waves back and forth. He walked along the beach, enjoying the sensation that the further he was from home, the freer he felt. He listened to the bubble and squeak of the bladder wrack (*Fucus vesiculosus*) strewn across the wet sand and clumped over rocks, stretching into the distance as far as the eye could see, the sheer scale of it making him feel small and isolated. But he was so used to feeling lonely that it no longer touched him.

Suddenly he remembered what it was that had bothered him earlier – the collective noun he'd been searching for in the back of his mind:

A murder. A murder of crows.

Something far across the sea caught his attention and he peered into the distance. A herald had appeared on the horizon; a dark cloud that was visibly growing in size.

And Scott understood immediately. He knew that cloud and he knew what it meant.

Chapter Forty-One

September 7th

Jerome was out of breath, hobbling through the forest in search of his son again. His hopes of finding him, however, were fading fast, for when he had checked Scott's room he discovered that most of his clothes were missing and so was his haversack.

Jerome went downstairs and checked the kitchen table and the windowsill above the sink – but there was no farewell note. He caught sight of the postman walking away and hobbled after him.

'Yes, I gave Scott a letter just a moment ago,' the postman replied.

'Was it from the bank?' Jerome enquired, eyeing him sideways.

'Well, I didn't really take much heed, to be honest,' replied the postman cautiously. 'But, yes, I think it may well have been. Looked like one of those slips with a PIN number inside it, which makes sense because I think I delivered a bank card yesterday.'

Jerome drew a sharp breath and the postman looked a little alarmed. 'Not that I pry, you understand. It's just that I can tell at a glance what these things are after all my years' experience.' He gave a disarming laugh.

Jerome grunted and the postman, sensing that something was amiss, made his excuses and left.

Jerome's heart denied what he knew in his head to be true, so he went off in a vain search that led him deep into the forest. Eventually, he stumbled upon the corrugated iron roof from his hen coop. He saw the flattened grass around it, saw the footpaths through the bracken leading to and from the farm and in the direction of the old oak tree. *So this is where he was hiding*, he concluded sadly. With a deep sense of shame, he grasped to what extent he had alienated his own son. There was no sign of him. It dawned on Jerome that there had been no sign of Bessie, either. It was a sobering thought that for the first time in his entire life he was alone in the world.

He hadn't expected to feel this way. All those years he and his wife had spent building a life for themselves. All their hard work, all their suffering, had now come to a bitter conclusion. His son had left without saying goodbye and Jerome knew with the utmost certainty that he would never see him again. He sadly pondered the outcome of all those years of tough love and wondered what went wrong. *Have I really been too hard on him?*

Jerome was well aware that he had knocked any open displays of emotion out of his son a long time ago, and he also knew that despite his mother's influence, Scott still shared a lot of his own characteristics – his brooding verbal celibacy for a start. Sometimes it was almost like looking into a mirror. He wondered how his son would fare in the world. Scott had neither friends nor a girlfriend. He was a loner. Jerome pictured him going off with his backpack and he wished him well. But now Jerome was a loner, too. He contemplated the strange twist of fate that had befallen them both, for now that they were apart, they shared more in common than ever before – a reflection of one another; like father, like son. The prospect of being alone filled him with a previously unknown dread.

He remembered how Elspeth always managed to remain calm in the face of such adversity, how she deftly made her way through each recession, through the foot and mouth epidemics and, of course, that fire. Even as she lay in the hospital bed, her life ebbing away, she was still able to retain some dignity as she gave her last confession to her husband.

'The fire was my fault, Jerry,' she said. 'I blamed you for it because you had been drunk that night, but it was all my doing. It's why I was so quick to get things sorted afterwards – I was trying to make amends.'

Jerome was utterly confused by this and thought at first that she was delirious, but Elspeth assured him that she was not.

'Several hours after you'd checked up on the cows that night, I was woken by something moving outside,' she explained. 'I went out to investigate. My initial thought was that it might have been a fox, so

I checked the hen coop, but it was quiet, and when I looked in on the sheep they were still, too. Finally, I checked up on the cows. Again, there was no sign of anything suspicious.'

He listened as she told of her feelings of relief and of how she went back indoors and upstairs to bed. When the next day the firemen explained to Elspeth and her husband what had caused the blaze, she realised with horror that it had been her fault, for she had been the last one to check up on the animals that night.

'When he told me that an oil burner had been left alight I stood there in shock, knowing that I had condemned our animals to a terrible, cruel death. So I took care of things after that because I never wanted to let you down again.'

He reassuringly stroked her forearm. She took his hand in hers and squeezed tight.

'You'll remember that I contacted the insurance company,' she continued, 'but they refused to pay out, so I sold off some things that we didn't need, including some old farming equipment and a derelict plot of land, in order to raise the finances to build a new barn.'

'I remember,' he replied distantly.

'It wasn't enough,' she confided. 'I had to sell off my late mother's jewellery.'

She gave a throaty laugh at his look of surprise. 'The loss of those cows had been bad enough, but having to part with my family heirlooms hurt me more than I cared to admit. However, it enabled us to continue with the daily running of the farm, and to be honest a small part of me felt that I deserved it for being so stupid.'

She cast her gaze down to the wedding ring on her finger and thought for a moment. Then she said quietly, 'I did resent you for a time, though. You took to the drink around then. You were weak when I needed you most. You were no longer my husband.'

Jerome smarted at such honesty and couldn't bring himself to look at her. He felt Elspeth tighten her grip and she began to speak with urgency. 'I told Scott that it had been your fault. I couldn't bear the idea of him thinking badly of me. I know how much he looks up to me.'

Her eyes met his once more and she said quietly, 'It might be why you two don't get on. I think that's my fault. I'm sorry.'

An uncomfortable moment passed between them. She stared at him tearfully. 'There, I've said it.' And she playfully rubbed his hand.

Jerome gave a steadfast smile and tried not to clench his fist.

'Look after Scott for me,' she continued breathlessly. 'He's so young and such a sensitive child. I think he will do well, though. He adores Bessie and he loves animals. I saw him just the other day mending a bird's wing and letting her fly off. He's such a clever boy. Be kind to him, Jerry. Don't drink around him. Please, promise me you'll be kind...' She trailed off, trying to suppress her anxiety.

Jerome smiled sadly. He was unable to say anything much, and so he just held her hand.

'You never did bring me those sunflowers,' she said, and managed to give him a good-humoured wink.

He chuckled at the memory and they both sat in silence for a while. When Jerome woke with a start the following morning, her hand was still in his, but it was cold and he knew that she was gone. Elspeth Jennings – the wife and mother; the canny businesswoman who knew when others were trying to undercut her; the strong-willed woman who even hammered some of the nails into the scaffold of the new barn, unaware that she was also hammering the nails into her own coffin by putting enormous strain on her heart.

But her legacy was still standing: the barn, fitted with windows and run by electricity, their expensive new milking equipment stationed inside, and the cattle, all alive and well. It was an achievement that Elspeth had been very proud of – a reminder of happier times.

Jerome flushed with guilt at what she would make of it all now. His heart sank at the thought that he had broken his vow to her, for Jerome knew he had been anything but kind to their son. He never told him that the inferno was her fault. He couldn't, because he didn't think his son would believe him, such was the animosity between them. Now he was gone. Jerome pondered the future. Without Elspeth or his son by his side, the odds against him seemed truly insurmountable this time.

He thought back to that last day in the field. Scott had seemed so keen to get the fire burning, and Jerome concluded shamefully that it was because his son was so desperate to get away from him. He pictured the ironic smile on his face once the deed was done, and he remembered the way he casually threw his bank card into the flames as a way of wiping that smile clean off. An act of unnecessary callousness that now left Jerome feeling utterly desolate.

Just then he was distracted by a movement in the undergrowth. His spirits lifted when he saw it was Bessie. She trotted up to him, wagging her tail, and he gave her a world-weary smile. In that moment he wished for a dog's life – unclouded by conscience or remorse, never thinking forward or looking back; only living in the moment; happy. She nuzzled his hand and broke out into panting. He noticed how humid it was. How close it felt. He looked up at the sky. It was overcast. All the signs were there of another storm approaching, right down to the metallic taste in the air. Coppery, like blood.

Jerome understood that the foundations of his son's impending desertion had been there for years, but he hadn't paid any heed to them. He remembered when he took him to the local abattoir. Scott was just 16. He was horrified.

What Elspeth had said was true. Over the years, Jerome had witnessed Scott mending the broken wings of birds countless times. Only now did he understand that rescuing the fox from the snare had not been some underhand way of marring his authority, but an act of kindness, and one of many that up until now Jerome had stubbornly ignored. He sighed heavily, the regret bearing down on him.

He looked at Bessie, who sat patiently at his feet, awaiting orders. 'At least you're still here,' he said, and bent down to pet her. He then led her out of the forest and headed back to the farm, all the while pondering how he and his son had been unceremoniously taken to the police station, and then separated from each other. He recalled the claustrophobic interview room and the bullying tactics.

'You dare to give me the third degree – you, a so-called *detective* who, judging by your well-manicured hands, has never done an honest day's labour in your life.'

It wasn't the best of starts, but Jerome wasn't going to be intimidated by anyone, least of all by the likes of Jack Russell.

'We're looking for someone with blood on their hands, Jerome. Know of anyone who fits the bill?' the detective remarked.

Jerome sat back in the chair at that moment, his hand casually resting on the desk. 'Jack Russell – what kind of a name is that anyway?'

'It's no worse than yours,' replied Jack with a smile.

'My forename is French,' Jerome said with an air of pride.

'Every day's a school day, isn't it, Campbell?' he heard the detective quip.

Jerome turned his attention to this *Campbell*. 'That one's wet behind the ears,' he pronounced, looking him up and down. 'A right mummy's boy, just like my son.'

'Yes, about your son. He seems rather frightened of you.'

'The only thing he's frightened of is work.'

'Yes, you said that before,' responded Jack.

Jerome watched as the detective started to pace the room. *Self-important sod,* he thought.

'But just how frightened must your son be if he runs away from you during the most violent thunderstorm in living memory? A storm that can knock down pylons – and does he come back the next day? No. He decides he'd rather stay in the woods than live with his own father. How do you explain that, Jerome?'

The farmer sat there, eyeballing the detective. 'Why did you take my walking stick from me?'

Jack stopped pacing the room suddenly and turned to him. 'I would have thought that was obvious, Jerome. Because it concealed a dangerous weapon, notably a knife hidden in the hilt. And you can't bring a dangerous weapon into a police station now, can you?'

Jerome felt incensed. 'I need that walking stick. I can't get around without it.'

Jack shrugged. 'It's beyond my control. Or, more accurately, it's the law.'

'Two stupid kids go missing and I get robbed by a criminal in a uniform,' Jerome grumbled.

'You don't like kids much, do you?' announced Jack.

Jerome looked at him for a moment, then said, 'If you're referring to my son then say so. It might surprise you to learn that I think Scott will do very well for himself in the future. He'll be someone to be reckoned with one day. Just like his father.' Jerome smiled broadly – anything to antagonise the crap out of the detective, anything to get the last word.

There was a knowing exchange of looks between the DCI and his officer, but Jerome didn't care. Nor did he care that neither of them looked impressed when, to further illustrate his son's good nature, he told them about the fox that Scott had rescued. He deliberately went on at length about how his son had let the fox go back into the wild once it was well again. Of course, Jerome had hated him for it, but turning the tale around served a purpose because he was determined not to be slighted. Hours later, Jerome was told he could go.

In other words, you don't have anything to pin on me, he thought with a smirk. 'When do I get my stick back?' he demanded.

'When we've finished checking it for fingerprints and blood,' purred Jack, with a smile.

Jerome hobbled out of the police station, bruised, but with his dignity intact. That was until Jack called after him, 'See, Jerome – I just knew you could manage without that stick of yours.'

Jerome thrust his jaw forward with contempt. The detective had managed to get the last word in. He wanted to kill him.

His thoughts were suddenly interrupted by Bessie, who was barking loudly. He looked at her and saw that she was pointed towards the field – the one that he and his son had burned down. Without warning, the sky lit up. A split second later there came a huge crack of thunder so loud that he and Bessie cringed simultaneously and a car alarm was set off in the distance. He looked up at the angry clouds and realised that he had been so engrossed with the events of the past that he had forgotten about the storm accelerating above him.

Bessie would not be placated, so he put her leash on. Immediately she started to drag him down the darkened country road. *What's wrong with you, girl?* he wondered, as she strained against him, panting with the effort of returning home post-haste. He could only guess that the storm had spooked her, and so Jerome allowed her to take the lead for once. Something about Bessie's fearful behaviour made him feel inexplicably spooked himself, and so he was relieved when the farm-house appeared amidst the trees, just as the first rain began to fall. He took her leash off and she darted into the living room, hiding under a table. As he closed the front door, he took one last look outside and felt a pang of worry about how his son might cope on such a night.

But as he hobbled into the hallway and opened the cupboard under the stairs, he felt his old self begin to manifest.

'Up yours, Jack,' he said, and fished out his spare walking stick, gave it the once over and slammed the cupboard door shut.

Chapter Forty-Two

September 7th

As darkness descended, and Jack waited on the rescue services to arrive, he noticed that the storm seemed to be moving away. The thunder was distant now and the rain long gone, replaced once more by the incessant heat. He sighed and tugged at his shirt collar, feeling harassed.

He thought back to his interview with Jerome and marvelled at how the old git had surprised him by defending his son. Scott Jennings – a boy who tended to sick animals and who fell apart at the touch of a button. He ruminated on this. It was telling that Scott did not utter a single word in Jerome's defence – on the contrary.

'I don't believe Scott's story about the axe,' he said immediately after the interrogation.

'No evidence has been found to support his accusation either,' replied Driscoll, who looked distinctly uncomfortable, having been summoned into Jack's private headquarters.

Jack regarded him, measuring him up and drumming his fingers against the desk top.

Driscoll, sensing this, moved away and picked up a paperweight and pretended to be interested in it, rolling it over in his slender fingers. 'So how did you guess that Jerome had a weapon on his hands?' he asked, more to break the silence than anything else.

'Just a hunch.'

'So you confiscated it from him.'

'I believe under the Criminal Justice Act 1988 I can do just that, yes,' replied Jack evenly. 'But this is not what I wanted to talk to you about.'

'Oh?' replied Driscoll with pretend innocence.

Jack raised his eyebrows expectantly. *Do I have to spell it out?* he wondered.

Driscoll waited.

Jack let his eyebrows relax and said, 'What's wrong with Clements?'

Driscoll smiled slyly and replied, 'I don't know what you mean.'

Jack slammed his fist on the table. 'Cut the crap, Driscoll.'

The officer looked startled. 'Sorry,' he said quietly, and placed the paperweight back on the desk. 'May I?' he asked.

'Of course,' replied Jack, gesturing for him to sit down.

'Please don't tell him I said this,' Driscoll began. 'He doesn't want anyone to know.'

Jack leaned forward. 'I promise I won't say anything to anyone about it, whatever it is.'

Driscoll took a deep breath. 'It's like this. A few months ago he found something, a lump. And, well, he kind of ignored it for a while but it got a bit... well, it's serious now and he needs to have it removed.'

'Cancer?' Jack asked.

'Yes...'

Jack sensed more was coming. 'And?'

'It's testicular cancer, sir.'

'Fuck,' whispered the DCI, and he sat back again, trying to take in all that the bad news implied. 'How far on is it?'

'Hard to say, sir. He's stopped talking about it. Worried it will interfere with his promotion.'

Jack smiled sadly. 'Why didn't he tell me?' he asked, his heart sinking with the thought of how mean he had been to him.

'Promotion,' repeated Driscoll simply.

'Does anyone else know?'

'Just his wife.'

And mine, Jack realised, his mind harking back to her phone call.

'I should advise you that I've caught him drinking a few times whilst on his medication. It might explain some of his erratic behaviour.'

Jack was taken aback by this at first and gazed steadily at Driscoll. He knew him well enough to know that he had ambitions for promotion, too, and wasn't squeamish in spreading dirt about anyone, regardless of their disposition, even his own boss.

'Okay, thanks Driscoll,' he said coolly. 'Tell him if there's anything we can do…' He left it at that, realising that whatever he said was ineffectual, given that he wasn't supposed to know about it.

Driscoll nodded and left the room.

Now it all makes sense, thought Jack, staring at the paperweight – of a fly trapped in fossilised amber.

Just then he remembered his son sitting in the back seat. 'We all have our crosses to bear, eh, Jamie?' he said quietly, and he looked up into the mirror, and there he was, waiting patiently, but with a sadness in his eyes such as he had not seen for a long time.

Chapter Forty-Three

September 7th

Helen was in the kitchen, making tea, music playing in the background. Satie. Alice's favourite composer.

Helen stirred the tea for a full minute before bringing it through on a tray to the conservatory where Alice was seated, the music echoing intimately throughout the house. She sat uncomfortably opposite her, the chair pinching at her ample hips. Once settled she asked, 'How are you today?'

She saw Alice blink and give her a smile. 'I'm fine,' she said. Helen could tell her cheerfulness was somewhat forced.

'You sure?' she asked, tilting her head to one side.

'I keep thinking about fires.'

'Fires?'

Alice shook her head, and flicked her hand as if to say, *Forget it.* Helen glanced at the vague outline of a muddy footprint on the kitchen floor. An enigmatic reminder of Caroline, who she hoped was being looked after properly in hospital.

'I've got something to tell you,' began Helen, carefully. 'It might be nothing but I thought you should know.'

Alice said impatiently, 'Fire away.' Then laughed involuntarily.

'You remember Caroline? The girl who stayed here?'

Alice looked confused.

Helen tapped the edge of her cup, trying to think of another route. 'The gardener,' she said simply.

Alice's face lit up. 'Yes, I remember her.' Then Helen observed a shadow fall across her face and Alice seemed lost in thought.

Helen shifted in her seat. 'Well, one day when I was walking up to the house, your house, I saw someone.'

Alice smiled patiently.

'I should have said something sooner but at the time it seemed harmless enough.'

She waited for Alice to signal that she understood, but there was nothing. Sighing heavily, Helen placed her cup on the table beside her. 'She was with a man that day. An older man.'

Alice absentmindedly sniffed at her tea. 'Darjeeling,' she murmured.

'I didn't want to intrude so I held back and waited at the side of the garden. I thought it was innocent at first...'

Alice smiled vacantly, as if enchanted by some fairy tale. She fingered an orchid that sat in a pot beside her, caressing it like some kind of precious pet.

Helen could feel herself growing impatient. 'Mrs Smith, they were in an embrace. And they were kissing.'

'That's lovely, dear,' replied Alice, and sipped at her tea. 'Too hot,' she muttered, and frowned with displeasure.

Helen was feeling agitated. 'She said his name. It was Mark, I think. Or it might have been Matt. I couldn't quite hear from where I was. Like I said, I didn't want to intrude. Do you think it means anything?'

Alice smiled again and said, 'I'm sure it's all perfectly harmless.'

'Do you know the man?'

Alice shook her head sadly. 'No, but I'm sure he's lovely. Alistair always chose nice girls.'

Helen sat forward and said, 'But this wasn't Alistair. It was someone else.' She sat back again, trying not to appear too anxious. 'Do you think I should contact the police? Tell them what I saw? It might be important.'

Alice smiled demurely, and said, 'I wouldn't be so concerned. It's all just dead birds and terracotta.'

Helen watched as Alice blinked furiously and stooped forward, the tea cup threatening to fall from her shaking hand. Helen rose awkwardly to help her, and placed the cup back on the tray. She watched carefully as Alice seemed to recover, but when she looked up it was with eyes that were devoid of any burden of knowledge or responsibility.

Helen felt her throat constrict. Through a tearful smile she wished in that moment that she could feel the same way. Her frustration was threatening to overwhelm her.

'This flower needs clipping,' Alice said, recovering. 'What do you call that now? Topiary?'

'An orchidectomy,' replied Helen sharply, and walked away.

Chapter Forty-Four

September 7th

'You told him?'

Colin was furious, his face scarlet, pacing up and down inside the mortuary.

'I had to,' began Driscoll. 'Jack wanted to know.'

'Then why didn't you lie to him, you fucking idiot?!'

'I think he's genuinely concerned about you,' replied Driscoll quietly.

'Bullshit,' snapped Clements. 'He just wants to find another weak spot so he can take advantage. Any excuse to hold me back.'

'I don't think it's like that at all, sir.'

'Oh and you know him, do you? You've worked here for how many years?'

'Six, sir.'

'Exactly. So you're in no position to tell me that you know him, because you don't. Not the way I know him. I've been here for almost two decades; you think I don't know him a wee bit more than you by now?'

That had the desired effect. *Clobbered into submission. That'll show him. Fucking wee upstart.* He saw that Driscoll was staring at him oddly and wondered if he'd just said that out loud. 'Your wife's worried sick about you,' Clements heard him say.

'Fuck it!' he shouted, his face feeling like it would burst, the sweat slick on his forehead. 'You think I'm mad, do you? Think I'm nuts? I'm not nuts, no way, not me.' He stomped about, and felt the tears welling in his eyes, blinding him for a moment. 'He's the one that's nuts. Let me tell you: he's not fit to work here. He's not a well man – know what I mean?'

'Sorry, boss, I don't.'

He stopped and looked at Driscoll, who was regarding him

with caution. Suddenly feeling reasonable, Colin said, 'Of course you don't. Why would you? You've only been here five minutes, but me? I've been here for ages. I know everything about everyone. All their dirty little secrets. And there's one dirty little secret that I know about him. Want to know what it is?'

'Sure,' muttered his officer. 'Anything for a quiet life.'

Colin smiled, ignoring the sarcasm. He strode up to Driscoll and looked him straight in the eye so that they were almost nose to nose. 'He talks to himself.'

A blank stare from Driscoll. 'We all do that from time to time, sir.'

Colin punched the metal surface of the nearby surgeon's table and then self-consciously massaged his knuckles. 'No, but have you seen him do it? It's quite a sight to behold, believe me. Entire conversations he has.'

'Well,' began Driscoll, 'I did catch him out once, but I don't think there's anything abnormal about it.'

'There is when it's actually a dead man he's talking to.' Colin smiled patiently, waiting for the penny to drop.

'Sorry, sir, I don't understand.'

'His son, Driscoll, his dead son, he talks to him. You get it? He still talks to him.'

Part Four

Chapter Forty-Five

September 8th

Alice was sat in her white chair in the conservatory, listening to the wind moaning gently through the eaves. Her myriad of plants were trembling as the breeze found its way in through the cracks in the seams of the windows. *A breath of fresh air at last*, she thought, getting up and humming to herself, welcoming the coming change.

Pulling her cardigan over her shoulders, she felt as if a great burden had been lifted. She could think clearly for the first time in ages. She recalled the fact that her son was gone for good, but Alice could not recall why the news of his death had not surprised her. She felt that there was something familiar about it, nothing more, nothing less. She decided to forget about it. *And I'm very good at that these days*, she concluded, and walked through the house to the front door. Before she opened it, Alice turned and looked around. The house seemed truly empty. No creaking floorboards. Nothing untoward.

'A house of Hades,' said Alice to herself. She frowned. 'That's not what I meant.'

'It's okay,' said Helen, smiling gently.

Alice was startled and clutched at her pearls. 'Where did you come from?'

'I've been here with you since lunchtime.'

Alice watched in fear as the woman with the long, black hair took her hands.

'Are you all right?' Helen asked.

Alice thought for a moment and then it dawned on her who this stranger was. 'I was going to go outside for some air,' she replied, sounding officious.

'Sure,' Helen said. 'Let me help you.' Alice stepped back a little as Helen opened the front door, then she let her take her by the hand.

Arriving in the garden, Alice watched with interest as the sky began to rapidly darken.

'Looks like thunder,' commented Helen.

'The air is different,' replied Alice knowledgeably. She smelled the breeze as it wafted across, ruffling her dress and her wispy, white hair. 'The autumn is here,' she concluded, and felt Helen looking at her oddly. *You know nothing*, thought Alice.

Just then there was a flash of forked lightning between the clouds. Alice stood stock still, but she saw Helen jump a little and she smiled supremely. Turning to her, she said sweetly, 'Perhaps you might want to go indoors.'

'I'm not leaving you out here,' retorted Helen.

Alice pressed her lips together with displeasure. 'I don't need you today,' she said flatly.

Helen replied, 'Yes, you do,' and Alice waited impatiently whilst Helen remained by her side. Finally, Helen lost her nerve and left her to it. She called out tersely, 'I'll make you some tea. Don't be long now.'

Alice ignored her and stared out across Hobbs Brae. The clouds were massing ominously above the rooftops and the birds were fleeing to their nests. The brown and red leaves were being tossed around by the wind, which was beginning to howl.

'Just as my garden was beginning to look rather tidy for once,' she remarked. 'I wonder if I should just burn it down?'

Helen, who had just passed her a cup of Darjeeling, leaned against the kitchen worktop and stared at her strangely. 'Burn what down?'

'The garden, of course,' replied Alice with exasperation.

'Why on earth would you do that?'

Alice faltered and looked around her. *How did I get in here?* she wondered, and lowered her eyes when she felt Helen analysing her with her gaze. 'I don't know. I thought I saw it somewhere.'

'What, on television?'

'Yes, that's right,' Alice lied. 'On television.'

Chapter Forty-Six

September 8th

Colin was standing inside his small office, watching the rain as it fell against the window, a tumbler of whisky in his hand. He sipped at it, savouring the warmth as it coursed through his body, trying not to think about his hangover, which was now thumping away at his temples.

He was resigned to fate. The bad news was out there now. There was no going back. He toasted himself in the reflection of the window and took another gulp.

'Your wife's worried sick about you,' Driscoll had said. *The only man I could trust,* Colin thought bitterly, *and now he's stabbed me in the back, too. He told Jack.* The Chief's words came back to him. *'And I'm sorry, Colin, but you're staying put'.* Colin had hoped his promotion might have been expedited given that Jack was on the verge of retirement but, no, Jack had obviously picked up the baton and told the Chief everything. *They're probably lining Campbell up for the job next; Jack's wee golden boy. Or maybe Driscoll. After all, he's more experienced.* He shook his head, knowing that none of this was really true. *The Chief told me I'd get Jack's job soon. I just need to believe him, that's all.*

He tried to cheer himself up by thinking back to the good old days, when he was younger and more dynamic, someone to be reckoned with. Not so bitter as he was now. He smarted at the whisky, which was beginning to burn his throat, and placed the glass on his desk. His tongue explored the roof of his mouth and found an ulcer. He winced at the pain. The side effects of his medication wasn't only a sore palate. He was experiencing mild delirium and paranoia. *Everyone's out to get me, especially Jack,* he had thought, but he knew it was just the drugs he had been prescribed. And the booze. He looked at his half-empty glass long and hard. Then he tipped the contents into the sink of the toilet next door. He caught sight of himself in the mirror. *I look haggard*, he concluded gloomily.

'That's the problem with being in the force for too long,' the Chief had once said, in a rare moment of candidness. 'It hardens you to stone. You become impervious to everything, including your nearest and dearest.'

'How do I tell her?' Clements had asked Driscoll in an unusually vulnerable moment. 'I feel like finishing it all.'

His sidekick didn't respond.

'No. I don't know the answer to that one either,' Colin replied. 'Fuck off. I want to get drunk.'

So he did. At the Crow's Beak he had drunk all night in front of the fire until the wee small hours, until he knew for sure that his wife at home would have lost patience and gone to bed.

How much of an excuse will this give Jack to replace me once and for all? he wondered in a drunken haze. '*Don't come back until you're feeling much better,*' he could hear him say, '*or better still, don't come back at all.' And if I do come back, how do I introduce myself? 'Hi, I'm Colin. And I have only one ball.'*

Finally, he tired of his own self-indulgence and staggered home; after all, he knew he would live. 'I'm not at death's door yet,' he muttered as he put the key into the lock of his front door again and again until he passed out underneath the letterbox. Hours later, he woke up with a crick in his neck and a blinding headache that made his ulcer seem like a birthday present. *What the fuck happened?*

He checked his phone. Jack had left a message. '*Talk to me.*' That was it.

He angrily filled up his tumbler with whisky again, all the way to the brim. 'Fuck you, Jack,' he said to the window. 'You come talk to me. Why should I go to you? To make you feel better about yourself? Why don't you get your fat arse out of that gilded fucking wankchariot you call an office and stoop down to talk to me for once, why don't you?' He picked up his glass. 'What's the point, anyway? I could never get a word in because you were always too busy talking to the dead. Weirdo.' He took a long swig and finished his glass, grimacing once more at the burning sensation.

Just then there was a knock at the door. Startled, he hid his whisky bottle and the glass under the desk and said gruffly, 'Come in.'

The door opened.

It was Jack.

Chapter Forty-Seven

September 8th

Alice sat in the conservatory. She contemplated her situation. *My son's girlfriend was here all that time working for me – and I didn't even know.*

She mouthed her name. *Caroline Baker.* A stranger who knew her son intimately. Alice tried to imagine what the girl could have meant to her if things had turned out differently. *Daughter-in-law* sprung to mind, but the term felt clumsy, like putting a plaster over a six-inch wound. The truth of the matter was that even with the benefit of hindsight, she still did not understand who Caroline was.

'I need to talk to her,' she had announced to Helen, who was making tea in the kitchen.

Helen suddenly seemed alarmed. 'Is that a good idea?'

Alice looked at her as if she was touched. 'Yes, it is. I want to know what she knows.'

Helen replied, 'As far as I can tell, she knows nothing.'

'She must know something.'

'I think you should forget it.'

Alice confronted her. 'I'm done forgetting,' she snapped. Then she saw the look of hurt on Helen's face. 'Look, it's just that I'm under the distinct impression that Caroline would rather have stayed here than been taken back to her family.'

She saw Helen pout as she stirred the tea, as if to say, *So what?*

Alice took the teaspoon out of her hand and threw it on the worktop, much to Helen's annoyance. 'Just before she was taken away she apologised for what she had done, said she was sorry for misleading me.'

'Exactly, Alice. And you want to talk to her? She lied to you. She stayed here under false pretences.' Helen then took a biscuit from the plate beside her and started munching loudly on it, steadily gazing back at her.

Alice felt like a gauntlet had just been laid down. 'I know, Helen. I know I'm not always there. But I was *there*.'

Helen looked away moodily and continued crunching on her biscuit.

'Besides,' Alice continued, 'I was *compos mentis* some of the time. And you knew what was going on. As far as I'm concerned we're all guilty, all of us are complicit in this... secrecy. We hid that girl and everyone was worried about her. Her family. They must think I'm a right nut job, practically stealing their daughter away.'

'Now you're being melodramatic,' sighed Helen, taking a slurp of tea.

Alice picked up the spoon and stirred her own cup, trying to think of another approach. 'I need to find out about the last movements of my son,' she announced firmly, and dropped the teaspoon into the sink with a clatter.

Helen said quietly, 'Remember what I saw, Alice. She was with that other man.'

'And?' queried Alice haughtily.

Helen avoided her eyes. 'And you might not like what you find out.'

As she sat there amongst her plants and flowers, Alice could hear the wind skirting around the house, the rain dancing on the roof. She could remember the scent of the fields and the brush of leaves on her skin. And now that rare occurrence when she could picture the garden in her mind's eye from a summer long gone, sunlit and beautiful, every flower wide open and the bees bobbing in and out of the foliage – when she was younger and in full control of all her faculties. Was it that same summer's day her mind kept returning to – the day they built *Alfred*? She could no longer tell. One memory lapsed and was replaced by another. Thoughts and images from the past were presented enticingly, all too briefly, as if marooned on the beach with little or no context, a mysterious artefact on the shore. Then swept away again by a riptide, to be submerged forever beneath the waves. But all her memories, no matter how deeply sunk they were, had one clear thing in common: her son.

And now a girl had appeared. Not a drowned memory, but solid, real. Yet just as intangible. She remembered those glacial blue eyes of hers, and she thought back to Helen's warning. She wondered if Caroline was truly capable of being culpable. She had to know. *Did she two-time my son? Did she, god forbid, murder him?*

Chapter Forty-Eight

September 8th

'How did we forget?'

Colin didn't know how to answer his partner's question, and instead just watched as the hedgerows flitted past. He was sat in the passenger seat with Jack, who was driving them towards Loch Ness, where William Smith was last seen.

'Remember when you captured that crook single-handed? The one with the blowtorch? That was amazing.'

Colin attempted a smile, but in truth he didn't feel like smiling. The entire conversation felt forced.

'I know you're trying to cheer me up and all,' he said, 'but why don't you just do this on your own? You obviously don't want me here stealing any of your glory.'

He watched as Jack's smile was replaced by an intense frown, his jaw gradually clenching. Abruptly, he pulled over and stopped the car. He turned and looked right at him.

'Listen to me. I don't care about any of this competitive stuff that's been going on between us. I don't care about whether I solve this case or you do. I don't care about what anyone else thinks, either. What I do care about is you. You've been my partner for almost ten years now. What happened to us? We were good together. The cases we solved. The criminals we put away. The lives we saved. Why are we throwing all that away now?'

Colin was surprised to see just how emotive Jack had suddenly become. *He actually means what he's saying*, he thought, but Colin couldn't help himself.

'That's a very pretty speech. You must have been practising that one in front of the mirror.'

'Fuck you, Colin,' snapped Jack, and he got out of the car, slamming the door shut behind him.

Colin watched po-faced as Jack strode backward and forward in the rain. The longer he did so, the more guilty Colin felt. 'Fuck it,' he gasped and got out of the car. 'Are you coming back in or are you going to keep pacing up and down like a cornered chicken?'

He smirked as Jack stopped suddenly and glowered at him, the rain trickling down over his shoulders, his breath visible in the cold. 'I've a good mind to punch your fucking lights out,' he snarled.

Colin immediately retaliated with a slap across his face. Before he knew it the deed was done and he was shocked by his own reflexes. He was about to apologise when suddenly a blow struck the side of his head and he staggered back. Colin regained his balance and a brief stare was exchanged between them. Blood boiling, he marched up to Jack. A split second elapsed and they were lashing out at each other, fists flying clumsily into the air, sometimes grazing a chin, or a brow, but never quite hitting their intended mark. Back and forth, tit for tat, until Colin tried to kick him and clumsily fell over, taking Jack with him. Into the mud they landed with a grunt and a curse, waging war against each other until exhaustion led to mutual surrender.

They lay there, trying to get their breath back, then Colin heard Jack begin to laugh. He sat up, wondering what the hell he was finding so funny, and caught the look in his eyes. The absurdity of it all. He too began to laugh, low at first, then it rose to fever pitch, until it grew hysterical, uncontrollable, the tears blinding him. Jack got up, still giggling, and offered Colin his hand. Colin allowed himself to be pulled back up onto his feet. He saw the muck all down Jack's front.

'Somehow I always end up in the shit,' Jack said, with a grin.

Colin smiled back, recalling the press reports on Jack's state of undress. 'Glad you got that out of your system?' he quipped, trying to wipe the mud from his trousers.

'My mum always used to say, "Make love not war". But you're such an ugly sod there was only ever one choice,' said Jack, beaming.

Colin laughed and then looked at him. 'Sorry,' he said through the rain, which was incessant.

Jack smiled and looked back at him, his eyes welling up with tears. 'No. I'm sorry.' He held out his hand.

Colin felt his throat tighten. He took Jack's hand and shook it. A moment passed between them and Jack was about to say something, but Colin was feeling raw and exposed.

'Right, enough of that now,' he said loudly, 'or people will talk.' He sniffed with the air of a proprietor.

They both got back in the car and listened to the rain for a bit, getting their breath back. The phone rang. Jack listened carefully.

'Matthew White has just been sighted,' he said, hanging up.

'Where?' demanded Colin, excitedly.

'In Loch Ness.' Jack winked at the irony.

'Then what are we waiting for?' replied Colin.

'Let's close this case,' declared Jack. 'Together?'

'Aye,' replied Colin. 'Together.'

Chapter Forty-Nine

September 8th

Alice felt restless, moved by the plight of the wind howling as if in anguish around her home, her sanctuary, the rain lashing, the trees creaking outside like spines of newly opened books.

Alice flicked through the pages of her memory and found something she had forgotten about. A chapter in her life that had been dog-eared for another time, which up until now she had dared not read. She got up from her sofa as if transfixed, walking on autopilot out of the living room, and made her way through the house until she came back to her favourite place, the conservatory. Her mouth twisted at the sudden and all too clear recollection of what took place there one night long ago. Something bitter sprang to life in her gullet, tightened its grip and squeezed the brine from her eyes – she was drowning in guilt that had been hidden in the depths for years.

Her husband, William, had been a popular bloke, solid and likeable, a hard-working trawler-man who could tell a good yarn or two – *Will* to his friends. A player of games, pool or darts usually, and always with a beer in his hand. *Nothing wrong with that*, she had thought at the time. *Goes with the territory. Besides, he earns a good wage, enough for both of us – so I'm not complaining. And if he gets his kicks from time to time at other ports then I don't mind as long as I don't know.*

She had always expected that one day she would find out about his extra-curricular activities and that it would hurt, but Alice felt well able to get over it; after all, they had made an unspoken pact about it. He was a player, but never a cheat.

However, she had not bargained on what his tastes were.

As she recalled the moment, Alice felt her stomach lurch, just as it had then, the bile rising in the gorge of her throat. She stifled a cry, placing a hand over her mouth. Then she shuffled towards the window and watched the branches of the trees violently thrashing against the glass. Alice denied herself the urge to stand outside, feel the wind and the rain push and pummel her body, the branches whipping across her back, again and again, flagellating the dirt from her soul.

Then something within her seemed to subside, as she accepted her guilt, her own culpability, and she watched, detached, as the pages turned and the memory unfolded before her.

'I've done something terrible,' he had confided in her, his thick fingers trembling, his brow forming a deep ravine.

She placed her hand on his arm and noticed the smell of salt water and beer that was sweating out of him. Cautiously, quietly, she asked, 'What? What have you done?' As she did so, she attempted a smile, but Alice had never seen such a look on his face, never seen him look so *serious*.

'I went with a boy,' he said softly, his lips trembling now too, large brown eyes cast downwards in shame.

Alice's heart jolted inside her breast. She composed herself and replied, 'You went with a boy? What do you mean – another man?'

She watched him closely as he seemed to think about this, and then he nodded.

'I'm sorry, Alice, I'm so sorry,' was all he could say, before he broke down into weeping. Alice stroked his head and reflected distantly that this was not the kind of game she was expecting.

Their marriage survived, but things were never quite the same after that. Then he disappeared. She spent the rest of her life frozen in that moment, never able to move on. Now her son was gone, too.

But there was something else.

'A boy,' he had said.

Did he really mean a boy – a child? And if so, who? Alice spent years trying to figure that one out, regretting that she had not been assertive enough to follow it up. She allowed herself a margin for error. *I must have misunderstood him. He was drunk. He meant another man. He did confirm that when I asked him.*

But since then she had wondered what became of him. The police never tracked him down. *Did he run off with that man?* Alice guessed she would never know. That was, until Helen said something odd about Caroline.

'She was with a man that day. An older man.'

If not Alistair, then who?

Alice didn't recognise Helen's description. But she had said his name was either Mark or Matt. It took her a few hours, but she recalled that someone called *Matt* had once worked for her husband. And he, too, disappeared around the same time.

Chapter Fifty

September 8th

The car pulled up outside a nursing home. Jack and Colin both got out and bounded past it. They went up a nearby flight of stairs as fast as their unfit legs could carry them. Once at the top, they saw a car park. And the back of a pub. A door was swinging to and fro in the wind and the rain, banging against the wall. They exchanged a look and entered cautiously.

Jack shouted, 'This is the police. DCI Jack Russell and... DCI Colin Clements.'

He glanced knowingly at his partner, and saw a smile spread across his face. Just then, footsteps were coming towards them, and a sound like metal scraping against metal.

From out of the shadows came a man dressed in white, two knives in his hand. Jack and Colin braced themselves and watched cautiously as the chef sauntered past them, oblivious to their presence, sharpening his blades. They saw he was wearing headphones.

Without a moment's hesitation, both Jack and Colin went straight back out again.

'Where to now?' asked Colin, breathlessly.

'He can't be far. Campbell said he only left moments ago.'

A police car sped past, its siren wailing.

'Follow that car?' asked Colin with mock politeness.

Jack grinned like a boy at a scrumping spree. His phone began to ring. 'Your turn to drive,' he said, climbing into the passenger seat and answering the phone. Colin drove hastily after the police vehicle, manoeuvring through the streets precariously, the wheels skidding loudly.

'Bloody hell,' growled Jack.

Colin laughed. 'This is great,' he announced. 'The old team back again.'

Jack said, 'That was Campbell. They've lost him.'

Colin caught up with the other police car, which was now parked in a street, and they both got out. There, running in the rain towards a lock up, were Campbell and Driscoll.

'Where did he go?' Colin shouted, jogging heavily after them.

Driscoll gesticulated wildly to an abandoned warehouse.

'Got back-up?' Jack wheezed, already out of breath.

'On their way, chief,' said Driscoll, and they stopped at the lock up doors. Driscoll looked at Colin and then at Jack.

'You can almost hear the cog wheels turning,' remarked Colin, exchanging a conspiratorial look with his boss.

Suddenly, Matthew appeared from behind the building, running at speed down the hill and past their cars, just as another police siren could be heard in the distance, growing louder.

'After him,' shouted Jack, and the two officers ran down the hill. Jack watched them. Colin turned to him questioningly. 'You go on, Colin,' he breathed. 'I'll catch up in a minute.' Colin nodded, and Jack watched him disappear in the rain.

A short while later, Jack arrived, and there was Colin handcuffing Matthew and reading him his rights. The other police car had pulled up and Matthew was escorted inside.

'Well done,' said Jack, placing a large hand on Colin's shoulder. 'Sorry, I couldn't keep up. Guess you'll just have to write in your report that you caught him in the end, without me.'

Colin smiled and said, 'No, Jack. We're a team.'

Jack caught sight of Driscoll watching them both. He had a sneer on his face. Reluctantly, he got into the police car, Campbell following him.

Colin caught his gaze and shrugged, before heading back to the car.

Jack stayed there a moment, in the rain, as it poured down, the sound like white noise all around him. There in the corner of the street, next to the derelict warehouse, stood Jamie, hands in his pockets, mid-length hair wet and bedraggled.

And he was smiling.

Chapter Fifty-One

September 8th

Matthew White was sitting patiently in the interview room at Hobbs Brae Police Station, watching as the small, red-headed detective and his fellow officers cast doubtful looks in his direction. He was well aware that *DCI Clements* had taken an instant dislike to him. The prejudice was all too firmly set in his marbled red-and-white stony face, and in those small eyes that hunted greedily for any signs of suspicious behaviour. He could tell from the way he slowly paced around the room that the detective was toying with him, but Matthew wasn't one for being easily intimidated. Nor was his solicitor. She was seated beside him, her paperwork on the desk. She was middle-aged with too much eyeliner, which made her stare seem like that of a ferocious animal. *Probably intentional*, Matthew surmised. Her heavy jaw was thrust forward, as if she was about to bite someone's hand off. He noticed that she wore a Cartier wristwatch. *Now that's intimidating*, he thought, with a smug smile.

'Matthew White, you have been detained as a suspect in our ongoing investigation to find the whereabouts of Alistair Smith. Is that understood?'

'Yes, my client understands why he's here,' answered the solicitor gruffly. 'And he's been advised of his right to silence,' she added, with a firm smile.

'So, you've been hiding for some time now,' the detective said, deliberately ignoring her.

'I haven't been hiding,' replied Matthew confidently, lazily fingering a plastic cup of water in front of him.

'We questioned all of your employees and not one of them knew where you'd gone. Neither did your family.'

Matthew glanced at his solicitor, who nodded. 'I don't have to tell them everything,' he replied with a smile.

He watched carefully as Colin grinned broadly, and said lightly, 'No, of course you don't, but it makes sense – don't you think? – to let your staff know where you're going to be, in case any business pops up that you need to deal with. And wouldn't your family be pleased to see you?'

'I have a supervisor to deal with work matters,' said Matthew, taking a swig of water. 'And I can see my family when I please.' *Touché*, he thought to himself.

He saw Colin stop, and begin to walk anti-clockwise. 'Odd that you didn't give your supervisor any instructions while you were away, but, never mind.'

'Like I said, I don't have to tell them everything.'

'Well, they only phoned you seventeen times so I guess it was nothing urgent. In the meantime, can you explain about your affair?'

'My what?'

'Your affair – with Caroline Baker.'

'You don't have to answer that,' said the solicitor coolly.

'It wasn't an affair. We were lovers.' Matthew saw the look of mock surprise on the detective's face. He knew he sounded a bit stuck up but he didn't care. The feeling of dislike was mutual and he saw no point in hiding it now.

'*Lovers?* I see,' replied Colin. 'The reason we ask is because she went missing in these parts and we believe you may have been the last person to have seen her.'

'Surely Scarface would have been the last person to have seen her,' replied Matthew, catching the eye of the solicitor, who flinched slightly and shook her head.

'Who's *Scarface*?' asked the detective.

'Alistair,' replied Matthew, with an insubordinate smile.

'He didn't mean that,' the solicitor interjected. Matthew saw the warning look in her eyes when she turned to face him. 'Did you?' she asked meaningfully.

'Guess not,' he said reluctantly.

'Why did you come here, if not to see your family?'

Matthew didn't want to reply so he didn't bother, and instead regarded the detective with a look of contempt. He watched as Colin smiled patiently and turned to the other two officers.

'Can someone jog Matthew's memory?'

'Nothing wrong with my memory,' chided Matthew, but it fell on deaf ears. The solicitor cautioned him by placing a hand on his forearm and giving him another look.

'Matthew White checked in to the Warm and Friendly hotel on the night of September the first, sir,' said the officer, who Matthew observed had greased-back black hair. He had a slight smirk on his face. Matthew took an instant dislike to him, too.

'That's right. September the first,' repeated Colin. 'The same night Alistair Smith disappeared.'

Matthew deflected the insinuation, leaned forward and said, 'But Caroline was found again, wasn't she?'

'Yes, but Alistair Smith was not,' replied the detective pointedly.

Matthew felt uncomfortable for a moment and tried to cover it up with a polite cough. 'I'm sorry to hear that,' he said, but he was aware how empty it sounded. He felt his solicitor looking at him.

'Well, I'm glad to hear that you're concerned about his well-being, Matthew.'

He could feel the detective was watching him closely, looking for tells, but he avoided his eyes.

'And here's another strange thing,' continued Colin. 'You checked in to the hotel under an alias. You called yourself *Jason Black.* Why?'

Matthew looked to his solicitor again. She nodded. 'I didn't want anyone to know that I was here, so I used a false name.'

'Well, this is all so damnably intriguing,' said Colin loudly, as if performing in front of an audience. 'Why did you use that particular name?'

Matthew shrugged. 'No reason.'

He saw the detective smile shrewdly. For a moment he felt a chink in his own armour, but he wasn't going to be outwitted and so he sat up straight and composed himself.

Just then, the door opened.

'For the benefit of the recording, DCI Jack Russell has just entered the room,' announced Colin, stepping aside.

Matthew froze as Jack strode in and sat down in front of him.

'Hello, Matthew.'

Matthew just looked at him. He was pissed that not one but two grunts were now harassing him. He turned to his solicitor and she gave him a shrug.

'You were arrested today because you tried to evade our officers when they came to routinely question you earlier. Do you understand?'

Matthew snorted. 'I'm not stupid.'

He watched as Jack leafed through some paperwork he had brought in with him.

'So you left your place of work on the morning of September the first with no instructions to your supervisor, then you made your way here, checking in to the hotel that night. You used an alias – *Jason Black*. Correct?'

'We've done this bit.' Matthew sighed.

'Why did you choose that particular name?'

'My client has already answered that question,' replied the solicitor.

'The reason I ask is because the name is identical to that of a child who died in this vicinity several years ago. The official story is that it was a domestic accident, but this was just a cover. In actual fact, the child was murdered and the perpetrator was never found. So, I repeat, why did you choose that name, Matthew?'

'You don't have to answer that,' said the solicitor sharply.

Matthew sighed loudly and said, 'I knew the kid's mum. And my mum had to console her. It just came into my head. Don't worry, I didn't do it. I was only a kid myself at the time.' He watched as Jack slowly and deliberately leafed through his paperwork again.

'For what purpose did you come here?'

'To protect Caroline.'

'Why?'

'I wanted to make sure that she was all right. I knew that we had split up but I wasn't convinced about her... *boyfriend*.'

'To clarify, that's Alistair Smith you're referring to?'

'Yes.' Matthew attempted a helpful smile, but felt a nervous tic in the corner of his mouth. 'I wanted to make sure he was looking after her properly.'

'I see,' said Jack, looking right at him, his voice reasonable, but his eyes intense, his face serious.

Matthew suddenly felt intimidated. He shifted in his seat.

'We observed your car on CCTV on the night in question. To all intents and purposes, would it be fair to assume that you were following Alistair and Caroline?'

'You don't have enough evidence to come to that conclusion,' the solicitor said impatiently.

Matthew hesitated. 'Like I said, I was worried about her.'

He watched as Jack locked his fingers together and peered at him over his knuckles. 'What is it that you were so worried about, Matthew?'

'Alistair's not a nice person. He's been in trouble with the police.'

He saw Jack turn slightly and raise an eyebrow at Colin.

'So, naturally, you had some concerns,' he agreed. 'And yet Caroline Baker has been with Alistair for over a year and is now carrying his child. Would it be out of the question to suppose that she was a good enough judge of character after all this time, and that perhaps your own concerns for her well-being were unfounded?'

'I don't think she knew about his past. He's not exactly going to tell her about it, now, is he?' Matthew smiled triumphantly. *One nil to me, smart arse*, he thought.

'Did she know you were following her?'

'No,' answered Matthew quietly.

'Could you repeat that, please?'

Matthew sighed impatiently, said more loudly, 'No, she did not.'

'Why?'

'She didn't want me around,' explained Matthew reluctantly.

Jack seemed to bat an invisible ball to Colin, who jumped in with, 'Maybe you should just have phoned her.'

Matthew observed Jack raise his eyebrows in expectation but he wasn't in the mood to play games.

'Oh,' exclaimed Colin, 'she didn't want you to phone her. How come? Were you being a pest?'

'I object,' said the solicitor loudly.

'No,' replied Matthew steadfastly. 'She just wanted some time to herself.'

'With Alistair, you mean,' said Jack.

'I suppose so,' Matthew replied, already tiring of the *good cop, bad cop* scenario.

'What about your car, Matthew?' asked Jack. 'I should explain that it was hauled away because we needed to check it out. Didn't you want it back? I mean, it's a very nice vehicle – a Porsche, I believe.'

Matthew stared at him, unmoved by his false politeness. He caught sight of the other two officers – Campbell, who kept a poker-straight face, and Driscoll, who gave another smirk.

Matthew smiled tolerantly and said, 'I figured I'd come and collect it sooner or later.'

'So you decided that you could manage without your car for a while,' concluded Jack. 'I'm curious, Matthew, to find out what you got up to when you arrived. I mean, you've been here for quite a while now, so how did you pass the time?'

Matthew began to grow impatient. 'I'm not here to pass the time. I'm here to protect Caroline.'

'From what, Matthew?'

'From Alistair.'

'Why?'

'I don't trust him.'

'That's not really a reason now, is it?' commented Jack.

'It's reason enough,' replied Matthew sullenly.

'But you haven't done a very good job of protecting her now, have you?' added Jack, who Matthew observed was beginning to take a leaf out of Colin's book. He could see the malignancy become increasingly transparent in the exchange of looks and the cruel narrowing of the eyes.

'I did my best,' he retorted.

He saw Colin smile disbelievingly. Matthew could read him like a book. He was envious. Not only did Matthew tower over him when standing, but his other physical attributes – muscular build, good looks and even tan – were the antithesis of the pot-bellied, bespectacled detective. It was obvious to him that DCI Clements was making a concerted effort to appear professional, at least whilst the tape was running.

'So what exactly did you do in order to *protect* her?' queried Jack.

Matthew thought for a moment. 'I watched everyone's movements.'

'*Watched everyone's movements*,' Colin repeated – his voice almost, but not quite mocking.

'So you were playing the detective?' asked Jack.

'That's a question you certainly do not have to answer,' said the solicitor firmly.

'Well, this is what the landlady at the Warm and Friendly told us. Margaret Crawford said she thought you were a detective because that is what you said you were. Didn't you? I mean, impersonating an officer of the law. Bit much, isn't it?'

'Hearsay,' the solicitor barked.

But Matthew dropped his guard. 'Yes, I suppose I was.' Then something caught his eye. He saw that the other detective was limping slightly. A moment later he left the room.

'Did you find anything interesting?'

Matthew felt his face redden a little. 'No. Except…'

'Yes?' Jack said softly, leaning forward.

Matthew felt a warning hand on his forearm again. He ignored it and thought back to the mysterious figure he'd seen in the field, surrounded by flames. A woman. Or a ghost. Maybe both. *But what does that have to do with anything?* he wondered. It seemed irrelevant now.

'I think my client is a little tired,' added the solicitor helpfully.

'This is all very intriguing, Matthew,' said Jack, snubbing her. 'The lengths you have gone to in order to observe your ex-girlfriend's movements – some people would call that stalking.'

'That's not what I was doing,' said Matthew emphatically.

'So what did you do, Matthew, when you realised you'd failed to protect her?'

Matthew watched as the detective punctuated this with a flurry of note-taking. He looked right at him, determined to get even. 'When I found out she'd gone missing, my suspicions were confirmed.'

'And what were your suspicions?'

'I don't believe he was ever truly capable of looking after her.'

'So what did you do next?'

'I searched the woods, where she was last seen.'

'And what did you find there?' enquired Jack.

'Nothing,' replied Matthew, with an air of disappointment.

'So would you agree that it's best to leave these things to the experts?' asked Jack, with an overt tone of insincerity.

Matthew didn't want to admit to any failure on his part and replied, 'No. I did my bit. I don't like the look of him. End of.'

'Plain old jealousy, huh?' quipped Jack, flicking through his notes once more.

'No,' Matthew replied indignantly. 'What have I got to be jealous of? I mean, look at him.'

'I can't, Matthew, because he's still missing.'

Touché, thought Matthew again, feeling uncomfortable.

He watched as Jack folded his arms and stared at him. He then seemed to lose interest and got up from his chair, before terminating the interview.

Matthew felt relieved as he was led through the corridors of the station and back outside into the daylight and fresh air. His car was returned to him.

'They found nothing incriminating,' the solicitor told him, her humourless disposition interrupted with a triumphant smile. 'You're free to go.'

It was still raining by the time he arrived at his parents' home. They were only too pleased to see him. Later that night he was standing upstairs in his old bedroom, his swimming medals proudly displayed on the shelves, his bicycle in the corner. He stared out of the window and reflected on how things had turned out. Matthew could easily recall how elated he'd felt when he had won his prizes. His parents had been so happy for him. He smiled at the memory, but his smile faded when he recalled the reason why he stopped swimming.

He wondered at the narrow escape he'd just had. And he wondered at the reaction from the detectives if they'd discovered that there had been a murderer in their midst.

Chapter Fifty-Two

September 8th

'We found blood.'

Jack allowed himself a brief moment for the news to sink in. 'Are you sure?' he asked, pressing the phone more firmly against his ear so that he could be certain that he heard correctly.

'Yes. We found some traces of blood on the blade inside the walking stick. It matches with Alistair's.'

'Thank you,' said Jack quietly, and hung up.

Moments later he was addressing the team and they were heading to the farmhouse.

'You all right?' Colin asked, pulling his seat belt over him in the passenger side.

'I don't know,' replied Jack. 'I feel I should be asking you that.'

There was a silence from Colin as they drove off. Then he said, 'I'm okay.'

'I saw you limping earlier,' replied Jack.

'Aye. Had to leave the room. I'll be fine.'

There was another silence. Jack felt Colin glancing at him.

'You always get like this,' his partner stated.

'Like what?' replied Jack, surprised.

'Down in the dumps. Whenever you're about to close a big case like this one. You get all maudlin.'

Jack smiled at his partner's astuteness. 'Yes. You're right. The thrill of the chase, I guess. Once the case is cracked, the thrill is gone.'

Colin smiled in agreement.

'*La petite mort*,' added Jack.

The detective looked at him questioningly.

'The little death,' Jack explained. 'The French say it's what happens after sex. Every time you make love a little part of you dies. It's their way of explaining the mild melancholy after the thrill of, well, a...'

'A good shag?' added Colin helpfully, with a mischievous grin.

'Yes, that's the one,' replied Jack, laughing.

A moment passed. He could feel Colin watching him again. 'There's something else,' Jack said.

'I knew it,' said Colin. 'What?'

'It just seems too easy, you know?'

They pulled up outside the farmhouse, another police car pulled up beside them. 'Well,' said Colin, unbuckling his seat belt, 'I reckon you deserve an easy ride on your last case.'

'I suppose so,' replied Jack, but as he approached the house he didn't feel convinced. The old doubts and fears were still there. Something about this case made him feel that it was going to be anything but easy.

Chapter Fifty-Three

September 8th

'How did it go?' asked Helen, one hand neatly clasping the other.

Alice put her shopping bag down on the worktop and seemed despondent. 'I wish I hadn't gone,' she replied distantly.

Helen smiled sympathetically. *I told you so*, she thought and then consigned herself to putting Alice's groceries away for her. Helen became aware she was being watched.

'You're being very helpful today,' Alice commented, with a tone that made Helen feel self-conscious.

'It's nothing,' said Helen lightly, and finished putting the last of the tins into the cupboard. 'Shall I make you some tea?'

Alice shook her head and sat at the table. Their eyes met. Helen could sense that Alice wanted to say something but didn't know how to begin, so she seated herself opposite.

'I'm sorry about how things have turned out,' she said, hands clasped once more.

'I went to see her family,' explained Alice.

'Good,' replied Helen, but she saw that Alice's eyes were filling with tears.

'What is it?' asked Helen softly.

'They didn't want to talk to me,' she wailed suddenly.

Helen instantly got up from her chair. Putting an arm around her shoulder, she asked fretfully, 'Why ever not?'

'It was the mother I spoke to,' began Alice in between sobs. 'She hated me. Looked at me like I was something she'd found under her shoe.'

'Then she's not worth talking to,' reassured Helen, and gave her shoulder a gentle squeeze.

'She said she didn't think that Alistair was good enough for someone like her daughter, and when I told her that both my husband and my son were missing – do you know what she had the gall to say to me?'

'No, what?'

'She said that I was an unfit mother.' Alice broke down again.

A sharp intake of breath. 'That's a terrible thing to say,' commented Helen.

'Maybe she's right, though,' said Alice, calming down. She looked at Helen wide-eyed. 'What do you think?'

Helen felt her heart fill with pity. 'I think you should ignore what that cow has to say and get on with your life,' she answered, pouring Alice a glass of water and handing it to her.

'Thank you,' said Alice quietly. Helen wasn't sure if this was for the water or for her supportive comment.

'She's nothing more than a gossip,' continued Helen, 'and gossips should never throw stones in glass houses.'

'I forgot to water the plants in the conservatory,' Alice said suddenly.

'Leave it to me,' replied Helen dutifully. 'I'll be back in a moment.' And off she went to tend to Alice's garden.

When Helen got there she stopped beside the table and grasped the back of one of the white wicker chairs, brooding about the situation that she now found herself in. Finally, she returned and said what had been on her mind for some time now.

'Do you remember when I told you that I saw Caroline with a man?'

Alice put her glass down and said, 'Yes, I do.'

Helen carefully considered her next move. Bracing herself, she swallowed, and said slowly and deliberately, 'I know you told me to forget about it, but I couldn't. It's none of my business I know, but if there's the slightest chance that it might help you to find Alistair then I think I did exactly the right thing.' She looked at Alice, whose forehead creased suddenly.

'What have you done?' she asked, her voice stern but nervous.

'I went to the police, Alice. I told them what I saw.'

Chapter Fifty-Four

September 8th

It was late and Jack was driving through the darkness of the countryside, the car headlights illuminating the road in stark and spectral contrast. He was supposed to be off duty, but for Jack there had never been any such thing. Besides, he couldn't sleep. The need for closure was simply too irresistible. He relayed all the recent events through his mind and cursed himself. *Why is it when I suspect that something bad is going to happen I always end up right? Why can't I be wrong, just for once?*

A strange case, this one, he thought. *A boy missing, presumed dead, and a girl with no idea of what happened.* And now, his forebodings confirmed – Jerome Jennings had disappeared, too. No sign of him at the farmhouse earlier that day. Nothing in the fields. The search party still hadn't found him. Jack left Colin in charge and drove back to the station in order to figure out what to do next.

Then there was the eyewitness account from Alice's carer.

'This man that you saw with Caroline, what did he look like?'

He noted how Helen Patterson had seemed very nervous. Almost timidly, she responded, 'He looked like a movie star.'

Almost certainly Matthew, he concluded. Now his team were looking for him again. Jack thought back to Matthew's capture near Loch Ness. They had already been there because of William Smith. Jack had reopened his case because every time Matthew showed up someone seemed to go missing. Caroline was being questioned again, too, now that her infidelity was known. But Jack felt sure there was something else, something indefinable, something that bound all the disparate threads together. As he flew down the winding lanes, he thought of Alistair and Caroline and he pictured himself and Rachel in their early years – youthful, naïve and in love. The world at their feet. A time when they were happy and had their whole lives ahead of them. He had just taken his first step onto the rungs of a promising career – a police officer patrolling the streets of Hobbs Brae.

Yet his rosy-hued memory didn't compare with what he had seen so far. Caroline seemed a trifle distant when informed that Alistair was quite likely dead. She was upset, but there was something about her reaction that didn't quite ring true. Initially, he had put it down to his own mistrust, for after countless years engaging with liars and criminals, he found it difficult to believe anyone anymore. He did reason that she was suffering from trauma, which was certainly the case. But something never seemed quite right. Now he knew why. She had been two-timing Alistair. It explained perfectly why Matthew would go to such lengths to track her, especially if there was a hint that he was still in with a chance. Jack had almost overlooked it, believing that Alistair and Caroline were probably very much in love, and this made him wonder. *Am I so resigned to my own marriage as having failed that I'm desperate to see someone else having a chance, no matter how unlikely?* He hummed to himself and shrugged his shoulders, adjusting to the fact that his life with Rachel was the one mystery he had never managed to solve.

He cast his mind back to the photo of her that sat in his study. Her smile, despite being made of steel, was an expression he hadn't seen on her face for years, but it was the person behind the camera who still haunted Jack's every waking moment – his son. The memory of Jamie's death was indelibly etched into his brain and seemed destined to obscure all sense of proportion forever. Even now, at the summit of his career, he was still being plagued by pessimism and self-doubt, still deliberately conjuring up imaginary conversations with his deceased son, which, if he was really being honest with himself, was symptomatic of someone suffering from depression brought on by grief. Jack wasn't yet ready to face up to that particular nemesis because he feared that it would destroy him. He felt vulnerable enough right now. He knew Rachel wanted desperately to talk about it, but he couldn't bring himself to do so.

Instead, his thoughts turned to Colin's wife. He wondered how Mrs Clements was coping. *Probably very well*, he reasoned. He could almost hear her now, talking in that clandestine tone of hers, party to her husband's dirty deeds over the years, for she was equally ambitious. There wasn't a local committee that she wasn't involved with. She knew everyone's business. He pictured Colin returning home to her at the end of each working day, only too eager to boast about his mean little endeavours. *She's probably keeping score*, he thought, and began tapping the steering wheel with frustration at Colin's lack of professionalism. Next in line for Jack's throne, he figured that Colin – always one for rubbing somebody up the wrong way – would lose that throne of his own volition if he wasn't careful.

Jack did feel sorry for him, but he doubted his cancer would make much difference, for Colin's biggest problem was his attitude. He thought back to those times that Colin had jumped the gun in the past, introducing himself to all and sundry as a DCI before he had even been promoted. Then there was Jack's clumsy recommendation to the Chief that Colin should not be the one to take Jack's place when he retired. But then something changed. They ended their little war. Jack named him a DCI. It seemed like a kindness, perhaps – the equivalent of giving a dying man one last wish. Except Colin wasn't dying. He was ill, but not out of the running. Maybe it was simply that Jack had decided it was time to close a few doors on his life. Clements was one such door. Jack smiled fondly. He wished Colin well, but he wasn't convinced that he would know how to use his new found power for the best. Colin enjoyed what limited power he currently had a little too much as it was. But when had it ever been any different?

Jack's heart skipped a beat when suddenly something flew past the windscreen and he swerved to avoid it, coming to a rest on a lay-by. In the headlights, he saw a crow perched on the hedgerow opposite, eyeing him curiously.

History repeating, he mused, and Jack wondered if it was the same crow that had nearly made him crash the last time. He was about to think of some method of retaliation when it spread its wings and flapped towards him, landing with a soft *clack* of its claws on the bonnet of his car. Jack peered at it menacingly through the windscreen, his distrust of the animal kingdom growing at an unprecedented rate. He could see the blue-black sheen of its feathers.

There was something in its beak.

Jack leaned forward, craned his neck and took a closer look. Then he saw what it was.

A human finger. Almost pecked to the bone. A sliver of flesh holding the joints together.

He sat there clutching the steering wheel, dumbstruck – the crow's feast and the implication reverberating around the fused bones of his skull.

His resulting shock spurred him into action and he tried to shift his bulk out of the car as quickly and quietly as possible, but no sooner had he stepped out of the vehicle than the bird flew off into the darkness, taking the startling evidence with it.

Jack ran over to where the crow had come from and peered over the hedgerow, where he saw nothing but endless fields, and beyond that the forest, barely registering in the gloom. Without a further moment's hesitation, he hurried back down the road on foot, trying to find a way in. He discovered a gate, but it was padlocked.

'Damn you, Jerome,' he breathed, knowing that he would have to climb over it. The gate was moving precariously under his weight, tilting this way and that. He hoisted his leg over and tried to maintain his balance before almost falling off the other side. Collecting himself, he began to walk across the field, searching for more clues, his heart beating double time with excitement. He knew now that he had never needed to see Caroline or hear her testimony because the truth had been staring him in the face all along. It was just that he couldn't see the wood for the trees.

He knew it was wrong not to call for back-up, but his pride had got the better of him because he was still stubbornly determined to design the perfect conclusion to his career.

A warning rumble of thunder sounded overhead, but Jack was now far too busy marching stealthily into the woods to notice; like a hunter, watching for anything suspicious as he went.

And again, that same old sensation returned. The one that made the hairs on the back of his neck stand up.

The feeling that he was being watched.

As he made his way through the forest, spurred on by the shocking evidence that he had witnessed, he knew that going it alone was dangerous – but he couldn't help himself. He had the bit between his teeth now and nothing was going to stop him. This would be the defining moment of his career. It would either elevate him above all the others in his field, or it would be the biggest mistake he would ever make.

He crept through the undergrowth, surrounded by the sound of rainwater dripping from the trees and landing heavily on the decaying forest floor. It put him on edge, for it sounded like the woods were filled with the pattering footsteps of unknown predators that could leap out from the shadows at any moment, so he was constantly darting a look over his shoulder. The inkling that he was being followed was never far from him. He stopped and listened, cautiously looking around. Nothing.

He was relieved when he finally came to a clearing and recognised the humpback bridge that arched over the river, looking like something from a Grimms' fairy tale. He crossed over it and followed the river's path upstream. In the dark it flowed silently past, molten and black, like some primal life form making its serpentine way through the forest. A sudden and dramatic flash of lightning lit up the trees skeletally, like some cartoon X-ray. Amongst them was the sapling that had held Caroline's DNA in its gnarled claws. It was now flanked on all sides by police security tape, which flapped listlessly in the wind, making it seem like the remnant of some former glory.

Something snapped sharply behind him. He spun round and stared wide-eyed into the darkness. A branch had been broken. *Definitely someone or something caused it*, he thought. *Or maybe it had rotted and fallen off, but how likely is that?*

He waited a moment and then moved on, until he was drawn to a strange green light seeping through the woods. He moved towards it and found that it was coming from an abandoned railway station. The empty platform and the rail track were glowing ghostly green – the unearthly light from the still-functioning signal head. The end of the line – a forlorn sight that served to remind him of his impending retirement. This, in turn, made him think of Rachel. And, of course, Jamie. Forever Jamie. Shaking his head with dismay, he turned and was startled to see a stag standing there on the tracks looking right at him, its horns silhouetted against the lime light. It remained there for a moment, watching him, then seemed to lose interest, walking on and disappearing into the trees on the other side, followed by a doe. *Might this have been what caused the noise earlier?* Jack wondered hopefully.

He followed the deer across the rail track and thought, *There's no turning back now.* Cautiously, he entered the woods opposite, walking gingerly through the thinning forest until he came to the edge of the treeline, where only a small fence stood between him and the answer he had seemingly waited a lifetime for.

He climbed over and found himself standing in one of Jerome's fields. It had only recently been ploughed and the rain had turned the soil to mud. Jack noticed that the thunder had died and was replaced by an eerie silence. He looked up and saw the clouds gradually giving way to a full moon and an infinite array of stars. He blinked and the stars blinked back. He saw one particular star moving steadily across the night sky. The sight made him hold his breath and he wondered if this was the star that Scott had referred to, the one that *moved differently from all the others.* He smiled at such innocence. It was, of course, only a distant man-made satellite, moving on its silent axis.

Another snap. He jerked his head in the direction of the woods.

'Who's there?' he shouted.

There was no reply, and the longer he waited, the more foolish he felt, so he continued walking for a bit and then instantly turned round, hoping to catch whoever it was in the act. There was no one there – only the empty field and the forest beyond.

He reached the top of the hill, where he could make out the silhouette of Alice's house, and down below, the moonlit pastures. Beyond, the distant streetlights glittering in the dark, like precious jewels embedded beneath the stratum of a sky that seemed almost subterranean. *Where to now?* he wondered, and realised that he no longer knew where to look. There were two options. *Should I wait until daybreak*, he mused, *or call for reinforcements?* He gazed at the mysterious moon high above, its ghostly image shimmering on the sea, hovering in between the ruins of the old abbey, like a question in need of an answer. 'Read between the lines, Jack,' he heard himself say.

Jack stubbornly fought hard with the idiotic idea of trying to crack the case himself. Finally, deciding that he wasn't Superman after all, he made his way back down the hill and soon he reached the edge of the forest once more.

Suddenly, there was a loud crack. Jack flinched but kept walking. The harshness of the sound seemed deliberate, as if someone was trying to get his attention. Nevertheless, he continued on his way. Before long, the tingling sensation at the nape of his neck unnerved him so much that he turned round.

Someone was standing there, under the trees, a shadow amongst shadows, watching him. Jack's blood began to charge through his beefy body. He was well aware how overweight and unfit he was, and he had nothing to defend himself with. All Jack had was his authority – for what it was worth under the circumstances – and his wits. They stood watching each other. It was as if a spell had been cast and neither party seemed to want to be the first to break it. Jack hesitated, then decided to make the first move and extended his palms up and outwards as a gesture of goodwill. Surprisingly, the figure took a step forward – but he couldn't make out who it was. Emboldened, Jack took a step forward too.

Then the figure was gone. Just like that.

Jack cursed himself. *I shouldn't have moved. It was too soon.* Then he realised. The figure was still there. It hadn't moved. It was just that the whites of the eyes had momentarily disappeared – and now he knew why. It was because they were averted, looking down, perhaps in fear or shame. Jack took another step forward.

The eyes reappeared in the darkness and something about their increase in brightness betrayed a wider, more apprehensive stare. Jack was now close enough to call out.

'It's all right.'

He took another step forward, hands still raised openly.

Suddenly the figure jumped over the fence and disappeared into the forest.

'Wait!'

Jack peered anxiously into the gloom, but he could not see anything. Now he was faced with a difficult choice – give chase or continue towards his intended destination. He knew he could live or die by his decision, but he had already determined which route he would take. There was never really any alternative. Once over the fence, he could discern the figure moving hurriedly through the trees, leading him back the way he had come. It struck Jack that whoever was ahead of him had stayed well in the shadows and did not want to be seen. Finally, Jack was out of the woods, sweating profusely and trying to get his breath back. He looked around. There was no sign of his quarry. Reluctantly, he walked with heavy, tired limbs back towards his car, which he could see in the distance.

It was then that he saw something else. A figure standing in front of his vehicle, watching, waiting. And the DCI looked back at the forest. And he realised with a sick feeling that he'd just made the biggest mistake of his life. For the figure in the forest had been but a decoy. Now he was trapped.

By their accomplice.

Chapter Fifty-Five

September 8th

Alice sat alone in the conservatory listening to the endless thunder as it toiled away in the distance, an angry act of god that would never be silenced, it seemed, echoing her state of mind. *It won't let me rest*, she thought, guiltily.

She couldn't help worrying, going over and over the events of her life. The threads that refused to be tied together, refused to make sense. Her faltering memory and her reliance on Helen only served to fuel her anxiety.

Did I enable a crime? she asked herself. She thought back once more to what her husband had said. '*I've done something terrible*', which implied more than just a one night stand or an affair — something far more sinister.

Then there was Caroline. *Helen did the right thing and went to the police. I did nothing. Maybe it's true. Maybe I am an unfit mother.* Her mind began to race. *Did that man come back here for her, or to exact some kind of revenge? What if he's still here somewhere? What if the creaking floorboards upstairs were him and not her?*

Alice panicked, running through the house, locking all the windows and doors, the thunder rattling still. Finally, she braced herself and listened. Satisfied that there was no one else with her, she hurried up the stairs and into her bedroom, locked the door shut and hastily slipped under the covers. She tried to sleep, but all she could think about were her husband's words, which now seemed to apply to her.

Chapter Fifty-Six

September 9th

The two men stood watching each other from a distance. No one dared to make a move. A sliver of apricot sky hovered above the surrounding hills as they both weighed up the odds, like gunfighters at dawn: at one end of the road stood Jack Russell; at the other end, beside the battered old red phone box, stood Jerome Jennings.

Jack wasn't sure how to react at first. All that anticipation, the need for closure, had finally been delivered.

How did he get his walking stick back? he wondered. *A spare?* Jack recalled how confident the farmer had been when he had confiscated the original from him. He was exactly the kind of person to have a back-up plan firmly in place – shrewd and conniving, that was Jerome. Jack noted, however, that his accomplice was nowhere to be seen. He reckoned Scott had been coerced into helping his father to ensnare him, though for what purpose remained unclear. Perhaps it was payback time for his heavy-handed interrogation of them both.

Not wanting to take any more chances, he got out his phone and called for help. *It won't take long for them to get here. After all, I had to make a detour on foot. Where I am now, they could get here easily by car*, he reassured himself, but his heart was racing with adrenalin for he was in real danger now. He reprimanded himself. *On the verge of cracking the case and I've fucked it up.*

Just then, Jerome surprised him by turning tail and hobbling quickly away down the hill, disappearing out of view. It seemed ridiculous, but it appeared that the old man was trying to make a run for it. Jack ran as fast as he could after him, until he reached his car. Fumbling for his keys, he got inside, all the while fantasising that he would turn the old bastard into roadkill if necessary, but as he pulled on his seat belt this rather desperate move of his opponent's suddenly seemed less so. There was something too rehearsed about it. As he switched on the ignition, he considered the possibility that he was being drawn deeper into the trap. Yet he had to make a move, otherwise he would lose him, so he drove quickly down the country lane in case Jerome tried to scuttle off the road and into the surrounding trees. As soon as he had driven up to the top of the hill, these thoughts were instantaneously banished when he saw Jerome running at full pelt towards him.

Jack swerved his car to avoid hitting him, but the light from the rising sun was blinding, and with a sudden sinking sensation he realised he had propelled his car off the road – '*Drive carefully,*' he heard Alice say. There was no time to wonder why as the hedgerows raced towards the windscreen and he crossed his arms over his face as the car crashed into a ditch, shuddering and shaking, glass shattering all over him. There was the sound of crunching metal and he felt himself being pitched forward as the tail end of the car lifted into the air in almost slow motion, and he braced himself as he was turned upside down. There followed a sickening jolt as the car landed on its roof, wheels spinning lazily in the air, then it slid, slowly down, into the mud.

Jack was dazed. He tried to move, but his body would not respond – and he cursed himself for being so reckless. And he cursed his *bad luck* and that *blasted crow*. And he cursed himself for not speaking to his wife. As he twisted and turned and tried to wrench himself free, he vaguely speculated on what had happened to Jerome's walking stick. *How could he run so fast?*

Jack stopped struggling at that moment, because the question required him to summon up the will to think and he was fighting the urge to pass out. So he remained stuck there. He could detect liquid trickling down his face, and he could taste something metallic in his mouth. He felt something warm and wet spreading across his lap – blood or piss, he wasn't sure which. All time and space and memories were fused together in a mess that he could not see his way out of. Jack knew somewhere in the back of his mind that he should be in pain, but he smiled dopily, because all he could feel was a mild discomfort and a warmth seeping through his body that sweetly suggested sleep.

Through the broken shards of the side window he thought he could see someone standing the wrong way up at the edge of the ditch, watching him, their inverted face dissolving in the molten halo of the sun. 'Is that Jamie?' he croaked, and he tried to call his name, but the words died in his throat. It broke his heart, because it felt as if a mirror had been held up to his soul. He sobbed dry tears, for he knew now that he had been selfish in grieving alone, that his decision had forced Rachel to do the same. And now he was about to die and Rachel would be more alone than ever, and he desperately tried to cry out, but he was fighting against a sudden and inexplicable preoccupation with how cold it had suddenly become. Jack was aware that this was the end. He wanted to scream.

No, not like this, please…

Everything blacked out for just a single second, then he saw the sun that never sets, his son, one last time, the vague red blob of the telephone box somewhere behind him, and he heard Colin say, '*You look like you've just seen a ghost.*'

And then DCI Jack Russell lost consciousness and all was dark, majestic and infinite.

Chapter Fifty-Seven

Margaret Crawford stood in the darkened hallway waiting for the hearse to arrive. She stared at herself in the mirror. It was an act of vanity that she had resisted for many years now, but on this occasion certain introspection was required. She wanted to take a good look at herself, not to see how she had aged, but to see what lay beyond the surface. She broke her custom and saw clearly the expression of mistrust that had set in – her way of dealing with the world.

'*Expect nothing*', her mother used to say, so she didn't, and now those words were etched on her face, in the lines and the contours of making do and disappointment. The once soft corners of her mouth now set firmly against whatever horrors the world had to throw at her; the constant frown that set the expression below the brow into one of contrariness, for she would not be moved on anything or indeed by anyone's plight – not anymore. *Suffer and suffer well* was her dictum, and she had followed it to the letter. She had turned the deed of self-sacrifice into an art form.

Once upon a time she had reckoned on being someone special – a high achiever. As a girl she had wanted to be a policewoman. Hard to believe now. Her father had been in the force, but he was cut down during the war. Margaret wept and wept when she heard the news, but her mother remonstrated her grief by telling her without a word of a lie that he *wasn't much cop* – no irony intended.

Margaret still dreamed of him for years after that and quietly maintained her hope of joining the force one day. But somehow the big day never came. She married Hugh. Not because she loved him but because her mother told her to. Hugh was dull, ordinary, worked in a grocer's shop as an assistant manager. The reason Margaret wasn't taken with him was precisely the reason why her mother was absolutely taken with him.

'He's soft, pliable – so you will rule the roost, as all women should.'

She went on to talk *sotto voce* about his good prospects. 'He'll be running that shop before long. Or rather, you will.'

They were married and stayed that way for the next 40 years, during which the shop closed and her mother died and life became something to be endured rather than lived. Hugh was not a bad man. He'd stayed faithful for the entire four decades, but all the while Margaret wondered what life would have been like if she had just waited a little longer, held on for something better – too late now, of course. A lifetime of listening to Mother and being the good wife had worn her heart out. Being a spouse to Hugh was a full-time job, for although he ran the shop for a time, he was useless at anything else. Forty years of finding his socks for him, cooking his meals, then keeping his failing mind occupied with various chores in the twilight years of his life. Her mother was right. She should have asserted herself from the start, but she had grown complacent as her heart's desire dwindled, until she realised too late that her existence, like that of so many women, meant revolving around the needs of men who were still boys at heart; the wars they tore into as if it were a game. The lives they destroyed in the process.

Even setting up the hotel business, although a brief respite from the grim realities of her married life, was simply more unending labour spent caring for guests who could be polite on arrival and monstrous by the time they checked out. Perhaps *Mummy dearest* had infiltrated her daughter's dreams with her own disappointments – why else would she repeat her mother's mistakes? But she was past caring now, for Margaret no longer had the energy to expend on the hotel anymore. In the end she had become her husband's carer and there was no time for much else – exactly as her mother had said it would be.

So when *Jason Black* booked in to the Warm and Friendly she was surprised to find herself fawning over him like a little girl with a crush. His good looks and stature reminded Margaret of her late father, but she could still hear her mother saying, '*soft centred, like all men, and as easily pushed about as dust on a mantelpiece.*' Margaret, however, couldn't help herself. His arrival was a welcome interlude from her humdrum reality, an intrusion that seemed almost exotic, particularly as the case he was in charge of had been so newsworthy.

'I'm investigating the disappearance of Caroline Baker,' he had said to her discreetly one night. 'But you mustn't say anything about it. It's a covert operation.' He gave her a wink and bared his white movie star teeth.

'You're a detective?' she exclaimed, then put her hand over her mouth, realising she had almost shouted it. 'I had no idea.'

She gazed at her reflection in the mirror. 'You still have no idea,' she said, disapprovingly.

It had all felt so exciting, breathtaking. She was playing hostess to a detective, and not just any detective, but a handsome young officer who was in charge of a very important case. It was even on the television. But now all she felt was her mother's disapproving stare bearing down on her. A distant rumble of thunder seemed to lend her a voice; her warning, ominous and foreboding, but ultimately a long way away and all too easily ignored.

She heard the car pull up outside. Dutifully, she adjusted her hat, then took one last look in the mirror. She heaved a sigh, wanting to get it over with. Thinking that she would pour herself a stiff gin and tonic when it was all over, off she went to bury her husband.

Chapter Fifty-Eight

September 10th

Rachel Russell was sitting by her husband's bedside in the hospital, watching him breathe. Her emotions fluxed with each rise and fall of his chest. There was hope, but it was all too quickly replaced by anger, because she felt he should have been better looked after by his own team. She replayed the conversation in her head.

'*I'm sorry, Mrs Russell*,' the Chief Superintendent began, '*but Jack had already decided to go it alone. He didn't call for back-up until it was too late. I don't know why he did it. But he has been known in the past for being something of a "hero".*' He smiled gently but firmly. He offered his condolences, but only as she was being shown the door.

So now she was angry at Jack too, and possessed of a sadness that resulted from the fact that she was in hospital again – the same hospital where her son Jamie had died after the car crash. '*History repeating*,' she heard her husband say – one of his pet phrases. *And that girl he found. Caroline. She ended up here, too. God, the irony.* It all seemed so unfair.

Perhaps worst of all was the loneliness.

There were cards from well-wishers sat on Jack's bedside table. A hastily written one from the Chief and another one from officers Campbell and Driscoll.

But then there was the bouquet of flowers she had found with its anonymous and spiteful message spelled out on a card:

R.I.P.

Who would do such a thing? she wondered. She knew from experience that Jack could be an easy target, given his job, but never before had she beheld something so personal, so nasty. 'Whoever did this has a real grudge against him,' she had said to the nurse, who explained that she did not know who brought it in, or when.

'Don't you keep a record of visitors?' she had asked, trying to keep the accusation from her voice.

'No, sorry,' the nurse replied.

'That's not good enough.' Rachel rebuffed her. 'That means anyone could get in here and do something, anything, to him.'

The nurse was young and without much experience, which made Rachel feel all the more frustrated. It was clear that the nurse had no solution to offer.

Rachel concluded with one of her own. 'From now on, the only visitor will be myself. I don't want anyone else to be admitted into his room.'

She called the police station. The Chief offered his *sincere apologies* once more and said he would check the hospital's CCTV footage so they could track the culprit down. The bouquet of flowers was taken away for fingerprinting, which at least made her feel a little better. She was doing something about the situation now. Fighting back, refusing to be a victim.

It was the unfairness of it all that got to her the most. It was akin to kicking a man when he was already down. Very few, it seemed, had come to assist her in ways that were helpful. There were some close friends and a couple of well-meaning but nonsensical relatives who suggested that Jack was a workaholic and had exhausted himself into an early grave. Rachel heard herself say, 'He isn't actually dead.' But no one was listening, apparently. The press had shown an interest, but she refused to play ball. *They're only after some local colour, nothing more.* The entire situation antagonised her. *Has everyone suddenly forgotten about all those lives he's saved in the past, all those people he's helped? Why do none of them come forward now?*

But that was the crux of the matter. Jack's job was pretty anonymous. Very few people knew of his plight, even more so now that the bouquet had been discovered and therefore security in the hospital had been tightened up. She thought about the *brat* that Jack had found and who had been at the very same hospital. Rachel wished she could swap their places now, especially as she had found out that the girl was probably not as innocent as she had at first seemed, given that she had been seeing someone else. Rachel managed to glean that information not from her husband, but from Colin's wife, who always had her finger on the pulse.

Rachel forced a smile and stroked her husband's face. Avoiding eye contact, she walked out of the hospital with as much dignity as she could muster. She retained a brave face all the way to her car, where she strapped herself in and drove off slowly and calmly. She stayed on course until she came to a quiet spot, where she pulled over and her sensible demeanour began to fall apart. Through almost painful sobs, she recalled how a junior nurse had explained to her in quiet and sympathetic tones that as well as a fractured neck and a broken femur, Jack had sustained a severe head injury. As a result of this he was in a comatose state. It was gently broken to her that the longer Jack was out, the longer it would take for his memory to recover. She immediately understood the implication – if her husband didn't awaken soon, it would be several weeks or even months before he recognised his own wife.

'He's lucky to be alive, really,' the nurse had said.

As Rachel sat there in the car, it seemed that Jack wasn't really alive – not with all those tubes coming out of him, not with his head and his left leg in plaster and the bruising across his chest. And the neck brace, the stitches and the dried blood.

It reminded her of the framed photograph that sat on her husband's desk: the photo of herself, taken a long time ago, when she was younger and happier. It didn't matter to Rachel that her husband thought enough of her to have such a keepsake in his private study. What did matter was the boy who took the photograph. Jamie – her absent, yet ever present, son, who they never spoke about or even alluded to, and who they both grieved for separately and in private. Every day, she still saw in her mind's eye the look of dead calm on his young face as he had lain in the hospital mortuary – and it was the same look that was on her husband's face now. It was a strange thing to observe, for Jack's facial muscles were so still; not a twitch, as if embalmed. After a lifetime of work, endless days away from home, and sleepless nights, Jack suddenly seemed unburdened, uncomplicated by the stress of daily life, and absolved of all his responsibilities. His much anticipated retirement had arrived a little earlier than either of them had expected, and he was finally getting the sleep that Rachel knew had evaded him for so long – and his grief seemed forgotten. It made him seem youthful somehow, and there was even the suggestion of contentment in the slightly upturned corners of his mouth. Rachel could see clearly and painfully her son in that visage. Her son, who died, aged only seventeen. Jack, however, had slipped into a coma and lived, if indeed his current state could be called living.

Her husband had always been obsessed with his work, but since the day of his son's death he had become even more so. Perhaps he blamed himself for it, but they both knew that their son's demise came about because he had only pretended to lock his seat belt into place. Deliberately flouting his father's authority had become second nature to Jamie and it was to be his final act for someone then crashed into their car. Death was instantaneous. It was that simple.

Rachel was faced with the unblinking reality that her husband had ended up almost as dead as her son. There was now the worry that increased with each passing minute that he might end up with no memory of what had happened either to himself or his offspring. It shocked her that she couldn't help but feel a little envious – Jack's obsession with his work was his way of trying to forget about what had happened. Now he could.

Did Jack deliberately crash his car into that ditch? she wondered guiltily. *Was he punishing himself? Trying to end his pain once and for all?*

She frowned and shook her head, knowing full well how unlikely that was, but her mind was racing for newer and more fantastical ways to blame herself. She couldn't help it. They had both made a pact of silence on the matter of their son's death and on Jack's ensuing depression. Her complicity in this had blinded her to the fact that the man she knew as her husband had disappeared at the same time. Now that he was out of action, she could see how flawed that complicity had been. But this was her chance to rectify it.

She started the engine and drove back to the hospital. As she flitted past the reception desk, the nurse who was stationed there gave her a smile, and she found herself smiling back, for whom better to find comradeship in than a nurse? With their sisterhood acknowledged through a tacit exchange, Rachel felt unburdened somewhat and promptly sat back down beside her husband, took his hand and held it, her wedding ring there for all to see, her dignity and pride intact. And she waited for him to wake up, for the amnesia to lift, for the day when they would look each other in the eye again and renounce their mourning – for the day when she would lead him out of the darkness and into the light once more.

Chapter Fifty-Nine

September 10th

Scott was hitchhiking his way to a new home. The air was clear, and despite the weight of the belongings on his back, he could feel the burden lifting from him as he neared his new destination.

The journey hadn't been an easy one, however. Scott had wandered aimlessly for days, drifting on the sidelines. He had no idea where to go or what to do next. Finally, he resorted to thumbing a lift. Only one person stopped for him – a loud and brash builder, who was driving a small van.

'So where you heading, son?'

Scott had no idea. 'Glasgow?'

'Sure,' replied the driver. 'Hop in. I can only take you as far as Dumbarton, then I'm heading elsewhere, okay?'

Scott nodded and smiled. The driver made small talk and Scott listened, clutching his haversack protectively between his knees in case things got ugly. He'd heard stories about getting into cars with strange men. The driver, who called himself Joe, asked Scott a few questions about himself.

'Where you from, mate?'

'I come from Hobbs Brae.'

'Never heard of it,' replied Joe, breezily.

'It's near Loch Ness, well it's just a short distance from there, I think…' He trailed off, and he could see that Joe was casting looks at him, his easy smile beginning to falter. As the exchange continued, Scott could feel his confidence sapping. *Why can't I speak properly?* he wondered. *I can barely hold a conversation.* He looked down at his hands, which were shaking, and he tightened his grip on the haversack.

The small talk rapidly got smaller and the silence loomed between them like a brick wall. Scott could feel the tension in the air.

His shoulders began to shake now, too, and he could feel his lip begin to tremble.

A service station came into view and the now spooked driver abruptly pulled into it and said sternly, 'This is where you get off.'

Scott took his bag and slinked away. He watched sadly as his lifeline drove off into the distance, abandoning him. He went to the service desk and asked, 'Is this Dumbarton?' The woman behind the counter looked at him as if he was nuts and said, 'You're about three hours away from there, pal.'

'Do you mean walking distance?'

'No,' she laughed, 'driving distance.'

He got some vague directions from her and continued on his way, mooching along the roadside, the cars whizzing past, the resulting blast of air pummelling him each time and threatening to knock him over. He stopped somewhere quiet to cry, all the while thinking about how much he missed his mother.

That night, he bedded down amongst some trees and dreamed of his father laughing cruelly at him. And the river, and the blood.

And, illuminated by a flash of lightning, the knife.

Chapter Sixty

September 11th

DCI Colin Clements felt as light as air, having just had confirmation of his promotion from the Chief Superintendent.

Not before fucking time, he wanted to say, but thought better of it.

Those three little letters that now preceded his name summed up all that he had strived for over the years – a sure sign of success and a certain social status, too. But these things were academic to a man like Colin, because for him it meant one thing and one thing only – it was an acronym of power.

He marched through the corridors of Hobbs Brae Police Station, carefully considering Jack's accident – a reversal of fortune that no one could have seen coming. Only days ago he would have welcomed such a gift. It had played right into his hands. With his boss quite literally out for the count, it meant that his upgrade had arrived early and the case was now fully under his charge. But since they had made up, the now expedited promotion left a bitter taste in his mouth. He had craved it for so long, but not like this.

It was a strange thing, though – carelessness was something he had never before attributed to Jack. Really, his old rival should have known better. He had been warned about taking on too much responsibility in the past many times before. And now he was out cold. Colin had mixed feelings about it, but his wife was very happy, deliriously so.

'Not that I wished Jack dead,' she said coyly, 'but a coma is the next best thing.'

'You are wicked, Mrs Clements,' he said, forcing a smile.

He thought of all the boxes and stacks of paperwork that he had been meticulously packing in his office – a boring task that he had surreptitiously started on long before he had even received the official news of his promotion. Now that it was a done deal, he had a renewed vigour and was looking forward to organising the rest of it all and reclining in his rather more spacious office opposite the Chief's own. He recalled a dog-eared volume on medicine that he still had from his student days. Sometimes he wondered how his life might have turned out if he had finished his studies and taken his Hippocratic Oath, but he quickly learned that helping others was never going to be enough for a man like him. Colin desired power, and he was never going to find that in the medical world – at least, not the kind that he craved. So, after much thought, he had decided on the police force. Looking back on it now, he had comparatively few regrets.

But Colin knew how much he owed to Jack. His old sparring partner had rescued him from many situations that were less than professional in the past, and so he was struck with a pang of guilt at how he had sunk so low and told Driscoll about Jack's son. It was not like him and it was ultimately pointless. He blamed it on his medication.

'Jack was and always has been something of a one man show,' his wife had said, over some wine, demurely clinking her pinkie against the stem of the glass and almost purring with delight as the Rioja slipped down her throat.

'Aye. I've always despised the way he tries to take credit for everything. There's an entire team working behind him and they barely get acknowledged.' He clinked his fork against the rim of his glass, as if to say, *Your turn.*

Narrowing her eyes with pleasure at this cruel bitching game, she said, 'I hear Campbell isn't too happy at being sidelined by someone such as yourself.'

Colin dropped his fork. 'How do you know that?'

Mrs Clements smiled as if in collusion with an unknown entity, got up from the table and, leaving the room, said airily over her shoulder, 'Perhaps you're more like Jack than you care to admit, dear.'

He thought about it for a moment, acknowledging the tragedy that had changed Jack and the illness that was now eating away at his own body. Their respective wives. And their sons. *Too much in common. Maybe that's all it ever was.*

Either way, as he now idly flicked through the case notes, he wryly observed that they had another similarity – neither he nor Jack had successfully located Alistair Smith, and despite being questioned again, there was still nothing definitive from Caroline Baker.

'Sure, she two-timed Alistair, but that's hardly a crime now, is it?' the Chief Superintendent had said.

'I need more time,' pleaded Colin.

'Time is running out and you have nothing more to go on. Focus on the evidence you do have.'

'Aye, okay. By that you mean Jerome Jennings.'

'Precisely.'

'What about Matthew?'

The Chief gave a stern expression. 'What about Matthew?'

'I received a call from the emergency services. He was found at the site of the car crash.'

The Chief raised an eyebrow.

'At first, they assumed that it was Matthew who made the emergency call, but they discovered that this was not the case.'

The Chief raised a hand, interrupting him. 'It was Jack who made the call. His voice can be heard on the recording.'

'Yes, he did call for reinforcements, but I'm referring to the car crash. Someone else found and reported the crash, and that person is unknown. The caller, whoever it was, cannot be traced. Matthew himself has claimed he made no such call. He just happened to be there, it seems.'

'That's very compelling evidence,' the Chief said, with a wry smile. 'And Matthew said that, did he?'

Colin smiled back. 'He's being very helpful with our enquiries. It's almost as if he wants to be caught. And he does seem to be in all the wrong places, Chief, at all the right times.'

The Superintendent leaned forward. 'Haul him in.'

Colin got up immediately, eager to get his hands dirty. 'Shouldn't be too difficult. What about Jerome?' he asked, almost as an afterthought.

'Jerome is being held in the interview room. Congratulations on finally tracking him down, by the way. He can sweat it out while you go and get Matthew. Driscoll will act as your partner.'

Some time later, Colin was interviewing Matthew. Driscoll was in his favourite position beside the door with Campbell. The solicitor with too much eyeliner was there too, her face like stone.

Colin began, 'So, Matthew, you were the sole witness to a near fatal accident involving one of our officers. What were you doing there?'

'I was following him.'

'You were following Detective Chief Inspector Jack Russell?'

'Yes.'

Colin sat down in front of him. 'Why?'

'I thought it best to observe him, see what he found. After all, my luck had run out. I never found Alistair.'

'You were looking for Alistair, not Caroline?'

'Caroline was found. I knew she was okay.' Matthew smiled confidently.

'Why were you looking for Alistair?'

'I had to know.'

'Had to know what?'

'Whether he was dead or alive.'

Colin smiled. 'Why would that interest you?'

'He's competition. I don't want him taking my girl again.'

Colin glanced at Driscoll, who narrowed his eyes shrewdly.

'You mean Caroline Baker?'

'That's right,' replied Matthew. 'I know she's pregnant but we're still together. She was never sure about Alistair and wanted to keep her options open. Her mother certainly didn't approve of him, so in the end she came back to the better man.' Matthew smiled supremely.

'*The better man.* I see,' replied Colin, with a smirk.

Matthew leaned forward suddenly and said, 'Between you and me, I think she was only after a bit of rough, know what I mean?'

Colin pretended to be in on the joke and gave a little laugh. 'Aye. I know what you mean.' He flicked through his notes, and eyed the solicitor, who was looking on edge. He wondered at Matthew's sudden change of tack. His demeanour was much more assured this time round. He seemed to be gearing up for something, though for what Colin did not know. Either way, he believed that Matthew was behaving like a contemptible snob. *We'll knock that out of you soon enough,* he thought.

'I see that you used to live in Hobbs Brae,' he commented, still looking at his notes.

'I did,' replied Matthew.

Colin suddenly looked up at him. 'You worked for Alistair's father, didn't you?'

Matthew blinked. 'I don't know what you mean.'

The solicitor's ears pricked up. 'My client doesn't need to answer that,' she said hastily.

'Fourteen years ago you worked for William Smith, yes?'

Matthew gazed at him steadily. 'Yes…'

'Did you know that he used to disappear at regular intervals?'

'I think we can take a break now,' the solicitor interjected, giving Matthew a meaningful stare.

Matthew blinked again, swallowed hard, 'No. I didn't know that.'

'Did you forget?'

Matthew coughed a little. 'Sorry, I don't follow.'

'Well, according to the notes from the investigation that took place at the time, you were questioned about this particular fact – so are you saying that the report is wrong?'

'I can assure you that my client is not saying that,' maintained the solicitor, who shot Matthew a warning look.

'No, of course not. I mean, they probably did tell me about it – but it was such a long time ago. And I can't remember every little detail.'

'A moment please so I can brief my client,' said the solicitor.

Colin watched with some amusement as Matthew had a whispered and somewhat heated exchange with his legal eagle. Once they had finished their discourse, he continued.

'Let me refresh your memory regarding those details that you can't recall. It seems that after his wife, Alice, reported him as missing, the police investigating the case discovered a little anomaly regarding her husband's clocking off habits. You see, he used to clock off, but he didn't always return home. Well, not right away. Instead, he used to disappear for two whole days, and only after this would he return to his wife. Do you have any idea where he might have been going on these little excursions?'

'No, I don't,' answered Matthew tersely, reaching for a plastic cup of water. Colin noted that his hand was shaking.

'Yet, according to the police files of the time, you were routinely questioned, as were all the crew, and had nothing more to add. There was no further evidence and eventually the case turned cold. And William Smith was never seen or heard of again.' The detective watched for a reaction. Matthew looked distinctly uncomfortable. Colin decided it was time to go in for the kill, so he leaned forward and said through a smile, 'You know the biggest mystery of all, Matthew? It's not just that people keep disappearing up here, but that every time it occurs, you just happen to be in the vicinity. Now, how do you explain that?'

'Objection!' shouted the solicitor.

Matthew shrugged, smoothed his perfect hair. *A self-comfort gesture,* thought Colin, and he decided to turn up the heat.

'I wasn't the only one at the crash.'

Colin was startled. He looked at Driscoll, who stopped leaning against the wall and moved closer. Campbell checked the tape was still running.

'There was an old man there. He had a walking stick,' added Matthew.

Colin and Driscoll exchanged looks once more. 'Would you recognise him if we showed you a photo or in an identity parade?'

Matthew snorted derisively. 'Hardly. It was dark. I could only see his silhouette.' Colin watched as Matthew looked expectantly at the officers. He didn't seem to be aware of the bombshell he had just dropped.

Moments later, Colin and Driscoll were marching down the corridors to speak to Jerome.

'Where did you find him?' asked Campbell, eagerly following in their wake.

'Hiding in the basement,' said Colin over his shoulder.

'With the rest of the rats,' joked Driscoll.

'Let's give him hell,' said Colin, and he opened the door. There was a solicitor there, dressed in a smart suit the colour of charcoal. *Good,* thought Colin. *If Jerome's got him in tow, then he must be feeling nervous.* The solicitor was young but his hair was dyed jet black, making his already pale face look anaemic. Colin was surprised to see Jerome standing in the corner.

'Why is he not sitting down?'

'My client has to stand from time to time because he has a herniated disc,' the suit replied loudly.

Bullshit, thought Colin, but he smiled and said, 'I see.' He then sorted his papers at the desk and said, 'For the benefit of the tape it would be helpful if he could at least step a little closer to the table in order for the microphone to pick up his statements.' He eyed the suit expectantly, and watched with good humour as he in turn looked at Jerome. The old farmer nodded.

'Mr Jennings wants to help with your enquiries in any way he can,' said the solicitor as Jerome hobbled over to the table, grimacing slightly as if in pain when he arrived, but casting a shrewd look at Colin.

Sitting down, Colin said, 'Jerome Jennings, you have been arrested on suspicion of the murder of Alistair Smith. Can you explain where you were on the night of...'

'September the first?' Jerome concluded. 'I already answered that question the last time you hauled me in here.'

Colin saw the solicitor raise his hand a little to silence him. 'I'm actually referring to the night of September the eighth, through to the early hours of the ninth,' the detective continued. 'Where were you at that time?'

Jerome looked at the suit, who nodded and smiled at his client, his bright red lips stretching across his slightly yellowed teeth, accentuating his almost vampiric appearance.

'I was in the pub,' said Jerome.

'And which pub was this?'

Another glance at the vampire. 'The Crow's Beak.'

Of course, thought Colin. He'd seen him there on many occasions, usually blind drunk and *on the border of disorderly*. He'd been arrested twice for his violent behaviour and he'd been done for possession of cannabis. But he knew if he brought it up now that the solicitor would dismiss it as irrelevant to the case in question. 'Any witnesses to corroborate this?' he asked, knowing there probably would be.

'Plenty,' replied Jerome predictably, regaining his usual mettle. 'It was a lock-in, see?'

'I think you will find his alibi is solid,' the vampire added with a smile.

Hours later and Colin returned with Driscoll from the pub.

'Well, that was interesting,' quipped his sidekick.

'Yes,' replied Colin. 'I quite enjoyed grilling everyone.'

'So, what do we do now?'

'We have enough evidence against Jerome for the murder of Alistair Smith. His blood is on the blade in his walking stick. And we now know that he lied about being in the pub that night. He has no alibi. No witnesses to say he was there. He's been in trouble with the police before. And let's face it, he was never the most likeable guy. Matthew, on the other hand, used to live in Hobbs Brae. So I'm sure he knows of Jerome and his reputation.'

'So you reckon he lied about seeing the old man at the crash site?'

'Difficult to say. Something odd is going on. We have evidence of foul play on Jerome's part. But Matthew does seem to have a history of being there whenever someone pops their clogs.'

'So this is two separate cases now?'

Colin shrugged. 'Fuck knows. My head's about to explode.'

'That's the drink talking,' sneered Driscoll.

'Shut it,' replied the DCI, 'or I'll demote you.'

Chapter Sixty-One

September 11th

Helen sat alone in her house watching television, the light dimmed, a big bag of crisps beside her. There was a bold, romantic drama series on and she was crying, not at the lovers' tragedy that was unfolding before her on the screen, but at her own life, and the way it had turned out.

'She's always been shy,' she overheard her mother say when she was still at school. 'Rubbish at algebra or maths in general. Excels in home baking. And eats far too much of it.' There was a brief pause. 'Very conscientious, though,' she said as an afterthought.

Being conscientious didn't give her the breaks in life that she had expected. Helen had savings, lots of savings. She had a nice home and the mortgage would be paid off in a few years' time. She had a well-kept garden. Food in the cupboard. Lots of food. It was her comfort. It made up for what she didn't have. She had no man. No children. She had desperately wanted a family of her own, but somehow it never happened. It was something exotic that happened to other people. Time and again she would watch young couples holding hands and pushing their prams and it would seem the easiest and most straight-forward thing in the world. But love was her algebra. She couldn't work it out.

And now, at the age of 46, she remained a virgin.

She could only dream of love and babies and relationships, which seemed to roll away from her with increasing speed, like the end title credits of television programmes.

She switched the set off and stomped heavily upstairs, taking her crisps with her. As she sat in bed reading a book, her thoughts kept drifting to the day she saw Caroline with that man.

Helen was usually so diligent, but she had delayed talking about it. She remembered saying to Alice that it was because she didn't want to upset anyone. In fact it was because Helen was worried that if she went to the police they would ask her lots of probing questions. She was concerned that they would find out about her true motives, but in the end she saw what she saw, regardless of whatever misgivings they might have had, and above all, it was the truth.

Yet Helen knew if she was being honest, really honest, she only went to the police because a small part of her that she had kept hidden was jealous.

Chapter Sixty-Two

September 11th

Margaret Crawford began to tear up the newspaper reports of the investigation that she had proudly collected over the past few days. She had read all the sordid details about Matthew White being interviewed as a suspect and she recognised his photograph. Margaret decided there and then that she would never let anyone cross her threshold again – especially if it was a man.

All she could think about was the fact that she was almost murdered in her own house. *There's been a psychopath prowling about and I could have had my throat slit or anything*, she thought, horrified. *Matthew White was nothing more than a fraud. Using a false name. Jason Black indeed*, she concluded bitterly, as she binned the last of the clippings. *And passing himself off as a detective? He couldn't detect flies in shit.* It disgusted her that the very man whom she had placed on a pedestal – *an officer of the law, for god's sake* – was a monster that she had given bed and board to. His handsome face had exuded decency and innocence. Now Margaret knew just how gullible she had been, and how vulnerable, for that very same face was now branded a suspect in the papers. Thankfully, *Jason Black*/Matthew White was now gone, though where she did not know – it still made her flesh creep that she had played hostess to such horror, that an *undesirable* had been stalking her hallways. *None of us are safe in our homes*, Margaret decided, and she shuffled through the hotel, shutting the windows and locking the doors as she went.

You were right all along, Mother, she thought. *Men – they always disappoint in the end.* She arrived in the gloomy reception hall and looked around. It was as quiet as the grave. Margaret then announced haughtily to her late husband Hugh that she was 'giving up this lark'.

To that end she put a *No Vacancies* sign on the window and carefully locked the front door before retiring to the safety of her bed.

Chapter Sixty-Three

Colin left the interview room with the formal arrest he had hoped for. On closing the door behind him, he punched the air in triumph. He had successfully put Jerome Jennings away.

'A great start to your new position,' said the Chief, 'provided we can make it stick.'

Colin felt himself flinch slightly, his feelings hurt as he watched the Chief saunter away down the corridor back to his office.

'Does that pompous oaf never give you credit for anything?' commented Driscoll incredulously.

'Still in love with Jack,' explained Colin. 'The Chief was his mentor.'

He thought back to the day he visited Jack in hospital. He had to show his ID before he was allowed into the ward. He smiled with an element of superiority at the security guard as he strode past him and into the room where Jack was being kept alive.

He sat there for a moment and stared, his feelings as mixed as ever. Envy at Jack's career. Guilt at the things he'd said behind his back. But in the end he felt only sorrow. 'No man should end up like this,' he said quietly to himself.

Just then, Jack's eyes flickered open for the briefest moment, and with a strain of desperation in his voice he croaked something that did not seem to make any sense.

'Crow's beak.'

Colin watched uncomfortably as Jack's body twisted slightly with the effort to stay awake, his fingers flexing, grasping at thin air. Then he fell back into unconsciousness. It was too much for Colin, and he left with tears in his eyes.

For the rest of the day he was perplexed. *What did he mean? What was he trying to tell me?* In the end, he decided that it was just the musings of a barely conscious mind.

But what if?

He sat in the Crow's Beak with Driscoll, watching everyone and everything, looking for a clue. As he did so, he could barely hear his subordinate, who was bitching about everything and nothing.

And nothing was what he came away with.

Chapter Sixty-Four

September 13th

Caroline Baker was sat between her mother and her brother in the back seat of the car as her father drove them out of Hobbs Brae. They sat in silence. There was nothing left to say. Her mother had done all the talking.

'We're taking a well-earned holiday in the south of France. You are coming with us. And you can forget about that job in the book-shop.'

'I've probably lost it now, anyway,' replied Caroline sullenly, but her brother gripped her arm so tightly it hurt, and she relented, much to her parents' satisfaction. *Bullies, all of them*, she thought.

It seemed that no matter what she did or tried, she was always destined to disappoint. It had become clear that her parents were more upset about her pregnancy than the fact that she had almost died at the hands of a maniac. She knew from the looks they gave each other that they did not believe her story and that they viewed the doctor's diagnosis of her trauma with more than a degree of scepticism.

She thought back to what had happened that night, but there were only snatches, glimpses: Alistair desperately, soundlessly shout-ing something to her; his hand reaching out; the wind and the rain...

The police had tried to jog Caroline's memory by showing her the car that Alistair had driven to Hobbs Brae – but to no avail. Yet she could still smell his aftershave occasionally, could still feel his pres-ence, as if he was watching over her even now, like some guardian angel. And she wondered what had actually happened that night. And she wondered if she would ever know. The not knowing exhausted her and it was why she had allowed her family to come and take her back home. She didn't have any fight left in her.

Caroline believed that she had got exactly what she deserved because she had behaved selfishly and cowardly. *I took advantage of a* woman with a mental illness. *Worse still, I betrayed Alistair.* She wept bitterly at what she had done. *For a time I thought I loved Alistair and I genuinely did, so much so that I was ready to bear his child. But now he's gone, I feel terrible, because I don't miss him as much as I should. He loved me and I betrayed him. I don't deserve anyone.*

Naturally, her thoughts turned to Matthew. She recalled how she had deliberately kept him in the background in case things with Alistair never worked out. She was caught between genuine love and love of surface. '*Deeply shallow,*' she heard Alistair say. But her mother preferred Matthew for precisely that reason. He had better prospects and he looked better. *Perhaps I'm more like my mother than I thought.* She wept all the more at the admission.

She hated saying goodbye to Alice and Helen, who had been so kind to her, and she prayed that the police had got it wrong somehow – that Alistair was still alive out there somewhere.

With her luggage half-heartedly packed in the boot, she glanced sideways at her mother, who was staring straight ahead, her lips firmly closed, eyes as hard as diamonds; her brother, texting moodily on his phone. She caught her father's eye in the mirror, but he quickly looked away, mouth set disapprovingly. The silence and the all-too-close proximity of her family were suffocating her. She felt the urge to scream or to run away, *anything but this.*

And it dawned on her that what she was feeling was displacement. She didn't belong in the here and now. Her heart belonged in the past and she wanted to go back and retrieve it. *Perhaps I will in time,* she thought, her head hung low lest her family pick up on what she might be thinking. *Perhaps I'll run away whilst on holiday, make something of myself and one day return home when I feel ready to call the shots.*

She paused to consider that perhaps Matthew's jealousy of Alistair was such that he might have been responsible for his disappearance. But Caroline knew that was not the person she had once loved. Matthew was vain, he was envious, but he wasn't a bad person. Besides, Caroline felt she wasn't special enough to make someone feel so passionate about her. *My mother made that clear from day one,* she thought resentfully.

Alistair loved me. He made me feel special. So why did I betray him? Am I just fulfilling my mother's ideals?

She thought of the kiss with Matthew in the garden that day. *What happened to me? Where did my heart go?*

She realised that she never did get to find out what the *special surprise* was that Alistair had in store for her. It took all her self control to stop bawling in front of everyone. So she sat tight, gripping her knees and looking down, into the past, her heart still lost somewhere in those woods, searching for the father of her unborn child.

Chapter Sixty-Five

September 13th

Jerome Jennings sat in front of the fire with Bessie at his feet, pondering the fate of the detective who had crashed in his car, and wondering why the police had thought that he was responsible. It was true that he disliked the uppity officer, but Jerome disliked most people and most people disliked him. Even the pub landlord had barred him on many occasions, but he spent a lot of money there and in a matter of days he would be allowed back in. Up until now he had never been branded a criminal.

His hopeless alibi and his hapless young solicitor weren't enough to convince them, not with the blood found on his walking stick. The red-headed little detective who took over from his predecessor never left him alone after that. Even though he liked to think that he was still as tough as old boots, Jerome was considerably shaken by recent events and was suffering more doubts than ever before. His existence marginalised and his profits diminishing, he wondered if it was time to get off the wheel now, for he was tired of crop rotations and agricultural cycles. In fact, he was tired of life itself. Jerome was lonely. He had no family anymore. His wife long gone. His son now, too.

As he watched the flames licking at the grate, he thought back to the night the barn had burned down. He wondered what it would be like to just torch the entire farm and maybe start anew somewhere else, a long way away.

He looked down at Bessie, who was sleeping soundly – the only member of his family who remained. He smiled sadly. He knew in his heart of hearts that he could never commit to such destruction.

He found himself visiting Elspeth's grave, the wind racing through the ruins of the old abbey and ruffling his shirt, the waves crashing in the distance. The roses in front of her headstone were wilting.

He looked around at the walls. Stoney. Cold to the touch. The bed equally so, despite the mattress. He snapped out of his fantasy and saw his situation for what it really was – a prison cell inside a police station. The reality of it all was finally beginning to sink in.

'They think I killed someone, Elspeth,' he declared despairingly. 'What's going to happen to me? To the farm, and Bessie?'

He wiped away a tear and tried to regain his composure, thinking to himself, *I'll do it tomorrow, Elspeth. Tomorrow is the day I begin again. Tomorrow I'll bring you sunflowers.*

Chapter Sixty-Six

September 13th

Rachel had murder on her mind.

She was mulling over the situation. The latest gossip was that her husband's crash was a suicide attempt because he had killed his son in a car accident. She knew instantly who the culprit was.

She sighed dejectedly, for despite being married to him for all these years, Jack had kept his thoughts locked away in an undisclosed place. God knows what was going through his mind now, if anything. The nurse had explained to her that the results of his progress were encouraging, but the intricacies of the Glasgow Coma Scale faded into obscurity, because all she could think about was the injustice of it all.

As she watched over him, and saw how decent professionals looked after his needs without prejudice, she began to defend herself, in small ways at first. Staring back for just a fraction longer than usual at whoever she caught eyeballing her. Not that they were. It just seemed that way. She felt almost as if the entire world was against her. Rachel soon realised with a heavy heart that without Jack she no longer amounted to much. Their lives were now so inextricably linked. This made her sad. She always thought that she was the stronger one, looking after her husband like a mother to a child, but now she realised that she needed him as much as he needed her. Rachel soon lost patience – never one of her virtues – and decided it was high time she fought back against the lies that had been perpetrated against her family.

Being married to a high-ranking detective had its advantages, for she had contacts she could call upon. Rachel thought long and hard about just who she needed most, and finally got in touch with the one person she could guarantee would help her.

She had arranged the meeting at a park in Inverness, not far from the hospital where Jack was being looked after. It was sunny – a nice day to be outside – and she needed the fresh air. Besides, it was good neutral territory. When she arrived to meet her contact, she wasn't surprised to find that his two henchmen were with him, too.

Christ, they're like a boy band, she thought, as she looked at the terrible trio: DCI Clements, flanked by his two officers. The one with the greasy black hair and sharp nose she knew as Driscoll. His dark, almond-shaped eyes upturned at the outer corners, giving him an almost feline disposition. *Though more of a leopard than a tabby*, she thought derisively. When she had encountered him on previous occasions, she had noticed that his eyes were always scanning everyone and everything, watching all the time. It was no different today, for he clocked her immediately, nudged Clements, and his stare turned predatory. She made her way across the grass in her flat, sensible shoes, catching sight of Campbell, the other henchman – hands in pockets, as if posing for a fashion catalogue. His constant desire to attract the opposite sex was humorous, but like Driscoll he appeared to have a constant agenda on his mind. She didn't like or trust any of them, and she had no idea what Campbell and Driscoll's forenames were. Right now she didn't really care because she had an agenda of her own.

'Well, well,' said Colin, smiling inscrutably, the light bouncing off his spectacles. 'I didn't think you'd ever come out to play again after recent events.'

'Well, I thought it's such a lovely day today, so why not?' she replied, smiling broadly and holding his gaze.

'Why not indeed,' he answered. 'So how can I help you?'

'I'll get to that in a moment. First, I wanted to congratulate you,' she said smoothly, offering her hand, which he accepted after only the slightest moment's hesitation. The physical exchange was brief, however, for his palm was clammy, and by withdrawing her own hand sharply, she wanted to get her point across – that this was a mere formality and she was now intending to run the show. She stepped a little closer to him and said, 'I need someone who can help fight my corner. Someone who will stand up for Jack and me.'

Colin's smile remained fixed in place, but she could see his cohorts were looking awkward. Indeed, Colin himself had begun to fidget a little, rubbing his palm against the side of his thigh – an age-old tell that he was uncomfortable around her. But, then again, he always had been. She knew the dislike was, and always had been, mutual.

'I know you have powerful contacts in the police force,' she stated.

Colin laughed a little. 'Well, hardly…' he began.

'Nevertheless, I need you to find out who has been instigating this barrage of deceit about my family. Can you do that for me?'

'Well, I can try – but I can't promise you anything,' he said, still smiling like the Cheshire cat.

She inched closer and, almost nose to nose, looked right at him. 'Don't try. Just do. Jack has looked after you very well over the years and I know about some of your indiscretions. Jack has never said anything to anyone about that and I don't intend to start talking about it now. You see, unlike a certain someone, I can keep my mouth shut. Of course, I know I can call upon you, because I feel it in my bones that we, I mean, Jack and I, can trust you implicitly.' She gave him a firm smile and he stared back at her, his facade crumbling, for he knew a threat when he heard one.

'How is he?' he asked, more to break the silence than anything else.

'Tell *Mrs Clements* she will be glad to hear that he's rapidly improving,' Rachel lied. 'Down, but certainly not out.'

Mr Clements smarted, and his eyes narrowed a little behind his spectacles.

And that was that – for the time being. They parted company and she returned to the hospital. Rachel knew that he knew she was on to him, but that was precisely her point: face the enemy and tell them that you know what they are up to. Ensure their co-operation. Silence them. Destroy them if need be. All she had to do was to say a few carefully chosen words and let him read between the lines, for she believed that the unspoken word could be just as easily coercive as its spoken or written counterpart. She learned that from Jack, or perhaps he learned it from her; she could no longer remember. Either way, it was a passive aggressive masterpiece and it would get him to heel.

As she sat beside Jack's bed, Rachel suddenly felt a dead weight lift. She was now free from all the dirt that had clung to her, burying her judgement under sediments of years past. It was time to move on, time to forget about Jamie. Their son was dead and nothing was ever going to bring him back.

For the first time she did not have any guilt about that. And it felt strange. A habit had been kicked. Now it seemed so easy. She could see clearly for the first time in years. There were possibilities now where previously there had been none. She still loved him, and always would, but he no longer occupied her whole heart the way he had done for so many years. He was still there, though: an eternally unruly teenager – now held firmly in place – a small splinter of pain and love, somewhere in the corner of her heart.

She stroked her husband's forehead, and she wondered just how much he would remember when he woke up. Would he even remember Jamie at all? She found herself hoping that he would not, for she now believed firmly, and with the benefit of far too many years of hindsight, that sometimes forgetting was actually a very good thing...

Chapter Sixty-Seven

September 13th

'A long time ago there was a man. A bad man.

And there was blood. Blood in extraordinary quantities.

I was an apprentice fisherman, eighteen years old. I worked for William Smith. On his boat. I went to the same school as his son, Alistair, though he was a good few years younger than me. Our lives have run in parallel ever since. At different times we both moved to Glasgow. At the same time we both went a-courting with Caroline.

It was fourteen years ago when it happened. There were five of us. Quite a rowdy bunch – they all drank a lot. Not on duty you understand, but, well, that's the life of a fisherman, I suppose. We used to set out at three in the morning and catch fish off the coast. It was hard work but... well, I don't need to tell you all this now, do I? You just want me to get to the meat. So I shall, in a moment.

But first of all let me tell you that, yes, I was looking for Alistair that night, as I had been every other night. And I did see a man in the woods, too. I followed him all the way until we reached the other side – and there was a field. I could see him walking across it, so I climbed the fence after him. I grabbed hold of the branch of an overhanging tree to steady myself, but it snapped off in my hand. I managed to land safely, but the man had heard the noise and turned round to see where it had come from. I stood my ground, hoping I couldn't be seen in the shadows. Just then he made some kind of threatening gesture with his fists, so I prepared to defend myself by taking a step forward and raising mine. I hoped that this would be enough to deter him, but he started to advance towards me. I thought he might attack me, so I picked up a heavy branch that lay at my feet and was prepared to use it as a weapon. But then the man advanced closer and shouted something. I didn't hear what it was, and didn't want to stay to find out, so I bolted back over the fence and made my way as quickly as I could through the trees. But when I looked over my shoulder, I saw that the man was following me. After a while I lost him.

A short time later, I was relieved to see him getting back into his car. I'd escaped. This, and the fact that the sun was rising, made me feel a little better about coming out into the open. But just as I was about to, I saw something odd – an old man with a walking stick, who appeared to be trying to run away from the man in the car, who was now revving up his engine as if he intended to run him down. I had no idea what, if anything, had occurred between the two men prior to this, but to all intents and purposes, it looked like I had stumbled upon an attempt at murder.

The man gave chase in his car, driving at high speed, and the old man seemed to be running for his life. They both disappeared over the hill. There was a screech of tyres, followed by a loud crash. I ran as fast as I could to help, and when I reached the top of the hill I saw the car lying upside down in a ditch. I never faltered, but when I got to the vehicle I saw that the old man was gone. I looked around but I couldn't see him. And to be honest there wasn't a moment to waste because I intended to rescue the driver, who must have been in a bad way – but then the police arrived and, well, you know the rest.

I don't expect the detective quite believed my story, but he has no evidence either way. I don't think he particularly liked me either. Being good-looking and successful has made me some enemies and I certainly think that the Clements guy was gunning for me.

But back to Alistair's father and me. We would clock off from work and he would take me to Loch Ness. Just the two of us. It became a regular thing and to be honest I'm surprised that no one noticed that a couple of days were unsubstantiated. Even my parents didn't realise. They thought I was still at work because he told me to tell them that. The first time was okay. He bought us some beer and we went out and did some fishing, and at night we would sit round the fire and he would tell me all his stories. He was quite a character, you see, and I was only young at the time. It was all perfectly innocent but… the next time he took me to the loch and… he forced me to… He said that if I told anyone then I would lose my job and my parents would disown me – so I never did. I know, I know, I was old enough by then to do something about it. Old enough to be termed *an adult*. But I wasn't ready for the kind of assault that took place. He could be quite violent. Once, I came back to work with a black eye. Only once. He quietly apologised to me but I was beyond all that then. Something inside me had died. I no longer knew wrong from right. And that's when it happened.

A few weeks later, we were out in the middle of the loch again. I had no idea why I kept going there with him, lying to my parents and knowing full well what was going to happen. But by now I felt spellbound, totally under his control. I had no way of fighting back. Well I did, but I didn't know it yet.

Anyway, we were out in the middle of the loch and he tried to attack me again, but I just snapped. I hit him... I picked up one of the oars and I hit him with it. It struck the side of his head. There was blood, and I remember the look of shock on his face as he fell overboard... He never surfaced. I watched as the blood pooled out from under the boat. I felt sick. The blood seemed to fill the entire loch. I still dream about it even now.

I knew what I had done. But I never looked for him. I was too scared. All I wanted was to go home.

I never told anyone about it. How could I? I was terrified. And yet it's strange. I realise now that without that horrific experience, I wouldn't be the person I am today. I was so desperate to shake off the feeling of shame, that I completely changed my image and left home to start a new life in Glasgow. Then I set up my own business. Then I met Caroline. All was well with my world. Until Alistair appeared – and the bad dreams returned.

I have suffered constant guilt for all of my adult life because, in the years since then, I couldn't help but wonder how William's relatives had coped. I sometimes believed that I had effectively destroyed their little family. I accepted that responsibility for years but not anymore. William was a monster. I simply put a stop to him. I was barely out of school and repeatedly tormented by someone who was not only my employer, but bigger than me and old enough to be my dad. And my life almost completely ruined as a result.

In fact, if I am being honest, and please believe me, I am, I still suffer even now. You may think that I'm a bit full of myself but don't be tricked. My looks and my success hide an embarrassing secret. I think one of the reasons that Caroline went with Alistair is because my sex drive has been affected. I must say, I was very jealous when I found out that Alistair had given her a child. I can still see William in my mind's eye leering into my face as he did those unspeakable things to me. The memories keep flooding back, time and again. Maybe Alistair was the better man. I don't know. But how could I tell Caroline that I was raped repeatedly by a bloke? She would have dropped me like a hot potato, especially if her mother found out. And her mother finds out everything. I did despise her for two-timing me but I don't blame her. Not anymore. After all, I had done the same to her, which was why she had left me the first time. She deserves to be happy. I realised that when she said her last goodbye in the garden that day at Alice Smith's place. She was very mixed up. She doesn't know what she wants really. I hope one day she finds peace. I really do.

I did want Alistair dead for a time, but it was never a serious thought. And it now seems that someone else has beat me to it. I'm sorry to say that I even pictured Caroline lying dead. I imagined her sprawled on the forest floor, with Alistair beside her, and myself standing over their bodies. I was jealous, you see. But returning here has been cathartic. And in the end, what's done is done.

I suspected that there might have been some kind of agreement between Alistair and Caroline – that they had set me up for what I had done to his father – but I was being paranoid, I think.

As for *Jason Black*, well that was a bit clumsy of me, but I have spent most of my adult life pretending to be confident even though I rarely feel it, so it seemed quite natural to take on somebody else's mantle, albeit the mantle of a dead boy.

Speaking of which, the ghost of William still haunts me even now as I sit watching the television with my mother and father. I glance at them nervously. I want to tell them what happened, and is still happening inside my head, but I can't. I'm still tortured by that bastard even now. And so on it goes – the endless replays of his demise, until I begin to smile, for there is a certain satisfaction in the repeats of William Smith's violent end.

It's all I can do to stop going mad.

Maybe it's better this way, for I know there was a very real risk that I might have done someone harm, perhaps even myself. A small part of me no longer cares. It's why I couldn't be bothered telling my supervisors where I was going. Sometimes I feel like ditching everything. I have this urge to build things up solely in order to knock them down again. My confidence is a frequently lost battle. And I know I've lost Caroline.

But a man with nothing to lose has everything to gain. So why not go out with a bang, why not get back at the person whose father put me here? After all, he hasn't been found. Perhaps he's still out there somewhere, in hiding, thinking himself untouchable.

But then again, so did William, and look what happened to him.'

Chapter Sixty-Eight

September 13th

Colin stood staring out of the bedroom window, a glass tumbler of whisky in his hand. The air outside was calm and still. Everything seemed at peace for the first time in ages. His wife and son were downstairs entertaining the guests, who were celebrating his promotion, but something about the festivities made him feel hollow. It was true that Jerome was safely out of the way and everything was *peachy creamy*, and yet something was missing.

Perhaps it was the knowledge that he had not entirely earned his promotion through honest hard work and that Jack's misfortune might have helped him a little. Or perhaps it was his growing guilt at the entirely unnecessary smear tactics he had allowed his wife to coordinate. Or perhaps it was because he had been trumped in the end by Rachel Russell.

Maybe it was something to do with the fact that Alistair had still not been found and that he knew in his bones that Matthew *whiter than* White was still very much a suspect, despite the fact that none of the mud would stick.

In the end, it was probably just the maudlin feeling he shared with Jack. *Another thing we have, or had, in common*, he thought sadly. He pictured him in the hospital, lying there, at death's door. He wanted to do right by him. He wanted to make him proud, despite everything, despite the arguments and the subterfuge and the dirty tricks. The case of Alistair Smith was closing, not yet, but soon, he hoped. The case of his father, William Smith, remained open. It was odd how things had turned. Colin had known that Jack had messed up that one and he had thought to use it against him, but somehow real life took over and all his feelings of revenge disappeared and now he was the one working on the case. He recalled Jack's words again.

Crow's Beak... But it was still as meaningless now as it was then. He exhaled heavily and took another swig from his glass.

He heard his son downstairs laughing and it made him sad. His son was leaving to work in Glasgow. His first job. Colin didn't want him to go, but he was following in his father's footsteps and so he couldn't help but feel proud. The party was as much for him as it was for Colin. Mrs Clements had been so keen to invite everyone they knew. A double celebration. A chance to show off.

'Mr Clements, where are you?' The shrill tone of his wife. *I swear she can read my mind sometimes*, he thought with a smirk.

'Coming, Mrs Clements,' he shouted back distractedly, for he had caught sight of something dark in the distance, above the trees. A smudge on the window. Perhaps a shadow or a cloud. In any case, he blinked and it was gone.

As he turned to leave, he shouldered the thought that a pall had been cast on the celebrations from somewhere unknown. Perhaps it was simply his own unfathomable doubt, or because the medication was making him feel unsettled, but as he walked back downstairs he could not shake off the feeling that it seemed somehow as if this was the beginning of the end.

Epilogue

Alice Smith wandered outside to look at the stars. The sky in between was inky blue and she could see the moon hovering above the ocean. She thought of her late husband and of how he had led another life that she did not know about, and Alice recalled that she had erected something in the field to remember him by, though she couldn't recall what that something was now.

She felt a chill and knew that she had forgotten her coat, again. She started to walk back indoors. Then she realised that she was already wearing it. Alice pulled it tight around her and looked out across the stark, moonlit fields.

The storm was long gone, it seemed, replaced by a much-missed cool night zephyr that teased at the wispy hairs on the nape of her neck. She sighed and watched the leaves begin to fall around her. The autumn was here, an invisible guest that had come to play in her garden, its refrigerated breath kissing her skin.

She pulled her coat collar up. And she wondered. *Where is he? Where is Alistair?*

Just then she noticed something on her dress. It was dark. A large bruise that covered the trim. On closer inspection she noticed that it looked like smoke damage. She lifted the hem to her face and smelled it. *It is smoke.* She had a vague recollection of a hot, sunny day. And there was a fire. And a blue cardigan. And then all at once it came to her...

Alice had been in a particularly good mood that day, but she didn't know why. She reasoned that it might have been because the sun was shining and the sky was azure blue, and so everything seemed as clear as a bell. Even the air coming in through the kitchen window was fresh and crisp, and as a result Alice seemed blessed with an unusual degree of clarity.

She felt moved to do something constructive and made up her mind that she was going out, so she set off upstairs to get her things. But when she was halfway there, she seemed to quite literally switch off, and when she came to, she had to flex her fingers because they were stiff from gripping the banister so tightly. It was then she noticed that the light had changed, and it soon dawned on her that some considerable time had elapsed. Alice struggled to remember what she had intended to do and was deeply disconcerted by the fact that she could not.

Her fugues were getting worse. Alice's doctor had once more spoken to her about her memory and *dementia* – but it meant very little to her. Even less so the words of the carer, who explained with an expression of mild awe and a tone of deep concern of how Alice had been sitting immobile in her wicker chair and staring into space for a full 45 minutes. She couldn't remember her carer's name. Right now it didn't matter. Alice was in too good a mood to let it get to her. She immediately saw the funny side, and as soon as she did so, she noticed Alistair's old blue cardigan hanging on his bedroom door on the landing. And she remembered.

She grabbed the cardigan and went briskly back downstairs, and, because it was getting noticeably warmer, she decided it would be a good idea to wear her coat. After much searching she found it by chance – in the fridge. Alice wasn't sure if she had put it there by accident, but it felt quite right to be wearing a cold coat on such a warm day, and so she finally ventured outside. But the sun was already well past its zenith, the shadows lengthening like black blades. Everything was bathed in a warm orange glow. The sun and the last sweet stench of summer were retreating from the onset of autumn. The leaves on the trees turning russet and red, the wind rushing through them, mimicking the distant sound of the waves crashing on the shore. The sight of such beauty immediately lifted her spirits.

Yet the splendour of it all was tainted by an acute sadness that she could not place. Alice could no longer remember what she had done that morning, or how the blue cardigan came to be in her hands. It disturbed her that she had lost so much time and did not know what she had done with it. But Alice knew that she had a purpose in coming into the garden. It's just that she didn't know what that purpose was. This was the cause of her sadness. She was losing something. She was aware of it sometimes, but it remained intangible and indecipherable, and so she was left with a persistent feeling of loss.

Then her purpose came back to her. While she had all her faculties temporarily intact, she held tightly onto the cardigan and marched down the garden path. Just then, Alice was stopped in her tracks by a strange metallic *rat-a-tat-tat* sound from somewhere behind her. She turned and looked up to see a large black crow goose-stepping like a sentry across the gutter on her roof, but she could not be delayed, for she had important business to attend to.

As she went through the gate and walked at a pace down the hill, the wind picked up and seemed to lift her senses. She beamed broadly, her face lit by the sinking sun, and she felt more alive now than she had in a long time. In her temporary lucid state, she knew her memory was being eroded. But Alice was aware that her illness was liberating her from time and all the usual constraints of her adult mind, which was now unburdened from such responsibilities and free to wander at large. She considered it a blessing in disguise.

And it was then that she saw the old disused field.

And the lone figure that stood at its centre.

Tears of recognition welled up in her eyes and Alice increased her pace. She'd been meaning to attend to the scarecrow for a long time now. She could vaguely remember when they built it together all those years ago. There was herself, all officious and earnest in her endeavours to build it correctly. And there was that strange little boy – *Moley*, he was called.

And there was her son.

She stopped. Alice could suddenly remember holding him, and how tiny he was and how little he weighed. A precious little bundle in her arms. She could even smell him, and the olfactory memory took her by surprise. Alice clutched the cardigan to her breast in order to remind herself of the reason why she was here – to give *Alfred* some new clothes. But, more importantly, to remove the lingering memory of her husband William, because she believed he had betrayed both herself and her son. Alice felt deep-rooted shame, for she had been in denial for years and now it had finally bubbled up to the surface. It was time to redress the balance. The scarecrow would no longer be a memorial to William.

It would be a beacon of hope for her son.

The clouds had turned the colour of fire, and the cold sea in the distance was warmed to amber by the embers of the sky. Time was marching on and so she marched with it down the remainder of the hill until she arrived at the field. Alice made her way through the shoulder-height weeds, the yellow rapeseed and the dying sunflowers, blinking furiously with the effort of concentration and the heat from the sun-baked soil. She could just make out *Alfred* in the distance, but she soon lost sight of him as she travelled down an incline, and, as she did so, Alice became aware that the edges of the sky were turning ultramarine. She was running out of time. So she increased her pace, hurrying through the vegetation towards *Alfred*. Alice felt sure she was almost there. After a few moments, she came out from the other side of the incline and saw that the sun was beginning to settle on the horizon. Her heart was racing, for Alice knew she was close because she could clearly hear the sea.

And there he was: *Alfred* – only 20 feet away.

She smiled with relief and negotiated her way through the thickening forest of dried flowers and twisted stalks that seemed to fasten themselves to her, but she swept them aside with the palm of her hand, the cardigan held tightly in her other. And then she stopped suddenly and looked around.

The scarecrow was gone.

Alice had only taken her eyes off it for a moment and was sure she'd walked the required distance. By her reckoning, *Alfred* should have been right in front of her. So Alice stood on her tiptoes and frowned when she saw that she had made no progress and that she was looking at him from a completely different angle. Alice clucked when she realised that she'd somehow managed to walk around him, and so she stumbled on. But it soon became clear that she was lost. Alice paused because she was no longer sure what she was doing. The reserves of her mind were running dry. The cardigan in her arms was rendered meaningless. She thought she could smell smoke, and stifled a cry of panic. She took a deep breath and closed her eyes. She opened them again when a breeze made its way across the field and rustled the weeds around her, sending a cold caress across her shoulders – and it was then that Alice realised that she had somehow lost her coat. So she gripped the cardigan tightly to her breast once more, and with a monumental effort she marched on, with her determination to succeed fuelled by the fleeting memory of her son.

She could no longer picture Alistair and she wondered if she would even recognise him if she saw him, but Alice clung to her absolute belief that they would be reunited some day; he would be safe in his mother's arms once more. This conviction kept her going, even though the light was fast disappearing and there was a strange mist forming all around her, and her memory was fading, her pace faltering...

High above in the darkening sky, the crows began to wing home to their nests, over the burning field, the scarecrow at its centre. And in the last dying moments of the day, a pattern could be seen in the rapeseed: a crop circle made by the figure of a woman wandering round and round in an undecided revolution; a concentric line that slowly tightened around the figure at the heart of it all. As Alice soldiered on, she seemed destined to orbit *Alfred* forever, blithely unaware of where her trajectory was taking her; of the chance encounter; of the reunion that was nearing ever closer – as somewhere in the distance there came the faint, almost imperceptible sound of distant thunder.

'Alice? Are you okay?'

Alice was startled and turned round to see a woman standing there beside her looking concerned. Her head was tilted to one side and she was smiling, but Alice didn't know who she was or why she was there. She seemed nice, anyway, with her long, black hair and her generous figure.

'You haven't been out here all night again, have you?' the woman asked.

Alice felt unsure how to react so she just smiled. It seemed the right thing to do somehow. The woman offered her hand and Alice took it, allowing herself to be shepherded from the garden.

'I was in the field,' Alice said, desperately trying to remember something, anxious to explain herself.

'Were you?' the woman asked politely as she waddled across the paving stones, leading Alice to the front door of a house that she did not recognise.

Alice was struck with an air of urgency. 'There was a scarecrow,' she said excitedly.

'Yes, there was a few days ago,' replied the woman, opening the door, 'but that's all gone now. The farmer burned the field down, remember?'

Alice nodded happily, not remembering at all, but eager to please.

'It was quaint, that scarecrow. Pity,' added Helen regretfully.

Alice stopped at the front door, the woman patiently waiting for her. She needed a moment. Something was there, something that needed to be sorted out. A stray thread on her cardigan. A thought. An idea not yet formed. She looked over her shoulder at Hobbs Brae, the sun shining high above the blackened field below. She was filled with a longing and something tugged at her heart. She stood there trying to figure it out, but the ember of her memory winked one last time and was gone, forever.

She was inside a room.

'Tea?' she heard a voice say.

Alice smiled uncertainly and nodded. 'Yes, please.'

'This way,' the voice said brightly.

Alice took her first few hesitant steps into another room, another world.

And a door was shut firmly behind her.

'Nothing ever ends, not really. Everything is a prelude, a prologue, to something else...'

Prologue

September 13th

'My name is Scott Jennings.

I am nineteen years old.

I am not sure what that means really as I do not think of myself in those terms – years. Only as someone who exists, who is real. Alive. More so now than ever.

I don't often get the chance to talk given my circumstances – living on a farm in the middle of nowhere with only a dog and a nonentity of a father for company. And everybody at school was so dumb, so I spoke as little as possible to them – and I include the teachers in that clause. So I talk to myself. Not out loud you understand. Inside my head. People think I'm strange. I know what they say about me. But I'm completely normal compared to some of the oddities that live around here. Margaret Crawford? Don't even get me started on her! Then again, you have to ask yourself, what is normal? Of course, I understand why people say these things about me – I'm a loner who doesn't talk much. But I see no need to conform to their wishes that we all behave the same way and mould ourselves into a persona that everyone finds acceptable. That's boring. And I have no desire to be liked – only respected – and therein lies the difference. I do not, and I repeat, *do not* ever wish to fit into their dull ideas of existence. They might want to move through their lives in safety-first goggles and down the middle of the road but that is a course I do not wish to take. I move off the beaten track and that is far more interesting. They probably all think I'm a bit dumb. My father certainly does. But by the time I'm finished here you will realise that I can express myself most eloquently. All of you.

When my mother died it was like the last page of a book I'd been reading had been torn out, and so I never got to know how that particular story was to end. She remains something of a mystery to this day. I am not ashamed to say that I miss her deeply and, yes, I probably am a little fixated on her given how abruptly she was taken from me. Dad didn't talk about her much. He couldn't. It only upset him. My mother nicknamed me *Moley* because of my passion for digging. I was always looking for fossils – a habit I've since grown out of – and our dog, Bessie, would nearly always join me on these little expeditions and would often trot proudly back home with a newly-found bone in her mouth. I kept some of these because her teeth marks were embedded in them and I found that fascinating. I collected all sorts of stuff – the bones from our dead sheep, which we occasionally found in the fields, tadpoles, pine cones and sea shells. My father frowned upon all this. He thought I was turning queer. I hasten to add I am not homosexual. I'm just not that interested in girls. They talk too much and are so *excitable*. All that noise annoys me so. My mother was the exception to the rule and was a prime example of what a woman should be. She was always the calm, quiet one when my father was losing his temper. I remember the one time when mum did lose it though.

I woke up in the middle of the night. I was always a light sleeper. My dad used to say it was because I didn't do any work but I never listened to him. I knew instinctively that something was wrong, so I crept downstairs and when I got to the kitchen I saw Bessie curled up asleep in her basket. She was only a puppy then and it moved me to hear the little, wet snuffling sounds she made as she snored. The moment I ventured outside I could smell warming timber and I could tell immediately that it was coming from the barn. I knew it must be on fire but I did not panic. Instead, I watched as a bat (*Pippistrellus pippistrellus*) darted past, disappearing into the darkness. But soon I was overcome with curiosity, and as I stealthily approached there was the smell of something else, like burned hair – and I could hear a commotion going on inside. The wooden walls were hot to the touch but I managed to peer through a crack and caught a glimpse of the flanks of the panicked animals parading past, to and fro, desperately trying to escape from the flames. I hasten to add I could not see the actual fire yet – only its effects. The cows were bellowing and screaming now. I'd never heard cattle make such a din. But soon I wasn't able to see anything because of the smoke that was now belching out through the gaps in the timber, and I was forced to stand back. I don't mind saying I was fascinated by this impromptu performance, this theatrical spectacle – so fascinated I decided not to intervene.

Just as the flames were beginning to lick through the seams of the barn my show was interrupted by the sound of voices. I leapt round anxiously and saw my parents hurrying towards me, approaching the scene of the crime. I stood dumbstruck for a moment, unsure how to explain myself. So I did what any innocent little seven-year-old boy would do.

I cried.

Mum took me in her arms and hurried me away from the disaster area and I was left a safe distance away while dad ran back into the house – *to fetch a pail of water.* Mum ran indoors after him but all their efforts were wasted. From my ringside seat, I could see that the entire barn was now ablaze. It seemed as if the gates of hell had opened up beneath it and the entire structure was about to be swallowed into the very bowels of the earth.

I could have alerted them sooner, I suppose – the barn and at least some of the animals might have been saved – but for reasons unknown at the time I chose not to. And because I had allowed nature to take its course, the responsibility for all this carnage was mine. And mine alone. It was the first time in my young life that I'd experienced power. And it had been the making of me. I just didn't know it, yet.

Later that same year my mother died, but not before I overheard her confessing that it was her fault. It seemed that mum had heard a noise earlier that night and had gone out to investigate – but found nothing. She had left an oil lamp still lit inside the barn. It was knocked over by one of the cows and, well, you know the rest. I was a bit put out by that if truth be told because it was really *I* who destroyed the barn, not my mother – but *c'est la vie.*

During the following months I had to tolerate my father grieving for her. I say *tolerate* because even though he was doing it in the privacy of his bedroom the noise was deafening. He had a cheek, to be honest. He never showed any such feelings when she was in life. I spent as much time away from him as possible and so I took Bessie for long walks and I drew in my sketch book and looked for more fossils, and like most young boys I became especially fascinated with dinosaurs. I can still recite the full Latin names – genus and species – of seventy-six of those fantastical creatures. Pretty useless, huh?

I guess my interest in nature was a predictable one, given my habitat, my circumstances. I might as well have lived alone on an island. As I grew up, I started reading about farm animals from a book my father gave me – no doubt trying to harness my interest into some kind of working practice – ever the thoughtful one when it came to such things. Needless to say, the book sat on my shelf gathering dust. But he nevertheless did play an important part in my development when he took me to the abattoir that day. He thought that I hated it, but between you and me, I was rather thrilled by it, so much so that I instinctively knew my response was about to border on the unnatural and I pretended not to like it at all. But in actual fact I have a fondness for the abattoir and have surreptitiously revisited it many times since.

My mother had given me an altogether more interesting book, also about animals – but this one contained chapters on biology and veterinary surgery. I loved to read and memorise all the Latin names of the bones and the vital organs. It proved particularly useful in time because one day I got to put all the things I had learned from it into practice.

I found an injured fox (*Vulpes vulpes*) in a hedgerow, near our farm. I carefully muzzled her with my old leather belt in case she thought I intended to do her any harm and tried to bite me in self-defence. I then gently picked her up and took her home. I kept her in my room upstairs – a fox in a box – and put a splint and a bandage on her leg, fed and watered her, and two weeks later, her leg as good as new, I let her go.

At least that was the official story – the one my father faithfully gave to the detective that day when he was being interrogated in the interview room.

The truth is far more spectacular.

In actual fact, I had set a snare to catch a rabbit because I had for some time wanted to put a little theory of mine to the test. Imagine my surprise when I discovered I'd caught a fox – and in perfect condition, too. Anyway, I carefully muzzled her as I've already said. Then I deliberately broke her leg before taking her back home. It sounds terribly cruel, I know – but I had a very good reason for carrying out this dreadful deed.

I wanted to see if I could put her back together again. I discovered I could. Two weeks later she was as good as new. It gives me the greatest pleasure and pride to be able to say that. I equate myself with the great and the good of the world: a surgeon; a saint; a god. And I've carried out this surgery many times since. On animals of all shapes and sizes. I'm an expert now. A shame I can't repair the detective – lying there all mangled and broken in a snare that I made just for him. Hard to tell where he ends and the car begins really. He tried to interfere with my development, you see, and I cannot allow that to happen. Ever.

Because I am only just getting started.

I love my home, and it will always have a special place in my heart, but there comes a time in one's life when one has to give up childish things and become a man. So I left. And with the benefit of hindsight it was exactly the right thing to do, even if it wasn't entirely through choice. My father threatening me with an axe might have had something to do with it. In any case, I require enrichment. And I'll never find that on a farm. I realise now that all my unnecessary surgery was a kind of training, a prologue, if you like, to what was to come. Which leads me to the night of the storm.

I had been hiding from my axe-wielding father when it reached a crescendo. A blinding storm of a kind I've never seen before. The clouds were moving en masse and I could smell the ozone in the air. The wind was howling, the trees creaking and groaning. The thunder cracked and the sky became a vast, moving ceiling, shifting and flickering with lightning. And the rain fell in sheets. It was a terrific spectacle. A piece of total theatre to rival that of the burning barn. And I had a front row seat. It was as if the elements had put on a performance especially for me. I could feel the wind on my face and I could taste the rain on my tongue and I was pulsing with an energy I hadn't felt before. I was superhuman, godlike. I wanted to fly, to spread my arms out and soar into the air. I couldn't fly, of course, so I did the next best thing.

I ran.

I ran through the undergrowth, speeding past trees, feeling light as air and my senses wide awake. Something primal had kicked in, on this most magical of nights. I raced under leafy roofs and bounded effortlessly over logs and thickets, and somewhere along the way I became a hunter, a predator hidden by the darkening clouds and the great noise of the oncoming storm.

Poor father. His walking stick taken from him. The detective was right to take it, of course. It was a dangerous weapon with that knife hidden in the handle. Not that my father would ever have used it as such. And, of course, he knew I would never do such a thing either. Poor father. He never did get to know me, not really. If only he knew the truth. Then again it's probably for the best, because I suspect the truth would kill him – if he were ever to find out that the walking stick that he had relied on for so long had taken a life.

Alistair's.

I killed him.

There. It's the very first time I've said it out loud.

You should feel privileged.

Remember when I said that people think I'm odd because I'm a loner who doesn't talk much? Well, let this be a warning to you all never to mistake my silence for weakness. After all, no one plans a murder out loud. It was easier than I thought, though – perhaps because everything seemed so unreal that night, that wonderful night. The storm blasting its way through. The driving wind. The driven rain. I saw Alistair in the woods, by the river, next to the humpbacked bridge. He looked lost. I watched, fascinated, as he blindly ran this way and that, crying out for his girlfriend. He did not see or hear me approach under cover of the storm. I have to admit at this point that I was a little apprehensive about what I knew I had to do, but I also knew that if I did not pursue this act of destiny when the chance had shown itself so fortuitously, then I never would. I repeat, what surprised me was how easy it was. His body was soft, accepting the blade with near resignation. I wasn't prepared for his cry of pain though and I quickly placed my hand over his mouth. And as I pushed the knife up to the hilt I tried not to see my mother's face as I remembered the way she used to say: '*the way to a man's heart is through his stomach*'.

Alistair fell to the ground, heavily, surprisingly so; just flopped right there on the spot. And, with the storm raging all around me and my hands soaked in another man's blood, I suddenly felt as if I had broken a sacred covenant and reneged against every rule in the cosmos. All nature abominated. All creation condemned. In my mind's eye, bells pealed and pandemonium ensued. I was the fallen angel.

And it felt good. It was my baptism. My metamorphosis was now complete. A new beginning was in the offing.

I had killed Alistair with kindness. It was an act of mercy. He was suffering, so I put him down. It was a momentous act that required great courage. A battle was going on inside me, you see. *Moley* the child was going to have to make way for Scott the adult. But *Moley* wasn't going to give up without a fight. He was crying, but I had to blink his tears away and get to work fast in case the girlfriend arrived on the scene. She never did. I never saw her that night, not that anyone believed me, but that's all academic now. Sometimes you tell the truth and you are treated like a boy who cries wolf. Under the bridge I observed with some degree of fascination Alistair's final few moments in this world, while the part of me that was still *Moley* could only look on helplessly, for this act of mine far surpassed anything that he had done up to this point and *Moley* knew that he would never achieve that level of greatness in his lifetime. *Moley's* last memory was of seeing me cackling quietly to myself as I watched Alistair's blood trail into the water. As Alistair died, so did *Moley*. Two birds killed with one stone.

The storm subsided very quickly after that and when I looked up to the heavens and saw the strange star traverse the night sky it was with the eyes of a man. The star no longer held any wonder or mystery for me because it was suddenly obvious that it was only a television satellite. But I held on to those naïve thoughts of *Moley's* because I knew their innocence would come in handy. And they did – but more of that later. In the meantime, I revelled in my own power, for I had committed a noble act.

Now all I had to do was to dispose of the body.

It wasn't an easy task. He was surprisingly heavy – a lead weight that needed to be shifted fast. I happened upon the idea of hoisting him over my back – a fireman's lift, I believe it's called – but it was easier said than done because, as you can appreciate, the ground was slippery and uneven. And his clothes were soaked through, which added extra weight. But my training on the farm meant that I could manage it. After all, I am young and strong – and stronger now that I have done away with *Moley*. I cursed each time I stumbled or slipped, but I made it to the top of the slope eventually, panting from the exertion. I arrived at the edge of our old, disused field. The one where Alistair and I once played. I searched his pockets and found his wallet, some loose change and his phone. I kept what little money he had and I later dumped the wallet and the phone into the fire. As for my weapon of choice, well, I cleaned all of my fingerprints from it and *some* of the blood off the blade, not all of it, as I needed to incriminate *daddy*. Then I slid it back into the handle and put the walking stick back where I found it in time for my father using it the next day. Then I went off to my hidey hole in the forest just as the proverbial cock began to crow.

I was very keen to get that fire going. And now I will tell you why.

The crows were having a field day. Like an army of dark, hooded angels, they perched on *Alfred's* shoulders, pecking and picking at him with seemingly casual indifference. Others flew lazily around him, their cries cracking the silence. Whilst *Alfred* stood silently at the heart of it all, his wooden frame tilted to one side, giving him an awkward elegance that would have been complete had it not been for the flies that swarmed around him. Moving as one, and constantly changing shape like a buzzing black amoeba. Blotting and darting to and fro. Teasing and shifting in writhing, hissing shadows. A vast black cloud that hovered above him.

Alfred's general demeanour made him seem isolated and lonely. A forgotten soul. A relic. A fossil. His coat was faded, weather worn, and full of holes created by hundreds of sharp little beaks. There was an old trainer hanging off his left foot. Some of his straw stuffing had fluttered to the ground, some of it taken by the crows to furnish their nests. Some of it attached to the heel of his sock. The cant of his wooden frame, and the way his head lolled almost apologetically to one side, seemed to give him the air of someone who once stood proud, for despite the vandalism of his stature, and the finger missing from his left hand, the head still managed to convey in its tilt a slightly defiant air, one of almost royal rebuke.

But of the head there was no face, no expression. Nothing but the eye sockets of the skull, which stared emptily from their sackcloth across the field. Alistair's skull. The jaw slackened, wide open, emitting a silent scream of anguish – because I stole his thunder.

You see, my father had no real power over me. I wasn't coerced into burning the field that day. I needed to burn the body. So it served my purpose to appear to obey my father. Clever of me. The following morning, I dumped the charred remains into the sea.

It may seem strange, but I kept the ring.

The one I found in a box inside his jacket pocket.

Presumably, he was going to propose to that girl. I did not feel sad about it though. I actually think I did him a favour. Nobody belongs to anyone, you see. I'm wearing the ring now as a keepsake. The box I disposed of in the same way as his other belongings.

And as for *Alfred*, well, what can I say? I think it's very neat that Alistair and I collaborated in the creation of *Alfred* when we were boys and that now as young men we have *collaborated* once more; only this time Alistair is no longer the artist, he is the work of art. *Alistair* has become *Alfred*. And I find that very amusing.

Mind you, I did come close to being caught at one point. Jack proved to be a worthy opponent. I actually developed a little bit of respect for Jack. And despite his good cop, bad cop tactics, which he could only have learned from watching way too much television drama, I still feel a strange kinship with him. He is most evidently lost, as we all are. Some over-inflate their egos to compensate for this discomforting fact – that Detective Clements is a prime example. Jack, however, is more accepting. He is plagued with self-doubt and anxiety, just like the rest of us. Witness him in the interview room that day. I observed him with the same level of detachment that a boy with a magnifying glass would observe an ant on a hot sunny day. I quickly picked up on the fact that the detective seemed to be trying too hard. His tough guy persona didn't quite ring true. It smacked of desperation somehow. Nevertheless, I knew I had to survive this situation if my work were to continue, so I behaved in exactly the way he so evidently wanted me to.

But allow me to digress for a moment. As I've said, the book my mother gave me had been exceptionally useful of late. And it proved exceptionally useful now. I'd read in the well-worn pages that an octopus can squirt ink into the water as a method of self-defence. It briefly hides inside this black cloud of bodily fluid, confusing its enemy for a few precious moments – and then it makes a quick getaway. Other animals play dead. And others urinate or defecate in order to quite literally throw their predator off the scent. As I sat there with Jack pacing around me like a dangerous carnivore, I decided that deliberately pissing myself was the order of the day and the most theatrical and therefore the most effective choice. Shitting myself was just too vulgar and messy a display to think about really. And I don't play dead for anyone.

I chose my moment carefully. I knew that Jack was about to take the interrogation much further, and that the shouting and the clenched fists and the generally unpleasant demeanour would soon give way to something uglier – the outcome of which could only be guessed at. But I knew Jack was soft. I also knew how badly he needed results. And that desperate men do desperate things. We both understood that he had to finish what he'd started. I was already prepared for it. I deliberately pissed myself right on cue. It had exactly the desired effect. One minute Jack was towering over me in his best attempt at intimidation, the next he was aghast at the sight of me quietly sobbing and sniffling as the piss trickled out the bottom of my jeans. I had successfully degenerated into a quivering wreck before his eyes. I had performed for him and I could see from my hidden vantage point that playing the innocent was working surprisingly well. I say *hidden* because I wore *Moley's* persona that day like one would wear a cardigan – I told you he would still come in handy for something. By drawing on his naïvety, I had succeeded in portraying myself as the victim in this case, not the perpetrator. In essence, I had mastered the art of falling apart. I immediately saw the flash of guilt in Jack's eyes, observed the shameful reddening of his cheeks and the stiffness of his walk as he exited the room. I had known all along that he did not have the stomach for this.

And I got away *Scott-free.* A wolf in sheep's clothing.

But don't get me wrong. I did leave him a nice bouquet of flowers. See? I'm not all bad.

I couldn't help having a giggle to myself on the way home. Really, I should have won an award for my performance. But I knew how lucky I was. I suspect Detective Clements would not have been quite such a soft touch.

But I'll get him soon enough. Make no mistake about that.

Jack Russell's trouble is that he's lost his edge. He's an old dog who's forgotten how to learn new tricks. But I wasn't so naïve that I felt my performance in the interview room had let me completely off the hook. Far from it. I had been observing Jack's movements for quite a while. I knew almost to the minute when he would go for his nightly excursions. He had been poking around in the forest for some time now, usually in the wee small hours, and as far as I was concerned he was getting too close for comfort. I knew he wouldn't give up his current hobby so I needed to concoct a way of getting him off my back. It took a while to figure out how to do this, but it all worked out well in the end. For me that is. My intention was to lure Jack onto the road where I could create the means necessary for a car crash to take place. I wanted to kill him from a safe distance, you see. Obviously, I did not want to be recognised, so I took my father's spare walking stick, and I even copied his stride so that it would look authentic. This was just in case Jack happened to survive. He would see my father and not me. I hasten to add that I did not wish my father to spend his last days in prison for a crime he did not commit, but I needed a sacrificial lamb and he fitted the bill perfectly. Besides, he had never done me any favours. I quite enjoyed the fact that the roles had been reversed, for now he was ensnared just like one of those foxes he delighted in killing. And it felt good. In the event that my plan fell through, I would have no choice but to dispose of Jack in exactly the same way I disposed of Alistair. But this was the hard option that I wanted to avoid, because I have to admit I was more nervous about this than any of my previous endeavours. I had never killed a cop before. And even though I thought he was a relatively easy target, his status intimidated me, hence my preference for the softer option of killing him from afar.

However, I didn't bank on a third party showing up, but when it turned out to be Matthew White then it all fell rather brilliantly into position – he was in the right place at just the right time. A useful scapegoat with a suspect history of his own if the papers were to be believed. Then again, the hacks would swallow anything, as long it contained an ounce of sleaze. Really, it's the press that are the pigs, not the police. In any case, I remained in hiding. I watched. And at one point I wondered if I would have to dispose of him too. But imagine my surprise and pleasure when Matthew inadvertently did my job for me by luring Jack right into my trap. Matthew had turned and fled as soon as Jack had sighted him and it was this chase that led Jack to me. The detective came out into the open, searching for whoever he thought was tailing him, unaware that Matthew was now in hiding. And it was here that I picked up the baton, as it were, and came out from my bolt hole, and did my best impersonation of dad. I pretended to hobble guiltily away, knowing that Jack would take the bait and follow me in his car. And once we were over the hill, I turned and ran straight at him. It was a huge gamble because I had dropped my disguise at the last minute, but it paid off – only I knew how difficult it would be to manoeuvre a vehicle down that hazardous stretch of road, particularly with that crumbling ditch running alongside. And I'm amazed to be able to say that it worked. The car overturned and I saw Jack lying mangled inside. It was then that I spied Matthew reappearing on the top of the hill and I suddenly realised there was a magnificent opportunity here. I went to the phone box and anonymously called the police, making it brief so I could get away as fast as possible without being caught. Then I hung up, wiped the fingerprints off, and with the trusty walking stick under my arm I darted out of sight. I headed back to the farm and I put the spare stick back in the cupboard.

All in a day's work – and the sun had barely even risen yet.

I know how lucky I was and how much I owed to Matthew.

My gamble was a dangerous one but it paid off in the end. Next time though, nothing can be left to chance.

When I killed Alistair I was troubled by guilt and the persistent feeling that I was being watched. In fact, I have been plagued with that notion since the burning of the barn. The trees seemed like silent conspirators and the wind whispered the promise of retribution. Even the pylons seemed like moral giants, ready to uproot themselves and lumber after me, firing bolts of electricity at my fleeing form. It all seems so childish now, but at the time I was persistently haunted by the idea that something was coming for me. I was living my life *in fear and trembling*. I smile with irony when I recall seeing that dark cloud above Alistair in the field. I convinced myself that it was merely a flock of crows, but deep down I was rather more convinced that it was the same cloud that brought the storm back... I realise now that it was only a halo of flies – after all, his body must have been decomposing rapidly in the heat.

I know now that these feelings of dread amounted to nothing more than my own paranoia, my own fear. Or to be more accurate – *Moley's*. I guess he was going to be a tougher cookie to crack than I'd at first thought. But *Moley* won't hold me back, not anymore. I dare say he may well come in handy at some point in the near future, but it will be entirely on my own terms. For I realise now that I have been singled out for a purpose. And that purpose is greatness. I was afraid of that calling but now I am positively revelling in it.

And now my voice has finally broken. I have evolved into something else. And it is something good.

So here I am. Surrounded by the standing stones of the dead, high on the hill of the Necropolis where the shadows are long and the tombs are encrusted with lichen and festooned with ivy. And all around me there are fond remembrances carved in Roman font. *Orbis de Ignis. In Memoriam*. And that old favourite – *Rest In Peace*.

And the sun is slowly rising on Glasgow's horizon. The buildings and the streets are dislocating in light, sections hovering in shards and splinters cut by the sun's rays. Already, I can see vehicles and pedestrians, all emitting their combinations of carbons monoxide and dioxide, which rise from the streets in puffs as they make their hurried way through the freezing fog, this petrochemical city of vapours.

And I can see a plane flying off to some distant destination. I can hear the traffic too.

And birdsong.

And the wind.

The dreamers are waking.

Some are making love.

Some are making breakfast.

Others are just making do.

Somewhere, a baby needs feeding or a school tie needs adjusting or a car needs starting. And, elsewhere, a promotion is in the offing, a lottery is won and a new child is born.

And perhaps it is a boy.

Which brings me back to Detective Clements.

It's his boy next.

His son. His eighteen-year-old son. About to suffer a sudden and somewhat abbreviated life, I think. Shouldn't be too difficult. And it'll teach the detective a lesson he'll never forget.

A case of what goes round, comes round, don't you think?

R.I.P, son of Clements.

There. It is decided.

I take a deep breath.

And I smile broadly.

A wolf in sheep's clothing.

It is the mask that I will wear for as long as is necessary.

For my story is just beginning.

And I have much work to do.

The sun is rising.

The city beckons.

A new dawn.

And I can already tell.

It's going to be a beautiful day…'

Acknowledgements

I would like to thank the following:

Franzisca Aarflot, for showing an interest at an early stage.

Maureen Allan, for unknowingly providing the antidote.

Russel D McLean, for his helpful analysis.

Michael J Malone, for pricking up my ears and opening my eyes.

Unbound, for accepting my strange little story.

Xander Cansell, Head of Unbound Digital, for his enthusiasm and support throughout the entire process.

Gavin Mitchell and Jennie Ensor, for their readings.

Dr Brooke Magnanti, for her kind words.

My editorial team (Annabel Wright, Rachel Rayner, Sally Sargeant and Molly Powell) for their constructive feedback and assistance with my many queries.

Peter McMullen, ex-Strathclyde Police, for his advice on the investigative process – any mistakes are mine.

And thanks to Emma Thomson for the 'sundowning'.

A huge thank you to my patrons, my friends and family for all their heartfelt support throughout the production of this book.

And a bigger than life thanks to my parents, without whom this book would not have been born.

Patrons List

Hagar A
Franzisca Aarflot
David Aitken
George Allan
Nikki Anderson
Jason Ballinger
Clare Barker
Stewart Borland
Ken Britt
Kimberly Burke
Lucy Burns
Ali Burns
Beverly Campbell
Carole Cassidy
Cazzikstan Cazzikstan
Andrew Chapman
Gaynor Cherieann
Runilla Chilton
Meagan Cihlar
Michael Clarke
Ian Clarkson
Mick Clocherty
Peter Collins
Anne Cunningham
David de Croy
Jenny Doughty
Dan Ellis-Jones
Jennie Ensor
Greg Erskine
Jelles Ffonk
Thomas Gemmell
Catherine Gemmell
Nicola Miller Gillies
Granny Grace
Ceri Gray
Vince Handley
Anne & Louis Hanlon-Bucher

Linda Hepper
Sandy Herbert
Moira Hogg
Paul Holbrook
Janice Holve
Samantha Jennings
Marjorie Johns
Stephanie Johnson
Michele Kane
John Kazek
David Keddilty
Richy Kenny
Shona Kinsella
Paul Kramer
Suzanne LaPrade
Anne Lehmann
Amanda Lloyd Jennings
Karen Macleod
David Manderson
Ottis Manning
Mike McConnell
Bren McCreery
Martine McDonagh
Stephen McGowan
Louise McKenzie
Julie Mclaren
Martin Mcnee
Dale McSaiyan
Lorenzo Mele
Gavin Mitchell
Virginia Moffatt
Colleen Mooney
Sam Morgan
Maike Muller
Maria Nunn
Jan O'Malley
Susan Piper
Shelley Prior
A Randall
Joanne Rewinski
Mihai Risnoveanu

Pauline Ritchie
Anthea Robertson
Guido Roessling
Gary Rooney
Alexis Roseman
J. David Simons
David Sismore
Wajoma Smith
Susan Soutar
Caroline Stammers
Kathryn Stevenson
Tabatha Stirling
Ann Taylor
Elizabeth Tucker
Annabel Wardrop
Sue Whitten
Derek Wilson
Stacey Woods
Susan Worsfold
Anne Marie Young
Marisa Zanotti

Jack will be back…